D1601261

A REGIMENTAL AFFAIR

This first world edition published in Great Britain 2004 by
SEVERN HOUSE PUBLISHERS LTD of
9–15 High Street, Sutton, Surrey SM1 1DF.
This first world edition published in the USA 2004 by
SEVERN HOUSE PUBLISHERS INC of
595 Madison Avenue, New York, N.Y. 10022.

Copyright © 2003 by Catherine Jones.

All rights reserved.
The moral right of the author has been asserted.

British Library Cataloguing in Publication Data

Jones, Catherine, 1956-
    A regimental affair
    1.   Great Britain. Army - Military life - Fiction
    2.   Great Britain - Armed forces - Women - Fiction
    3.   Love stories
    I.   Title
    823.9'14 [F]

ISBN 0-7278-6049-6

Except where actual historical events and characters are being
described for the storyline of this novel, all situations in this
publication are fictitious and any resemblance to living persons
is purely coincidental.

Typeset by Palimpsest Book Production Ltd.,
Polmont, Stirlingshire, Scotland.
Printed and bound in Great Britain by
MPG Books Ltd., Bodmin, Cornwall.

A REGIMENTAL AFFAIR

Catherine Jones

3 1336 06623 8248

I am indebted to a number of people who gave me help and information about the life of long-suffering army wives. If there are mistakes in this book, it is not the fault of the following: Emma Brambell, Sarah Buckley, Cathy Carter and Jan Smith, to whom I am very grateful.

G inny Turner was surrounded by chaos. On the floor of her room was a suitcase piled high with clothes, mostly various sorts of army uniform, but with a number of skimpy outfits that bore witness to Ginny's off duty retail habit. By the bed was a packing case half-filled with books, CDs, walking boots and a tennis racket, while a hockey stick balanced precariously in the corner. Her skis were propped against the end of her bed until she could work out how the hell she was going to fit them in a tea chest. Music blared from her radio and Ginny herself was lying on her back on the bed wearing a T-shirt and shorts, her left knee crooked with her right foot resting on it, nattering into her mobile phone.

'I know, it's a pisser isn't it? I mean, two weeks' notice to move. It's all very well them saying "exigencies of the service", but it still means I'm the one getting mucked about. Still, even though this new place I'm going to is in the back of bloody beyond, I'll still have more to do than you have where you live.' There was a knock on her door. 'Hang on a mo,' she instructed. She held the phone away from her mouth as she yelled, 'Come in!' The door opened and an attractive young man poked his head round and tapped his watch. She looked at her own. 'Oh shit.' She re-clamped her phone to her ear. 'I'm sorry, Netta. Gotta go. I'm late. Ring you tomorrow. Yeah, hugs to all the kids and love to Petroc. Bye.'

Smiling apologetically at her visitor, Ginny bounced off her bed, flicked her phone shut and switched off the radio. 'I'm so sorry. I was chatting to my sister and forgot the time. Give me two ticks and I'll be there.'

'It's your farewell party.'

'I know, I know. But let's face it, if you lot haven't got used to me being late by now, when will you?'

Tim Benson nodded and gave her a lopsided smile. He wondered how could anyone so utterly organized at work be so shambolic in her social and private life?

As soon as he left, Ginny stripped to the buff and concentrated on getting ready for her final night out with the other single officers before her departure from her current unit to a new posting, via a spot of leave. She only had herself to blame for being so late this time – her excuse that a phone call had delayed her had been a fluent lie. The truth was she had spent too long going through an old photo album she'd found as she'd been packing. She instantly remembered what it contained and had flicked eagerly through it to find a few specific shots. She'd whizzed past the snaps of her earlier exploits in the army until she found what she had been looking for; pictures of the last time her path had crossed that of Bob Davies. Then he'd been a junior captain, not long married and a new father, and in the two years that Bob, his wife and Ginny had all been together at Tidworth she had got to know them quite well. Well, not his wife. Ginny had been wary of Alice. There had been something about the woman that Ginny had taken against almost from the outset. She had never been able to put her finger on it precisely, but she had an inkling that Alice had not entirely approved of her. Not enough to refuse her offer of babysitting Megan, but enough to subtly cut her at the few social events they attended together. It had been very hurtful, and if Ginny hadn't liked Bob so much she would have told Alice where to get off when she'd asked her to babysit.

To start with she'd liked Bob simply because he'd been kind to her. She'd been the newbie in the unit – and the only girl – and consequently had been largely ignored by most of the other officers. The blokes seemed to resent a woman living with them in the mess – some sort of macho idea that having a woman around would cramp their style. Consequently she'd felt shunned and lonely, which hadn't been helped by the fact that her sister had got a job on the Isles of Scilly and her parents had been stationed in Washington. It wasn't her style to complain and she'd told no one just how friendless she'd felt. Instead she'd just thrown herself into her work and got on with things.

Somehow Bob had guessed that she wasn't the happiest

2

person in the regiment and had wheedled out of her the reason why. She had been touched that he cared. Not only that, he was also the one who had bothered to find out that she had been a county hockey player before she joined the army, and who'd had the courage to suggest that she should be included in the regimental hockey team – a suggestion that had been vindicated when she had become the team's highest goal scorer that season. That, more than anything, had given her status in the unit and had helped to integrate her with the men. But more than that, whenever Bob came across her he made a point of talking to her. He had a knack for making her think he really cared about her, unlike the other blokes who only just about tolerated her. She knew it was an act – he was married with a kid – but she didn't mind. It was just lovely to have someone take an interest in her when everyone else dear to her was miles away. She knew that if it hadn't been for him she might have easily thrown in the towel and resigned from the army. It was one thing being perfect military material – outgoing, sporty, courageous – but it was another thing entirely being able to prove it when surrounded by blokes. She knew it was directly down to Bob that her first unit had accepted her eventually, and she was incredibly grateful. Furthermore, young and naive as she was, she had been deeply flattered that this older, good-looking man had taken the least interest in her, and it wasn't very surprising that over the months they had been posted together she'd found that gratitude wasn't her only feeling regarding him.

In the ten years since, Ginny ought to have grown sufficiently in self-knowledge to realize that Alice's antipathy towards her might have stemmed from the fact that Alice realized what Ginny's feelings were too. And if she had been further inclined to a moment of self-examination, Ginny might have realized that in the exuberance of youth she had probably not been as discreet as she thought she had. Then he had been, and possibly still was, an absolute hunk. Not only that, but he had a terrific sense of humour and shared Ginny's thirst for extreme sports and adventurous training, which had thrown them together on several occasions. She had enjoyed his company and had searched it out – which had probably been the main source of Alice's resentment – but never with any sort of alternative agenda. She might have been young and naïve but she wasn't stupid, nor was she a marriage wrecker. But when looking at the photos and recalling the events of a decade ago, Ginny had not bothered with any analysis beyond wondering, yet again, what on earth had possessed Bob to marry Icy Alice and, more intriguingly, to stay married to her. She'd always felt that Bob would be sensational in bed, but Alice? Hardly. Which had led Ginny to allow herself an indulgent fantasy involving Bob. Immersed as she had been in her thoughts, Ginny had completely lost track of time, and even when her sister had called she still hadn't realized how much of the evening had slipped past unnoticed.

Guiltily she snapped the album shut and dumped it in the box, trying to banish her inappropriate daydream about her future boss from her mind. But as she zipped herself into a tiny denim skirt and pulled a slinky top over her head, she couldn't ignore the quiver of pleasure she felt at the prospect of seeing him again. Only a couple of weeks to go, she thought, as she abandoned the muddle of her room and went to join her friends.

Ginny wasn't the only person on the move. The next morning, Alice Davies gazed at the exterior of her new quarter and felt a deep sense of satisfaction. It was as Bob had described it on the phone, only better – and bigger. Montgomery House was mock Georgian with three floors, and was by far and away the largest house she and Bob had ever been allocated in their fourteen years of married life. It looked stylish and opulent, and Alice felt that her carefully accumulated period furniture was going to look wonderful in such surroundings. She had worked long and hard for this moment, longer and harder than anyone except Bob would ever know, and at last she had achieved her ambition. She was the commanding officer's wife. She was top of the pecking order on the patch. She had the biggest and swankiest house and didn't she feel smug. It was rare for Alice to feel like that, as she wasn't one for very strong emotions. She didn't really approve of them, as strong emotions always left her feeling uncomfortably out of control. But today she didn't care. She was unbelievably happy and she felt the fact that the weather, despite it being only March, was bright and sunny too could only bode well for the next two years.

The door was open and Alice wandered into the cool hall. She liked the black and white chequered tiles. Very 'stately home', she thought. She felt a momentary prickle of irritation that Bob was nowhere to be seen, but then she supposed her husband and the camp commandant were still busy with the march-in. As so often before during the course of Bob's military career, he had gone on ahead to the new posting, leaving her to tie up the loose ends of the previous one. This time had been no different, although on this occasion Alice had had to wait at their old quarter to allow the departing CO and his wife the courtesy of leaving without feeling that their replacements were breathing down their necks.

The hall was big, with a sweeping staircase curving elegantly down from the first floor. Alice imagined herself descending it in a stunning evening dress – the envy of the other, junior wives. She peeked through the door on her right; the drawing room. Nice enough, she thought. She didn't much go for the colour scheme, but it had a fabulous fireplace and two big French windows that led out into the garden. Not that the fact she didn't like the decor was the least bit of a problem. She would get Bob to repaint the walls before they got properly unpacked. She considered the curtains. They would do at a pinch, but with any luck the quarter might be due for some new ones. Excitedly, Alice opened the doors to the rooms downstairs and found with mounting delight that the promise the exterior had offered did not disappoint. The reception rooms were all beautifully proportioned and the kitchen was like something out of a glossy magazine.

She returned to the hall and ran up the stairs. At the top she met Bob.

'I saw you arrive but I was a bit tied up with the march-in. Anyway, I thought you would like to have a look round without me getting underfoot. What do you think of it?'

'It's wonderful. Absolutely lovely.'

'I thought you'd like it. Good journey?'

'Fine. No problems at all. I passed the removal van about twenty minutes ago, so I expect they will be here soon.' There was a discreet cough from behind Alice. She turned around.

5

'Hello, Mrs Davies. I'm Mr Wilkes, ma'am. I'm the camp commandant. Welcome to Salerno Barracks.'

Alice shook his hand. 'Thank you Mr Wilkes. I'm sure we'll be very happy here.' And she meant it, she was certain of it.

Mr Wilkes departed, leaving Alice to explore the rest of the house and to choose a bedroom for her daughter, Megan. With six rooms other than the master bedroom, Alice hardly knew where to begin, but with only two weeks before Megan came home from school for the Easter holidays, she had set herself a deadline to have the house straight by then.

Down the road, in a much smaller quarter that had a number rather than a name, three women were watching their small children play with Duplo bricks and animals while they drank tea.

Maddy Greenwood, plump, dark and pretty, leant forward to right a drinking beaker before juice leaked on to her carpet and said, 'So she's here then. Does either of you know what she's like?'

'Never met her,' said Caroline. 'Somehow our paths never crossed.' She set her mug down on a coaster and pushed her shoulder-length blonde hair behind her ears. 'But I've heard things.'

'Tell,' said Josie.

Caroline leaned forward slightly and said, 'Well, it is only gossip—'

'So?' said both the others in unison.

'I've heard she's a bit of a control freak.'

'In what way?' said Maddy.

'She doesn't drink, for a start.'

Maddy and Josie exchanged significant glances. An army wife who didn't drink! Was there such a thing? Certainly no one they knew was teetotal. Maybe they knew a few who stopped indulging when pregnant. Quite a number didn't mind staying stone cold sober to drive their husbands home from mess functions, but not to drink – ever?

'Anything else?' asked Josie.

'I don't know if it's true, but ages ago I heard she keeps a note of every dinner party she's ever had, who attended and what the guests ate.'

6

'You're kidding,' said Maddy with a shriek of disbelief.

'I said I didn't know if it's true. I'm just repeating what I heard.'

'Scary though.'

The three women exchanged more significant glances.

'Oh God. You don't think she's the sort to think any wife who doesn't have a full-time job has to be involved in good works?'

Josie and Caroline groaned. They thought Maddy was more than likely right, and as none of them had gone back to work since they had had their first children, they knew they were all equally vulnerable. They could see stints of duty on regimental committees beckoning.

Alice was busy directing the removal men when the doorbell rang. She hurried happily down the wide, shallow stairs, taking pleasure from the feel of the polished, curved banister rail under her hand. She had always longed to live in a house with such a staircase and now she did. Bliss. She ducked slightly as she got halfway down to see who was standing on the doorstep of the open door.

'Sarah!' She ran down the last few stairs and proffered her cheek for her visitor to kiss. Alice's and Sarah's husbands had both been at Staff College together, and the wives had been neighbours.

'Hi Alice. I thought I'd better drop round and see you now you've arrived. Everything OK?'

'It's wonderful. Bob told me that you and Alisdair would be our neighbours again.' Alice looked past Sarah at the row of officers' quarters. 'Which one is yours?'

Sarah pointed. 'Third on the left. The one with the blue Ford Galaxy.'

Alice noticed that the quarter allocated to the regiment's second in command was pretty small compared to hers. Well, rank has its privileges, she thought smugly. She turned her attention back to Sarah and hoped her tiny moment of gloating hadn't shown.

'So how long have you and Alisdair been here?'

'About three months.'

'Great. So you'll be able to give me the low-down on all

the other wives. I'm looking forward to meeting them for coffee.'

Sarah shifted a little uncomfortably. She knew Alice's firmly held views about the role of army wives. She hedged. 'Quite a few go out to work.'

Alice's mouth tightened in a small but involuntary grimace. She really didn't approve. She knew she was old-fashioned but she'd been brought up to believe that the role of officers' wives was to look after the wives of the soldiers. Her mother and her mother's friends had been only too aware of that, and Alice couldn't see why it should be different for her generation. 'Oh. Well, I suppose it's only to be expected these days.'

'Boarding school fees mean most of us have to,' said Sarah.

'Do you work too?' Alice was surprised. She would have thought that Sarah, as the wife of the second in command, would have been far too busy to be able to work as well.

'Only part-time.'

'Hmm.'

A man's voice called down from the landing above. 'Excuse me Missus, but do you want the bed put together?'

'Hang on a sec,' Alice called back. To Sarah she said, 'Look, now I know where you live I'll drop round when it's a bit less chaotic. Lovely to see you again.'

Sarah returned home. Duty done.

'So has she changed?' asked Alisdair Milne that evening when he got in from work.

'What do you think?' Sarah snorted.

'But you used to be friends. When you lived next door you used to think her ways were quite funny.'

'That was when she was my neighbour. Now she's Lady Muck, lording it as the CO's wife, and I don't think it'll be quite so amusing.'

Sarah walked into the small and somewhat tatty kitchen of her current quarter. Alisdair followed.

'Gin?' She held up the bottle.

'Please.' He watched as Sarah busied herself with the glasses and the ice. 'So what has she done to upset you?'

Sarah picked up a knife to slice a lemon. 'Look, I know this is going to sound really bitchy, but you know I went to see her this afternoon?'

'You said you were going to.'

'Well, when she asked which house was ours you could see the triumph written all over her face that we have been given this poky little box and she is there in Montgomery bloody House.' Sarah sloshed two generous slugs of gin into the glasses.

'Surely not.'

'Trust me. You weren't there.'

Alisdair sighed. It would make his life so much easier if Alice and Sarah got on. But what the heck. Part of him knew that Sarah's sour grapes were caused by a modicum of jealousy. Alisdair knew that she would have quite liked to have been the CO's wife herself but Alisdair could have told her years back that it was never going to happen. Even when they had been cadets together, Bob had always shone as the star. He was always going to be the winner if it ever came to direct competition between the two of them. And now it had. Bob had been picked as the CO and Alisdair was his sidekick. Personally, Alisdair didn't mind one bit. He really liked Bob and almost from the start he'd resigned himself to being in his contemporary's shadow. But Alisdair didn't envy Bob on every level. Alice, if rumours were to be believed, was a bit of an ice maiden, but that was Bob's problem not his. Alisdair didn't think he would like to be married to someone like Alice. For one thing, she was so damn perfect. Everything she did, she did amazingly; cooking, flower arranging, painting, restoring furniture. She'd been a bit of a joke at Camberley – Alisdair remembered hearing from Sarah how the other wives used to take the mickey out of her when she wasn't around. Well, perhaps Alice's dedication to being the perfect army wife had paid off although, Alisdair reflected as he sipped his drink, Bob would have more than likely made it to the top even if he'd been married to a nymphomaniac floozy with communist tendencies.

'And there's another thing.'

Alisdair turned his attention back to his wife. 'Miaow,' he said.

Sarah had the good grace to look a little shamefaced. She

9

laughed. 'OK, OK. But honestly, even you'll agree that she can't be normal if she is directing removal men dressed like she's about to go to a garden party at Buck House. I mean, surely if she was halfway human she'd be wearing old clothes – jeans even – but I swear the jumper she had on was cashmere and her skirt must have set her back at least a hundred pounds if not more.'

Alisdair didn't argue. What did he know about fashion? He was either in uniform or jeans and sweatshirts that Sarah bought for him from Marks and Spencer or some such place. But it went against the grain for Sarah to be disloyal to his boss's wife. 'Well, she's only supervising them, isn't she? She's not humping the boxes around herself, is she?'

Sarah took a noisy slurp of her gin. 'Huh.'

Alisdair gazed out of the kitchen window. He thought it best not to say anything right now – Sarah probably wouldn't appreciate it – but he would have to remind her at some stage that whatever views she expressed in the privacy of their quarter should not be voiced to the other wives. It wouldn't be good for the regiment if the soldiers got to hear there was hostility amongst the wives on the officers' patch. He deliberately changed the subject. 'I don't suppose either of the kids have been in touch today?'

'Will might have emailed. He had a match today so he'll probably want to let you know how he got on.'

It was the excuse Alisdair was looking for to stop this conversation. 'I'll go and check, shall I?'

'Please.' Sarah reached forward to the radio on the window sill and flicked it on. The voice of a Radio Four announcer told them it was six o'clock. Sarah took another sip of her drink and began to get supper ready while Alisdair wandered into the dining room that doubled as his study when the kids were away at school.

As always, the room was in chaos; bills, letters and papers were strewn across the centre of the issue oak table. The telephone directory was lying open at one end of the table and the computer dominated the other. It was no wonder they never had people round to dinner. It was too much effort to clear the room so everyone could eat at the table. Alisdair walked round to the machine and switched it on.

As the system booted up he wondered briefly what sort of fist Bob would make of being CO. He certainly had a hard act to follow. His predecessor had been immensely popular and his wife, a dizzy blonde, had by all accounts endeared herself to all and sundry by throwing outrageously boozy and amazingly fun parties. Alisdair and Sarah had arrived just in time to be present at the previous New Year's Eve bash, which had served to prove that the reports had not been exaggerated. Somehow Alisdair didn't think that Alice was going to plough a similar furrow. He reckoned things were going to be very different on the patch from here on in.

Megan Davies removed the towel from her head and studied her reflection in the mirror on the wall of the bleak bathroom.

'Shit!' said Zoë with a mixture of awe and horror.

Megan felt a frisson of nerves jangle her stomach. This was going to cause trouble – trouble in a big way. She'd known that it might from the moment she opened the bottle of dye, but she hadn't expected the end result to be quite so . . . what? Dramatic? Outrageous? Well, it was certainly that. Her auburn hair was now jet black.

'What is Miss Pink going to say?' whispered Zoë.

Megan met her eyes in the mirror and said coolly, 'She can say what she likes. It's done now.'

'She's going to be mad though.'

Megan shrugged. 'So what's the worst she can do? Gate me? Big deal. Term ends in a fortnight, there's no more exeats, and I'm broke so I can't afford to go out anyway.'

'Well . . .' began Zoë cautiously. She stopped and wondered if she ought to continue.

Her apprehension, despite her outward bravado, made Megan snappy. 'Spit it out.'

'Expulsion?'

Megan's eyes widened in horror for a split second. Then, 'Nah. No way.'

Zoë looked sceptical.

'Of course not,' emphasized Megan, more for her own benefit than Zoë's.

'She expelled Tasha.'

11

'Yeah, but she was *very* drunk.'

'True.'

'And she'd been caught smoking twice.' But even so, Megan's confidence wavered. She had been no angel in her time at Downton Manor. OK, a couple of things had been unintentional. The broken window really hadn't been her fault, nor had she meant to drop the block of sodium into the water, it had just slipped out of her fingers. Still, on the positive side, the explosion had been quite spectacular and worth the enormous rifting she'd had afterwards. But the rigging of the school's public address system on sports day so that Nirvana had belted out over it was entirely down to her, as was her idea of writing HELP! SAVE US! in three-foot-high letters in weedkiller in the middle of the hockey pitch. Still, smoking was still considered almost the worst thing Miss Pink's young ladies could get up to, with drinking just pipping it to the post. None of the girls thought that Miss Pink even knew what drugs were – except possibly as the American term for medical preparations.

'And what will your mother say?' Zoë voiced a thought that was already present in Megan's mind.

'She'll be cool.'

Zoë's eyebrows shot into her hairline. She'd met Mrs Davies on several occasions and knew precisely what she was like.

'Well, she'll get used to it.'

Zoë's eyebrows stayed up.

'Eventually.'

Zoë remained silent.

'When it grows out.'

'Yeah, that's more like the truth.'

At Montgomery House, Alice had cleared away the supper things and was now sitting at the table in her kitchen surrounded by half unpacked boxes, piles of china, crumpled newspaper and other evidence of the chaos of moving. Part of Alice wanted to get on and clear up the mess but she had firmly decided that she had another task taking priority that evening. Accordingly she had dispatched Bob off to the scullery to plumb in the washing machine and dishwasher, while she got on with organizing her first social occasion. Even before she had moved in she had ascertained the best days for 'borrowing' the mess staff to help her out, and now she was checking those dates against her diary and the regimental forecast of events. She sighed as she went through the possibilities of one date after another. Eventually she decided there was no alternative; she would have to have her coffee morning for all the officers' wives the day after Megan got back from school. It was that or postpone meeting all the officers' wives for nearly a month. She hoped Megan would understand – and after all, they would have the rest of the holidays together. Before Alice began to write out the details of the invitation on to her engraved 'At Home' cards, she promised herself that she would make it up to Megan with a couple of treats – shopping sprees or cinema trips to make up for having to be otherwise engaged on their first day together. Ignoring the grunts and occasional swear word from Bob as he struggled to shove a recalcitrant dishwasher into a tight space, she began to write out the cards in careful italics. Bob could get one of the clerks to deliver them tomorrow, first thing.

It was at about ten the next morning that the phone rang at Montgomery House.

'May I speak to Mrs Davies?' asked a cultured voice.

'Speaking,' replied Alice, recognizing the voice of her daughter's headmistress and instantly steeling herself for the worst.

'This is Miss Pink.'

'Yes.' Alice tried not to sound too dispirited. She just managed to stop herself from asking what had Megan done this time. It was unfair to Megan to automatically assume there was a problem, except that there had been exactly that on too many previous occasions.

'I am calling to ask if you were aware that Megan planned to dye her hair?'

Alice was momentarily lost for words. 'Dye?' The shock made the word come out in a squeak.

'I take it from that you were not.'

'Well . . .' Alice wanted to lie but she had been caught on the hop.

'Apart from the mess she has made of her own hair, I'm afraid we are going to have to add the cost of replacing several bath mats and towels to your bill, as they have been irreparably damaged.'

'How?' Alice was feeling shell-shocked.

'The black dye your daughter used was permanent.'

'Black?'

Miss Pink either didn't hear Alice or chose to ignore her. 'In view of the nature of your daughter's latest misdemeanour I have gated her until the end of term. I thought you should know.'

'Yes.'

'I look forward to seeing you for the end of term service a week on Friday.'

'Yes.'

'Goodbye.'

Alice was left saying goodbye to a dead line. Black? How could she! How could she show her daughter off to the other wives at her coffee morning if she looked like some sort of freak? She'd just have to tell Megan to stay in her room. Alice knew that under normal circumstances only a heavy bribe would induce Megan to put in an appearance but, knowing her daughter as she did, there was no guarantee that the little minx would stay out of sight. In fact Alice knew that, just to be contrary, Megan would make sure she was highly visible.

Making a quick decision, she phoned regimental headquarters. She'd have to have the coffee morning in the mess. Megan wouldn't make an appearance there. She had her fingers crossed that the invitations were still in Bob's briefcase so she could retrieve them and rewrite them. After a couple of rings the adjutant answered.

'Captain Greenwood speaking.'

'This is Mrs Davies. Is my husband still there?' She hoped that Bob hadn't already left for his visit to brigade headquarters that was going to take him away for most of the day.

'He's with the RSM, Mrs Davies. He told me he didn't want to be disturbed.'

'It's urgent.'

Richard Greenwood sighed. The previous evening Maddy had told him about the rumours she'd heard and, together with intelligence gleaned from other officers who had served before with the Davieses, he reckoned she wasn't a woman to be argued with.

'I'll put you through.' Anyway, if Colonel Bob didn't want to talk to her he could tell her himself. It was too early in his relationship with the new CO to end up playing piggy in the middle between him and his wife.

A minute later the CO put his head round their interconnecting door. 'Richard, those invitations I asked you to send out.'

'Sir.'

'Have they gone?'

'They were delivered to the company offices straight away, as you requested.'

'Damn. The memsahib seems to have changed her mind about the venue, but I'll tell her it's too late now.'

Colonel Bob withdrew back into his office and, after a brief word with his wife, resumed his discussion with his most senior warrant officer. Richard glanced at the invitation to his own wife, which was sitting in his in tray, and wondered for a fleeting instant what the problem was, but the phone rang again and Maddy's social calendar ceased to concern him.

Maddy was putting her daughter, Danielle, to bed when Richard came home.

'Hi darling. Hello sweetheart,' he said quietly as he entered the bedroom.

'Dada,' cooed Danielle sleepily.

Maddy tucked the quilt over the toddler and wound up the mobile so a tiny flock of fluffy sheep danced round in a circle above her daughter's blonde curls. Richard leaned over the cot rail and dropped a kiss on her forehead. 'Night night gorgeous. Sleep tight.' He gazed at his daughter and tried to imprint the image on his mind. He'd had word of some important news that was going to affect the entire regiment. He hoped that he would be able to hide the secret from Maddy until the news became official. He loved Maddy to bits but she wasn't the soul of discretion, and if she got a hint of what was going on it would be round the married patch before you could say, 'What secret?'

Danielle turned on her side, stuck a fat thumb in her rosebud mouth and shut her eyes. Her parents tiptoed out of the room and shut the door.

'I've got a letter for you,' said Richard as they descended the stairs.

'Me?' Maddy was curious. Overseas their post was delivered to the unit and distributed to families via husbands, but on home postings they got their mail through their letter boxes like everyone else. 'Who's it from?'

'CO's wife. It's in my briefcase.'

Richard fetched his bag as Maddy went into the kitchen and began to dish up their supper.

'It's spag bol,' she called through the open door. 'OK?' She didn't wait for her husband's reply as she dolloped large ladles of spaghetti on to two plates sitting ready on the Formica work surface.

'Great,' said Richard, returning to the kitchen as he unzipped his document case. He rummaged briefly inside it. 'Ah, here it is.' He passed Maddy a stiff cream envelope.

Maddy wiped her fingers on a tea towel and took it. 'Nice stationery,' she commented as she ripped it open. She scanned it quickly and groaned. 'Oh God. I knew it.'

'What is it?'

'It's a summons from Alice Davies.'

Richard couldn't see what was wrong with that. 'That'll be nice, dear,' he said blandly.

'No, it bloody won't.'

'Don't be silly.'

Maddy chucked the invitation on to the worktop and began to put the Bolognese sauce on the plates. 'I'm not. I told you what Caro said about her. She sounds awful.'

'I expect Caroline was exaggerating. You know what she's like. No need to spoil a good story with the truth.' Out of loyalty to his new boss, Richard kept quiet about the stories *he'd* heard.

Maddy laughed. 'Well, maybe. Come on, grab a tray.'

Richard did as he was told and followed Maddy into the sitting room where they settled down in front of the TV with their supper.

'By the way, we've been told that Ginny Turner is being

16

parachuted in to the post of regimental admin officer. She's arriving in a couple of weeks.'

'That's great,' said Maddy indistinctly through a mouthful of spaghetti. She'd been good friends with Ginny when she had been dating one of Richard's friends. She swallowed. 'Poor cow didn't get much notice though, did she?'

'No.'

'Why was that?'

Richard knew perfectly well but couldn't say. The regiment needed to be up to full strength by Easter to be ready for preparations for a future event, but if he said anything about that Maddy would smell a rat. Safer to blame the system in general rather than a future event in particular. 'You know what the army is like.'

A snort from Maddy indicated that she knew only too well. She slurped up more spaghetti. 'Still, it's an ill wind.' She swallowed noisily. 'Tell her to get herself round here as soon as she arrives. I'll have a bottle of wine open. Won't it be great to have Ginny here? Just think, a year with a live wire like her for company.'

Richard kept to himself the news that both he, Ginny and the rest of the regiment would be gone for at least six months of the year that Maddy was so looking forward to.

At Montgomery House things were rather more formal. Alice was also getting ready for supper but, unlike Maddy and Richard who were happy with trays on their knees, she was putting damask place mats on her mahogany table and lining up crystal wine glasses with the tips of the knives. They might be surrounded by half unpacked possessions but that was no excuse to allow her standards to slip.

She glanced at her watch. Good, Bob would be home soon. Apart from anything else she wanted to tell him about Megan's latest misdeed and ask his advice about moving the coffee morning to the officers' mess. Would sending out a note to everyone to say the venue had changed make her look foolish and disorganized? But would that be better than Megan swanning around looking like some sort of punk rocker? God, this was turning into a nightmare. She'd made her plans carefully to make sure she would have the maximum possible attendance of all the officers' wives, and now she was going to be embarrassed by her daughter in front of them all. Really, Megan was the limit! Bob would have to have a word with her.

Feeling more than a little irritated, she had just finished arranging the table to her satisfaction and was returning to the kitchen to check on the potatoes dauphinoise when she heard her husband's key click in the lock. She decided the potatoes could manage on their own for a few more minutes and crossed the hall to greet him as he walked through the front door.

She offered her cheek for Bob to kiss and said, 'Bob, you'll never guess what Megan has done now.'

'Hmm?' Bob took off his beret, kissed her and dumped his case on the hall table.

'Bob?' Bob wasn't usually this distracted when he came home.

'Sorry dear. Just had some news from the brigade commander today.'

'Oh?' Megan's hair was sidelined.

'Let me get changed and I'll tell you.'

Alice watched her husband make his way up the stairs. Whatever the news was, it sounded as if it might be rather serious. She wondered what it was.

Over the course of their meal she recounted Miss Pink's telephone call and tried to put her curiosity to the back of her mind. Bob didn't seem that concerned, and his only reaction was to comment that it would grow out soon enough. Alice changed tack and prattled on about her day – the boxes she had unpacked, the way she was arranging Megan's room, the disagreement she'd had with their cleaner. She would return to the subject of Megan when Bob had less on his mind and could be relied upon to take a more appropriate stance. In the meantime Alice had tired of waiting for Bob to tell her the news which was obviously bothering him.

'So,' said Alice as she placed her knife and fork together in the centre of her plate. 'Are you going to tell me what is on your mind?'

Bob sighed. Not a good sign, thought Alice.

'I had two pieces of news today. One good, one not so good.'

Alice moved her plate a few inches further on to the table and rested her wrists on the edge. The 'not so good' bit sounded as though it was going to be rather worse than that.

'The good news is that Virginia Turner is being posted in as regimental admin officer. She arrives next week.'

'Oh, that will be nice,' said Alice non-committally. She struggled to remember who on earth Virginia Turner was. Bob had obviously come across her before and thought well of her, but the name didn't mean much to Alice. She gave up and admitted defeat. 'Have I met her?'

'Yes. Of course you have. She babysat for us a couple of times when Megan was little.'

'Oh, goodness.' Alice remembered now. 'Ginny.'

'Yes, Ginny,' said Bob with a smile.

Alice tried to look pleased, but she didn't think that this was good news at all. Frankly she hadn't much liked Ginny. In her opinion she'd been a bit fast and she'd suspected that Miss Turner had been more than a little free with her favours. Yes, Bob had thought highly of her then, perhaps too highly. He'd certainly talked enough about her; her skiing, her windsurfing, her adventurous training expedition to the Andes. She tried not to let her feelings show. 'Still Turner,' Alice observed snakily. 'So, not married then? I would have thought she might have settled down a bit by now.'

'Well, I don't think settling down is Ginny's style, do you? I can't see her with a brood of kids and a pile of ironing.'

Alice, slightly nettled because her husband had just – albeit unwittingly – belittled her homemaking skills, was about to make a bitchy comment about Ginny not being able to catch a man when she thought better of it. Even Alice knew that all the single officers (and, she suspected, some of the married ones) had been panting after Ginny when their paths had last crossed, and she didn't think that things would have changed so very much in the intervening years. She'd been a stunner then and probably still was.

With an effort, Alice smiled. 'No, you're right dear. Children and ironing wouldn't be up Ginny's street at all.'

'On the downside we had some not-so-good news.'

Alice waited expectantly. She raised her eyebrows slightly to encourage Bob to get on with it. What did he want, a drum roll?

'The regiment is being sent on an emergency tour.'

Alice felt as deflated as if she had been given an exquisitely wrapped box only to discover that it contained crumpled newspaper and no present. 'Oh no!'

''Fraid so.'

'When, where?'

'Kosovo. Two months' time.'

'Two months! But . . .'

'I know. I know.' Bob had been expecting this reaction. It was the main reason he'd put off telling her for as long as he'd been able. Alice had always known that separation was an inevitable part of army life, but it didn't prevent her from resenting it. And perhaps they had had more than their fair share of it over the sixteen years of their marriage. 'We weren't due for a tour for quite a while but things change. There's more trouble brewing in the Balkans and we're available. But don't go telling anyone till I've had a chance to tell the rest of the regiment.'

Alice began to clear the plates. Bob could tell from the set of her mouth and her silence that she was upset. He didn't like the way the family was going to be split up for months any more than she did. She stacked their plates and hurried out into the kitchen. She didn't trust herself to speak.

But Bob was mistaken that Alice was distraught at the thought of so many months apart. That was not what was making her feel very close to tears. This posting that had promised so much was now looking much less appealing. If the regiment was away on an emergency tour, there would be no official visits from the top brass and – and this was her biggest disappointment – no chance of a royal visit. She had really hoped that at some time during her stint as CO's wife she would have to host a member of the royal family. Now hopes of that were fading fast. If the men were going out to Kosovo the last thing her husband would be thinking about would be future social events, and Alice knew that a visit from one of the royals often took between a year and eighteen months to organize. By the time Bob got back and could be persuaded to

20

think about such things it would be too late. Even if he did pull his finger out, the chances were that they would be on their way to yet another posting and her successor would get the benefit. Really, life was so unfair. Ever since she had heard that Bob was to take over the regiment she had imagined herself at the helm of numerous impeccable social functions. Well, there would be none of that for at least six months. Damn. Alice's annoyance at the curtailment of her social plans pushed the news of Ginny's impending arrival to the back of her mind.

Sarah turned the cream envelope over in her hand. She recognized the distinctive calligraphy and had a pretty fair idea of what it contained.

'Good God almighty, she didn't waste much time then, did she!' Sarah remarked as she stuck it, unopened, on the cooker hood.

'I'm not with you,' said Alisdair, who was reading the sports page of the paper.

'Alice.'

'How do you mean?'

Sarah sighed. 'She's only been here a matter of hours and she's already getting the invites out to show us mere mortals how proper entertaining should be done.'

'Oh.' Alisdair turned the page. He obviously hadn't taken in a word.

Sarah shook her head. Really – men! She poked the potatoes to see if they were done. 'Anyway, why were you so late tonight?'

'Ah.'

Sarah drained the spuds over the sink and began to mash them. '"Ah" sounds ominous.'

Alisdair folded up the paper. 'This mustn't go any further – at least not till it's official.'

Sarah stopped mashing and focused her attention on her husband. 'What's official?'

'We're going to Kosovo. Six-month emergency tour.'

Sarah considered the news for a few seconds. She didn't trust herself to speak until she'd taken a couple of deep breaths. 'Soon?'

'The beginning of June.'

'That's soon enough.'

'So suddenly, it all got very hectic today.'

'And will stay that way till you go.' Sarah had been an army wife long enough to know all the implications. There was a mountain of stuff to do, especially as they didn't have that long in which to get ready. Getting every scrap of equipment repaired, regimental documentation to be brought completely up to date, vaccinations to be organized, training to be undertaken, briefings on the local situation to attend . . . The list would make sure that every minute of every working day (and a good bit of their leisure time) would be taken up until they actually departed. And with a shiny new CO at the helm and still finding his feet, most of this would devolve to his second in command – Alisdair.

'So I'm afraid—'

Sarah had already worked out the personal implications for the family. 'The Easter holidays are going to be a non-event.'

'Yes.'

Sarah returned to mashing the potatoes. 'Can't be helped,' she said, trying to hide her disappointment. Damn and blast the bloody army. She took her frustrations out on the spuds.

Ginny dumped her suitcase in the lobby of the officers' mess and looked around. She recognized some of the pictures and the silver from the last time she'd visited the regiment, when they had been based on Salisbury Plain and she had been dating one of the subalterns. It was a bit like visiting one of the pad's houses after they had moved. It didn't matter what their new quarter was like; to all intents and purposes it was exactly the same as the previous one, it was just the colour of the carpets and the shape of the rooms that changed. You'd see the same house plants, the same pictures, the same rugs – everything arranged, as much as circumstances allowed, in the same way. Ginny supposed it was some sort of defence mechanism devised by the wives so it didn't seem as though their families had been uprooted quite as often as they had been.

She looked around for signs of life and could hear and see none. She wandered along a corridor leading past the dining room and heading, she hoped, towards the kitchens. There was bound to be someone there at this time – lunch was

22

going to be served in under an hour. Behind her she heard a door slam. Ginny turned around and recognized the emerging figure immediately.

'Richard!'

'Ginny?'

She walked towards him and kissed him heartily on both cheeks. 'Great to see you. I'd heard on the grapevine that you were here. And what's this I hear about you being a father now?'

Richard grinned broadly. 'Hard to believe, isn't it? You'll have to come and meet her.'

'What's the baby's name?'

'Danielle. But she's hardly a baby any more, she's eighteen months old.'

'And is she beautiful like her mother?'

'Yeah. Happily my genes seem to be the recessive ones.'

Ginny laughed. 'Christ, that was a lucky escape for the kid.'

Richard smiled. 'It'll be good having you here. Should liven the place up a bit.'

'Does it need livening up?'

'Not at the moment. We're all far too busy.'

'Busy? On a peacetime posting in the UK?'

'But the CO wrote and told you?' To be more accurate, Richard had actually written the letter containing the news but the CO had signed it.

'Told me what?' asked Ginny suspiciously.

'That the regiment's off to Kosovo in a couple of months.'

Ginny narrowed her eyes as she considered Richard's bald statement. Then she laughed. 'Good one. You nearly got me going then. Yeah, right.'

'But surely you got the letter?'

Ginny thought back. Yes, she had had a letter from Bob and she'd read the first bit about how much he was looking forward to her serving in his regiment and how demanding the job would be and how he thought she was more than up to the task and blah, blah, blah. And then? And then she remembered throwing the letter on the bed and deciding to read the rest of it later. Had she? No, obviously not, or she would have picked up the news about their deployment to Kosovo.

'Um, well,' she hedged.

Richard smiled encouragingly.

'Well, I did get it, but . . .'

'You didn't read it.'

'No. Well, you know what that sort of letter is like. I mean it's usually all bullshit, isn't it?'

'Usually, but not always.'

'Yes, well.' Ginny had been caught out and felt a little foolish.

'I mean, didn't you think it odd that your posting was so sudden?'

Ginny had to admit to herself that she had wondered about that, but her curiosity had been submerged in the chaos of her round of farewell parties, all of which had had to be crammed into a somewhat short time frame. Ginny shrugged and wrinkled her nose.

'So, do you want a hand with your kit?' asked Richard, sensing Ginny's embarrassment and tactfully changing the subject.

'Please. It's all dumped in the hall at the moment. I was looking for someone to tell me where to find a room.'

'I'll take you to the mess manager's office. He'll get you organized.'

Twenty minutes later Ginny was hanging clothes in her wardrobe, wondering if she liked the way the furniture was arranged in her new bedroom and getting used to the news that she was off to Kosovo in the near future.

Well, she thought, abandoning her unpacking and sitting on her bed, now she knew why her posting had suddenly been brought forward, why there had been all the urgency. Just as well she didn't have any compelling personal reasons for wanting to stay in the country. Footloose and fancy-free, that was her. Not that she really wanted to be that way, but suitable men – or to be precise, suitable, *unattached* men – seemed to be getting scarcer and scarcer. She sighed quietly at the thought. Part of her fancied the idea of a stable, long-term relationship. The trouble was that it had been OK being 'madcap, love-'em-and-leave-'em, good-time Ginny' when she was twenty or so, but she was getting a little old for that role now. And all the guys that had kept her company, who had accompanied her on expeditions and on skiing holidays had, one by one, drifted into marriage and domesticity and left her to carry on her life of single irresponsibility. The men that swum back into the availability pool, their marriages falling apart as they often did in the military, always seemed to carry so much emotional baggage as a result of the ex-wife's infidelity, their own infidelity or whatever, that they could hardly be considered a prize catch. Yesterday's leftovers was a better description, thought Ginny.

Furthermore, she didn't think that six months in some godforsaken NATO outpost was going to improve her chances of finding Mr Right. The only people she was likely to come across were the chaps in the regiment, and the chances were that the single ones would be miles too young for her, and her contemporaries were bound to be married and therefore off limits. Thirty-one wasn't old, for God's sake! But all the men of her age had wives and kids, or hang-ups and alimony payments. Perhaps, she thought dully, she had left it too late. Heigh-ho. Middle age as a spinster didn't seem very appealing, but that was what beckoned. She looked in the mirror. There were the beginnings of some lines around her mouth. Little ones that she'd got from pursing her lips when she concentrated. If she didn't watch out she'd soon be a *wrinkled*, middle-aged spinster, just like all the unmarried female officers she had laughed at when she had been a cadet.

Feeling down, she wandered over to the window and looked out. Not too bad a view, she thought – better than the last place she'd lived in where her room had looked out across dustbins behind the mess kitchen to a busy main road and a row of dreary, run-down shops. This time her room was at the front of the building so she looked across a large lawn. A screen of mature chestnuts was on the left and beyond them she could glimpse the parade square. A road led off the square, across the top of the lawn in front of her and then curved around into the small estate of officers' houses with their neat front gardens, hanging baskets and people carriers or estate cars in the drives. All those officers had managed to find the time and the right person to marry, she thought. Perhaps she ought to make the effort this time when she came back from Kosovo. She'd make someone a good wife – and she'd be a good mother, she was certain of that. She sighed again. Wasn't it funny how lonely you could sometimes be, even when you lived in a bustling place like an officers' mess.

Bob wasn't a heavy smoker and he still had five cigarettes left in the packet on his desk – more than enough for the afternoon – so he knew he was kidding himself when he popped into the mess on his way home for lunch that the sole reason for the detour was to buy some fags. Richard had let slip that whilst in the mess, carrying out his duties as Wines Member, he had run into Ginny. As Bob neared the front door of the mess, he finally admitted to himself that he was hoping to see Ginny and that he was just curious to see if she had changed at all in the last ten years. That was all.

And he needed cigarettes, didn't he?

On entering the bar he saw that it was empty apart from a couple of young subalterns drinking orange juice and poring over a motoring magazine. Walking over to the bar he noticed a feeling of disappointment welling up inside him. Oh well, he'd just get his cigarettes and go home. Anyway, if the poor girl had only just arrived it was a little unlikely that she would already be propping up the bar. One of the young men glanced up and saw Bob as he passed, and they both leapt to their feet. With a casual hand gesture to signal they could sit down, Bob made a mental note to get Richard to spread the word that he didn't expect junior officers to jump to attention every time he made an appearance in the mess. After all, the mess was their home and he was, in some respects, a visitor. He'd have said something then and there but for the life of him he couldn't remember their names. He filled in a chit for twenty Silk Cut and handed it to the steward.

'Sorry, sir,' said the young lad serving him. 'I've run out. I think we might have some in the cellar. I'll just go and see.'

'In which case I'll have a tomato juice while I'm waiting.'

'Yes, sir.'

The steward returned the chit to Bob for him to sign for the drink and busied himself mixing the juice with Worcestershire sauce and adding ice and lemon. With nothing else to occupy him, Bob watched and then accepted the proffered drink. The barman excused himself to fetch the cigarettes.

'So, sir,' said a woman's voice behind him, 'still not drinking at lunchtime I'm pleased to see.'

Bob spun round. 'Ginny!' She hadn't changed a jot, he noticed instantly. Still as slim, still as blonde, still as pretty. 'How lovely to see you again.' His feeling of disappointment was replaced in a heartbeat by real happiness.

'It can hardly be a surprise,' she replied. 'You knew I was arriving today. In fact I've already been told by Richard to report to your office at two o'clock for my initial interview.'

'Hardly necessary though, seeing how well we know each other.'

'You could have dispensed with the formality.'

'I didn't want you to think I was ignoring you.'

'As if.' She raised an eyebrow at him and smiled. Bob had forgotten how devastating her smile was.

The two young officers finished their drinks and drifted off to the dining room in search of food. The barman hadn't returned with his cigarettes and Bob was suddenly very aware that he and Ginny were alone and he found the thought oddly disturbing.

'Settled in?' he asked somewhat abruptly, clearing his throat.

'Ish,' said Ginny. 'Although there's not too much point in making myself feel completely at home. Seeing as how I'll just have to pack everything up again soon.'

'No.' The barman returned and handed Bob his Silk Cut. 'Right, well, um . . . I'd better get off home or Alice will wonder what has become of me.'

'How is Alice – and Megan, of course?'

'Alice is fine. Megan's at public school.'

Ginny looked aghast. 'My God! So grown-up.'

'You must come round and meet them again. Megan'll be back soon and Alice was so pleased to hear you'd been posted here.'

Ginny didn't say anything. She had a feeling that the last few words were a lie. She could not imagine that in the intervening ten years Alice Davies would have revised her opinion about her.

Bob left the bar and Ginny ordered a lemonade from the steward. Taking her drink, she picked up a tabloid to read but, although she looked at the headlines, she didn't take in a single word. She was far too busy thinking about Bob. She decided that the two wings of grey that had appeared at his temples made him look very distinguished, but that had been the only change she could see. His fringe still fell almost into his eyes as it had done ten years previously. When she had been talking to him she had wanted to push it off his face and she had only just managed to refrain. She recalled the time when they went on a climbing expedition together and they had been alone on a ledge while they waited for the other members of their party to join them. She had allowed herself to do it then and she remembered how soft his hair had felt. Bob had looked surprised and then he had leant towards her. She was certain he was about to kiss her when they were interrupted by one of their fellow climbers appearing from below. Bob had grinned at her a little sheepishly as he moved away again. Ginny had wondered then, and since, if he had been embarrassed about almost getting caught or allowing his feelings to show. Ginny sipped her lemonade, gave up any pretence of reading the paper and admitted to herself that she still fancied him like mad. She knew it was wrong and she knew it was unwise but she couldn't help it. She plonked her drink firmly on the table. No, not unwise, she told herself. Completely stupid. Bob was off-limits and was going to stay that way.

When Alice saw Megan's hair it was every bit as hideous as she had imagined it would be. No wonder Miss Pink had been so annoyed. It was not the sort of advertisement she would want for her school.

'I'll make an appointment at the hairdressers to get it dyed back,' said Alice as they drove home from the school. Megan said nothing. 'What on earth possessed you? And black!' Megan still didn't reply. 'Well?'

'Well what?' she said with a deep sigh.

'Don't you take that tone with me.'

Megan sighed again. 'But I like my hair this colour.'

'Of course you don't.'

Megan raised her eyebrows in exasperation. 'I wouldn't have done it if I hadn't wanted it to be this colour.'

'We'll get it dyed back and that is that.'

Megan didn't argue but Alice knew she actually had to get her daughter to the hairdressers. That was another matter.

'It's a shame nothing can be done before tomorrow.'

'Why's that?'

'I'm having a coffee morning for the other wives.' Bob had persuaded Alice that she might as well hold her function at Montgomery House. As he had pointed out, they could hardly confine Megan to her room for the whole of the holidays and so there was no point in altering things as people were bound to come across Megan and her hair at some point.

Megan groaned. 'Gross.'

'Well, if you're going to be like that about it you can stay in your room.'

'That's what you'd like isn't it?'

Megan might be the teenager from hell, thought Alice, but she wasn't stupid. 'Not really. I was rather hoping you might help out.' Alice was hoping nothing of the sort.

'Huh.'

Alice was finding Megan's monosyllabic grunts increasingly irritating but she knew it would be better not to rise to the bait. 'I hope you're not going to be like this for the whole of the Easter holidays. You don't want your father to go off to Kosovo with a memory of you doing nothing but sulk.'

'What would he care?'

Alice almost snapped. It was only the fact that she had both hands on the steering wheel with the car doing seventy along a stretch of dual carriageway that stopped Alice from slapping Megan's thigh. 'He would care very much. And I'm not going to stand for you spoiling his last few weeks at home.'

Megan didn't reply, she just glowered at her mother.

They didn't exchange a further word for the remainder of the two-hour journey. When the car pulled up outside Montgomery House, Megan got out, slammed the door and dragged her case from the boot. Alice had expected her to comment on her new home at the very least. Really, that child was the limit sometimes.

Alice locked the car and opened the front door. 'Your room is at the top of the stairs on the left.'

Megan didn't answer, she just thumped up the stairs, banging her suitcase against the paintwork. Alice breathed deeply and refused yet again to take the bait.

Megan threw her case on the bed and looked at her room in disgust. Pink – again. Why did her mother have this fixation with pink? Every room she could remember, and there had been a few, had been painted pink. God, it was so twee. But that was their house all over; all frills and knick-knacks, with dainty little ornaments littering the surfaces. Megan vowed that when she had a place of her own she would have absolutely no clutter. Nowhere. Ever. And no pink.

Megan propped herself up against her pillows and angrily studied her new room. At least it was a decent size. Better than the last place they'd lived in at any rate. It was odd seeing all her things arranged differently, although it was still completely recognizable as her room. Or rather what her mother's idea of her room should be. Pink and frilly, with a white and gold dressing table to match her white and gold headboard, chintzy cushions scattered on her pink counterpane and pink curtains at her window. But all the pink plastic toys that Megan had longed for with a passion when she was little had never materialized – the Barbies, the My Little Ponies, the Sylvanian Families. Alice had made no secret of the fact that she considered them naff, and instead Megan had been given dolls with beautiful clothes and porcelain faces, a designer doll's house, a wooden rocking horse with a horse-hair mane and tail, all of which were still in her room, still pristine, still ignored, still unloved, still unwanted.

At least, thought Megan crossly, she'd managed to make her mother see sense about her clothes. A stand-up, knock-'em-down, drag-'em-out row in John Lewis had put paid to Start-Rite shoes, tartan kilts and coats with velvet collars. She'd stamped her foot and cried, her mother had been ashen-faced, shushing and embarrassed. Megan was a little embarrassed herself at the memory – after all she had been eleven at the time and hardly of an age to be throwing a tantrum in public, but the ploy had worked. She knew her mother would crack before she did and after ten minutes (although it had seemed infinitely longer) she had got her mother to agree to

30

take her to Top Shop. She hadn't needed to set foot in John Lewis since. And now, thank God, she was like the rest of her classmates when out of uniform, indistinguishable in baggy jeans, skimpy tops and hooded sweatshirts.

She pulled her case towards her and flicked open the catches. The lid sprang open and Megan reached in and pulled out the latest *Cosmo*. She thought it better if she stayed out of her mother's way for a while. She immersed herself in an article about body piercing – if she was going to get her belly button done she needed to know the possible pitfalls. She'd just finished that and was about to start doing the 'How Sexy are You?' quiz when there was a knock on her door. Guiltily she stuffed the magazine back in her case. Mum would not approve. 'Yeah,' she called.

Her father opened it. 'Hiya Megs. Got a hug for your dad?'

Megan scrambled off her bed and ran over to him. She put her head on his chest as he folded her in his arms. His khaki jersey was scratchy but she didn't care and it smelt as it always did – a faint mix of cigarette smoke and his aftershave.

Bob ruffled her hair. 'Hmm. Not sure about the colour.'

'Don't you start as well,' she mumbled into the wool.

'Your mother giving you a hard time?'

'What do you think?' Megan looked up at him. 'You know what she's like.'

'It's only 'cause she wants the best for you.'

'No. It's because she wants me to be like Princess Eugenie.'

Bob laughed. Megan knew he agreed with her but that he couldn't say so. They both knew Alice pored over anything to do with royal children in her glossy magazines.

'So, do you approve of your new home?'

''S OK.'

'It's big.'

'Mum must be in seventh heaven.'

'Probably.' They both laughed again. 'I've got to go back to work. I only popped back to say hello to you. It's a bit busy at the moment.'

'Yeah.' Megan resented the army with a vengeance. She hated the way it was always taking her father away from her.

'So why don't you come downstairs and make your peace with your mother?'

'She still mad at me?'

'She's calmed down. I think the hair was a bit of a shock.'

'Yeah, well . . .'

'Not quite as you planned either, eh?'

'Of course it was.' Megan couldn't hold her father's steady gaze. 'Well, not quite,' she finally admitted.

'So let your mother pay to have it sorted out. It'll make her happy.'

'Maybe.'

'She could probably do with a hand too. She's up to her ears in baking in the kitchen.'

'Coffee morning tomorrow. She told me.'

'Well, I'd best get back to the office. See you at supper.'

Her dad left the room. Megan stared after him. She wished he didn't have to go away. Six months meant he was going to be away for the summer too. Back for Christmas. Well, hoo-bloody-ray. There was still the problem of eight weeks in the summer with only her mother for company.

At seven thirty Ginny called it a day. She'd been in the office since eight that morning and, apart from a toasted sandwich that she had grabbed from the mess at lunchtime, she had worked solidly. Maddy and Richard were expecting her for 'kitchen supper' and she owed it to her hosts to have a shower and change out of uniform before she went round. She grabbed a pile of papers that Colonel Bob had asked to see and wandered along to his office.

'He's just left,' Richard informed her, seeing her standing in the doorway. He was busy clearing his desk and locking the safe.

'Oh, he wanted these.' She waved the sheaf of documents.

'Leave them on his desk.'

'No. I'll drop them in to Montgomery House on the way round to yours. He said he wanted to see them today.'

'Would you like me to do it?'

'No, it's OK. He may want to ask me questions about a couple of things.'

'OK then. See you later.'

Ginny left regimental headquarters and scooted back to the mess. In record time she showered, changed, repaired her make-up and tidied her hair. Squirting a puff of perfume with one hand she grabbed the papers with the other and left her room just as the grandfather clock in the entrance hall struck eight. A couple of minutes later she rang the bell of Montgomery House. She hoped she wasn't interrupting supper or anything; eight was an awkward time to be calling.

An odd looking waif with jet black hair opened the door. 'Yes,' said the child.

'Megan?' Surely not.

'Yes.'

'Really?'

Big sigh. 'Yes.'

Ginny remembered her manners. 'God, I'm sorry. You must think I'm dreadfully rude. Except that the last time I saw you, you could only have been about two, two and a half.'

'Oh.'

'I used to babysit you.'

'Oh.'

This conversation was proving too much like hard work for Ginny. 'Is your dad in?'

'Yeah.'

Perhaps it wasn't cool to be chatty when you were thirteen.

Megan left the door open and Ginny stepped into the hall. From a room on the right Ginny could hear a murmur of voices, then Megan reappeared and told Ginny to go into the sitting room before disappearing upstairs.

'Come through here, Ginny,' called Bob. 'Come and say hello to Alice.'

Ginny followed the direction of the CO's voice. Ginny noted that Alice's taste hadn't altered a jot in the intervening years, only now it was on a grander scale. Even more she seemed to be trying to recreate the drawing room of some stately home. There were more ornaments, more little tables, more silver photo frames, more antiques, a big overmantel mirror on the wall and natty tie-backs on the curtains. Ginny thanked her lucky stars she didn't have to clean and polish this lot. She pitied whoever did. Somehow she didn't think it was Alice these days.

33

She switched her attention from the room to her boss's wife, sitting on a rather uncomfortable-looking Queen Ann chair, stitching a piece of needlework and watching an opera on BBC2. Very country house, thought Ginny cattily.

'Hello, Alice. How lovely to see you again.' She hoped she sounded sincere.

'Ginny. How nice. Bob told me you were here. Have you settled in all right?'

'I was about to ask you the same.'

There was a brief silence and the two women smiled at each other with their mouths but not with their eyes.

'Can I offer you a drink or something?' said Alice.

'No. I can't stay. I'm late already.' Ginny switched her attention to the colonel. 'I've brought those papers you wanted.'

'Oh, surely they could have waited until morning,' interrupted Alice.

'I did ask to see them today,' said Bob with a slight smile to Ginny, as if to apologize. Alice sniffed.

Ginny felt the sooner she got out of there the less she would upset Alice. She didn't care about Alice's feelings but it wasn't a good idea to antagonize the boss's wife in front of the boss – even if you knew that he liked you. 'Right, well I'd better go, leave you in peace.'

'Off somewhere nice?' asked Bob.

'Supper at Richard and Maddy's.'

'That'll be fun.'

Ginny nodded. She thought she had detected a hint of wistfulness in his voice. She didn't think Alice went in for 'fun' evenings somehow. Once again Ginny wondered why Bob had married Alice. She just didn't seem his type. Perhaps she had been more of a live wire in her youth.

Maddy pushed the bottle of Beaujolais across the table to Ginny. 'Help yourself.'

'Cheers.' Ginny upended it and poured the last of it into her glass.

'I'll get another,' said Richard.

'Not on my account,' said Ginny. 'I think I'll have to go into work tomorrow.'

'Not going to Alice's coffee morning?' asked Maddy.

'I'm not qualified. I'm not one of her wives.'

'Lucky you,' muttered Maddy. 'With the men away I can see it's going to be such fun here having Alice in charge. It almost makes me want to rush out, find a childminder and get a job.' Richard cleared his throat to get Maddy's attention and frowned at her. 'What's that for?'

'Well . . .'

'Oh don't be such a stick in the mud,' said Ginny, who understood exactly what was going on. 'We all know that Colonel Bob might be the best boss in the world, and I know you're the most loyal adjutant ever, but it doesn't stop his wife from being a royal pain in the arse.'

'Hear, hear,' said Maddy. 'And Ginny hardly has any dealings with her, so if she thinks that . . .'

'How are your folks these days?' said Richard, deliberately steering the conversation a new way.

'Dad's still working for the Foreign Office and Mum is still trailing around the world after him.'

'Where are they at the moment?'

'Australia. Mum loves it because the sunshine suits her rheumatism. I get the impression Dad is a bit bored. I think he'd like somewhere more challenging.'

'Like?'

'Moscow or Beijing, that sort of place. The worst diplomatic crisis in Oz in recent years was when their prime minister put his hand on the Queen. Hardly major league stuff.'

'And your sister?' asked Maddy.

'Oh, Netta doesn't change. You know her. She's either just given birth, just about to or announcing she's pregnant.'

'I remember,' said Maddy. 'How many kids has she got now?'

'Four. Number five is due around Christmas.'

'Good God. How does she manage it?'

'It's being stuck in the Isles of Scilly. I don't think she's got anything else to do except shag.'

'And change nappies,' said Maddy with feeling. 'Five. And the oldest can't be more than six.'

'She will be seven when the baby is born.'

'There you go Mads,' said Richard. 'You ought to take Netta as a role model and give Danielle a brother or sister or two.'

Maddy gave Ginny a sideways look of faintly amused horror. 'In your dreams, sunshine. One more is my limit.'

'Well that's an advance,' said Richard. 'A couple of months ago it was still "never again".'

When Bob walked into the mess bar a few days later it was crowded. Perhaps not surprising, considering that it was nearly time for dinner, but normally it would not be quite so packed. The single officers would often book out from the evening meal in order to go into the nearest town to see a film, catch the train up to London to go to a club or just stay in their rooms to watch TV. However, he had warned the regiment that he was going to call a snap twenty-four-hour exercise within the next few days and effectively all leave had been cancelled until it was over, thus gating all personnel, including the single officers. It had caused some rumblings throughout the barracks but, even if the wives remained unhappy about the forthcoming tour of Kosovo, there was mostly a buzz of excitement amongst the officers and men alike. The thought of going somewhere in the world where they would be training for real, not just going through the motions, had given them all a very real sense of purpose. As one had put it, 'It'll be nice to stop rehearsing and get on with the performance.'

Silence fell when the men noticed the colonel.

'Carry on,' he called to them all. 'Don't mind me.' As he walked to the bar and began to write out a chit for cigarettes the noise began to climb back to its previous level. He was aware that Ginny was sitting at a table on his left, surrounded by a small group. Without looking in her direction he consciously began to eavesdrop.

'I still say that as soon as the exercise is over we ought to go. We're bound to get a couple of days off and Alton Towers will be almost empty. The public schools have broken up but the state schools haven't.'

'But it's for kids,' said one of the group.

'You obviously haven't been on any of the rides,' retorted Ginny. 'I tell you, there's a couple there where you are seriously advised to wear incontinence knickers.'

The colonel turned away slightly to hide a smile. Ginny was still as outrageous as she always had been.

The group dissented and made excuses about duty trips to parents and time to be spent with girlfriends.

'But if you lot don't go I either have to go on my own—' she noticed the ironic grins. 'Yeah, I know. I'm really sad. Billy No-mates,' she chanted in a sort of sing-song. '*Or,*' she continued, 'I have to stay here because I really haven't got anywhere else I can go. You lot can all piss off to your relations but mine all live too far away.' One of the young officers mimed playing a violin. 'Oh, naff off,' she said good-naturedly. 'Just because you lot are a wussy bunch of losers who get scared.'

The steward handed the CO his cigarettes and Bob left.

'Bye, sir,' a number of his subordinates called after him. Bob gave them a cheery wave and went home to put to Alice the idea that had been forming in his head.

'No,' Alice said. 'I really don't think it's a good idea at all. Besides which, all those awful rides'll make Megan sick.'

'I think she'd love it. Why don't we ask her?'

'Because if we do . . . Well, I just don't think we should.'

'What you mean is that if we ask her and she wants to go you really haven't got a leg to stand on.'

'Nonsense.' Alice saw the look on Bob's face. 'Well, not nonsense. I would just rather she didn't go.'

'Why, for heaven's sake?'

'I'm sure the place will be full of dreadful people and if she doesn't enjoy it she'll spoil Ginny's fun. Anyway, I can't see Ginny wanting to be saddled with a thirteen-year-old for the day.'

'I don't think she'll mind. I expect she'll be glad of the company.' Bob sensed that Alice was running out of ideas as to why Megan shouldn't have a day at a theme park. He knew that she didn't want Megan to go because she was a snob and didn't approve of such places. More than likely she would have them filed in the same category as holiday camps, bingo halls and coach tours. 'Why don't I ask her? She can always say no.'

Alice was a poor loser. 'OK,' she said tartly. 'I can see that you've made your mind up regardless of what I think. I don't know why you bothered to ask my opinion. You obviously don't want it.' She gave him a cold stare and returned to the kitchen where she banged about noisily as she finished preparing dinner.

Bob went into the hall and phoned the mess.

When the steward told Ginny it was the colonel on the phone she assumed it was something to do with work, although she was puzzled that he'd said nothing when he'd come in for his cigarettes. She took the call.

'Look,' said the colonel, 'I hope you don't mind but I heard you were planning to go to Alton Towers.'

'Yes,' said Ginny slowly. She didn't have a clue where this was leading.

'And you thought you might end up going on your own.'

'Yes,' even more slowly.

'Well, I think Megan might like to go, and I'm really too tied up here to think about taking her and . . .' Ginny heard the colonel pause. 'And I don't think Alice would really want to drive all that way.' Ginny translated that as 'Alice would rather die than go there.'

'So would you like to take Megan? We'll pay for her, of course, and go halves on the petrol,' she heard him add quickly. 'Be honest though,' he said. 'I really don't want you to feel obliged to take her just because it's me asking.'

'You mean I shouldn't feel intimidated by your rank, Colonel,' said Ginny with a chuckle. 'Don't worry, I'm not.' But all the same she wasn't sure what to say. On one hand she really wanted a day at Alton Towers, but on the other hand she didn't want to go on her own. But was Megan the company she wanted? The impression she had got from her one recent encounter with the teenager was of a sulky, monosyllabic weirdo. Still, if Megan wanted to go, the chances were she was going to try and enjoy herself and consequently she might turn out to be good fun. And surely it would be better to go with Megan than go on her own – or stay in the mess.

'Do I take it from the pause that it's a no?'

'No, not at all. I'd love to take her. I wasn't sure she would want to come with me. She doesn't really know me.' A bit of an exaggeration, thought Ginny. She doesn't know me from Adam.

'I don't think that'll matter. I haven't said anything to

Megan yet. Of course there is the possibility that she has got other plans.'

'You mean, that she wouldn't be seen dead in the company of someone as ancient as me.'

'Not at all. And as for ancient – hardly.'

'Flatterer.' Ginny took advantage of their informal conversation to ask a question that she could not have done under other circumstances. 'So does this mean the rumour that the exercise is tomorrow is kosher?'

'You might think that but I couldn't possibly say,' said the CO, doing a very passable imitation of a well-known TV villain. 'And please don't say anything to anyone else – whatever your suspicions.'

'You can trust me, Colonel.'

'I know.' There was a pause. The silence extended another couple of seconds. Ginny got the distinct impression that the colonel was about to say something else and had thought the better of it. The CO cleared his throat. 'Yes, right. I'll go and tell Megan and let you know her answer.' She wondered what he had really been going to say.

Ginny wandered back into the dining room to continue her meal. She felt ridiculously pleased that the colonel trusted her so much that he was happy for her to look after his only child for a whole day. What was it about the man that with just a few words he could make you feel so good? He'd always been able to do that, she thought. He had a knack for making the person he was focusing his attention on feel special. It probably explained why he was now the rank he was, unlike many of his contemporaries who were still majors.

'What's your map reading like?' Ginny asked Megan, who looked more normal now her hair was back to being auburn. The grapevine had passed on the news that Alice had been less than thrilled by her daughter's foray into home hair colouring and Ginny had wondered how long she would take to get it sorted. The answer, apparently, was next to no time.

'Dunno,' said Megan.

'Well, you're going to have to learn on the job then.' If Megan was coming along she could make herself useful. 'Here,' said Ginny as she pushed the road atlas on to Megan's lap. 'Watch and learn.' Ginny traced the route from the barracks up the country to the theme park with her finger, reading out the road numbers and the major towns that they would go through en route. 'OK, got that?'

'Think so.'

'Now you show me.'

Megan obediently did as she was told.

'Good. I'll be all right until we get past Birmingham, then you've got to take me across country.'

'I think I'll be able to do it.'

'Good,' said Ginny as she turned the key in the ignition and slipped the car into gear. She turned the car round and headed out of the barracks. Once she was on the main road she felt she could attempt a conversation with her passenger. 'So, how are the holidays going?'

'OK I suppose.'

'Got to be better than school, surely?'

'Anything's better than school,' said Megan with vehemence. 'Our head is called Miss Pink and . . .' And what followed was a long spiel about the unreasonableness of the school, the regime, the rules, the teaching methods . . .

'So do I gather that you don't much like it there?'

'Haven't you been listening?' shrieked Megan in indignation.

'Joke.'

'What?'

'I meant it as a joke.'

'Oh.' Then in a quiet voice, 'Sorry.'

'Don't worry about it.'

'I just thought you were like Mum. She never listens.'

Ginny didn't know quite how to respond. Part of her, the part that remembered Alice's many subtle social cuts, longed to know more about the home life of Alice, but part of her felt she shouldn't encourage family disloyalty.

'I'm sure she does really.'

'You don't know her.'

'True. I expect she's very busy though.'

'Busy climbing the social ladder.' Ginny pretended to be too busy overtaking to answer. She felt she was getting into dodgy territory. 'She wants Daddy to be a general.'

'Your father is perfectly capable of becoming a general by himself,' said Ginny a touch brusquely. Wanting the dirt dished on Alice was one thing, but Colonel Bob was off-limits, even if he was Megan's dad.

'That's as maybe, but Mum isn't taking any chances. She's been at it ever since they got married. There's never a weekend when she isn't throwing some sort of party or dinner. I'm sure Dad must hate it. It's not his scene at all.'

'I'm sure your father would say so if he didn't like it.' Whatever else Ginny thought about Bob, she was sure he wouldn't put up with things he hated just for a quiet life.

'Huh.'

Ginny decided to change the subject. 'If you look in the glove compartment you'll find some CDs. How about some music?'

Megan opened it and rummaged. 'Hey, you've got Nelly Furtado's latest. Great!' She slotted the disc into the player. Ginny smiled. The subject of Alice was closed, but fancy Alice being such an ambitious schemer. Maybe she wasn't so icy after all.

'Did you have a good time?' asked Bob when Megan finally arrived back at about eight. The way she tumbled through the front door meant that the question was pretty well rhetorical. Ginny, following more sedately behind, looked shattered.

'It was so wicked. Honestly the best fun ever.' She turned to Ginny. 'You enjoyed it too, didn't you?'

'It was brilliant. We had a great time.' She suppressed a yawn.

'Come on in, Ginny. You look beat. Have a drink to unwind after the long drive.'

'Thanks. That's really kind of you, Colonel.'

Ginny followed Bob through the house into the kitchen. 'I'm in here at the moment. I don't use the sitting room when I'm on my own.'

'No Alice?'

'She's out at some committee meeting or something. Lord knows what.'

The kitchen was warm and bright. In the corner the TV was tuned to a quiz show. Ginny thought how unlike her last visit to the house this was – no needlepoint and improving programmes tonight. When the cat's away . . .

'What can I get you?'

'Got any beer?'

'Course. Megan, run into the garage would you. There's a case of Stella there. And bring one back for me too.'

Megan obliged.

'Glass?' offered Bob.

Ginny raised her eyebrows. 'I thought you knew me better than that.'

Bob laughed. 'There was just a chance you might have gone down with a dose of sophistication.'

'Yeah, right.'

Megan returned, gave her father the beers and helped herself to a glass of cola.

'So, tell me all about it.'

By the time Megan had finished her blow-by-blow, ride-by-ride account of the day, Ginny and Bob were on to their second beer.

'It sounds terrifying,' said Bob.

'It's not really,' said Ginny. 'The vertical drop ride is a bit of a thrill.'

'Christ, it sounds like hell to me. I'm far too old for that sort of thing now.'

'Don't be silly,' said Ginny.

'That's very kind of you,' said Bob smiling at her warmly. 'Still, as long as you both had a good time.'

'We did. Now,' said Ginny putting her empty can on to the table, yawning and stretching like a cat so her shirt came out of the waistband of her trousers and displayed her flat midriff. Nonchalantly she tucked herself in again and said, 'I think I had better get back to the mess and leave you in peace. I'm pooped.'

'Thanks ever so much for taking me, Ginny,' said Megan with real gratitude in her voice. 'It was fantastic.'

'I enjoyed your company too.' Ginny put her arm round Megan's shoulders and gave her a squeeze. Megan looked up at her and smiled. 'Bye Megan.' She ruffled the teenager's now normal hair.

Bob stood up to accompany Ginny to the front door. 'And

I must give you my thanks too. You've obviously been a real hit with Megan.'

'She's a nice kid.'

'It's not her mother's opinion of her at the moment.'

'But that's it, I'm not her mother. I gave her a fun day out. I don't have to do any of the heavy-handed parental bit.'

'Thanks anyway, Ginny. I really appreciate it.' Then he leant forward and gave her a light kiss on the cheek. 'Night,' he said.

'Night,' said Ginny, stunned. She got back into her little car and drove it round to the mess. She sat in it for a few minutes in the car park. She wondered briefly about the kiss. The colonel wouldn't go around kissing his other officers like that, now would he? But then his other officers hadn't looked after his daughter all day, nor were they women. She rubbed the spot his lips had touched and told herself that she didn't fancy him one jot. Except the trouble was, she knew she was lying.

'If I hear one more word about that blasted woman,' said Alice, 'I think I may very well scream.'

Sarah was a little taken aback. When, in the local shop, she'd asked Alice how things were, she'd expected an answer to do with how she was settling in to her new quarter and whether or not she had got everything straight and how the business of redecoration was progressing.

'Which woman?' asked Sarah a little uncomfortably.

'Ginny Turner,' snapped Alice. 'Ever since she took Megan to Alton Towers I have heard nothing, but nothing, except how wonderful Ginny is.'

Sarah rather liked Ginny. They'd met briefly a few times in the mess bar and from what she'd seen, Ginny had seemed very good company. 'I expect Megan was rather flattered that Ginny took her at all.'

'It's not Megan who is banging on about her,' said Alice. 'It's Bob! All it's been for days now is Ginny this and Ginny that and Ginny the other.'

'Oh.' Sarah was at a loss to know exactly what to say. Alice was obviously insanely jealous that Ginny should have scored such a hit with her family. But what Alice said reminded Sarah of events in her own family a few years previously. Her sister had had a disastrous first marriage and, despite the fact that she insisted she was happy with her husband, Sarah could remember how often the name of a work colleague had cropped up in her sister's conversation. It had been Graham this, and Graham that and Graham the other, and in the end it had transpired that there had been a lot of 'the other' with Graham. Sarah couldn't help wondering if Bob had been smitten with Ginny's more than obvious charms. And frankly, she thought, if you were married to Alice, who wouldn't be?

As quickly as was decent, Sarah finished her conversation with Alice and returned home. Alisdair was where she had left him, sorting out his kit after yet another training exercise.

'You'll never guess what?' she crowed as she sat on the bed beside his pile of combat kit.

'What won't I guess?' asked Alisdair mildly, busy checking items off against a list as he repacked his webbing.

'Bob Davies is sweet on Ginny Turner.'

'Don't be ridiculous.'

'Bet?'

'Where on earth have you got this daft idea from?'

'Alice herself.' Sarah recounted their brief conversation.

'Doesn't prove a thing.'

'You only think that because you're not a woman. Woman's intuition, you'll see.'

'Well, don't say anything to anyone else. Personally I think you're barking up the wrong tree and spreading a rumour like that won't do anyone any favours. Besides which,' he added, a decidedly chilly tone creeping into his voice, 'I don't understand why you are so completely anti Alice. OK, she's a bit of a dinosaur. OK, she likes to see herself as Lady Bountiful but she's harmless enough, surely?'

Sarah knew she had gone too far – Alisdair was cross. And perhaps she was being a little unfair taking so much delight in Alice's annoyance over Bob's attitude to Ginny, but there was pleasure to be had in seeing her discomfiture. She was always so bloody perfect, so certain of her own superiority, so sure that she was so much better than anyone else, that she alone knew the right way of doing things – so it was nice, just once, to see Alice wrong-footed. Still, it would be best not to voice this to Alisdair.

'Well, maybe,' she said, hoping she sounded contrite.

'The last thing Ginny needs is for a rumour to start up that things are more than platonic between her and Bob just before we all go off on an emergency tour. You know the ideas some of the wives get about their husbands being stuck in some godforsaken place with a handful of females. It's no good telling them that most of the girls with us have their own husbands, fiancés or boyfriends. There are some wives who believe that their men can't be trusted to keep their trousers zipped for a second once they are away from home. Any talk about Ginny – or any of the girls in the regiment – is only going to make things worse.'

Sarah rolled her eyes. 'OK, OK. I get the picture.'

'Good, lecture over.'

A week later things in the regiment were still hectic. Weekends and weekdays had blurred because the men were given a day off when their punishing training schedule permitted, which didn't necessarily mean a Saturday or Sunday. It looked as if they were not even going to get a break over the Easter weekend and all the families had been warned to put any plans for the holiday on hold. Maddy didn't mind too much. With only a toddler to cope with and no school holidays to take into consideration it didn't really matter to her, but she knew it was difficult for the families with older children. She knew Sarah's two, Will and Jenny, were less than thrilled by the dull Easter they were faced with.

Maddy was in the kitchen feeding Danielle her lunch and listening to some music. She hummed along to the new number one as she helped her daughter push chunks of fish finger on to a spoon. She heard the front door click.

'Richard,' she called. 'In the kitchen.' She heard the sound of stuff being dumped in the hall.

'Hi sweetheart. Hi gorgeous,' he greeted them as he walked into the kitchen. He wandered over to the radio and turned the volume down a little.

'Meanie,' said Maddy. 'We can hardly hear it now, can we Danny?' Danielle didn't comment. She was too busy trying to grab the last bit of fish with her pudgy starfish hand.

'Got a letter for you.'

'Oh God, not another summons from Alice. I haven't recovered from the coffee morning yet.'

Richard grinned. 'No I don't think so. This is from the livers-in.'

'Oh, that's different. Gimme!'

Richard returned to the hall and found the envelope. Maddy wiped her fingers on a tea towel and ripped it open.

'Brill! It's a party.'

'That sounds fun. When?'

'The Saturday after Easter. We'll have to get a babysitter. If all else fails I expect Ginny would let us put Danny to sleep in her room. We can take it in turns to pop up and see how she is.'

'Yeah. Actually that would be the best idea. Then it means there's one more babysitter for the others.'

Danielle had finished her main course and was banging her spoon on the tray of her high chair to signal she was ready for some pudding. Maddy took a yoghurt out of the fridge and removed the top, licked it, pronounced it 'scrummy', and gave it to her daughter.

'So have you finished for the day?'

'Yeah. Considering it was supposed to be a day's leave I suppose I'm lucky that I only had to work half of it.'

'Poor babe.'

'It wasn't just me that was at work on a day off. Most of Regimental HQ was in – the colonel, Ginny, the chief clerk.'

'Alisdair?'

'No. But he's been working so much overtime this last fortnight he's barely been home at all.'

'Poor Sarah.'

'She's OK.'

'She may put a brave face on it but she hates the idea of yet more separation and the fact that Alisdair has been working round the clock. Will and Jenny haven't really seen their father this holiday.'

'How do you know?'

'Wife talk.'

'Ah.'

'You should say "ah" indeed. Us wives could give the Signals a run for their money when it comes to communications.

Our jungle drums and grapevine can beat any of your radios hollow when it comes to transmitting intelligence.'

'I don't doubt it, especially knowing how much you gossip. How was the toddler group today?'

'Danny had a great time, didn't you poppet?' Danny raised her eyes at the sound of her name but she was far too engrossed with her strawberry yoghurt to make more of an effort by way of acknowledgement. 'It was good. I suppose about twenty turned up. No one was sick, no one threw a tantrum. Even the kids were quite well behaved.'

Richard smiled. 'Sounds like fun.'

'Well, it's good for Danny to get out to play with other kids. Caro and Josie's two are nice friends for Danny, but Josie's Pip will be off to nursery in the autumn and Caro thinks Mike is due a posting soon, so they'll be off too.' Maddy sighed. 'Let's hope some other people with kids move in soon or Danny'll be the only toddler on the patch.'

'But I thought that's why you take her to the toddler group in the village. So she can make friends with kids who will be here for the duration.'

'Yeah. But we'll move one day, won't we? I suppose all I'm doing is prolonging the agony.'

'That sounds very defeatist.'

'It's not meant to be. It's just we had a new member join today and she told me that she'd bought the cottage on the green – you know, the one by the bus stop that we both said would be our dream house if we ever stop moving round – and I suppose I'm just a bit envious, that's all.'

'We'll get our dream house one day.'

'Yeah.' But Maddy wasn't convinced. Still, this was no time to be down in the dumps. Richard didn't need her being a misery guts along with everything else. 'Anyway, this new mum is lovely. She's called Taz – s'pose it's short for something – and she and I had a long chat. She's moved here from London and her little girl is nearly the same age as Danielle. They played together quite nicely.' She smiled at her daughter as she said this and Danielle, who had finished her yoghurt, held her arms out to be lifted down from her high chair. Maddy got a damp cloth and quickly wiped her hands and face before lifting her out. 'There you go, darling,' she said as she lowered Danny to the floor. Danielle stood for a few seconds before dropping on to her hands and knees and crawling into the sitting room.

'I do wish she'd walk,' sighed Maddy.

'It's not as if she can't. She's just idle. She can go quicker on all fours, so why should she bother with the effort of walking.'

'All the same, at the toddler group, all the other children over about a year can walk. Taz's little girl walked at ten months apparently.'

'And who's Taz?' asked Richard, who hadn't been listening properly.

'This new woman I told you about. The one who bought our dream house.'

'Oh.'

'And the really good thing about becoming friends with her is that I expect I'll be able to visit her and see if the house is as nice on the inside as it looks on the outside.'

'Mum?'

'Yes, Megan.' Alice silently wished her daughter called her 'Mummy' rather than 'Mum', but she knew full well that if she said anything it would make Megan even more contrary. She put down her magazine to give her daughter her complete attention.

'Mum, there's a party in the mess the weekend before I go back to school.'

'I know, dear. Your father and I have been invited.'

'Oh.' Megan looked astounded. Alice ignored her implication that the livers-in wouldn't want her and Bob at their party.

'So, what about the party?'

'Nothing.'

'There must be something or you wouldn't have mentioned it.'

Silence.

'For heaven's sake, Megan.' Alice was beginning to get annoyed. She had been particularly enjoying an article on life with the Grimaldi family in Monte Carlo and she wanted to return to it. 'Why on earth would you be interested in a grown-up party anyway?'

48

'Because Ginny has invited me.'

'Don't be ridiculous.' Alice returned to her magazine. How on earth had Megan got that idea into her head?

'She has,' insisted Megan.

Alice lowered her magazine again. 'Megan, I don't know why on earth you think that someone like Ginny would want to invite you to an adult party in the officers' mess, but I can assure you that you have got the wrong end of the stick. She just wouldn't have done.'

'But she has, look.' Megan hauled a piece of card out of her jeans pocket and stuffed the creased and dog-eared scrap into Alice's hand.

Alice read it. That bloody woman, she thought vehemently. What on earth was she doing inviting a young girl to a party that would no doubt end up as an exhibition in intoxication and bad behaviour – and without asking her parents' permission first.

'Well, you'll have to decline.'

'That's not fair.'

'Fair or not, young lady, that's what you are going to do.'

'But she wants me to go.'

'Of course she doesn't. She's just being polite.' She's just stirring things more like, thought Alice.

'Who's just being polite?' said Bob from the doorway into the sitting room.

'No one, darling,' said Alice smoothly.

'Ginny,' Megan butted in angrily.

'How is she being polite?'

'She has invited Megan to the party the single officers are holding next Saturday.'

'Is that so bad?'

'I don't think it is suitable for Megan, that's all. She's too young.'

'Mum. I'm nearly fourteen.'

'You are *only* thirteen,' riposted Alice. 'My point exactly.'

Bob sighed. The judgement of Solomon was needed here. 'Perhaps if she just went for an hour or so. Till ten o'clock.'

Megan opened her mouth and looked as if she was about to protest but Bob shot her a warning glance. Megan shut her mouth again. Alice might just be persuaded to compromise, to

49

allow Megan to put in an appearance, but it would be foolish to hope for more than that.

'I'll see,' Alice conceded grudgingly.

Sarah finished writing the details of the party in her diary and went through into the sitting room to talk to Alisdair. The television was on and Will and Jenny were glued to some daytime soap. She'd tried remonstrating about the waste of time such programmes were, only to get withering looks from the two teenagers so she had given up. However, she picked up the remote control and turned the volume down so she could speak to Alisdair without shouting.

'I've had a look at the date of the mess party. As it doesn't kick off till half past eight, why don't we have a gang of people round for a few drinks first?'

'That sounds like a good idea. Who have you got in mind? Apart from Bob and Alice that is.'

'Ha ha, very funny.'

Alisdair gave her a long look. 'Actually, I'm serious. If we're having people round it would look most odd, not to say rude, if we didn't invite them. They can always decline but we must make the offer.'

Sarah was about to open her mouth and tell Alisdair to stuff that idea when she remembered his disapproval of her gossip about Bob and Ginny. But then the devil in her got the better of her and she couldn't resist making a snide comment. 'My, we are being grown-up and responsible these days.'

'Look, I know you don't get on with Alice that well but Bob is my boss and he's also my friend. Furthermore, as his second in command we have to work hand in glove and if we fall out the regiment just won't function properly. We're about to go to Kosovo which, and I shouldn't have to tell you this, isn't going to be a picnic, and I really don't need you stirring it with his wife or giving me a hard time at home.'

'Mum, Dad,' said Will, staying glued to the box, 'if you're going to have a row could you do it in the kitchen. Jen and I want to watch this.'

Sarah felt her face redden with shame. Alisdair was right, of course he was. And he was tired. And she was being a complete cow. And in front of the kids who were having a rotten enough holiday anyway. 'I'm sorry darling. You're right. Of course we will invite them. And who else? The rest of the patch or just the RHQ officers and their wives?'

'Well, I think we owe hospitality to quite a few people. When was the last time we had anyone to supper?'

Will rolled over, grabbed the remote and with a loud sigh pointedly turned the volume up again.

Sarah decided to ignore this and just raised her voice a notch. 'God, not everyone. We'd never squeeze them all in. Let's just have the Greenwoods, Alice and Bob – we could have the doctor and Josie too. I know they're not really RHQ but they're a nice couple. And we ought to have Caroline and Mike. I know they're not RHQ either but as they live next door I really think they ought to come. And what about Ginny?'

'But she lives in. Won't she be helping get the mess ready?'

'She can always say no. Besides, I think I'd like to get to know her better. She seems fun.'

'She is. A great girl.'

'That's settled then.'

'Have you two finished?' said Jen. 'We want to watch this and we can hardly hear it. If you want to natter can you go next door?'

Taz held the door of her Regency cottage open wide so Maddy and the buggy could squeeze through.

'Tight fit,' said Maddy, desperately hoping she was going to make it without scraping the paint.

'I don't think builders in the late eighteenth century had come across pushchairs. I don't think they factored that need into their designs – along with decent plumbing and draught-proof windows.'

'That was said with feeling.'

'Oh, don't get me wrong. I love this house to bits, but it needs a heap of work done on it and I can only afford to do it bit by bit.'

Maddy noticed the 'I' rather than 'we' but didn't say anything. Perhaps Taz was a single mum. Or perhaps there was a Mr Taz but he was away. Not that Maddy cared one way or another; it was no business of hers after all, but she was curious by nature. She resolved to find out. Especially

51

as she knew exactly what exorbitant sum the house had been advertised for in the local papers so there had to be some money from somewhere.

Taz showed them into the sitting room. Maddy gave a little gasp of delight.

'But it's so pretty.'

'It is, isn't it? It's the reason that I couldn't resist buying this place, despite its faults.'

The room had the most wonderful ceiling of ornate plasterwork, which had been painted in white and the palest shade of yellow. On the floor was an oriental rug in shades of pale green and the chairs had been upholstered in a green and yellow Regency-stripe fabric. Dark green velvet curtains hung at the windows and on the walls were three big watercolours of country landscapes. The whole room looked wonderful and harmonious but because it was very simple it also looked child-friendly. No little tables to bump into or tempting ornaments to handle. Frankly, with a toddler in tow, Maddy was quite relieved.

'Where's Amelia?'

'She's upstairs having a rest, but I expect she'll wake up any minute now. In fact,' she crouched down to talk to Danielle, 'shall we go upstairs and see if Amelia's awake and you could find some toys to play with? Would you like that?' Danielle nodded vigorously. 'Good. Let's go upstairs shall we?' She held out her hand to Danny who grasped it firmly.

'Shall I come?' said Maddy hopefully. She longed to see more of the house.

'Of course.'

Taz obviously guessed Maddy's wish because as she led them across the hall to the stairs she pointed out the dining room, the kitchen and her study.

'Oh, you work,' said Maddy as they began to mount the stairs.

'Yes. Don't sound so surprised.'

'Sorry, did I? It's just that most of the mums I know don't.'

'Lucky them. Most of the mums I know have to.'

They reached the landing and Taz showed Maddy some bright plastic crates full of toys. Danny instantly occupied herself by pulling out one after another and then discarding each toy in turn as the next plaything caught her eye. Carefully shutting the stair gate, Taz went in to see if her daughter was waking up and left Maddy and Danny with the toys on the landing. Maddy couldn't resist a peek into a couple of rooms before she joined Taz in Amelia's bedroom. The toddler was just stirring in her cot. Taz pulled the curtains and woke the child properly.

'Let's change this nappy shall we,' she said when Amelia had finished rubbing her eyes and yawning.

'So what do you do?' asked Maddy as Taz got busy with a clean disposable and some talcum powder.

'I do some freelance stuff for a couple of big London companies. I work from home and fax or email my stuff in.'

'Interesting.'

'Paperwork. But it pays the bills.'

It certainly does, thought Maddy as she wondered how much it had cost to get this house looking as it did. There was a possibility that the decor might have been like this when Taz had moved in, but the matching bedding and curtains, the pictures on the walls and the beautiful nursery furniture had all cost a bomb. Whatever it was that Taz did, it paid very well. Or perhaps it was her man's job that was so well rewarded. She had to find out.

'So, um, what does your husband do?' she asked as casually as she could.

'No husband. That's why I work.'

'Ah.'

'And yours?'

'He's an army officer.'

'Really? How incredibly interesting.'

'It isn't, you know.'

'Let's take the little ones downstairs and get them something to drink and you can tell me all about what it's like to be an army wife over a cup of tea.'

Maddy was flattered that Taz should be so interested. No one else she knew was the least bit interested in her lifestyle. All the moving, separation and the grotty quarters didn't seem like a good topic of conversation to her, but if Taz was keen to know then Maddy was quite prepared to give her the low-down, warts and all.

After Maddy had gone, Taz made sure that Amelia was happily occupied and went back into her study. She dialled the number of the features editor at the *Mercury*. As she expected, she got put through to Minty Armstrong's voicemail.

'Minty. It's me, Taz. I've had an idea for a feature. How about something on army wives? "The Birds in the Barracks", that sort of thing. The article about the Earl of Knightsbridge is done. I'll fax it through tomorrow. Give me a ring when you've read it.'

She put the phone down. If Minty liked her new idea for a feature, she knew she'd probably have to admit to Maddy that she had been more than a little economical with the truth when she had said what she did for a living. It wasn't exactly paperwork – more that she worked for the papers. She wondered how Maddy would react when she found out that her new friend was a top flight freelance journalist.

By the time the day of the party came round, Sarah and Alisdair's pre-party party had grown like Topsy. Her plans for a select gathering had been ditched and it had degenerated into a big get-together. By the time most people had arrived there was standing room only in her sitting room. As she brought through a tray of sausage rolls and pushed her way into the centre of the room she thought with a little disappointment that, for a lot of people, they weren't making much noise. She began handing around the nibbles, telling her guests not to worry about crumbs on the carpet while Alisdair distributed more wine and beer. She hoped that as the drink flowed the decibels would increase. It was a good mix of people, she thought, so there was no reason why they should be so subdued. Perhaps it was that everyone was tired with all the training the regiment had been doing recently, or perhaps it was the imminent departure of the men that was making them all feel less than jolly. Well, whatever it was, all Sarah could do was to fix a smile on her face and try to make the best of things and hope the party livened up in the near future, otherwise it would be a dull bunch moving across to the mess in an hour.

She did a quick headcount to see if everyone had arrived. Bob and Alice had yet to put in an appearance and Maddy was still over in the mess trying to get Danielle to go to sleep in Ginny's bed, helped by Ginny herself. The doorbell went.

'I'll get it,' she mouthed over the chat to Alisdair as she thrust the tray of eats into Caro's hand and asked her to make herself useful.

She pushed through her guests and escaped into the cool calm of the hall. Feeling a little flustered, partly through entertaining so many guests but partly because the entertaining wasn't going as well as she had hoped, she brushed some flaky pastry crumbs off her dress and opened the door. She was confronted by a tall, slim blonde wearing a leopard-print bodysuit, high heels and a chain belt. The sight was so extreme that Sarah almost didn't recognize Ginny. Bloody hell, she thought.

'Sarah, I'm so sorry I'm late.'

'Ginny. Wow!'

'God, is it too much? Maddy says like I look like a reject from the cast of *Cats*.'

'No, no.' Sarah was faintly nonplussed. She had thought almost exactly what Maddy had, but what a reject! 'No, not at all. I'm just envious. If I wore a bodysuit I'd look like a sack full of snakes – all lumps and bumps and bulges.'

'No you wouldn't,' said Ginny, running her eye up and down Sarah's size twelve figure.

Sarah spotted the eye movement. 'Yeah, but what you don't see is the whalebone underneath holding it all together. In a bodysuit you have to rely on skin and muscle to keep it all in shape.'

'Sarah, that's *so* not true. You want to put your trust in Lycra – I have. Honest.'

Sarah found herself irresistibly drawn to Ginny. There was something so disingenuous about her – and so outrageous.

'Come on in. You'll catch your death in that outfit if I keep you standing on the doorstep any longer.'

'No chance of me popping my clogs,' said Ginny, picking up a large cool box that Sarah hadn't noticed until that moment and stepping over the threshold. 'Only the good die young.' She plonked the cool box down on the hall carpet as Sarah shut the front door behind her. 'And Maddy sends apologies. Danielle is refusing to go to sleep, the minx, so she sent me over to explain. I was going to stay with Danny and let Maddy join Richard, but Maddy wouldn't hear of it. Anyway, I thought that as I couldn't bring Maddy at least I could bring this.' She indicated the cool box. 'I hope you don't mind or take offence but everyone's so knackered after Colonel Bob's training regime I thought we could all do with a bit of rocket fuel.' She whipped the top off the box and revealed half a dozen bottles of ice-cold champagne. 'If I'm out of order please say so, but I think nothing gets an evening off to a flying start like a glass of fizz and I thought I'd like to make a contribution to events.'

Sarah was momentarily lost for words. Gin . . . Wow . . . Gosh . . .'

'I'm sorry. It was crass of me. You've got everything arranged and I'm going completely over the top, as usual.'

'No. It's wonderful. It's too much.'

'Why?'

'Why?' Wasn't it obvious? Most guests felt they were being generous if they brought one bottle of wine round. But *six* bottles – and champagne! 'It's just so extravagant.'

'Look, I'm single, I'm off to Kosovo in a short while, I'm not going to spend money on petrol, drink or clothes for six months. Do the sum. I think you'll find I can run to a few bottles of fizz.'

'Well, if you're sure.'

'Actually,' said Ginny putting the lid back on the box. 'You're right. What was I thinking about?'

'Oh.' Sarah felt a little cheated. Perhaps she shouldn't have protested so strongly. Her face fell.

'Joke!' said Ginny, whipping the top off again with a huge grin. 'Your face is a picture. Come on. Let's get some corks popping.'

Sarah led the way into the sitting room with Ginny following behind already unscrewing the metal cage off one of the corks.

'Drink up,' called Sarah. 'Ginny's—' But the cork popped with a satisfying bang before Sarah could finish and Ginny grabbed a nearby glass to stop the white foam from falling on to the carpet.

'Who's for champers?' called Ginny. There was a chorus of assent and the noise level instantly rose. Well done Ginny, Sarah thought.

Alisdair came and stood beside her.

'You don't mind?' he said into her ear.

'How could I? It was all a bit flat and now it's zinging. Does she always have this effect?'

'Don't know, but I wouldn't be surprised.' The doorbell rang again. 'I'll go. It's probably the colonel.'

Sarah didn't vie for the privilege of letting in his boss. She just hoped that now her drinks party had taken off the arrival of Bob and Alice wouldn't kill it stone dead.

Sarah, hot and puffed from a recent stint on the dance floor with Alisdair, was recovering with an ice-cold cola at the mess bar, chatting to Maddy and Richard. As she talked she was aware of a commotion developing in the ante-room, clearly visible through the open double doors that divided the two rooms. At the centre of the kerfuffle appeared to be Megan and Ginny. She let her attention wander as she wondered what on earth was going on. A group of young officers and their girlfriends had formed a circle round Megan who appeared to be engaged in some sort of gymnastics. As Sarah watched it appeared that Megan, egged on by the gaggle of young subalterns, was trying to teach Ginny how to do a backwards walkover. Quite why Ginny wanted to learn this gymnastic feat during a party in the mess Sarah didn't know, but it was providing a great deal of entertainment for their audience. As Sarah watched, Megan bent over backwards into a crab and then gracefully raised one leg so her toe was pointing at the ceiling, then she kicked it over her head and stood up. There was a round of applause and Megan made a little mock bow.

Sarah suddenly realized she had been so engrossed in watching Megan that she had no idea what Richard had just said to her. She turned her attention back to him and apologized.

'I'm sorry. I am just mesmerized by what is going on over there. Look.'

Richard and Maddy turned and followed her gaze.

'Good God, what does Ginny think she's up to?' shrieked Maddy as she watched Ginny bend over backwards.

'I think the technical term is a backwards walkover,' said Sarah. The three of them moved away from the bar and into the next room for a better view of the spectacle.

Ginny was trying to follow Megan's example, but although she had managed to get herself into a crab, all she could now achieve were some pathetic little hops. The foot that remained on the ground never lifted more than an inch off the carpet while the one that was supposed to be pointing balletically at the ceiling was waving around like a tree in a gale. There were a number of observations from the group watching her about 'lack of muscle tone' and the fact that she couldn't accomplish something so simple that 'even a child could do it'. Eventually she collapsed with laughter in an untidy heap on the mess carpet.

The noise from the disco in the dining room was drowned out by yet more ribald and raucous comments from her audience of subalterns, and Megan was persuaded to demonstrate the gymnastic move again.

'Goodness,' said a voice that cut across everything. Alice was standing in the door leading into the hall, watching her daughter.

'Oh God. This'll put a damper on things,' whispered Maddy to Sarah.

'Come along Megan,' said Alice. 'I don't know what you think you are doing but it's time to go.'

Megan stood up and looked a little shamefaced.

'It's all my fault, Alice,' said Ginny. 'Megan said she could do a backwards walkover and I asked her to teach me. It's something I've always longed to be able to do.'

Alice looked disbelieving. 'Really?'

The group of subalterns and their girlfriends seemed to decide en masse that now was the moment to check out the disco. They drifted away to the dining room where the beat of the music thumped and the lights flashed and where they would be safe from Alice.

'Yes, well . . . Anyway, you'd better do as your mother says, Megan, or she won't let you come out with me tomorrow.'

Alice raised her eyebrows at Ginny. 'Tomorrow?'

'I hope you don't mind, but I promised to give Megan a

slap-up tea before she goes back to school on Tuesday. It is OK, isn't it?'

Judging by the look on Alice's face it was far from OK, but she was wrestling with the knowledge that it would be extremely churlish to say so.

'Well, yes. I suppose so.'

'Great,' said Ginny, apparently completely unaware of – or choosing to ignore – the ice in Alice's voice. 'I'll collect Megan at three. Bye.' And, giving Megan a peck on the cheek, Ginny skipped off to the disco.

'Bob, you're going to have to do something about Virginia Turner,' said Alice as she removed her make-up. She had her back to her husband but she watched him in the mirror of her dressing table.

Bob folded up his trousers and hung them carefully over a hanger before he replied. 'Is there a problem?'

'Oh, for heaven's sake. Her behaviour, and the influence she's having on Megan. Of course there's a problem.'

'But why?'

Alice swivelled round on her dressing-table stool so she could look at Bob directly and not via the mirror. 'I don't think it's healthy. To be frank I wonder what on earth Ginny's intentions are?'

Bob laughed. 'What, you think she's hell-bent on corrupting our daughter?'

'I don't know what she's up to, but I don't like it. It's not as if they can be real friends – look at the age difference.'

'So what are you saying, that you think Ginny has befriended Megan for some dark reason?' Bob shook his head. 'Are you suggesting that Ginny is some sort of rampant lesbian with designs on our daughter?'

'Don't be so disgusting Bob,' snapped Alice. 'Of course I don't mean that.'

'Well I really don't see what you do mean.' Bob bent down to remove his pants and socks and threw them in the washing basket. 'Come on, let's get into bed,' he said as he pulled on his pyjama trousers.

'Just look at Ginny's behaviour in the mess tonight; those

59

ridiculous gymnastics. And she was making Megan behave badly too.'

'Oh, for heaven's sake. It was a party. If it had been some formal mess function with some visiting VIPs, I might have thought Ginny was out of order. But it was a party thrown by Ginny and the other single officers in what is, if you think about it, their home. We were the guests and I think they were entitled to behave as they liked.'

'But she was setting such a bad example to Megan. Megan will think that it's OK to go into an officers' mess and get up to those sort of high jinks.'

Bob climbed into bed and pulled the duvet up to his chin. He yawned heavily. 'I don't think Megan will think anything of the sort. She knows the difference between a party and a formal function.'

'And I don't. Is that what you are saying?' Alice slapped some moisturizer on to her face, her irritation evident in her body language.

'No, not at all. Look, Megan is going back to school in a couple of days. The next time she comes home, Ginny and the rest of us will be in Kosovo. She won't see Ginny for six months and by the time they meet up again Megan might have decided that she'd rather mix with people of her own age. But let's not make an issue of something that may die a natural death all by itself.'

'So you don't think I should stop Ginny taking Megan out to tea tomorrow?'

'No. And if you do, you are going to have to be prepared for a row with Megan. She's looking forward to it.'

Alice gave in. Perhaps Bob was right. And she really didn't want yet another row with Megan. The holidays had got off to a bad start. She didn't want it to end in acrimony as well. She slipped into bed beside him.

'Come here,' said Bob snuggling up next to her. Alice reached across to the bedside lamp and switched it off, then moulded her body to fit into the curves of Bob's.

'It's not late,' she murmured.

'No, it's not,' Bob murmured back as he began to caress her gently.

*   *   *

60

'Can I write to you?' asked Megan, not very clearly as her mouth was full of scone and jam and cream.

'Of course you can, if you'd really like to. I'd love it. I adore getting letters. My family are hopeless letter writers and if you keep your word I expect you'll be the only one who'll keep me in touch with what's going on,' said Ginny. 'I shall want to hear all about the awful Miss Pink and Zoë and everything. Oh, and any gossip you hear. And I'll write back and tell you lots of exciting stuff about balancing the regimental accounts and documentation checks and—'

'Silly,' said Megan giggling. 'There'll be lots of wild things happening in Kosovo.'

'I hope not,' said Ginny. 'I'm going out there for a rest after all the stuff your dad has put us through recently. The last thing I'm looking for is excitement.'

'It won't be dangerous, will it?'

'I don't think so – hope not. Anyway, let's not talk about Kosovo. Let's talk about you. What do you want to do when you grow up?'

'You sound like Mummy.'

'Bloody hell!' said Ginny before she could stop herself. Megan shrieked with laughter. 'I'm sorry,' said Ginny, trying not to laugh too. 'I shouldn't have said that. It was rude of me.'

'No it wasn't. You were just being honest. Personally I'm scared stiff I'm going to grow up to be like her.'

'I doubt you'll do that. You're the spitting image of your dad. I expect you'll turn out like him.'

'That's a relief. I don't mind the idea of being like him. He's cool.' Megan took another scone off the plate and began to pile it with jam and cream.

'I didn't think grown-ups could be cool.'

'Course they can,' said Megan. She took a big bite of her scone and chewed thoughtfully. 'You are.'

'Thanks.'

'No, I mean it. You're not like most grown-ups.'

'Probably because I haven't grown up myself.'

'No, don't be silly, but you aren't like the others.'

'Yeah, but I don't have kids. I expect that makes all the difference.'

'Do you think?'

'My sister Netta's younger than me and she's much more grown-up. She does all sorts of responsible things like going to bed early, and staying sober at parties and—'

'Dull,' pronounced Megan.

'And getting up at six most mornings because she's got four kids under seven and another on the way.'

'Four!' Megan coughed and spluttered a few crumbs on to the tablecloth. 'And pregnant.'

'Yup. But because she's a mum she's very sensible. Doing all the things I should be doing, like saving for a rainy day and paying a mortgage and eating healthy food.' There was a small pause, then with a perfectly straight face Ginny added, 'Pass the cream.'

Megan grinned and moved the cream out of Ginny's reach. 'You could start with the healthy eating now.'

'Could I? And you could find yourself walking home.'

Megan handed over the little cut-glass dish. 'Put like that . . .'

'Thanks. More tea? I think there's some in the pot.'

'No. I'm nearly stuffed.' Megan looked at the last morsel of scone in her hand, thought about eating it but then changed her mind, lowered it on to her plate and looked at Ginny. 'Gin?'

'Yeah?'

'Why are you so nice to me?'

'You're a nice kid.' Which was true and easy to say. Ginny didn't add that it gave her an excuse to see more of Bob; that she liked the thought that she was doing something for him. He'd always been so good to her, it was nice to be able to do something back, even if it was indirectly. 'And I like kids. Just 'cause I don't have any of my own doesn't mean I don't like them. Ask Netta – she'll tell you I'm a terrific aunt.'

'So, why haven't you got any kids? If you're such a terrific aunt, wouldn't you make a great mum?'

'Ah, but being a mum is a full-time job. Being an aunt is easy. I can come and go as I please and just do the fun things, like hand out presents and organize treats. And anyway, I've been too busy having a good time I suppose. And I haven't met anyone I want to settle down with.' Which was a lie, thought Ginny. She could settle down with Bob given half a

chance, but that wasn't an option. She would just have to look
for someone just like him. Fat chance there were two the same
on the planet. The thought put a cloud over her sunny mood.
To disguise it she concentrated on piling a spoonful of jam on
to another scone.

'I wish you were my mum,' said Megan in a quiet but
resolute voice.

Ginny didn't know what to say. She wished she were
Megan's mum too, with all the implications that went with
it. It was almost as if Megan had read her mind. She toyed
with her cup of tea for a few seconds while she considered the
best form of words. 'I wouldn't be me. I mean, if I were your
mum, Megan, I'd be different. I'd have to be. I would have to
do things like set a good example and think of your future and
all the things your mum does for you – all the dull, everyday
stuff. And I'd have to say that you couldn't do certain things
so we'd probably end up shouting at each other. We couldn't
just have fun like you and I do. Think about it, I'd have to
do all the dreary stuff like making you do your homework or
ticking you off. It wouldn't be the same thing at all. But I tell
you what.'

'What?'

'How about I'm a sort of fairy godmother?'

Megan gave her a puzzled stare. 'What, glass slippers and
pumpkins?'

'No, silly. I mean nice treats on your birthday – trips to
theme parks, girls' days out together, shopping trips.'

Megan's face was radiant. 'Wicked, that sounds like so
much fun.' Then her face fell again. 'But you'll be away for
my birthday.'

'When is that?'

'October.'

'We can do something together when I get back. We could
go up to London together in the Christmas hols. Would you
like that?'

'Lush.'

Ginny took that to mean yes. 'I'll have to clear it with
your mum.'

Megan groaned. 'You'd be better asking Dad.'

'Maybe, but I think this is one for your mother to OK. If

63

I go to your dad he's almost bound to say yes because he probably hates shopping, wouldn't think it was any sort of big deal. But your mum . . . Well, she might have plans of her own.' Probably nothing that Megan would like, but that was between Alice and her daughter. 'Right, well, if you've finished we'd better get back.'

After Ginny had dropped Megan back at Montgomery House and received effusive thanks from Megan and rather more restrained ones from Alice, she returned to the mess. Richard was walking through the hall as Ginny opened the front door.

'There you are,' said Richard.

'Looking for me?'

'Yes. You've been out.'

'Well done Sherlock. Nothing gets past you, does it?' said Ginny with a laugh. 'I took Megan out for tea. She's off back to boarding school on Tuesday. I thought I'd make sure she had a good feed before she gets put back in the slammer.'

'I think most kids get more than gruel these days. Parents who are shelling out fifteen grand a year in fees expect to see their little darlings looking fit and healthy when they spring them.'

'I'm glad to hear it. When I was at school the food was gross.'

'Good, so you probably still need to make up the shortfall in your diet.'

'I doubt it. I've just put away more scones and cream than I care to admit to.'

'Then you'll just have to find some more space. Maddy has sent me to find you. She's bought a chicken the size of a small ostrich and she wants you to come over and help us out.'

Ginny gave it a couple of seconds of thought. 'OK, but only on the condition that you let me bring the wine.'

'And you thought I was going to argue?'

'Nah.'

'So what's this with you and Megan?' asked Maddy as she stirred the gravy.

'I like her. Is that a crime?' said Ginny defensively.

Maddy didn't miss the tone. 'And . . . ?'

64

'And what?' Ginny's voice rose slightly in indignation at not being completely believed.

'I quite agree she's a nice child, despite her mother, but there's twenty years between you for heaven's sake.'

'Honestly, it's completely innocent. I just like her company.'

'So your friendship with Megan isn't designed to piss off Alice.'

A smile played across Ginny's face. 'Appealing though the idea is . . . No.'

'Or designed to increase your standing with Colonel Bob and improve your chances of promotion?'

'No!' Ginny was almost offended. Did people see her as a scheming promotion-seeking manipulative cow? Then she realized Maddy was joking. 'Oh well, I'd better come clean. Actually . . .'

'Thought so.' They both laughed.

'If you really want the truth it's because I had a fantastic day out at Alton Towers and I suddenly realized that there's a whole heap of great things to do but that, if you don't want to look a complete prat, you need a kid in tow.' And it would sound so wet to say she liked to think that she was making Megan feel special the way Bob had done it to her in the past, when her own life had been less than wonderful.

'But you've got all those hundreds of nieces and nephews.'

'And they live all those hundreds of miles away.'

Maddy stopped stirring and poured the gravy into a jug. 'Point taken.' Maddy scraped the last of the gravy out of the roasting tin and put the wooden spoon in the sink. 'Well, there's only one thing for it then, isn't there?'

'What's that?'

'You'll have to produce a few of your own.' She opened the kitchen door and yelled at Richard that she was ready to dish up and would he please come and carve.

'Don't you start. I've just had Megan telling me I would make a great mum.'

'And so you would.'

'Which is all well and good but I don't even have a boyfriend at the moment.'

'There must be someone you've got your eye on?'

'No,' said Ginny, thinking it was no good having your eye on someone if that someone wasn't available.

Richard came into the kitchen and began to carve the chicken. Maddy went into the dining room to put Danielle into her high chair and there was a fluster and a flurry of activity that didn't involve Ginny. She stared out of the kitchen window and thought about the one man who made her feel good and warm and happy every time she saw him. The man against whom she had compared every other suitor who had come into her life, and against whom they had been found wanting. They had all been too immature, too skinny, too fat, too timid, too macho, too bumptious . . . No one ever came close. She thought about the absent-minded kiss he had given her and she wondered if he ever thought about it too. She wondered what a proper kiss would be like. She wondered what it would be like to be seduced by him. God, Alice didn't deserve him.

'Ginny!' Maddy was staring at her, looking puzzled.

'Sorry – I was miles away.'

'You certainly were. I said, would you make yourself useful with the corkscrew.'

'Oh, of course.'

'So what were you thinking about? It was obviously something rather nice, judging by the stupid smile on your face.'

Ginny felt herself blush. She certainly wasn't going to tell her best friend that she had been having a private fantasy about her boss. How weird would that make her look? She sighed.

'The wine,' said Maddy, handing her a bottle of white and giving her another hard stare. 'And could you uncork it today?'

'I've got to go up to London this afternoon,' said Bob as he got in at lunchtime.

'London? Really! When was this decided?' said Alice, cross that Bob was asked to pack yet more into his frantic schedule.

'I had a phone call this morning. I've got to go up for an intelligence briefing. It's not something that can be done over the phone.'

'No, I suppose not.' But Alice still sounded huffy. 'I suppose this means you'll be late back.'

'Probably. You know what the traffic is like on the motor-way.'

'As if I don't see little enough of you as it is.'

'I can't help the traffic, can I?'

Alice smiled sheepishly. 'I'm being unreasonable aren't I? I'm sorry.'

'I'll give you a call if I'm going to be later than about six. How's that?'

'Fine. Right, well, I'd better get on with lunch.'

Bob's driver pulled up at the door to Montgomery House just as Bob finished his soup.

'You're early,' said Bob.

'I've been listening to the traffic reports, sir. The motor-way's a nightmare, there's been a pile-up, so I thought we'd better get going as soon as possible, if that's OK with you.'

Bob grabbed his briefcase, kissed Alice and left.

'Have they cleared the accident yet?' he asked as they left the barracks.

'They didn't say. They should've done. It happened a while ago, but you know what these things are like.'

Bob certainly did. They drove on in silence as Bob, in the back of the car, studied some papers and Corporal Finnegan concentrated on driving. It was an honour to be the CO's driver and Finnegan prided himself on the smoothness of the ride he tried to give his boss. After about twenty minutes or so they slid up the slip road and on to the motorway. The traffic seemed to be moving normally enough and they sped along at a steady seventy. Bob returned to his papers and Finnegan switched on the radio and tuned it to the local station for the traffic reports. Between the records the announcer began the list of hold-ups on the routes into London.

'Did you hear that sir?' Bob shook his head. 'It's still slow moving,' he said over his shoulder to Bob.

'Good thing you took the initiative and made me leave early. How are we doing for time?'

'Not too bad if things keep moving. We should get to the MoD with about twenty minutes to spare at this rate.'

'Good.'

They barrelled along for another ten minutes or so and Bob was beginning to think that the radio reports had got it wrong when he saw brake lights start to come on ahead. A couple of cars put their four-way flashers on to make sure that the unwary or inattentive didn't drive into their boots and Finnegan sighed. 'Seems like this is it, sir.'

'At least it looks as if it's still moving,' said Bob hopefully. 'Even if it is a bit slow.'

Bob glanced over Finnegan's shoulder and saw they were doing thirty. On the wide road it seemed as though they were crawling along at barely more than walking pace though. He sighed. He really didn't want to be late. The meeting was important and there were going to be lots of top brass there. It would be humiliating if he were the one to keep everyone waiting.

'Do you think the fast lane might be a better bet?' he asked Finnegan.

'We could give it a go.' Finnegan indicated and managed to slide out into the line of traffic moving past on the outside. A couple of vehicles ahead of them, in the middle lane, was a heavily laden lorry. 'That doesn't look too safe, does it, sir?'

'Lord, no,' said the colonel realizing instantly what Finnegan was talking about. The stacks of pallets on the flatbed of the lorry had either been badly loaded or they had slipped backwards and the ones at the back were hanging over the rear end. From their perspective they could see that there was apparently nothing – no rope, no straps – securing them. They seemed stable enough at the moment but should the lorry have to brake suddenly it was almost a racing certainty that they would go flying backwards. But from directly behind the lorry the danger was not so obvious. The colonel tried gesticulating at the driver of the car next to them and in the same lane as the lorry to warn him but he stared steadfastly ahead. The line of traffic they were in was moving slightly faster, and slowly they overtook that driver, who still refused to look in Bob's direction, and drew level with the next – the one directly behind the truck, a little Volkswagen.

It was a woman behind the wheel. Bob waved urgently. She looked at him for a second, then frowned and fixed her eyes ahead again. Bob wound down the window and tried again. 'Drop back,' he yelled. She looked at him again, waved two fingers at him and mouthed a word. Bob thought she'd said 'pervert'.

'I'll ring the police on the mobile,' he said. 'Perhaps they can pull this lorry over before the worst happens.' The traffic in their lane began to speed up as the cars got past the slow lorry and now Bob's staff car was almost alongside the cab of the truck. Bob rummaged in his case for his mobile. He switched it on. Ahead they could see the reason why the traffic was moving like treacle. On the hard shoulder were the battered and bent remains of several trucks that had been involved in the earlier crash – the one that had caused the initial problems on the motorway.

'Just look at all those bloody motorists rubbernecking,' muttered Finnegan. Bob was about to ring the police but was also distracted by the sight of the aftermath of a serious pile-up. In the slow lane a transit van braked suddenly for no apparent reason. The car behind it nearly ran into it and swerved into the middle lane. Beside them the lorry driver hit the brakes instinctively. Bob whipped round in his seat and saw the pallets fly, almost in graceful slow motion, off the back of the flatbed and descend on the traffic following.

'Bloody hell!' he said in horror. Over the sound of the radio and the engine they could hear the tortured shriek of metal, the squeal of brakes, the smash and crash of vehicles impacting and the scream of tyres on the tarmac. The lorry stopped – the driver had obviously realized what he had done. The slow lane was suddenly empty as the traffic ahead of them disappeared into the distance, but nothing else came through.

'Pull over,' he ordered Finnegan. The driver cut across to the hard shoulder as Bob called the police. Succinctly he gave the details, asked for all three services and said he thought it was a major incident. By the time he had finished his staff car was at a standstill.

'Let's see if they need any help.' He and Finnegan ran back the thirty or so yards to the chaos. The driver of the lorry was out of his cab, crouching down in front of it, as white as a sheet, motionless. Obviously shocked by what he had done, but otherwise unharmed. Bob ran round the back of the truck. The Volkswagen was under a pile of broken, splintered wood. The bonnet of the car behind that was deformed into a ridge, the windscreen shattered and the driver had blood oozing from a cut on his forehead, but he was dabbing it with a hanky. He was OK. He could wait.

On the other side of the motorway, traffic roared passed but as far as Bob could see on his side was a stationary sea of metal. Bob turned his attention to the Volkswagen. It was almost completely submerged under a mountain of pallets. The windscreen was smashed and the roof had been stove in. He peered through the window but the crazed glass and the covering of shattered wood meant that the interior of the car was oddly dark and he couldn't see much detail, but the woman – the one who had called him a pervert – was lying sideways across the passenger seat. Her face was a mess, covered in blood, but he couldn't tell how seriously hurt she was. He tried to pull open the driver's door but it was completely jammed. He'd have to try and get to her through the windscreen. He wanted to know if she was still alive. The way she looked it was possible she was dead.

It was then that he became aware of the smell of petrol. He pulled at one of the broken and smashed pallets lying on the bonnet. A splinter from the rough wood ran into his hand. He ignored the pain and threw the heavy pallet down beside the car.

'Finnegan,' he yelled. 'Get the extinguisher from the car.' Finnegan hesitated. 'Now!' Bob roared. Finnegan set off like a greyhound from a trap. Then Bob raced to the front of the truck. 'You,' he said to the shocked lorry driver. 'You're going to help me now.'

'Uh?' said the trucker. Bob grabbed the bloke by his collar and dragged him to the back of his truck. 'Your bloody pallets. Now you are going to help shift them.' There was no hint of a request in Bob's voice and the lorry driver was so stunned at being given orders by a complete stranger that he pulled himself together and began to haul the shattered wood off the Volkswagen.

A flicker of movement caught Bob's eye. The bloke with the cut head was trying to light a cigarette. Bob ran round the car and leaned in through the broken window. He grabbed the matches and the cigarette.

'Oi,' said the man. 'You can't do that.'

'I can,' said Bob, grinding the cigarette into fragments. 'Petrol,' he added by way of explanation as he returned to the pallets. But even as he returned, a tongue of flame began to lick out from the rear of the little Golf.

'Finnegan!' he yelled.

'Here, sir,' panted his driver.

'Deal with that,' he ordered, pointing at the fire.

Finnegan hit the button on the extinguisher and a jet of foam squirted out. He bent down to get near the seat of the blaze. He could see a pool of petrol that spread from the rear of the Golf, under the car behind and which was trickling under other vehicles towards the hard shoulder.

'Get everyone out, Colonel,' he yelled. 'If this really goes, this extinguisher'll be useless.'

The man with the bleeding head understood the implications of what Finnegan was saying and put his shoulder to his own door. It burst open and he scrambled clear.

'Hey, you,' yelled Bob, 'give me a hand.' But the bloke pretended not to hear and headed for the embankment at the side. 'Bastard,' muttered Bob under his breath as he redoubled his efforts to free the trapped woman. He tore at the pallets, the rough wood ripping skin from his fingers, knuckles and palms as he did so. As he worked he ignored the fact that his hands were becoming wet with blood. Beside him Finnegan seemed to be keeping the fire under control. 'How's it going?' he asked his driver.

'It's fine. I just don't know how long this extinguisher will hold out.'

Shit, Finnegan was right. It wasn't a big one. 'Have you got one?' he asked the truckie.

'Yeah, in my cab.'

'Well, get it man. Get it!'

The lorry driver didn't need to be told twice – he was already gone. Bob pulled the last of the pallets off the bonnet of the car and slung himself on to it, reaching in through the window to check on the woman inside. He managed to reach her wrist. Yes, there was a pulse. Faint but steady.

'Sir,' called Finnegan. 'I'm running out.'

Bob looked to his left and saw the flames appear level with the rear window of the car. He slid back so his head was out of the car again. 'Where's that bloody truckie with his extinguisher?'

'He's disappeared.'

God, another coward doing a runner, thought Bob. 'We've got to get this bird out,' he said. 'I know we shouldn't move her but she'll burn if we don't. Give us a hand.'

Finnegan threw his extinguisher away and ran to the front of the car.

'We're going to have to drag her out through the windscreen.' Bob slid over the bonnet again to the passenger side. He tried the door. It opened a few inches, enough for him to be able to squeeze his upper body inside. He disregarded the ripping noise he heard from the sleeve of his jacket. He pushed in as far as he could, then he levered the woman upright and undid the safety belt. 'Here,' he said as he lifted her arms and shoved them forward to where Finnegan could reach them. As he did so, he glanced up. The flames were really getting a grip now and the smell of burning rubber and fuel was nauseating. Finnegan, leaning in through the front of the car, grabbed her wrists and pulled. Her bottom left the seat and her body moved upwards and tipped forward. Bob slid further into the car and grasped her by her waist. He pushed while Finnegan pulled. She came to a stop. Her knees were stuck under the steering wheel.

'Bloody hell,' muttered Bob. It didn't help that he was beginning to panic. The fire was getting stronger. He knew that, in the main, cars didn't blow up like they did in films, but there was always the exception that proved the rule. And if this one went up he was not in a position to be able to extricate himself with any speed. He forced himself to think calmly.

'Come on, sir,' called Finnegan. 'I can't hold her much longer.'

Bob pushed himself another few inches into the car and felt at the base of the seat with his left hand. There, that was it. He pulled the lever up sharply and the driver's seat shot back about six inches. With a final heave, Finnegan got the woman far enough through the windscreen that he no longer had to support her weight.

Relieved, Bob wriggled back out of the passenger door and clambered over the front of the bonnet so he could help

Finnegan carry her away from the Golf. Just as they were laying the young woman on the ground there was a dull crack and the passenger compartment filled with flame and smoke.

'Blimey, mate,' said the lorry driver. 'You were lucky. I thought you were a goner there.'

'Where the fuck did you get to?' Bob's relief at his escape now translated into anger.

'Looking for this,' said the driver, aggrieved. The last pillock who drove this truck didn't put it back in the right place.'

'Oh.' Bob wasn't sure he believed him.

The woman on the ground began to stir.

'Thank God,' he murmured. He stared at the mess that her face had become. He hoped that it was mostly superficial but her pretty looks were now an ugly mask of blood. He patted her hand abstractedly. He didn't know what to do. He couldn't do anything, but he felt it would be wrong to leave her. She was injured, possibly badly, and she didn't need to be abandoned too.

She opened her eyes. She looked groggy and dazed but Bob knew it was a positive sign that she was conscious.

'Hi,' said Bob. 'How do you feel? You've been in a bit of a crash.' She nodded and winced. 'Lie still. There's an ambulance on the way,' he said confidently. He hoped to God there was although how they were going to get through the tailback was anybody's guess.

She kept her eyes on him. Then she said, 'You tried to warn me.'

'Didn't do a very good job, did I? You thought I was some sort of weirdo.' It was a poor effort at humour, he knew, but he wanted to do something to make her feel a little better.

It was difficult to tell if she was smiling with all the blood on her face but her eyes seemed to. Her gaze moved from his face to his hands which were holding one of hers. 'Were you in the crash too?'

In the distance Bob could hear the approaching wail of sirens. 'No. I came back to help.'

'But your hands . . .' she said.

He turned his battered, bloody hands over and examined them and thought they looked in no worse a state than her face. Although if his hands ended up with scars it wouldn't matter much. 'They're just scratches really. No permanent damage,' he said, hoping the same was going to be true for her. He could see blue lights making their way along the hard shoulder. It was an ambulance.

'Look,' he said. 'I'm going to leave you to the professionals now. I'm sure you're going to be fine.'

The woman looked backwards to see what Bob was looking at and saw her car. 'Oh my God,' she whispered.

'It's OK,' said Bob. 'We got you out of it. The main thing to remember is that you are all right. It doesn't matter about your car. What matters is you.'

'Thank you,' she said. 'Thank you. I don't even know your name.'

'It's Bob,' he said as he stood up. 'Come on Finnegan,' he said quietly to his driver. 'We're late enough as it is. There are plenty of witnesses. If we slip away now we might still make that meeting.'

'Shouldn't we stay?'

'I think we've done our bit.' The two men slipped away just as an ambulance crew arrived.

The motorway was amazingly clear for much of the remainder of the journey up to London, as the majority of the traffic was stuck behind the accident. They arrived in Whitehall with a couple of minutes to spare. Bob used them to clean himself up and, with the exception of his hands and a rip in the sleeve of his jacket, there was little to show for his involvement in the incident.

Ginny was organizing her kit for Kosovo in her room. There was a pile of military kit in one corner, which she had to take, and in another one was a pile of things she would like to take. The problem was she only had a large rucksack, her webbing and a kitbag to pack it all in. The accommodation would be spartan and cramped, with very little room for the personnel, let alone their possessions, and if the soldiers were being restricted to taking the bare minimum then the least the officers could do was set an example. Ginny sighed and gave up. She'd have another go at weeding it in the morning. Right now she was too pooped to think straight. She flopped on her bed and pressed the remote for her television. The news was on.

She watched the images of world events, reporters spouting meaningful commentaries, pictures of the great and the good and the not-so-good and the downright bad, and forgot about her own worries and problems. Her lack of a man in her life hardly rated a mention in the greater scheme of things. The national news ended and it was time for the local news. Ginny looked at her watch – six thirty. She decided she'd watch it then go down to the bar for a drink before dinner. It was the usual round-up of stories about school kids raising funds for some worthy cause, a shop that had won a national award for being the best butcher in the country and a report from the pile-up on the motorway because one of their camera crews had been caught up in the ensuing traffic jam. They had filmed the chaos – the dozens of wrecked cars, the broken pallets, the burnt vehicle from which, according to the reporter, 'one woman had a miraculous escape'. Ginny thought it was like watching an episode of *Casualty* as she watched the shots of the woman being lifted into the back of an ambulance. Her face was a mess but she was conscious and she smiled wanly at the camera.

The camera turned to the reporter for her to do her piece. She wittered on about the police charging the lorry driver, the length of the hold-up, the number of cars damaged and any other statistics she could think of. Finally she said, 'But if there is any good to come out of this horrific incident it is that it seems there was a modern day good Samaritan passing. The woman who was dragged from her burning car, moments before it was engulfed in flame, would like to thank the man who rescued her. She doesn't know who he is beyond his first name, which is Bob. Other witnesses at the scene say his action was truly heroic and he risked his life to save her. So if you are watching, Bob, please get in touch with our studios so she can thank you personally. This is Sheila Manners, reporting for *Midlands Tonight*.'

Ginny hit the off button, and hauled herself off her bed. She could do with a good Samaritan herself, to rescue her from spinsterhood, she thought. Preferably one on a white charger who would come galloping up to carry her off and ravish her. Fat chance! She dragged a comb through her curls, checked her make-up, touched up her lipstick and went down to the bar.

There were half a dozen officers already there when she arrived. But she didn't feel especially sociable so she remained by the bar, mulling over her own thoughts rather than joining them at their table. She leaned against it, both elbows resting on its mahogany counter and twiddled the stem of her glass.

'Penny for them,' said a familiar voice.

She felt her heart dance. 'Colonel.' She turned and smiled at him. 'Can I get you a drink?'

'No thanks. I've just dropped in for some cigarettes on my way home. I'm already late and Alice will give me hell if I stop here to gossip. Besides which, Finnegan's waiting outside.' As he spoke he pulled a pad of bar chits over and began writing.

'What on earth have you done?' gasped Ginny, catching sight of his mangled hand.

'You should see the other guy,' joked the colonel. 'It looks worse than it is. Just a few scratches.'

'Doesn't look like that to me.'

Bob handed the chit to the barman who already had the cigarettes ready for the CO.

'You've just been to London, haven't you? Were you involved in that pile-up?' said Ginny, a suspicion forming in her mind.

'Yes, to the first. No, to the second. Finnegan and I were very lucky. We were just ahead of it.'

'So is it you?'

'Is it me what?'

'The good Samaritan. You were all over the local TV news.' Ginny recounted the story she had just seen and how the injured woman had described her rescuer and his injured hands and how she wanted to thank him.

Bob groaned. 'Well, for God's sake don't you ring in. Going to Kosovo in a few days is all I can cope with right now. I haven't the time to make hospital visits so some bird can say thanks.'

By the next day, the news that it was the CO who was the good Samaritan was fairly common knowledge around the regiment, as was the injunction not to contact the TV studio. Not that anyone had much time to give it much thought. The CO was off to

76

Kosovo with the advance party at the end of the week and most of the regiment was going a week later. Everything was far too hectic and everyone was far too busy for it to be an issue.

Maddy took Danielle to the toddler group as usual. Despite everything she wanted life to continue to be as normal as possible. She was pleased to see Taz there. With Ginny going away she had decided that Taz would be a great replacement. The children played happily as Maddy collected coffees for herself and Taz and filled beakers with squash for the two toddlers, and then she settled herself down for a good gossip. For a while they chatted about their daughters, then Taz asked Maddy about Richard going to Kosovo.

'We'll cope. I mean, not that we've been separated since Danny was born, but it'll be the third time since we got married. And that's not counting the courses and all the rest of it.'

'Really? So much?'

'Are you sitting comfortably? Let me tell you.' And Maddy launched into her favourite subject – the trials of being an army wife. As she talked Taz reached into her handbag and, unseen by Maddy, switched on her tiny tape recorder. 'People think that soldiers are some sort of modern day heroes but . . . Oh, and talking about being married to a hero,' she said, remembering something she'd been planning to tell Taz after she had finished her monologue. 'We've got a real live hero in the regiment.'

'Oh, who?'

'The CO. You know that piece on the local news yesterday about the car crash on the motorway?' Taz nodded. 'Well it was Bob Davies who went back to try and rescue that woman.'

'Well I never.'

'Of course, he doesn't want it to get out. He's got enough on his plate what with Kosovo coming up shortly. You won't tell anyone, will you?'

'You've got my word,' said Taz. 'Besides which, who on earth would I tell?'

As she left the toddler group shortly after eleven, using the pretext that Amelia needed a nap, she thought that if it was a slow news day it was just the sort of thing the *Mercury* or the *Messenger* might like. It was worth a try.

*   *   *

77

Ginny could hear the CO yelling from her office at the other end of the corridor in RHQ.

'Someone told them. I want guts for garters,' he thundered. The phone calls from the press, wanting confirmation about the story, had started about midday and by mid-afternoon he had taken his phone off the hook and ordered Richard to do the same. 'Anyone who wants us can get us via the chief clerk or Alisdair.' Ginny had heard that Finnegan had been the prime suspect for a while but eventually he'd managed to convince the CO that it wasn't him.

'Let's face it Colonel,' said Richard. 'It could be anyone.' The CO was forced to agree, but he issued an order that no one, *no one*, was to talk to the press about this or any other matter without getting permission from RHQ. He knew that he couldn't stop the wives from giving interviews if they were so inclined, but he made it clear to the troops that if they did they might find their next posting was the Falklands or somewhere equally out of the way. There was no doubt in anyone's mind that he meant it.

The only thing left for him to do was to warn Alice and Megan to expect to see him in the next day's papers. Megan thought it was 'cool' but Alice was horrified. Bob had tried to comfort her with the thought that as they were ex-directory she wouldn't get called, and with their house being in a barracks there wouldn't be any pictures.

'This story can't last long with nothing much to go on,' he said.

Maddy was delighted when Taz asked if she could pop round. Apparently Amelia had been pestering her to play with Danny since they got home from the toddler group and she wondered if it would be OK to bring her over. Maddy had nothing planned to occupy the afternoon and thought this was a grand idea. She rang the guardroom to organize access for Taz into the barracks. A quarter of an hour later they rang to say that her visitor had arrived but it seemed to take an inordinately long time for Taz to appear on her doorstep.

'I got lost,' she explained. 'I never did know my left from my right.' Maddy accepted this. She was as bad.

The next day Lieutenant Colonel Robert Davies discovered

that the *Mercury* had dubbed him 'Colonel Car Crash' and, what was more, had a picture of him entering his house. His rage hit new heights. He became incandescent when his new name appeared to strike a chord with the public. Local radio rang and asked for interviews with Colonel Car Crash, and the local TV company wanted a shot of him at the bedside of the rescued woman. Even a couple of the broadsheets ran the story when it also came out that he was just about to embark on an emergency peacekeeping tour in Kosovo. It was good PR for the army but Bob had more than enough to cope with without this sort of limelight.

'Thank God I'm leaving the country tomorrow,' he said. At least once he was in Kosovo they'd leave him and his wife alone.

Ginny had a window seat on the elderly RAF VC-10 that was transporting the regiment out to Kosovo. From thirty-five thousand feet the ground below resembled a multi-coloured map more than real terrain and Ginny could clearly see the green and brown of the Italian coast give way to the startling blue of the Adriatic. From her bird's eye position she could see minute ships, mere dots, plying across the sparkling water like tiny insects crawling across a blue carpet. The sea then became dotted with dozens of islands – the Dalmatian coast, she assumed – and then they were flying over land again. Almost there, she thought with a slight frisson of apprehension. She felt the pressure in the cabin change as they began their gentle descent into Kosovo and she looked out of the window with increased interest, wondering what it would be like to live and work in a place that had been the scene of such a recent and bloody war.

The temperature on the ground was pleasantly warm when they disembarked at Pristina airport. Well, it was called an airport but the reality was a large concrete shed, a cluster of sundry, tatty buildings, and a motley collection of air-craft, all military. Hardly Heathrow, thought Ginny. A tractor towing a rickety assembly of trailers rattled over towards the RAF passenger jet ready to collect their luggage, and by the terminal were a group of men, all in scruffy jeans, waiting to move the bags from the trailers to the ancient conveyor belt that was the Kosovan equivalent of a luggage carousel.

Ginny and the rest of the troops lounged around in the sun as they waited for everything to be sorted. It all seemed so normal and pleasant. It was hard to imagine that this was a country that had torn itself apart, neighbour against neighbour, so recently. Ginny and the others lay in the warm sunshine and took their ease, with nothing to do until their kit had been unloaded. Their boredom was relieved as they watched another military transport in United Nations livery come in and there was another flurry of activity as a couple of helicopters took off from the other side of the runway. Then their gear arrived at the terminal and bedlam ensued as they all scrabbled to find their own stuff and take it to the waiting convoy of buses.

They drove through the main town. Ginny was surprised by how normal it all looked. She hadn't been quite sure what to expect but it hadn't been this modern, bustling town with gleaming buildings of glass and concrete. But it wasn't long before they left Pristina behind and drove out into the country. Again it all looked so normal. The fields were cultivated, there were crops and cattle and prosperous-looking farms, and then they drove into a village. Superficially it could have been any foreign village; houses topped by roofs with wide eaves to provide shade from the intense summer sun and protection from the heavy winter snows; balconies and verandas for the inhabitants to siesta on; shady, dusty trees growing in scruffy yards; and side roads consisting of little more than compacted hard core. Cats dozed on the tops of walls; a couple of scrawny dogs nosed about a pile of rubbish and the locals pottered about, shopping, chatting on street corners, sweeping dust off the front steps to their houses. But in amongst this placid normality were dozens of reminders of more brutal, vicious times. There were burnt-out shells of buildings, pockmarks on the walls where bullets or mortars had struck. There were splash marks in the concrete where heavy ordnance had landed. The minaret of a mosque was lying shattered on the ground; there were patches of weedy rubble where buildings had been completely destroyed, and yet around these scenes of destruction and violence, life was continuing as before. One house, completely roofless, was clearly still inhabited as there was washing drying on the line in the unkempt garden and a child's trike parked by the open door. Presumably, whatever had happened to the house had left the ground floor or the cellar habitable.

Richard, sitting in the seat behind Ginny, leaned forward to talk to her. 'The houses that are untouched mostly belonged to the Christians. The ones that have been trashed belonged to the Muslims and the Albanians.'

And Ginny realized it was obvious now that Richard had pointed it out to her. There were little groups of completely wrecked buildings, then beside them, or on the other side of the road, were groups of untouched ones. Ginny had thought that the destruction had been random – the luck of the draw – but now she could see that it had been carefully, sadistically targeted.

Although there were numerous reminders of the recent fighting, the people were trying to eradicate them as fast as their meagre resources would allow. A couple of buildings had been patched up; new roofs were replacing the war-damaged ones. Some of the bullet holes had been filled in with new plaster and, in places, the rubble had been bulldozed away and new buildings were going up. But Ginny wondered if it was the old inhabitants returning or others moving in, taking advantage of the vacant possession. She didn't think many would be inclined to return to their old villages if their neighbours had driven them out. The scars of the fighting were being removed but would the human scars be so easy to shift? Somehow she doubted it.

It was a couple of hours later that their coach drew up outside a large brick and breezeblock building. It had once been some sort of industrial unit – a factory or a warehouse – but now it was to be their home while the soldiers patrolled the local area, keeping the different ethnic groups apart, stopping them from settling scores or wreaking revenge. As a new home it looked far from inviting but as it was situated at the head of a wide valley it did command a spectacular view across the countryside to the distant mountains that brooded against the far horizon.

Ginny looked around the bleak room that was to be hers and sighed. She supposed she was lucky to get a room to herself, but with its bare concrete floor and breezeblock walls it was the most unwelcoming place she had ever lived in and, with only just enough space for her camp bed, one of the smallest.

Richard put his head round the door. 'Lucky you. Luxury.'

'Huh,' said Ginny.

'You've at least got a window, mine hasn't.'

'That's all I've got. What's your place like?'

'Same stunning range of matching soft furnishings, carpets and wall coverings as yours but bigger so I get to share with five others.'

'Ugh. And no window! You'll need your gas masks at the ready, won't you?'

'I hope to God no one smokes. A naked flame in that sort of atmosphere could be dangerous.'

'Lethal,' agreed Ginny. She pushed her kitbag into a corner and began to assemble her camp bed.

'I'll let you get on and sort yourself out. Don't forget the CO's briefing. At five.'

'I won't.'

For Ginny, life in Kosovo was not that different from her life back in Britain. The job she did, to all intents and purposes, was much the same – basic admin didn't change just because the location did – and she was surrounded by the same faces as before and working much the same hours. The weather was undeniably better than back in England and Ginny, with very little in the way of entertainment, found that most of her leisure time, when she wasn't trying to maintain her level of fitness, was spent reading books and improving her tan. Every now and again it was necessary for her to go to the main British base to get cash for the soldiers' pay and deal with sundry other admin jobs. She looked forward to these trips as they relieved the boredom of her normal routine.

Late in the autumn, Ginny was in Richard's office checking with him which would be the best day for her to do her next run back to base.

'Whichever,' Richard had said. 'It's all the same to me, to be honest.'

'How about tomorrow?' said Colonel Bob from the doorway.

'Why?' said Ginny turning round.

'I've got to go too. It makes sense for us to go together and save a journey.'

Ginny couldn't argue with that logic.

'Right. I'll meet you at oh eight hundred out the front.'

Ginny went back to her office feeling happy. She couldn't deny it – a day in Bob's company would be a whole heap better than a day in the company of a squaddie driver. She looked forward to the morning . . .

'So, where's Corporal Finnegan?' asked Ginny the next morning as she shoved her briefcase in the back of the Rover and climbed into the passenger seat.

'I gave him the day off. I quite enjoy driving and there didn't seem much point in dragging him along. Besides which it would have been a squash with three of us in the front.'

'True.' And the back was mostly taken up with the radio set, although there was a seat for a radio operator, but the ride in the rear was desperately uncomfortable and with the sort of roads they would be travelling over it would have been a nightmare.

'Do you know the way, Colonel, or would you like me to map read?'

'I'm fine,' said Bob as he slipped the vehicle into gear and drew away from the building. 'I hope you've got plenty to do. I've got a meeting at two which won't finish till three at the earliest.'

'I'm sure I'll find something to keep me out of trouble till you're finished,' she replied. A whole day away from the claustrophobia of their billet. Bliss.

Ginny tried not to clutch the seat of the Land Rover as it wound up the side of the valley. On her right was a steep forty-five-degree drop through woods to the valley floor a couple of hundred feet below. The view was stunning and Ginny tried to concentrate on that rather than on the parlous state of the road and the rapidly approaching dusk. Occasionally the road crossed a bridge as a stream hurtled its way down the mountain to join the main river that gushed along the valley floor. Bob changed the gears down into second as the road steepened. The engine roared and Ginny tried to ignore the dodgy highway with its crumbling verges, potholes and occasional rocks scattered along it from the hillside above.

'Not so far now,' he said loudly over the racket.

'Good,' yelled back Ginny, hoping she sounded unconcerned. She squinted out of her window at the sun, dipping behind the ridge across the other side of the valley. 'I don't think we're going to make it back before dark though.'

'Not to worry.'

'No.' But Ginny was worrying. She didn't fancy the prospect of driving in pitch dark. For, out here in Kosovo, when night fell it was very dark indeed – no street lights, no ambient light from big towns, nothing. She looked across the valley again. The sun had almost gone leaving just a small sector of orange glowing on the frontier between land and sky, but the line through the trees that marked the passage of the road was still just visible. It wound south down their side of the valley, then traced a path across the head before turning through 180 degrees to double back northwards before finally climbing out of this valley over the opposite ridge and dropping down into the next one. Not far as the crow flew, but still a fair way by road, Ginny could see the gap in the trees where the road finally crested the ridge. As she looked, something flashed. The last rays of the sun had reflected off something up there. Probably another vehicle heading down the road towards them.

Suddenly the sun dipped behind the ridge and deep shadow engulfed the road. Above them the sky was still pale blue, although deepening to almost navy if you looked east. But in the valley it was quite dark. Bob switched on the headlights. The road flattened out for the moment and Bob changed the gears back up to fourth. The noise from the engine subsided somewhat. They bowled along the road as it followed the contours rather than climbing up them. The darkness increased and colour quickly drained out of the vegetation that surrounded them and the scenery assumed a rather sinister and threatening atmosphere. Ginny shivered.

'You can't be cold, surely?'

She wasn't – the heater was belting out heat perfectly efficiently to combat the late autumn evening chill. 'No, someone's just walked over my grave, that's all.'

Bob chuckled. 'Vampire country, eh?'

'Something like that.'

They drove on in companionable silence with the Land Rover making its distinctive high-pitched whine, the kit in the back of the vehicle rattling about, and sometimes the tyres scrunching noisily on the loose stones and gravel that had accumulated at the edge of the road. Now and again, through the scrubby woods and across the valley, they could see a flash of the headlights of the car or truck that was heading down the road towards them. Then the road would twist and the lights would be lost from view. Ahead, in their lights, a sign warned them that the road was going to start winding again. Bob dropped the gears as the road first took a very sharp bend to the left followed by a hairpin to the right. Ginny swallowed and kept her eyes staring ahead as they crawled round another promontory sticking right out from the side of the ridge. She tried not to think about the drop beside her, now just a black abyss. The road, barely more than a glorified track, wound in and out of a series of clefts that lacerated the ridge from top to bottom. Ginny judged that they must nearly be at the head of the valley by now.

Without warning, blazing headlights on full beam came round a corner.

'Shit,' yelled Bob, blinded. There was a terrific roar and a lorry, going far too fast, thundered past them. Bob slammed on the brakes and the rear of the vehicle slewed slightly. Then the front wheel hit the grit on the narrow verge and the slight loss of control deteriorated into a full-scale skid. Ginny's heart raced as she watched Bob frantically spin the steering wheel to try and regain control, then with a sickening lurch the Rover slowly tipped over the edge. Ginny grabbed on to her seat belt with both hands and shut her eyes as they gathered momentum. The Rover bounced and slammed its way down the incline. Outside, Ginny could hear the crack and creak of tree branches as they ploughed their way through the wood. She was being thrown around increasingly violently. Her head made an appallingly vicious contact with the side of the vehicle. Pain and light exploded in her brain. She clenched her teeth to stop herself from crying out. Then, with a ferocious jolt, the nightmare roller-coaster ride stopped and there was silence apart from a hiss from the engine compartment.

Shaking and trying not to sob, Ginny opened her eyes. They were at a crazy angle – she was almost hanging in her seat, but they hadn't rolled over. She could feel a warm trickle of blood seeping down her face to her neck and under her shirt, but apart from her head she didn't think she was hurt anywhere else. Tentatively, she loosened her grip on her safety belt. Her palms were sore – she must have dug her fingernails into them. Beside her Bob groaned.

'Bob?'

'Huh?'

'You OK?'

There was a long sigh. 'Yeah. And you?'

'A bit battered but yeah, I think I'm OK too.'

'I think we'd better get out of here if we can.' Ginny could hear Bob scrabbling at his door. The angle the Rover had ended up in meant it would be easier to get out of his side than hers. Ginny reckoned that if Bob could open his door they could just fall out of it on to the ground. The passenger door was almost above her and she didn't think she would be able to budge it if they couldn't get out of Bob's.

'Bugger. It's jammed.' She heard a thump and felt the vehicle move slightly as he tried with more force to open it. 'Nope. I can't shift it. How about your door?'

Ginny tried to open it but she couldn't find enough purchase to push it open and not slip down her seat. 'I think we're just going to have to crawl out the back.'

'OK. Let me go first.' There was a click as Bob unbuckled his seat belt then Ginny could here him grunting and mumbling as he turned himself round and began to lever himself over the back of his seat and into the rear of the Land Rover. It was so dark she could only just make out the pale shape of Bob's face. 'God, I should have lost weight. I'm too fat for this sort of malarkey.' There was another grunt. 'Remind me to go on a diet when we get back to base.'

Ginny noted he said 'when' not 'if', and knew he was trying to cheer her up by being positive. 'OK, Colonel.'

There was a scrabbling sound then silence then Bob called from the back, 'OK, your turn.'

Ginny undid her belt and nearly fell on to the driver's seat. She banged her knee on the gear stick and her shin connected with the dash. Pain shot up her leg. 'Fuck,' she swore under her breath. Wedging one foot against the dashboard she twisted her body round and grabbed both seat backs then, ignoring the protests from her sore leg, she levered herself over them and into the back of the vehicle. She thumped her arm on a sharp corner of the radio set and swore again.

She could see Bob, silhouetted against the slight remaining brightness in the sky, peering under the canvas roof. 'Mind you don't hit yourself on the radio,' he said.

'Very funny,' snapped Ginny. She didn't feel like joking. She was sore and hurt and, although she was deeply relieved she was still alive, she was shocked and shaking. With a final shove she pushed herself to the tailgate and heaved herself over it. Bob caught her as she almost fell on the rough ground, her trembling legs not properly able to take her weight. Bob holding her made her feel so much less vulnerable and she was acutely aware of his arm around her waist. She leant against him for support.

'Are you all right?' he said, turning her slightly so she was facing him.

Ginny nodded, trying to put a brave front on things, despite her aches and cuts. But a wave of nausea overwhelmed her and she suddenly felt even weaker and very giddy. 'No,' she mumbled, shaking her head. 'I need to sit down.' Her legs gave way and she sat down suddenly on the ground. She leant against a large rock for support.

Bob crouched in front of her and took her hands in his. 'Where do you hurt?'

Ginny felt tears welling up. Shock, self-pity, relief? Ginny didn't know but she gulped them back. This wasn't the moment to give in to emotion. She breathed deeply and regained control. 'I banged my head. I think it's cut.'

Bob let go of her hands and changed his position from crouching to kneeling. He examined her temple. He was so close Ginny could feel his breath on her skin. She shut her eyes. She had fantasized about this proximity for so long, but now it was happening and it felt all wrong.

'I can't see a bloody thing in this light. I'm going to see if there's a torch in the Land Rover.'

Ginny, still with her eyes shut, listened as he got up and

then rummaged in the back of the vehicle. There was some clattering and then, 'Eureka!' Ginny opened her eyes. Bob was back beside her clutching a torch in one hand and a first aid kit in the other.

'Now I can get a proper look,' he said. With great care he pushed Ginny's hair back from her temple and examined her head. 'Nasty,' he pronounced after a few seconds. 'It looks quite deep. I think the doc'll want to put a stitch or two in it when we get you back. In the meantime I'm going to bandage it up.

'OK,' said Ginny.

'You're going to have to make yourself useful and hold the torch for me. Can you manage that?'

'I think so.'

'Good girl. I'll try not to hurt.' Bob handed Ginny the torch and clasped his hand over hers as he got her to direct the beam on to the correct spot. Then he busied himself with a sterile pad and a bandage. 'There,' he said finally. 'Perfect. You look like a war hero. Or should I say heroine?'

Ginny switched off the torch. The beam had begun to have a yellowish tinge to it. It looked as though the batteries weren't in their first flush of life and Ginny didn't want to waste them. She smiled weakly at him. She still felt shaky but didn't think she was going to faint any more. And more than feeling a bit flaky, she was beginning to feel chilly. A light breeze stirred the damp evening air. She thought that, considering the time of year and how high they were, the temperature was bound to drop still further. She shivered slightly.

Bob sat beside her and leant back against the rock too. 'Well, here's a how-de-do.'

'Another fine mess you've got us into,' responded Ginny picking up on the movie quote theme.

'That's more like it,' said Bob looking at her and smiling. 'You had me worried for a minute.'

'I feel a bit better now,' admitted Ginny. 'Less wobbly.'

'Good.'

'So now what?'

'First of all I'm going to see if we can get a signal through. Frankly I don't hold out much hope. Reception in such a deep valley is always dodgy and now we've slid halfway down it I don't think we stand a snowball's chance in hell, but we've got to give it a shot.'

'And if we can't radio for help?'

'Stay put and hope someone finds us or try and walk out I suppose?'

'Right,' said Ginny slowly and with an obvious lack of enthusiasm.

'Got a better idea?' The colonel sounded sharp. The worry about their situation had made him short-tempered.

'No, Colonel,' said Ginny contritely.

'For God's sake, call me Bob. This is hardly a situation that demands formality.'

There was a small silence. Ginny broke it to show there were no hard feelings. 'So which do you think we should do? Stay or go?'

'I don't know. We could try to climb back up to the road but there's a lot of loose stones and scree and the torch isn't going to be good for much longer. Personally I think we're in more danger of a fall and injuring ourselves if we try to go straight up than if we follow the contours back to the road lower down. But even if we do that, the terrain isn't good and if one of us twists an ankle or something . . .'

'We're really in the shit.'

'Not elegantly put, but succinct.'

'And if we stay?'

'I don't know how obvious it will be from the road that a vehicle has left it. It may be that the first vehicle along in the morning will spot our trail of destruction and send a search party to look for us. Alternatively it could take them ages to spot where that bloody truck ran us over the edge.'

'They'll miss us back at base.'

'But they won't send out a search party till daylight. They'll probably assume we've had a breakdown and are holed up in the vehicle overnight.'

Ginny thought quickly about the options outlined by Bob. 'I think we should stay here tonight and see if anyone comes for us in the morning. If they haven't by midday then we've still got a good few hours of daylight to get to the road. To be honest, I still feel a bit groggy and I really don't fancy the idea of trying to negotiate these woods in the pitch dark.'

'My view exactly. Well, let's see what we've got to make ourselves comfortable for the night. I'm afraid it's not going to be much.' Bob got to his feet. Ginny started to stand up too. 'You stay where you are young lady. I'm perfectly capable of finding things on my own. Besides which, we've only the one torch.'

Ginny slumped back against the rock again. Even that small amount of exertion had made her head spin. She listened to the noises coming from the Rover again. She heard Bob try to make contact using the radio. He made a number of calls for help using various frequencies, but the silence when he switched it to 'receive' and a couple of sotto voce swear words seemed to indicate he had had no success. After a while he gave it up as a waste of time. A few minutes later he returned holding a combat jacket, a tarpaulin and a twenty-four-hour ration pack. 'The radio was no good – couldn't get any sort of signal. The whole radio might be knackered for all I know.' He threw his booty on the ground by Ginny. 'Not much, but at least if it rains we will keep dry and there's a bite to eat.'

He unfolded the tarpaulin and spread it out. There would be plenty of room for the two of them underneath it. Then he sat down next to her so they could examine the ration pack together in the torchlight. A tin of sausages and beans, an oatmeal biscuit, some marge and jam, a chocolate bar, boiled sweets and a tin of stew was what they found.

'Enough to keep us going,' announced Bob. 'Are you hungry?'

'I could fancy a bit of chocolate.'

Bob handed her the bar. Ginny broke it in two and handed one half back. Bob switched off the torch again to conserve the batteries. They munched in silence. When they finished Ginny rubbed her hands together to keep the circulation going.

'Are you cold?' asked Bob.

'A bit,' admitted Ginny.

Bob reached forward and pulled the tarp up so that it covered them up to their chests. 'Tuck it round your legs,' he ordered. 'Keep out the draught.'

Ginny arranged the waterproof sheet and Bob did the same. As he did so he shuffled up close to her. 'Shared body heat,' he said. 'Best way of keeping warm.' Ginny didn't say anything.

Blast her previous fantasies. Her heart was pounding. She hoped to God he couldn't hear or feel it.

The sky, where they could see it through the trees, was completely black except for a speckling of stars, and apart from the rustling of the branches the silence was total.

'Have you noticed that since that wretched lorry, there hasn't been another vehicle on this road?' said Bob.

'No. I shouldn't think it gets much traffic, even in daylight,' said Ginny.

'How do you feel now?'

'Not so cold.'

'Good.'

Ginny felt the conversation was stilted because they were both thinking how potentially awkward their situation was. She decided to grasp the nettle.

'This'll get the rumour-mongers talking, won't it?' she observed lightly.

'The commanding officer spending the night with a strange woman, you mean? Well,' he turned to look at her, his face inches from hers, 'I don't mean strange like that, not strange peculiar . . .'

'I should hope not,' murmured Ginny, acutely and achingly aware of how close he was. Bob moved towards her until their lips met. Ginny felt such a surge of ecstasy course through her body it made her feel quite dizzy. Bob's arms moved round her and pulled her close to him. Ginny felt her body bend so she moulded against the contours of his exactly and then she, in turn put her arms around him. She had fantasized about them kissing more times than she cared to think about and now it was happening and it felt wonderful. Far, far better than in her dreams. She could hear the blood pounding in her ears as she shut her eyes and sank into the perfection of the moment.

But then Ginny came to her senses. Yes she had longed for this; yes she wanted him, but not while he was still married to Alice. 'No,' she murmured. 'This is wrong. We mustn't . . .'

'How can something that feels so right be wrong?' whispered Bob.

'But it is. You're married.'

'Oh, Ginny. Let's not think about that now.' Bob pulled back and used his right hand to lift Ginny's face so she had

91

to look at him. 'Ginny, I've adored you from the moment I first set eyes on you. I've never met anyone more vital, more vivacious, more beautiful than you. Even though I love Alice, I sometimes find myself wondering how things would be if I'd met you first? These last few months, having you so close and yet so inaccessible, have been more difficult than you could possibly imagine.'

Ginny gave a little groan. No, this wasn't right. Yes, it was words she wanted to hear but not with Alice in the picture.

'No, Bob.'

'But Ginny, you must have known how I felt?'

'I knew you liked me, were kind to me.' She became bolder. 'And I fell for you when I first saw you. You're the reason I'm still single. Every man I meet I compare with you, and no one ever comes close.'

'Oh, Ginny. I want you so much.'

Suddenly the tears she had managed to choke back earlier welled up again. She had spent more than a decade longing for this moment and now she had finally been granted her wish, she was overwhelmed by it all. And she was also crying for all those lonely years of unrequited love, the nights she had spent with other men while imagining that it had been Bob beside her in bed. And she was crying because, try as she might, she knew that Bob shouldn't be risking his family's happiness and his career for a night with her. She dragged a hanky out of her sleeve and blew her nose but still the tears coursed down her face.

'Oh, Ginny,' said Bob folding her in his arms again. 'Ginny, I had no idea that you felt the same way.' But Ginny didn't answer, she couldn't. She buried her face in his heavy woollen jumper and the tears flowed harder. He kissed the top of her head and gently rocked her back and forth to comfort her. 'Ginny, Ginny, Ginny,' he whispered as he patted her shoulder and tried to soothe her. But her silent, shoulder-shaking sobs continued to rack her body.

Eventually her tears subsided. Her silent sobs died to nothing and she lay quietly in his arms.

'Oh, Ginny. What is it? What has made you so unhappy? Surely if I love you and you love me and we're together . . . ?'

Ginny gulped and blew her nose. 'I'm not unhappy. Not

really. It's wonderful to know that you feel the same way about me as I do about you. But nothing can come of it. We can't have an affair. Just think what would happen if Alice found out.'

'It's a risk I'm prepared to take.'

Ginny raised her head from his chest and looked at him. 'Are you?'

'Yes.' Bob felt a degree of tenderness towards her that he didn't think he'd experienced since he'd held Megan as a newborn.

She rested her head against his chest once again. 'Do you remember the time we went climbing together?'

'Yes.' There was a pause. 'I wanted to kiss you then.'

'I know, but Staff McLean appeared.'

Bob remembered and nodded. He'd thought about that moment on any number of occasions. 'I think that's when I first fell in love with you.'

'I didn't mean that to happen.'

Bob squeezed Ginny gently and dropped a kiss on the top of her head. 'You always seemed so bouncy, so full of life. I imagined you had a hundred men dancing attendance on you. I thought I was just another bloke amongst dozens who had fallen for your charms.'

Ginny looked up at him again. 'But you were the only bloke I wanted. Still want, but . . .' She paused.

Bob rubbed her shoulder distractedly. 'But you don't think it would be right,' he finished. 'No one need know.'

'But they would. Eventually someone would notice. You know what the regiment is like for gossip.'

'Not if we're discreet.'

Ginny felt herself weakening. He was so sure and she wanted him so badly. And he was the one taking the risk. She didn't have the strength to resist. She wanted him, ached for him too much to hold out. She stretched up slightly and kissed him again on the mouth. 'If you're sure,' she said when they drew apart again. 'If you're certain no one else will ever know, then no one will get hurt.' She snuggled down under the tarpaulin and laid her head against his jersey. He could feel his heart pounding against his ribs. Ginny must be able to feel it too. She picked up his left hand, draped over her shoulder, and began to kiss his fingertips. Then Ginny began to lift up her sweater. She felt Bob's entire body stiffen in anticipation. She gently took his right hand and placed it on her shirt over her breast. 'Feel me,' she said. 'Feel how much I want you.'

Bob began to caress her hard nipple through the fabric. He heard Ginny groan with pleasure. Bob almost did too as a surge of passion rippled through him from his fingertips to his toes. Then, finally giving in to his own overwhelming desire, he began to undo her buttons.

When they were both naked they knelt, facing each other, on the damp leaf mould that formed the forest floor. The chill, still air seemed to heighten the eroticism of the moment and they pressed forward so their bodies touched from breast to thigh. Every movement of her hands, every flick of her tongue sent shivers of delight racing up and down his body. Bob could feel the hardness of his erection sandwiched between him and her flat stomach and he revelled in the sensation as they kissed again. Then they sank sideways on to the ground and Bob's hand moved down her flanks to her thighs and slid between them. Ginny was deliciously damp. Bob was afraid that he might come too quickly for her.

'Take me,' she whispered. 'I can't wait.' But he just smiled and bent his head so he could suck at her nipple. He had to get her to fever pitch too. His fingers felt the muscles in her pelvis tighten deliciously. She shuddered with pleasure and arched her back slightly and his finger slipped inside her. 'Oh, God,' she moaned. 'Please, now.'

Bob rolled on his back and Ginny rolled on top of him. She grasped his erect penis in one hand, lifted herself slightly and then lowered herself on to it. It was Bob's turn to groan. Ginny spread her knees slightly so she could spear herself as deeply as possible then she arched her back slightly as she leant forward so her breasts dangled provocatively over Bob's lips. He pulled her forward slightly and took one in his mouth. He felt her pelvic muscles flex once more. Bob responded with a thrust of his pelvis. This was unbelievable, he thought, almost drunk with lust and desire. Ginny began slowly to raise and lower herself. Bob continued to suck her nipple with his mouth and he kneaded the other one with his hand. Then suddenly he knew that if he didn't take control he would come before she did. He pushed her off, flipped her on to her back and with an almost ferocious thrust he took over. Almost instantly he knew that he'd succeeded. He felt Ginny shudder and writhe as the hot waves of orgasm rushed up her. Ginny's body arched as the powerful feelings took complete control of her. 'Oh, God!' she yelled.

Bob made one last, long thrust and then he too felt his own orgasm overtake him. It was so intense as to be almost painful, and shuddering and shaking he collapsed on top of her.

When his breathing had settled, Ginny began kissing him again. 'Don't think you're getting any sleep tonight,' she whispered. 'If you think that was good, just wait and see what I've got planned next. Now we've both got the urgency out of our systems, I'm going to tease you until you beg me for it.'

Her hand slipped down to his groin and Bob knew from the expert touch of her fingers that she was as good as her promise. 'Be gentle with me,' he groaned.

'Possibly, but when you find out what I want you to do to me, you may change your mind.'

'Hi, Alice?'

The line was bad but Alice could still recognize her husband's voice. 'Bob. I wasn't expecting a call.'

'I know but I wanted to assure you I am OK in case you heard the news from anyone else.'

Alice felt a prickle of worry. 'What news?'

'I was in a pretty bad accident yesterday. Some bloody local lorry driver ran the Land Rover I was in off the road. The Rover is a write-off but I got out with nothing more than a few bruises.'

'Oh, Bob! How dreadful. Was anyone else hurt?'

'Ginny Turner got a bad cut to the head. It needed five stitches but the doc says she'll be all right. No concussion or anything.'

Alice tried to sound pleased that Ginny had escaped relatively unscathed. 'Oh good.' Even she could hear that she had failed.

'We were pretty lucky. It could have been a lot worse.'

'It sounds as if it was bad enough.'

'The worst thing was getting rescued. We ended up halfway

down a mountain and it took the regiment a while to track us down.'

'You poor thing. You must have been so worried.'

'I think we were lucky that it wasn't bad weather. If it had happened a few weeks later on in the year . . . I mean, it snows heavily here.'

'Exactly.'

Alice told Bob all her news, most of which was inconsequential stuff, and then the time of their rationed phone call had ticked away, so she hung up. She was glad Bob had told her categorically that he was all right. The CO being in a car accident was the sort of news that the other officers would be sure to tell their own wives, and if Alice had heard the intelligence second hand she would have been worried.

She looked at the clock. Six. Time to go round to Sarah's for the meeting to organize the wives' club Christmas party. She gathered up her file, notebook and handbag and pulled the front door shut behind her. On the way to Sarah's she met Maddy heading for the same destination.

'No Danielle?' asked Alice.

'I've left her with Caroline. I don't think she'd have much of a contribution to make to the meeting.'

Alice smiled in approval. Very sensible. So many wives thought that they could take their children along to anything, like some sort of fashion accessory, and that their babies and toddlers would be welcome. Frankly, Alice thought that there were any number of functions for which it would be better to leave the children behind, but sadly she seemed to be in a minority these days.

Sarah's front door was open but Alice rang the bell anyway.

'Come in,' called Sarah from somewhere inside. The two women stepped over the threshold.

'Cooee,' called Alice.

'I'm in the dining room.'

Alice led the way along the hall and looked round the door. Sarah was struggling to lift the computer monitor off the table and put it on the sideboard, but she had got into a tangle with various flexes and she was balancing the monitor on the edge of the table, supporting it with one hand while she tried to disconnect the wires with the other.

Maddy immediately darted forward and lent a hand.

'Phew,' said Sarah as the muddle was resolved. Maddy dumped the keyboard and speakers beside it.

'At least we've got a table for the meeting now,' said Alice, wondering why on earth Sarah hadn't got herself organized earlier. Fancy leaving things to the last minute like this!

Sarah looked at her with a little annoyance as if she was aware of Alice's thoughts. 'I'll go and put the kettle on. I expect you would like tea, wouldn't you, Alice?'

'Thank you. That would be very nice.'

'And a glass of wine for you, Maddy?'

Maddy shot Alice a half guilty look, then with a self-conscious smile she said, 'Lovely.'

'Red or white?'

'Whatever.'

'I've got both open.'

Alice's eyebrows shot upwards. Wasn't it enough to have one bottle of wine open, but two! And to be drinking on her own . . .

'Red then please.'

When Sarah returned with a cup of tea and two glasses of wine, the three women sat down around the table.

'Before we start,' said Sarah, 'I just want to say how sorry I was to hear about Bob's accident. Thank goodness he's all right.'

Alice thanked Sarah for her concern and then brought the meeting back to their plans for a Christmas party for the wives. It was an annual event and usually consisted of a seasonal meal followed by some sort of cabaret act. The previous CO's wife had organized a troupe of male strippers which had been a huge success with everyone but, success or no, Alice had no intention of allowing anything as bawdy as that while she was in charge.

'Thank God that's over,' said Sarah to Maddy after she had seen Alice out.

Maddy sighed. 'It was a bit heavy going, wasn't it?'

'I don't know about you, but I need another glass of wine.'

Maddy glanced at her watch. 'I should really be going. Caro's got Danielle.'

'Give her a ring. See how Danielle is. If she's still awake, go and get her. You can put her to bed here and then go home when you're ready.'

'You sure?'

'Course. I wouldn't suggest it if I wasn't.'

Maddy made the phone call while Sarah got the wine.

'Caro's just putting the kids in the bath. She said to give it twenty minutes and then come and get her. But I may take her straight home.'

Sarah shrugged. 'It's up to you. But if you'd like to stay I wouldn't mind the company.' Sarah poured two generous glasses and handed one to Maddy.

'So what was this about Colonel Bob getting hurt?'

'Haven't you heard?'

'Evidently not,' said Maddy, taking a slurp of her wine.

Sarah recounted the details she had heard.

'It sounds dreadful!' said Maddy.

'I think it was pretty serious. But the really interesting bit is that Bob and Ginny were stuck on the side of this mountain for about eighteen hours – and all alone,' she added archly.

'Poor things,' said Maddy with sympathy.

'And there was no one else,' hinted Sarah again, heavily. 'They were alone. Together. Overnight.'

Maddy put her glass on the table slowly. Her mouth dropping open equally slowly as the implication sank in. 'It doesn't mean a thing though, does it?'

Sarah shrugged meaningfully and took a sip of her own wine. 'Maybe.' Then, with a niggle of guilt she remembered Alisdair's injunction that she shouldn't spread rumours about her suspicion regarding Bob and Ginny. 'No, you're right, probably not. I mean Ginny had had a bad bang on the head.' She giggled and had another slurp. 'I expect she had a headache.'

Maddy laughed too. 'I tell you something, I'm not going to have a headache for weeks after Richard gets back.'

'Me neither.'

'Only five weeks to push.'

'Hooray!'

Taz was sitting at her desk in her study, a CD playing Mozart quietly, working on a feature for the *Mercury*. She'd had a phone call from Minty Armstrong earlier that day asking if there was any chance of the feature about army wives that she had proposed earlier in the year.

'It's just that there's that court case coming up about army widows' pensions, and with the profile of army wives being raised it would be a good time to run it.'

'I have probably got most of the material. It's just a question of cobbling it together. But I don't want to be too specific about names and places. I've made some really useful contacts here and I might lose the lot if they find out.'

'God, that doesn't matter. Make them all up if you want. Jo Public isn't going to give a damn whether it's the Foot-and-Mouth Regiment or the Queen's Royal Dog Walkers.'

'Right. Well, in that case I can probably let you have two thousand words by tomorrow.'

'Great.'

Colonel Bob put the top on his fountain pen, laid it on top of the papers he was perusing, and squeezed out from behind the desk in his small office. After consuming four cups of coffee that morning to keep himself awake after a restless night, he was bursting for a pee. He left his office and turned toward the loos. On his way he passed Ginny's office and glanced in. She was sitting at her desk, beavering away. She must have sensed that she was being watched for she looked up. Her face was transformed by a smile. She slid her eyes quickly across to her clerk who shared an office with her to see if she was looking and, discovering that she wasn't, Ginny blew him a kiss. It had been two weeks since they had made love that night on the mountain and their affair had since continued, albeit under very difficult circumstances. But last night they had almost been caught and, despite Bob's earlier assurances that they could get away with their liaison, that if they were careful no one would know, their near miss had so frightened Bob that he had been brought to his senses.

What had he been thinking of, trying to continue their affair in the claustrophobic atmosphere of their location? They had managed a number of trysts but each had been far from satisfactory. Their passion had overcome the discomfort of making love out in the cold surrounding countryside or on the floor of a nearby derelict building but their main difficulties had stemmed from their departure from and return to the factory. Neither was exactly a low profile member of the regiment and it was nigh on impossible for either to slip away unseen. Then, last night, there had been a mass exodus of the officers to a pizzeria in a nearby town. Ginny had declined, complaining of a headache, and the colonel had done the same, complaining about pressure of work. As soon as a decent interval had passed, Ginny had crept along to Bob's room. Their love-making had been passionate and energetic and not entirely silent. It was only minutes after Ginny had left to return to her own room that the regimental medical officer had knocked on the colonel's door to inquire if he was OK. One of the soldiers had heard groans as he passed by the window and had been concerned about the colonel's health.

Bob had blustered something about doing press-ups and sit-ups in an effort to keep fit and the exertion had caused him to grunt and groan a bit. The doctor believed him – especially as he was still flushed and sweating and only dressed in shorts and a T-shirt when he had answered the knock on the door.

But the call had been close enough, Bob decided. After the doctor had gone Bob had sat on the bed feeling very shaken. What if the doctor had come five minutes earlier? What if the soldier had heard more than just a few groans? Bob thought back. Had Ginny been very vocal? He didn't think so, but he couldn't be sure. Supposing the soldier had put two and two together? Supposing he was, even now, discussing what he had heard with his mates? The thought was terrifying. The news would be round the regiment like wildfire and Bob's career would be finished. Well, there was a chance that that scenario wasn't being played out, but Bob knew he couldn't take any more risks. He would have to end the affair. And yet Bob was captivated by Ginny and the thought of giving her up was a desperate one. With her he had discovered joys and pleasures that he had never even come close to with Alice. Her love-making was almost clinical; the box of tissues handy on the bedside table for the 'spills', as she called them. No shouting and shuddering and crazy excitement with her. Not like Ginny. Would he be able to cope with basic, formulaic, boring and predictable love-making – the only sort in Alice's repertoire? Bob sighed. He didn't know, but what he did know was that he couldn't carry on with Ginny. If the army found out, if Alice found out, he'd be finished.

Alice, he knew, might not be the perfect wife in bed but in almost all other ways she had done him proud. No one could fault her dedication to his career, her unerring knack for charming senior officers. Bob's recognition of her abilities at entertaining, conversation and generally just knowing how to behave in almost any circumstance had been one of the things that had attracted him to her in the first place. He'd always been ambitious and he knew that a good wife could be of use as he made his way up through the ranks, and Alice had seemed ideal. The perfect wife for any officer. He had loved her – he did still – but he had never been sure that he had ever been *in love* with her. But it had been enough for him to ask her to marry him. It had come as a bit of a blow to discover that her background wasn't quite as pukka as he had thought, but then he had reasoned that if he hadn't guessed, who would? And he'd been proved right.

Then he met Ginny. And for over a decade he had resisted his desperate desire to possess her. He had been faithful to Alice even when temptation had almost proved too much but finally he had given in. And now it must stop again. No matter that it would break Ginny's heart. No matter that it was going to tear him apart. It had to be done. Bob had sat on his bed and been adamant that he would interview Ginny the next day and end it.

Bob continued on along the corridor towards the loos thinking that this was probably going to be one of the hardest things he had ever done. And he thought that, apart from hurting Ginny terribly, he was also making a sacrifice himself. He was going to have to give up all those wonderful sexual acts that Ginny performed. As the thought entered his head he became aware of a sudden erection. He pulled his heavy duty uniform jersey down to make sure it hid his crotch – he didn't want anyone to be aware of the bulge in his trousers – and hurried on to the lavatories.

When he got there he knew it was useless to try to pee. He'd have to wait until the old man decided to relax again.

He stared out of the half-open window and tried to make his mind think about the scene in front of him, soldiers going about routine duties, rather than Ginny. After a few minutes he felt more comfortable and wandered over to the urinals. As he peed he wondered how Ginny would take it. Surely she would understand? But at the back of his mind was a niggle that was not nearly so confident. What had she said? That he was the reason she had not married? That no one else had come close? That had been all very flattering but he couldn't, in his heart of hearts, believe that it was entirely true. He knew Ginny of old and she had always had a fondness for exaggeration, for gilding the lily. He didn't doubt that she had once fancied him and perhaps, in the past, it had been something more than that. Surely in the intervening years she would have forgotten about him, and she had just told him she hadn't because emotions had been running so high that night. He hoped so. He'd heard stories about people who got obsessive about their lovers but surely Ginny was far too sensible to go down that path. He sighed and offered up a silent prayer that she was. This was going to be difficult but time was not going to make it easier. He had to be straight with her. Their affair was over. He had made a ghastly mistake by starting it and what had happened was to be consigned to the past. Bob zipped himself up and squared his shoulders. This was it.

He stopped at Ginny's door. The set of accounts still held her attention. Whatever else anyone could say about Ginny, no one could fault her administrative skills. Bob had never known a unit to run as smoothly as the regiment did at the moment. Everything from the accounts to the documentation, from the soldiers' courses to their leave arrangements, was running like oiled clockwork.

'Ginny,' he said.

As she looked up a smile transformed her face from simply pretty to beautiful. 'Colonel,' she replied.

'Hmm . . . I need to talk to you for a moment. Would you come along to my office when you've got a minute?'

'Sure, sir. Do I need to bring anything? Diary, notebook?'

'No, just yourself.'

Ginny stood up and followed him along the corridor. Bob was holding the door open for her. She stepped into the tiny room that served as his office. In front of her was space for a couple of wooden chairs, then his desk and a decent, comfortable swivel chair behind it. Bob shut the door behind them. Ginny turned round to face him, and threw her arms around Bob. They knew that when the CO's door was shut, everyone in the regiment understood that, under almost no circumstances, was he to be disturbed.

Bob could feel her quivering with nervous energy and excitement as she pressed against his body. He hoped to God his body wouldn't let him down just at this minute by responding in the obvious manner. Bob extricated himself from her embrace and sat down on one of the hard wooden chairs. He took Ginny's hand.

'Sit down, we need to talk.'

She lowered herself on to the chair facing him, their knees almost touching.

'Ginny, there's something I have to say.' He paused, uneasy and unsure of quite what to say. 'About recent events.'

Ginny's brow creased in a frown of puzzlement. 'Events?' she queried.

'You know what I mean.' He looked away, embarrassed at mentioning it.

She understood the body language. It was unmistakable. 'You mean our love-making?' she said, slowly and deliberately.

'Yes.' Bob shifted uncomfortably. 'But it can't happen again.'

'Why not? I thought we agreed, as long as Alice doesn't know, no one will get hurt.'

'Ginny, it still means deception and I can't lie to Alice. She's my wife. I've been married to her for sixteen years. I can't do this to her.'

'But that's not what you said on the mountain. I was the one who reminded you of your marriage, if you remember. Why this change of heart?'

'I can't hurt her. If she found out it would destroy her.'

'You can't hurt her, but you can hurt me. Is that it?' said Ginny bitterly.

'I don't mean to. But you must have known that it couldn't be forever, that it would end one day?'

'But why? Why so suddenly?'

Bob recounted the visit by the doctor the night before. 'It was too close. It's too risky. There's too much at stake.'

'Too much at stake for you, you mean. You're shit-scared about what a rumour of an affair might do to your career. You know that if the brass get to know about this, you might find yourself out of a job. Go on, admit it. You know as well as I do what a dim view they have of liaisons between senior and junior officers.'

'Ginny—'

'Don't,' she snapped. 'I didn't want us to have an affair. I didn't want this to start. It was your doing, and I knew it was wrong. God, I should have listened to myself. I should never have let anything happen.'

'Oh, Ginny. Please don't make things harder for me,' said Bob.

'Why not? What makes you so deserving of an easy time?'

'Please, Ginny. You can't possibly despise me more than I do myself.'

'I wouldn't bank on that if I were you.'

'I know I'm being a bastard—'

'Yes.'

'But—'

'But nothing.' Ginny shut her eyes for a few seconds while she composed herself. Then she looked at her hands in her lap as she said quietly, 'Fine. It's over. And don't worry, Alice won't find out from me.'

Bob sighed, partly with relief. 'Thank you, Ginny.'

Ginny looked at him, a puzzled expression on her face. 'But I thought you loved me.'

'Ginny, you are the most remarkable woman I know. I have never had such erotic experiences. Memories of them will live with me forever. And there will always be a place in my heart for you.'

'But not in your life.'

'You must have known that couldn't be possible.'

'No, I didn't. I had hoped that you would quietly divorce Alice one day and marry me instead.'

Bob took her hands again. 'It isn't just Alice though, is it? There's Megan as well.'

'Yes. I see.' Ginny's voice was devoid of emotion. She looked pale and defeated. But Bob was glad that she wasn't sobbing her heart out like she had on the mountain.

'I know what I've said must be hurtful—' He was interrupted by a small snort of derision from Ginny – 'but in time you'll see it's for the best. You'll understand that we've done the right thing.'

'There's no "we" about this, Colonel,' said Ginny icily. 'Whatever this is about, it isn't about *us*, it's about *you*.' She stood up, her mouth set in a tight little line. 'If that is everything, I've got a mountain of work to get through, so if you'll excuse me . . .' She shut the door behind her as she left. Bob slumped in his chair. Part of him was relieved that the unpleasant interview was over but part of him felt dreadful that he had caused so much pain. If only he could put the clock back, if only that damned accident had never happened, none of this would have done either. Wearily Bob rose from his seat and reopened the door. Ginny was hurt and angry, that was obvious. He hoped to God she didn't decide to do anything rash. And he hoped, even more fervently, that she wasn't going to go and cry on anyone's shoulder.

'Cheer up,' said Richard as he plonked himself down next to Ginny at dinner that evening. 'Maybe it'll never happen.'

'Yeah,' said Ginny dully. 'And maybe pigs will fly.'

'It can't be that bad.'

Ginny gave him a long look. 'Oh, yes it can.'

'Sorry.'

Ginny didn't say anything, she just forked up another mouthful of lamb curry and chewed it morosely.

'I had an email from Maddy today,' said Richard, changing the subject on purpose. 'Apparently this year's wives' club Christmas party isn't going to be a patch on last year's.'

'Oh?' But Ginny wasn't really interested. After all, it looked even more certain that she was never going to be a wife, so what possible interest could a wives' club Christmas party hold for her? She couldn't even manage to hold a man for long enough to have a decent affair, let alone get him to marry her.

'Yeah,' said Richard, carrying on regardless. Ginny wasn't sure if he was too stupid and insensitive to see that she was disinterested and happy to wallow in her own misery, or whether he had spotted that she was unhappy and was making an effort to cheer her up. Because of the way she currently felt about the male of the species, she assumed it was the former. 'Yeah, last year they had the "Sheratons", a "Chippendale" tribute group. Maddy says this year Alice is booking a conjuror. Can you believe it? You can imagine what all those women are like after their men have been away for the best part of six months – a conjuror is hardly likely to fit the bill.'

'No.'

'Maddy says she and Sarah are trying to persuade Alice to let them book a stand-up comedian as well.'

'Oh.'

Richard shook his head as he gave up the struggle. Ginny was glad. She had never felt less like making polite conversation in her life. Even if it was with an old friend like Richard. She finished her curry and took herself back to the tiny, cold and dreary room that was her bedroom. As the only female officer she had the privilege of a room to herself. On most days she felt that the privilege only served to isolate her, but tonight she welcomed the solitude.

She sat on her camp bed and leaned against the cold breezeblocks behind her. She felt angry and upset. She had tried to stop the affair from happening. She had tried to resist him. She had known in her heart that it was a terrible idea, but he had persuaded her and raised her hopes of making a future life with him. And now her fears had been realized. He had been forced to make a decision and she was the one who had been left high and dry. Her anger grew as she thought about his rejection. He'd told her that he preferred that cold snob of a frigid wife to her. Her! How dare he? Ginny's hurt and humiliation turned to total rage. She felt tears of self-pity and indignation prick at her eyes. All those years she had compared her other men friends to his maturity and humour and looks and found them wanting. Not that she had been celibate – far from it, to be completely honest – but she had never looked for any sort of long-lasting relationship with any of her suitors. She had seen the ideal man for her and if she couldn't have him then she wasn't interested in a poor imitation. So her boyfriends

106

had come and gone and she had continued to hope that fate would deliver Bob to her. And she thought that her dream had materialized and her prayers had been answered, but now everything was ruined. Everything had turned to dust. She had been spurned as if she was some schoolgirl with a teenage crush. Bastard. Bastard! Well, so what if people guessed what had happened? He deserved to have his career wrecked. He'd wrecked her life after all. In fact, she might even start a rumour. That would show him, if everyone started gossiping about the two of them. Even if the brass didn't find out, it would put the wind up him. It would scare him shitless. And what would his precious bloody Alice say when she found out? Huh? Well, that would serve him right. Ginny sat on her bed and wallowed in vindictive, spiteful thoughts until she exhausted them and reality re-exerted its grip.

It was all very well wanting to get her own back but, realistically, what would she achieve? Petty revenge might be all well and good in the short term, but then what? She would alienate him forever. He was hardly likely even to speak to her, let alone form a relationship with her if she had wrecked his career and his marriage. She might gain some short-term satisfaction from the act of vengeance but he would despise her and she would lose him forever. Damned if she did, damned if she didn't. The stark truth was that he didn't want her, he wanted Alice. And where did that leave her? She sniffed. It left her in a bloody awkward position, that was what. With a sigh, she admitted to herself that she had got it all wrong. By revealing her feelings for him she had left him with only two options – her or Alice. He had made his decision and now she was the one with precious few options. Either she could stay in her current posting and accept that every day she would have a reminder of her humiliating rejection, or she could go, put this behind her and try to make a better fist of the rest of her life. With a leaden heart she realized that it probably wasn't even an option for her to stay with the regiment. Loyalty was a two-way thing, and she certainly didn't feel any towards Bob – and she was pretty certain the only loyalty he might feel for her was guilt-induced. There was no way they could continue a proper working relationship under those circumstances.

Even if her professionalism managed to rise above their

difficulties, could she really bear to see him every day? Could she pretend nothing had ever happened, accept that she was going to see Colonel Bob constantly but just try to put everything behind her and get on with it? Or, and this was the sensible course of action, she could ask for a posting for personal reasons. The trouble was, there were pitfalls that came with both options. If she stayed put, either she or Bob might say something indiscreet, or someone within the regiment might put two and two together. And she had already been on the receiving end of a comment about the two of them spending the night together. She had laughed it off with the retort that she wasn't *that* desperate for promotion. But it was from that sort of remark that rumours grew. Alternatively, if she asked for a new posting she would have to give a reason and the only reason she could give would be 'personal reasons' – often a euphemism for needing to get away from a failed love affair, although her postings branch probably wouldn't pry as to exactly what her reasons were. This would remove her from the regiment but there were people who were bound to be curious about whom she had been having an affair with. Even though she might be safely out of the regiment, someone was bound to come up with the right answer sooner or later. Well, that wouldn't be her problem. If she acted with dignity and left without a fuss she could hardly be blamed if things subsequently went wrong. Her reputation might take a beating but the person it was really going to hurt was Bob if the story got out. His career would be history, and possibly his marriage too. The desire to hurt, to hit back, reasserted itself with this thought. 'Serve him right,' she muttered angrily. 'Bastard.'

Her eye rested on the rough shelf that she had fixed up to serve as dressing table, desk and bookcase. Lying on it was the last letter from Megan. True to her word Megan had written regularly. Not frequently, but regularly. Seeing the letter reminded Ginny that there was another complication in this business. She was the innocent victim in all this. It wasn't Megan's fault that her father had the hots for one of his subordinates and her mother was frigid. If the affair became public Megan would be hurt beyond belief and Ginny couldn't do that to her. She was genuinely fond of the kid but she could hardly continue their friendship. It would be impossible for

108

her under the circumstances. Ginny stared at the letter for a while and wondered how she was going to deal with this added complication. She would have to find ways of avoiding her until another posting came up. But what would she say if Megan did corner her and asked what was going on? She didn't think she would be able to lie to Megan, but she could hardly come out with the truth. Which would be less hurtful: to tell Megan that she didn't want to be friends with her anymore or to tell her that she and Bob had fallen out? Either way, it was a mess. But one thing was sure, she would have to let Megan down in the Christmas holidays. Now that circumstances had changed, there was no way that Ginny could contemplate taking Megan on the promised shopping spree to London. She sighed deeply. Why were things so fucking complicated? she thought angrily.

She picked the letter up and began to reread it. It was full of news about the school's forthcoming production of *The Pirates of Penzance*. Megan had managed to land herself a small solo part and it also appeared she was helping out with wardrobe. She apologized that with the play and the ridiculous amount of prep they were now given every evening, she wasn't sure whether she'd be able to write to Ginny much more before they all came back from Kosovo. Ginny put the letter down again, thanking her lucky stars that with Megan so busy, she might not notice the lack of letters from herself. Even Ginny's egocentric attitude and odd set of personal rules didn't allow her to carry on a correspondence with her ex-lover's daughter. She might be able to pretend everything was just as it was before she went to Kosovo as far as the grown-ups in the regiment were concerned but she wasn't going to start lying to Megan.

At least that had forced her to come to a decision. She would have to go. She couldn't hang around the barracks with the frequent possibility of running into Megan.

Sarah picked a copy of the *Mercury* off the news-stand at the Naafi. She glanced at the headlines and popped it in her shopping basket. She knew Alisdair hated the rag but she was a secret fan. It always had such wonderful, juicy stories that the broadsheets never ran. It would be her treat for today, she promised herself.

On her return home she discovered the post had come. She picked it up off the mat and flicked through the letters as she shut the door. She noticed they consisted either of junk, bills or circulars, so she chucked them on the hall table as she walked into the kitchen to make herself a coffee. Once she had her drink she took the mug and paper into the sitting room and settled herself down. She scanned the front page and saw a succession of gloomy stories about war, pestilence and famine. She knew she ought to read them but it was just too depressing. Ignoring her conscience she turned to the inside pages.

NO QUARTER was the headline on the women's page. 'The tough life of army wives,' it said in smaller print. Sarah folded the paper and began to read the article avidly. Like most people she liked reading about things that concerned her. 'God, that's so true,' she muttered as she read about the nausea of moving every couple of years. 'Oh, yes,' she agreed as she got to the bit in the article about careers being almost impossible to follow. 'Exactly,' she said when she read about senior officers' wives who wore their husbands' ranks more prominently than their spouses and liked to lord it round the barracks. 'So like bloody Alice,' she murmured. In fact, she began to feel that everything that was mentioned in the article seemed to strike an unusually familiar chord. Even down to the fact that the husbands were in Kosovo. She reread the feature but there were no names or places mentioned to give her a clue that this was anything more than coincidence. She decided that life for army wives was obviously a shared experience and scarily similar for all of them, regardless of place or regiment.

Still, thought Sarah, the article would make a good topic of conversation at the wives' club coffee morning she had promised she would attend later that day. She tore the page out of the paper and put it in her handbag.

'I'd like a word, Colonel, please,' said Ginny from the doorway.

Bob looked up from his desk warily. He wasn't sure he wanted another confrontation with Ginny. The one the other morning had been harrowing enough and he'd been deliberately avoiding her since then.

'Come in. Sit down,' he said. Ginny entered his tiny office

and shut the door behind her. Hell, thought Bob, this looks ominous. She sat down on the edge of the chair. She looked distinctly uncomfortable and edgy.

'Colonel.'

'Yes.'

Ginny swallowed. 'I want a posting.'

'Oh.' Bob wasn't entirely surprised. 'I don't suppose I need to ask you on what grounds?'

'Personal reasons.'

'Yes. I thought as much.'

'When you speak to my postings branch, could you ask them to make it sooner rather than later?'

'You can't go before the end of the tour here.'

Ginny gave him a stony look. 'I may be an embarrassment for you to have around, Colonel, but I'm not stupid. Of course I know I'll have to finish here first.'

Bob felt his face flood with colour. He wasn't used to being put down like that and it was unpleasant. 'No.' Bob fiddled with his fountain pen while he regained his composure. 'Is there anywhere you would particularly like to go?'

'I thought the south of England, the far south-west if possible. I've relatives that way – my sister and her family.'

'There will be questions asked. Do you want me to suggest that as a reason – that you need to be nearer your sister?'

'Why not?' said Ginny tiredly. 'The truth isn't an option so does it matter what the lie is?'

Again Bob felt a twinge of shame. 'Right,' he said and took the top off his pen and made a note. 'I won't pretend that I like this decision of yours. Even though you've only been serving with the regiment a short time I can see the contribution you have made to it has been valuable. You'll be a hard act to follow.'

'Do you want me to tell my successor that she may be expected to fulfil other duties apart from pushing paper about? She might not be quite as good at sex as me but I could give her a few tips.'

'That was uncalled for,' said Bob quietly. 'And I think you are forgetting that whatever else has happened between us, I am still your commanding officer.'

It was Ginny's turn to blush. 'Sorry,' she mumbled.

111

'Apology accepted.'

'Thank you.'

'Is there anything else?' Ginny shook her head. 'If you could ask Richard to pop in and see me on your way out?'

'Yes, sir.'

A couple of minutes later Richard appeared in his boss's office. 'You wanted me?'

'Sit down, Richard. Ginny has just announced she wants a posting.'

'Good heavens. What brought that on?'

Bob looked him in the eye. 'I think it's got something to do with her sister, but I didn't like to pry too much. She'll be with us until we return from Kosovo, naturally.'

Richard nodded thoughtfully. 'Well, that could explain things.'

'Explain what?'

'Why she's been so moody. I thought it might have been something to do with the accident but if she's worried about Netta it makes much more sense. It just didn't seem in character for Ginny to be rattled by an accident. Nerves of steel that one. But her sister? They are very close.'

Bob felt a twinge of worry. 'I didn't know you knew her sister.' He hoped he sounded casual. If Richard was au fait with Ginny's family, the lie about the posting might easily get found out. Talk about tangled webs!

'Oh, I've not met her. But Ginny's always talking about her and her huge brood of children.'

'I didn't know.'

'Yes, she's got four and a fifth on the way. Perhaps it's all a bit much for her. Perhaps her health isn't too good. I'll have to ask Ginny if that's what she's worried about.'

'Well, as I said, I wouldn't pry too closely. Ginny wasn't very forthcoming.'

'Oh.' Richard was surprised. 'Oh, if you really think so.'

'Mmm, yes.'

'Have you seen this in the *Mercury*?' said Sarah to Maddy as she pulled the newspaper clipping out of her handbag like a magician with a rabbit. The regimental wives, or those that could be bothered to turn up, had gathered in the ante-room of the sergeants' mess for the monthly wives' club coffee morning. The decor always reminded Sarah of a steak and chips restaurant – red plush upholstery, lots of wood panelling and a dark red and black swirly carpet. Still, it was warm and comfortable, the coffee was hot and the mess chef had produced a tantalizing selection of cakes and biscuits.

'You don't mean to tell me that you get the *Mercury*?' said Maddy.

'Only when Alisdair's away. When he's home I wouldn't dare, but I just love the gossip in this one, don't you?'

'Totally. Anyway, what is it that's so fascinating?'

Sarah passed over the article. While Maddy was reading it, Caro joined them and peered over Maddy's shoulder.

'She's got it absolutely right, this woman,' said Maddy. 'Especially the bit about COs' wives.'

'Ssh,' warned Sarah, who was aware that Alice was only a few yards away.

Maddy glanced up and saw the danger. 'Oops,' she said. She finished reading and handed the article to Caro who was only halfway through.

'God, this bit about the CO's wife!' squealed Caro in a stage whisper, snorting back a giggle. 'It's Alice to a T. God, isn't it scary to think there's more than one like her?'

'Terrifying,' said Maddy. 'Hey, do you think it's what happens to you when your old man gets to be a colonel?'

'Hope not,' said Sarah, who was nearer the prospect than the other two. The three of them suddenly got a fit of the giggles and dissolved into peals of laughter.

'Dunno where she got her stuff from but it's spot on,' said Maddy, regaining control of herself. 'All those things that drive us all nuts. I almost felt I could have written that article.'

Caro finished it and handed the cutting back to Sarah. 'So what's the connection between this woman – what's her name?'

Sarah glanced at the byline. 'Tabitha Alabaster.'

'And the army?' finished Caro.

'It doesn't say. She doesn't name names though. Not proper ones,' said Sarah.

'Hardly surprising,' said Maddy. 'I mean it's hardly very complimentary, and if the CO finds out which of the wives in his regiment has been talking to the press, he's bound to have the husband in for an interview without coffee.'

'Who would have an interview without coffee?' said Alice, shoehorning her way into their group.

'Oh, nothing really,' said Sarah.

'Not one of your husbands in trouble, surely?'

'No nothing like that,' said Sarah. 'We were just talking about the dangers of talking to the press without permission.' She hoped the other two would realize she was deliberately keeping the subject general. She didn't think Alice would appreciate the newspaper article.

'Why, has someone been selling their soul?'

'Hardly,' said Caro. 'Just some article Sarah saw in the *Mercury*.'

Alice raised her eyebrows. 'The *Mercury*? Fancy reading that.'

'Yes, well,' said Sarah, wishing Caroline hadn't delivered that bit of information to Alice. She shot her a look and Caro looked faintly sheepish for a moment.

'Was that what you were reading just now?' asked Alice.

Hell, thought Sarah. She really hadn't wanted Alice to see it but she could hardly deny it now. If Alice read it she might guess that they had all been giggling about her – in a roundabout way.

'Can I see it?'

'Of course,' said Sarah, pulling it out of her bag again. She handed it over and as Alice turned her attention to the clipping, Sarah raised her eyebrows at the other two women as if to say 'now we're for it'.

They stood patiently while Alice read through the feature. They could tell by the tightening of her lips when she got to the bit about the CO's wife. Sarah wondered if Alice would realize the cause of their laughter. But then she consoled herself with the thought that Alice seemed to have the self-knowledge of a baked bean and so probably wouldn't.

'Well,' said Alice with a disapproving sniff, 'it all seems very disloyal. Fancy talking to the press like that. And as for what some of the wives said about other wives to this reporter, really!'

For 'other wives', read the CO's wife, thought Sarah. 'Yes,' she said out loud. 'I expect half of it was made up. You know what journalists are like.'

'Actually, I'm pleased to be able to say I don't,' said Alice tartly. She handed back the cutting and moved off. She had gone about two paces when she stopped and turned back to the group. 'But you're quite right, I would imagine that the army will take a very dim view of the wife who talked to the press. I would imagine her husband will be in very hot water.' And then she swept off.

'That told us,' said Sarah rolling her eyes. 'I think she guessed what we were laughing about.'

'Oh, who cares,' said Maddy defiantly. 'Silly old bag. You know what they say: if you can't take a joke you shouldn't have joined.'

'Weell,' said Sarah. 'Maybe we were a bit unkind.'

'No, we weren't. Right, more coffee anyone?'

'Any other news?' asked Maddy. Her voice sounded tinny over the satellite phone link.

'Oh, yes. Ginny's asked for a posting.'

'A posting! No! Why?'

'Dunno. She's been really low since the accident. There's obviously something troubling her. To begin with I thought it might be a reaction to having such a close call—'

'I can't see Ginny getting post-traumatic stress,' said Maddy.

'Exactly, but it now seems as though it might be something to do with Netta.'

'She's not lost the baby?'

'Maddy, I haven't a clue. I don't think so, but Ginny's really withdrawn at the moment. Colonel Bob doesn't think we ought to pry, but I don't know. What do you think? You're a woman, surely you have an idea.'

'It's a bit difficult to know from this distance. I mean, if I was talking to her face to face it would be different. And if it was Netta's baby I can see Ginny being a bit upset, but it's not the sort of thing that would make her depressed.'

'Yeah, you're probably right. It must be something else but goodness knows what. She's just so miserable. Not like her normal self at all. And she's been like that for about three weeks now – ever since the crash in fact.'

'When is she due back?'

'In a fortnight. I'm sending her home with the first lot.'

'How about I arrange to meet her at Brize Norton?'

'Would you?'

'Course. Danny and I could do with a trip out. Tell Ginny it's all fixed. Don't take no for an answer.'

'Maddy, you're a star. See if you can't work your magic on her and cheer her up.'

'OK. Love you.'

'And you. Big hugs to Danny.'

Richard put the phone down feeling a little better. Ginny's listlessness and general unhappiness was really beginning to worry him. He'd never known her like this. Her work was fine. In fact, it was better than fine as she didn't seem to do anything else but work, eat and sleep. She never relaxed with the others. When the junior officers had gone into the local village for a pizza she had just shaken her head and muttered something about catching up with a backlog of work. When they'd tried to organize a volleyball match – a sport Ginny excelled at – she had refused to take part, saying she wasn't in the mood. Everything about her seemed so out of character it was almost as though the woman the recovery team had rescued off the mountain was some sort of changeling. A couple of times Richard had asked her if she wanted to talk about what had happened and had been shocked at the ferocity with which she had declined. Not wishing to be told to mind his 'own bloody business' again, he hadn't pried any more.

Richard had asked the REME captain who had dragged the Land Rover back up the slope if he thought the accident had been particularly bad. The captain had voiced the opinion that it might have been nasty but not so bad as to leave a lasting mental scar.

'I mean, I'm no expert, but I've seen lots worse, honest,' he'd said. 'It didn't roll for a start. It would have been a bit of a roller-coaster going down that gradient of slope but no one got badly hurt. Usually it's when there's a death or really serious injury that the surviving victims seem to go through some sort of guilt trip. But then that's men. Dunno about women. Perhaps they get upset by more minor ones.'

Perhaps women *were* different, thought Richard. Perhaps

they reacted differently to that sort of brush with danger, but he was no psychologist. He didn't know. He asked the doctor but he refused to give an opinion unless he examined the patient, and as she hadn't asked to see him there was nothing he could do.

'Well, tell her *you* want to see her,' he had snapped in exasperation.

'On what grounds?'

'You want to check how her cut is healing up.' But Ginny had told the doctor it was fine and said she wasn't going to take up his time.

Even though it was still two weeks away, Richard felt relieved that Maddy was going to have a chance to talk to Ginny. Ginny's misery was so deep it was almost tangible, and he was very worried about her. He hoped that talking to another woman might unlock whatever the problem was. The other officers didn't seem to care, or perhaps they didn't notice, but then Richard didn't think they knew Ginny as well as he did. It was so completely out of character he knew there had to be something serious behind it. And despite what Colonel Bob had said about it being to do with her family, Richard had a sneaking suspicion that there was more to it than that. A little part of his brain was telling him that it had more to do with the day of the accident than anything else. He couldn't help asking himself exactly what had happened the night Ginny and Bob were trapped together on the mountain, and he couldn't help finding that he reached the same answer every time. Then he dismissed his notion as preposterous and put the whole thing out of his mind.

'Maddy!' called Ginny across the concourse of the RAF airport.

'Ginny!' Maddy rushed forward, Danny toddling behind as fast as her fat legs would carry her.

'It's so good to see you again. And look at Danny! How she's grown. And so good at walking – running even.' Ginny threw down her bags and swung Danny up in her arms then, almost crushing the little girl, she hugged Maddy. 'It's so good of you to come and collect me. I could have easily got the coach back with the lads.'

'No way. And I want to have a chance to catch up on all the news. To find out what it was really like out there. Richard is hopeless at that sort of thing. God, it'll be good to have you back. It's been like death warmed up in the barracks with the regiment away.'

Ginny smiled. 'It'll be good to be back. Even if it's not for long. You know I've asked for a posting?'

Maddy stepped back so she could look at Ginny properly. 'Yeah, Richard said. Why? You've only just got here.'

Ginny shrugged. 'It's just not working out. Personalities and stuff.' Maddy didn't say anything. Ginny shuffled and then picked up her luggage. 'Come on. Where's the car?'

Maddy settled Danny in the baby seat while Ginny stuffed her kit into the boot. She slammed it shut and plonked herself into the passenger seat as Maddy got in and switched on the engine. 'I hope you haven't any plans for tonight,' said Maddy. 'I've got a casserole in the oven and a couple of bottles of red that need dealing with.'

'As long as I can have a bath first, I don't care what I do.'

'Fine. I'll drop you at the mess. You can sort yourself out then come on over to my place.'

'That'll be great. Now, tell me what's been going on while I've been away.'

Maddy drove and chatted and filled Ginny in on all the wives' gossip and quizzed Ginny about what all the men had been up to. She was longing to ask Ginny about the accident and the real reason behind her request for a posting, but she decided that to broach difficult questions like that might best be done later, over a couple of glasses of passable claret. Behind them in the child seat, Danielle dozed, and under the wheels the miles passed.

It was mid-afternoon by the time they drove into the barracks. When Ginny had left, the trees had been in full leaf and the sports pitches had been bright green. Now the trees were bare and the grass looked drab. The place looked dreary and lifeless and somewhat unkempt. Ginny felt irrationally disappointed. She'd been so looking forward to coming back, but this bleak, wintry scene wasn't what she'd had in mind.

Maddy dropped her at the front door of the mess and Ginny promised she'd be round in a couple of hours as she dragged her luggage up to her room. On her way up the stairs she listened for sounds that there might be someone else in the mess, but the silence was as deep as the carpet. Her room was as she had left it but it smelled musty and damp. She dropped her bags and wandered over to open the window. A bit of fresh air would help remove the staleness. Despite Maddy's effusive welcome, despite the happy chat in the car – despite everything, Ginny felt very lonely.

She looked at her pile of belongings, she looked at her other possessions that she had been separated from for six months, and thought that it wasn't much to show for thirty-odd years on Earth. She asked herself what she had achieved. And if she disappeared off the face of the earth tomorrow, who would mourn her passing? Netta was wrapped up with her family in the Isles of Scilly. Her parents she only saw once in a blue moon. Yes, they would be sad for a while but then they would carry on and she would slowly fade out of everyone's memories. It would be as though she had never existed. And if she didn't disappear tomorrow, what had she to look forward to? Well, that was almost more depressing – a lonely old age was all she could envisage. No significant other. Ginny grimaced to herself. She didn't want that, but somehow she didn't seem to have a knack for finding the right sort of man. Most of her friends had managed it. Maddy had managed it. God, even Alice had managed it. Why couldn't she? She kicked her bag full of dirty washing out of her way and went to run a bath.

She was feeling more upbeat by the time she got round to Maddy's. Danny was already in bed, Maddy had candles lit in her sitting room, there was a delicious smell of something wafting from the kitchen and she was greeted with a glass of wine.

'This is more like it,' she said appreciatively after she had taken a sip of her drink. 'The mess is like a morgue. Not a soul around.'

'No one else back?'

'I was the only officer in this group. I think most of the rest are coming back next week with Richard and the CO.'

'Home in time for Christmas, that's something anyway,'

119

said Maddy, settling herself on the sofa and putting her feet on the coffee table.

'I suppose.'

Maddy caught the hint of sadness in Ginny's voice. 'Your parents staying in Australia for the holiday?'

Ginny nodded. 'And it's too risky to go to Netta's at this time of year. If the weather gets too bad, the choppers don't run and I could be stranded for days. Besides which, it'll take me the best part of two days to get there, and two days back, and the holiday is only a week.'

'Well, join us for Christmas.'

Ginny took another sip of wine as she considered this offer. 'I couldn't really. You don't want an outsider around on a family day.'

'But you're not an outsider. You're one of our oldest friends. And anyway, I wouldn't be able to enjoy the festivities if I thought you were languishing all alone in the mess.'

'I'll have plenty to keep me busy. I thought I'd volunteer for duty officer. There's no point in anyone else doing it.'

'You can do duty officer from here. The guardroom can just as easily ring our number as the mess one if they need you. Please.'

'Well, only if you let me help with the cooking and clearing up,' said Ginny, weakening.

'Done. Now you sit here while I dish up.' Maddy handed Ginny the remote for the television and pottered out to the kitchen to serve up supper. Ginny didn't much want to watch the TV. She'd done without it for six months and hadn't really missed it. She put the remote and her drink on the table and stood up. She wandered over to the mantlepiece to examine the photos displayed there. She couldn't help noticing one of Alice's engraved cards. It was addressed to Richard, Maddy and house guests. 'At Home. Drinks. December 25th, 12.00–1.00 P.M. Casual.' For a ghastly moment Ginny thought she'd have to go along too if she was Maddy's house guest. But then she remembered that if she was duty officer, she should visit the cooks preparing Christmas lunch for the other duty personnel. It would be the ideal excuse to get her out of the embarrassment of seeing Bob anywhere other than the office. And she didn't think she could face seeing Megan either.

'That was scrummy,' said Ginny appreciatively as she mopped up the last of her gravy with a forkful of mashed potato.

'Easy-peasy,' said Maddy. 'I just did as the recipe book told me.'

'All the same. It was the best meal I've had in six months.'

'That doesn't surprise me. You've lost an awful lot of weight. You look positively anorexic.' Maddy had been bursting with curiosity as to the reason for Ginny's sudden decision to leave the regiment. A discussion stemming from Ginny's weight-loss might be the gambit that would succeed.

'I could have done with losing some.'

'No you couldn't. You're like a rake anyway.'

'Well . . .'

Maddy gave the discussion another prod in the right direction. 'So what's bothering you? Is it Netta?'

'Netta?' Ginny was flummoxed.

'Oh, sorry. It's just that Richard said . . .'

'Richard said what?'

Maddy took a sip of wine. She felt she was just about to make a faux pas. 'He phoned me from Kosovo. He was really worried about you. He said that he thought it was something to do with the accident, but then when you asked to move on and you were ever so miserable, he thought that it had something to do with Netta.'

'Oh. Well, I did say it was for personal reasons.'

'Is it?'

'Sort of.'

Maddy looked at her, a small frown creasing her forehead. 'Ginny, I'm only asking because I'm your friend. Whatever it is, you can tell me.'

There was a silence while Ginny thought. 'I'm just miserable, that's all. I don't seem to fit in. It's my fault I suppose, but I feel I'd be better off elsewhere.' She glanced up at Maddy to see if the lie had been accepted.

Maddy hid her disbelief as best she could, but she thought it sounded like a monster whopper. 'But everyone loves you. You're the most popular person I've ever met.'

'Not really. It's all a front.'

Maddy didn't understand. 'That doesn't make sense. You

121

can't fake being popular. Either you are or you aren't. And you are.'

Ginny shrugged. 'OK, so perhaps they do quite like me. But it's only because I work so hard at it. And for what? It's all very shallow – meaningless really. I still don't really fit in. I'm not right here.' She still didn't look at Maddy.

Maddy twiddled her wine glass by its stem and willed Ginny to meet her gaze. 'So why don't you tell me the truth? And don't tell me it's something to do with the accident, as I simply won't believe you. Someone has said or done something to hurt you, haven't they? That's what's at the bottom of this.'

'No,' lied Ginny, still staring at her plate.

'Have it your way.' She topped up their glasses and then put their plates on a tray. 'Pudding? Cheese?' she offered.

'Nothing for me. I'm stuffed.'

Maddy took the laden tray out to the kitchen. When she returned she brought with her a fresh bottle of red. 'So tell me,' she said, putting it on the table by the nearly empty one, 'how did the accident happen? All I heard was that you were run off the road and ended up halfway down a mountain and were lucky to escape with your lives.'

'That sounds a bit more dramatic than it really was,' began Ginny, and she launched into a description of the events. 'And the only thing that was really damaged,' she finished, 'was the Land Rover. It was a write-off.'

'And you? Weren't you hurt?'

'Not really. I got a cut on my head that bled like a stuck pig, but then head wounds do.'

'Weren't you frightened?'

'If I'd been on my own I might have been, but Colonel Bob was there.'

Maddy grinned. 'Better him than a spotty subaltern. I mean, if you're going to be in a fix, at least you picked someone fanciable to be in a fix with.'

'What do you mean?' asked Ginny angrily.

Maddy was surprised at the sudden ferocity of her reaction but she'd had a glass of wine too many to realize she ought to back off. 'Well, you've got to admit that he's a great looking guy. I mean, if I wasn't married to Richard I would fancy him myself.'

'Well, I don't. Understand?'

Maddy took another gulp of wine. 'OK, OK. But all I'm saying is that if I'd been stuck with him all night . . .'

'Well, you weren't. I was and you can keep you smutty innuendoes out of it.' Ginny slammed her glass down on the coffee table with such force that she was lucky it didn't break. As it was, some wine slopped over on to the polished surface.

Maddy's eyes were wide with shock at Ginny's outburst and she leaned back defensively. 'Sorry, sorry. I take it all back.'

Ginny breathed deeply a few times. 'No, I'm sorry. I overreacted.'

Despite Maddy's slightly befuddled state, cogs began turning. 'Ginny, when you were stuck on this blasted mountain, did he have a go at you? Is that what has made you so upset and angry? Did he assault you?'

Ginny, calmer now, almost laughed. 'No, he didn't "have a go at me", as you put it.'

'Oh.' She sounded almost disappointed. 'I just wondered if that was why you want to get away from here so badly?'

'No.' She said the word with finality, hoping that would be an end to Maddy's interrogation.

But Maddy wasn't to be deflected that easily. 'So what really happened to upset you? Something or someone did while you were out in Kosovo, because right up to the moment you left here you were having a ball.'

'Nothing. As I said, I don't fit in and I'm fed up with being the only woman in the mess.'

Maddy snorted and nearly lost a mouthful of wine. 'You? Hating being the only woman in the mess? Christ, this one's got bells on! I wish you'd be straight with me. I'm your best friend and if you can't trust me who the hell can you?'

'Indeed,' said Ginny.

'So?'

'I . . .' She hesitated. 'No, I can't.'

Maddy felt a puff of elation. Ginny was weakening.

'Why can't you?'

'If I told you that, you'd work everything out. There are too many implications.'

Maddy might have had a bit too much to drink but she

was still in full possession of her woman's intuition. And besides which, she suddenly remembered Sarah's deduction about what might have happened while Ginny and Bob had been stranded, and she put it all together with Ginny's reaction a few seconds earlier. 'So if the colonel didn't have a go at you – was it mutual?'

Ginny sagged, defeated, her body language confirming Maddy's suspicions.

'Oh, Ginny.' She found it hard to believe how stupid Ginny had been. 'You didn't?' Ginny nodded. 'And it's ended in tears.' As if an affair with a married man who was also your boss could end any other way.

'It hardly even started.'

'What? You came on to him and he told you where to go?'

'No. It was mutual. In fact, it was me that tried to resist. Not very hard, I admit, but I did try. No, it was hearts and flowers when we were stuck on the mountain – and for a while after – but then . . . Well, something put the wind up him, and he decided that it wasn't such a good idea after all. So it was bye-bye Ginny, and close the door behind you on your way out.'

'You mean he told you to ask for a posting?'

'No, that was my idea. I got an interview in his office and he told me that he couldn't lie to Alice. There was no way we could carry on seeing each other and that whatever had happened between us was to be forgotten.'

Maddy longed to play devil's advocate and ask Ginny how on earth she thought it would have been possible for them to carry on. If the wives didn't gossip, the soldiers would. Privacy was almost non-existent and an army barracks was more close-knit than a Norfolk village.

'Do you love him?'

'I thought I did. In fact, after that first night together, I thought he felt the same way about me – he said he had since he first met me. And, do you know something, I actually believed him. I'd adored him from the beginning, but it was only after he said that that I realized I might have been *in* love with him But now . . .' Her voice trailed into silence and her eyes looked suspiciously moist.

'Oh, Ginny.' Maddy knew Ginny was foolish and misguided, but she was also aching with pain and Maddy felt for her.

Alice was getting ready for bed. She had pulled back the curtains as she always did before she got into bed and was taking a minute or two to look at the moon shining over the barracks. As she stood by the window she saw a figure walk a little unsteadily down the road towards the officers' mess. She wasn't sure, but she thought it might be Ginny Turner. She knew the first contingent of the regiment was on its way back from Kosovo, so it was quite likely. She made a little subconscious moue of disapproval. The girl had only been back five minutes and already she was drunk. Really, she ought to have more self-control.

Alice turned away and climbed into bed. She looked at the pillow next to her and wished Bob was back with her. She had been terribly lonely while he was away. She didn't have any real friends on the patch and no one called or dropped in on spec like they did with the other wives. Frequently she had stood at the drawing-room window and watched the toing and froing between the houses down the road and had felt completely isolated. She had always felt that it wasn't the CO's wife's place to be the most popular person on the patch, but she had hoped that if she ever found herself in such a position the other wives would find her approachable and would wish to include her in their get-togethers. But they hadn't. She had had to admit to herself that she wasn't wanted. With a stab of jealousy she recalled that Ginny had only recently got back and already she was in the thick of things. It was so unfair that the little trollop was so fêted. Of course, thought Alice angrily, she bought affection – all that ridiculous champagne she had provided at Sarah's house. And wheedling her way into Megan's life as a way of endearing herself to Bob. Alice made a mental note to put an end to that friendship just as soon as she could. She wasn't having a continuation of Megan's hero worship when she came home for Christmas.

Alice turned over in bed and tried to make herself comfortable, but her irritable thoughts stopped her from relaxing. Why did she allow Ginny to wind her up so? It was ridiculous. It

125

wasn't as if Ginny could possibly provide any threat to her position within the regiment. So what was it about the woman that she found so grating? Alice thought about it and decided that it was Ginny's confidence. And that's the problem, she admitted to herself. She had never had much confidence herself, and to see Ginny waltzing around the place, cocksure and self-assured, never putting a foot wrong socially, stuck in Alice's throat. Alice knew that was why she always tried so hard to do things properly – she was scared that she might make a gaffe. And more than anything she was scared that if she made such a slip the other wives might guess that her background wasn't top drawer. John Major might have decreed that Britain was a classless society, but no one had bothered to tell the army and Alice knew only too well that some of the wives were monumental snobs who would probably have a field day if they discovered what her pedigree – or lack of it – really was.

Maddy watched Danielle playing with Amelia as Taz recounted the latest problems she had discovered with living in a period house. Outside Maddy's house the rain hammered on the double-glazed windows and the wind buffeted the scrubby bushes in the back garden, but the sitting room of the bland army quarter was warm and cosy as Taz detailed her latest tussle with the planning authorities over her 'unreasonable' desire to have new windows that excluded draughts.

'Speaking as someone who would kill to live in her own home, a home of her choice, you've come to the wrong woman for sympathy,' she said with raised eyebrows as Taz finished.

'Oh, it's not so bad is it? I mean, if you have a problem, all you have to do is lift the phone and someone organizes everything for you. You don't have to decorate or worry about maintaining the heating system, and at least your house is weatherproof.'

'I know, I know, but it would be nice to experience the pitfalls of owner-occupancy, believe me.'

'And still looking on the bright side, I could never aspire to living in a great big place like Montgomery House, but you might.'

'True, although if I get my way, Richard will have left the army long before he's old enough for that.'

'And what would he do if he did?'

'Lord knows, but anything that doesn't involve endless bloody separation.'

'When is he due home?'

'Only a few more days now. He'll be back in time to help with the Christmas shopping, that's for sure.'

'You must be so looking forward to it?'

'I should co-co. I mean, it doesn't matter how strong a marriage is, it can't help if the two partners are always getting split up.'

'Distance makes the heart grow fonder,' offered Taz.

'Yeah, but out of sight, out of mind. I just feel it's all too easy for the blokes to find a bit of casual nookie when they're away for so long. And if they're clever and don't go boasting about it, who's to know? Certainly not the wife.'

'Does it happen much?'

Difficult to say. But I know for a fact that there's been at least one extramarital affair this tour.'

'Really?' Taz's curiosity was more personal than professional. 'How do you know?'

'Because the "other woman" has told me so.'

'Heavens.'

'Well, it's not really an affair. More of a several-night stand but even so . . . I reckon that once a man has strayed and got away with it, he's quite capable of straying again.'

'And would he?'

'I doubt it. He's got too much to lose.'

'It's an officer then?'

'No, I can't say. I've said too much already.' Much too much, thought Maddy. But then, what was the harm in telling someone not remotely connected with the army? Still, just to be safe she added, 'You mustn't breathe a word of what I've told you to anyone. I was told this in confidence and I promised I wouldn't repeat anything, so if this gets out I'll be right in it.'

'OK.'

Maddy changed the subject and asked Taz about her plans for Christmas.

'I'm staying at home. It's going to be Amelia and me and no hassle.'

'No relations?'

'My mother's dead and I'm not sure where my father is. He walked out on Mum when I was about twelve and I haven't seen him since.'

'I'm sorry.'

'Don't be. He was a bastard anyway and I'm quite glad Amelia doesn't have to have anything to do with him.'

'Still, it doesn't sound like terrific fun.'

'We'll be fine. Amelia will have a great time with the presents but she's far too young to know about any other sort of Christmas that she might be missing out on – you know, one with lots of people and crackers and stuff.'

'Even so, it'll be dull for you.'

'I don't know. There'll be no one to squabble over which film I want to watch, no one to criticize my cooking, no one to tell me I've eaten too much. You see, there are lots of advantages.'

'Look, tell me to take a running jump if you want to, but how about you come over to ours and have lunch with us? You and Amelia can have a lazy morning opening pressies and you can go home after to watch whatever film you like on TV, but I've got a vast turkey on order and it's too much for us and . . .' Maddy stopped and looked imploring. 'It'd be such fun. And you'd meet Ginny. She's stuck here with nowhere to go, too. Go on, do say yes.'

'I will when I can get a word in edgeways.'

'Really? Magic!'

'Yes, I'd love to. To be honest, I was really just putting a brave face on things.'

Ginny was in her room watching her portable TV when she heard a knock on her door. Eagerly she yelled for her visitor to come in. As all the living-in mess officers had disappeared to friends and relations for the holiday, and Ginny had stood down the mess staff as she was more than capable of rustling up beans on toast for herself, she hadn't seen or spoken to a single living soul for almost twenty-four hours and she felt a little stir-crazy. More than once the previous day she had considered going round to Maddy's but she was afraid that, charming though Richard was and as welcoming as they both always were, she might be surplus to requirements. After six months of separation, Ginny had no doubt that her friends had lots of catching up to do which would include quality family time, and her presence would surely cramp their style. So Ginny had retreated to her room with the TV guide and a bottle of wine and no hope of human contact till Christmas lunch at Maddy's the following day. The door opened and Megan poked her head round it.

'Hi Ginny,' she said, a trifle shyly. 'I'm so sorry I haven't been to see you before.'

'Megan!' She tried to sound pleased but inwardly she was really groaning. When the school holidays had begun and Megan had not put in an appearance, Ginny had really hoped that Megan had got fed up with hanging around a woman just about old enough to be her mother, and had found some friends of her own age. It would have simplified life more than somewhat. 'Long time no see,' she added, hoping she sounded regretful and not pleased about their lack of contact.

'Mother has had me doing so much stuff at home. And insisting that all my holiday work got done before Christmas so that it's all out of the way. I can't see what difference it makes when it gets done, as long as I do it, but you know Mum,' grumbled Megan.

Not half as well as I know your father, Ginny thought grimly. But she dismissed that and said, 'How did the *Pirates of Penzance* go?'

'Great. Well, the parents didn't throw things at us or boo, so, yeah, great I suppose.'

'Thanks for your letters.'

'Sorry they tailed off a bit at the end.'

'That's OK. You were very busy.'

'Yeah, I was a bit.'

'So was I.'

The conversation was desperate, but Ginny didn't want to encourage Megan to stay. What she really wanted was for Megan to get the hint that she wanted to be on her own. No, being on her own wasn't really what she wanted; company would be wonderful, but not Megan's company. The trouble was, Ginny didn't want to have to spell it out. The last thing she wanted to do was to be brutal to the poor kid. The situation between Ginny and her dad wasn't Megan's fault, but there now seemed every likelihood that she might end up getting hurt too.

The TV programme came to an end and a noisy theme tune blared into the room. 'I'm not interrupting anything?' said Megan hopefully, looking at the television and the glass of wine.

'Well . . .' It was obvious to anyone with half an eye that Ginny had only been loafing. 'I was sort of planning on a really early night. You know, long soak in the bath, leg wax, eyebrows, that sort of stuff.' Ginny expected her nose to shoot forwards, Pinocchio-like and poke Megan's eye out.

Megan looked crushed. 'Oh,' she said in a small voice.

And Ginny knew that her young admirer was desperately hoping that she would mention something about the shopping spree they'd planned six months previously, but Ginny had already decided to forget about it. She was banking on the fact that Megan was probably too polite to bring the subject up. Please God, she is, prayed Ginny silently.

'Right, um, well . . .'

'Have a lovely Christmas,' said Ginny. 'I'm sure you will.'

'Yeah. 'Spect so. And you too. Bye.'

And after Megan had shut the door, Ginny realized that never before in her life had she felt such a complete heel.

Despite the cold, Alice had the door to her house propped open so that her guests for drinks on Christmas morning wouldn't have to wait on the doorstep. Bob was dispensing good wishes and mulled wine in large quantities and when Richard, Danielle, Taz and Amelia arrived, the house was already packed with people.

'Come in, come in,' yelled Bob over the hubbub of noisy conversation. 'Put your coats on the stairs, Megan will take them up for you. Have a drink.'

'Colonel, this is Taz. A friend of ours,' said Richard as he took the proffered glasses and passed one to Taz. 'I'm sorry Taz,' he admitted, 'but I don't know your other name.'

130

'Forget it, Taz'll do nicely.'

The colonel and Taz shook hands. 'No Maddy?' he asked.

'She's coming along in a sec. She's just putting the potatoes on.'

'Great. Take the little ones into the dining room, there's some Disney videos for them to watch and some squash and biscuits.'

Taz and Richard did as they were bid and found that Sarah's two children, Will and Jen, had been bribed or co-opted into providing a babysitting service. The racket in the dining room was nearly as loud as the one created by the parents, but the children seemed happy enough. Danny and Amelia were a little apprehensive at first about being left, but a bowl of crisps, the promise of juice and the lure of the video proved too tempting and Taz and Richard were soon able to escape. They were making their way out of the room when they bumped into Sarah who was coming to make sure Will and Jen were coping.

'Hi, happy Christmas,' she said to Richard.

'And to you. Sarah, let me introduce Taz to you. Taz this is Sarah, Sarah this is Taz. Taz is a friend of Maddy's, she's spending the day with us.'

Sarah extended her hand. 'Taz, that's a name I haven't come across before. Is it short for something?'

'Tabitha, but I hate it. It's fine in Beatrix Potter books but not for a grown-up.'

'Tabitha – how unusual. Although it's the second time I've come across the name recently.'

'Really?'

'And now it's going to bug me all day as I can't for the life of me remember where I heard it. Still, never mind.'

Sarah continued into the dining room and Richard and Taz joined the rest of the party. A few moments later, Maddy caught up with them.

'This is a good crowd, isn't it?' she said, looking around. 'I'd have thought most people would have gone away for Christmas.'

'I think the men want to be at home with their families,' said Richard. I don't think they're interested in hurtling round the country seeing their relations.'

'Is Ginny coming along to this do when she's done her bit as duty officer?' asked Taz.

'I don't think so,' answered Maddy who knew full well that Ginny had no intention of putting in an appearance. 'I left the back door open for her so she can get out of the cold if she finishes before we get home.'

'Wasn't she invited?'

'Yes, but I think because she has to be strictly teetotal she felt she'd be a bit of a party pooper.'

Taz accepted the explanation. There was no reason not to, really. Maddy introduced her to more of Bob and Alice's guests and Taz was particularly glad when she got to meet Alice herself. Maddy was surprised to see how easily Taz was able to get Alice to chat about what it was like to be married to the boss and to live in Montgomery House, but like most people, Alice was only too happy to talk about herself. Seeing Taz was being entertained, Maddy wandered off. She was just collecting another glass of mulled wine when Sarah cornered her.

'Just the person,' said Sarah.

'Oh?'

'Your friend Tabitha—'

'Who?'

'Tabitha.'

'I don't know a Tabitha.'

'Yes you do. She's over there, talking to Alice.'

'Oh, you mean Taz!'

'Yes, but her real name is Tabitha.'

'Is it? Good Lord, I didn't know.'

Sarah sighed and started again. 'Your friend Taz, what's her surname?'

'Gracious, I don't know. Hardly surprising considering I didn't even know Taz was short for Tabitha. Why do you want to know?'

'No reason really, except that I'm sure I heard the name Tabitha somewhere else recently and it's such an unusual name I wondered if it's the same person but in another context.'

'So what was the surname of this other Tabitha?'

'That's the stupid thing, I can't remember, but I'm sure I'd know it if I heard it.'

'Why don't you ask her, see if it's one and the same?'

'I will if I get the chance.' But every time Sarah got within hailing distance of her, Taz seemed to be swept up in a new group of acquaintances. It almost seemed to Sarah that Taz was avoiding her, but it must have been coincidence.

The guests began to drift off again and Maddy and Taz caught each other's eye and signalled that they would meet by the front door. They thanked their host and hostess and Maddy thought she detected a faint chill from Alice towards Taz. As soon as they were clear of the house, Maddy asked Taz what she had done.

'I'm not sure. We were getting on like a house on fire and then I asked her if Bob had been Colonel Car Crash.'

Maddy groaned. 'God, no wonder she wasn't a happy bunny. She hated all the attention that brought. It was OK for Bob, he'd buggered off to Kosovo, but she just loathed the interest all the papers took, trying to make him out to be some sort of superhero.'

Taz, who knew exactly what the press coverage had been as she had been directly responsible for a certain amount of it, lied fluently. 'Whoops,' she said. 'I had no idea.'

'I wouldn't worry about it too much. She's pretty well over it now, but I should have warned you that it might have been better not to have mentioned it. Of course, the fact that he's just had his very own car crash out in Kosovo might have made things even more sensitive.'

'Noted for future reference.' But Taz had noted more than just the tip about ways not to upset Alice. *Another* car crash, she thought. Now that was interesting. There might be some more mileage in Colonel Bob yet. Or perhaps not. She'd have to see. She rather liked the friends she had made in the regiment – and in the village. She didn't want to have to move again because she had made herself too unpopular to stay.

They had reached Maddy's quarter by this time and they went to the back door, left unlocked for Ginny. 'Anybody home?' called Maddy as they went in.

'Hiya,' said Ginny, coming to meet them in the kitchen. 'I've only just got in myself. How was the party?'

The smell of turkey filled the air and the house was warm and inviting. Maddy bustled about, simultaneously regaling

Ginny with the details while Richard popped the cork of a champagne bottle.

'I'll be under the table soon if I have much more. I seemed to have quite a few glasses at Alice's,' said Taz.

'Does it matter? You live close enough to walk home and there's not a problem with you leaving your car here overnight.'

'Oh, go on then you sweet talking man.'

Richard filled her glass, persuaded Ginny she could have one glass of fizz and the regiment would still be able to survive, and went into the kitchen to help Maddy. Ginny and Taz were left to supervise the children in the sitting room, which was hardly arduous as there was a mountain of new toys to keep the pair of them amused.

'So, you're in the army?' said Taz as an opening gambit. She was, even for a woman, more than usually curious. It was one of the reasons she had become a journalist, as she loved to pry into other people's lives. Faced with the novelty of meeting a female soldier, her inquisitiveness reached new heights and she was quite brazen in her desire to get the low-down from Ginny on the life of women in the army.

Ginny looked down at her khaki uniform skirt and then up at Taz with raised eyebrows. 'Actually, I like to wear this colour because it suits my complexion.'

Taz looked a little sheepish. 'Sorry. Of course you are. Bloody stupid question really. But what's it like?'

'Much the same as any job, except that I don't have to think about what to wear when I get up in the morning.'

'But seriously?'

'There's a lot of paper-pushing on a routine day. Probably like most other office jobs, but then on top of that we go on exercises, emergency tours, go and fight foot-and-mouth disease, keep the peace in Ireland, go to war . . . When the phone rings you honestly never know what's going to happen next. And then you just get used to a job and a group of colleagues and you're posted off somewhere else.'

'Sounds fascinating.'

'It isn't really. Even the unusual becomes routine after a bit. I used to get a real buzz out of learning to fire guns, but now it's another piece of personal training that I have to fit into an already busy schedule.'

134

Taz was impressed. 'You fire guns?'

'Well, what do you think I would do if the enemy made a sudden advance and overran my position? Offer them tea and biscuits?'

'Sorry, it's just such an alien world.'

'That's OK. I suppose I'm just so used to it now that it seems quite normal.'

'So how many women are there in the regiment?'

'About a dozen.'

'Doing what you do?'

'Not really. I'm the only officer. The others are clerks and PT instructors and cooks and drivers.'

'What's it like being the only officer?'

'What's this,' said Ginny with a laugh, 'the Spanish Inquisition?'

'Gosh, I'm sorry, it must seem like it. It's just so interesting.'

'You need to get out more if you think my life is interesting. Mostly it's quite boring. And as for being the only female officer, well, it's OK. It can get quite lonely in the mess. No one to gossip with, no one to go shopping with, no one with a spare pair of tights when you've laddered your last pair.'

'So, did you go out to Kosovo?'

'Of course.'

Of course she had, thought Taz. Then she began to add some things up. Like the news from Maddy about the affair. She had heard it from 'the other woman', and who was Maddy's best friend amongst the officers? On top of that she knew very little about the army, but she did know that liaisons between officers and other ranks were extremely rare and utterly frowned on. If an officer had had an affair when in Kosovo, she thought that it was a racing certainty that Ginny was 'the other woman'. Interesting, she thought. In fact, she thought more than that. She wondered who the man had been. Not Richard obviously, but who? She didn't care a jot about the information professionally. For a start it wasn't the sort of thing that any newspaper would be the least bit interested in. 'So what?' would be the reaction of any editor in the land. She just wanted to know for her own satisfaction. She was a journalist and being curious was one

135

of the main things that made her tick. She wondered how she could find out.

Taz Alabaster decided she was going to throw a New Year's Eve party. Since she had moved to her new house, she had got to know a few families in the village via the mother and toddler group and these, together with her new friends in the regiment, would provide more than enough people for a good gathering. On the day after Boxing Day she began ringing round. By the end of the morning she had got to the end of her list and had received a gratifying number of affirmative replies. The cynic in her suspected that her popularity had more to do with her provision of free booze and food than a deep-seated desire to spend the festive evening with her. Still, what the heck? It would be a fun evening and she wouldn't have to worry about babysitters. One thing about being a single mother was that it had taught Taz to be extremely organized in her life. She had never had the luxury of being able to rely on others to look after her child, put food in the fridge or even to wire a plug, so the little business of planning a large party was no problem at all.

Having organized the people, Taz worked out the food and drink requirements and made a comprehensive list of shopping for her and Amelia to get on their next visit to town. With that done she worked out a list of adult party games. She wasn't sure about this last bit – she didn't know if her guests would be up for making public fools of themselves or if they would be too sophisticated for that sort of thing. Well, she would have them ready if things flagged a bit. But the last thing she wanted was for her first party in the village to be a flop. Although, the following day, as she unloaded the sixth case of wine from her car, she thought that 'flop' was not going to be the most likely adjective applied to her party.

New Year's Eve arrived and Amelia obliged Taz by demanding her afternoon rest bang on cue and allowing Taz to complete the last-minute preparations – moving furniture around, hoovering carpets, pre-cooking the rice, spreading garlic butter on the French sticks and other minor, but time-consuming tasks. Just as Amelia announced lustily, via the baby alarm, that she had finished her nap, Taz reckoned she had everything under control. She brought Amelia downstairs, played with her, fed her, played some more, pottered about in the kitchen while her daughter watched a Disney cartoon with rapt but uncomprehending attention and then, having put her biddable child to bed, she waited for her guests to arrive.

By nine o'clock she reckoned that everyone had turned up. The noise level was gratifyingly loud – Richard and Alisdair had taken it upon themselves to keep everyone's glasses topped up, the food seemed to be disappearing at a steady rate and her guests seemed to be thoroughly enjoying themselves. With everything under control, Taz was free to indulge in her favourite pastime of people watching, though on this evening she had a particular agenda – Ginny watching. She also had a digital camera hung on a loop round her wrist. Whilst she circulated and exchanged the occasional word with her visitors, she snapped shots of her guests and kept a close eye on the main subject of her curiosity. Taz couldn't help herself. She was burning with inquisitiveness to know all the prurient details about Ginny's affair. She didn't want them with a view to selling the story, she just had to know. Of course, Taz could not be sure that the other half of Ginny's liaison was present, but there was a fair chance. And in that event, Taz was absolutely certain that if Ginny's ex-lover were present, sooner or later she would give something away, let something slip. And Ginny was all the more likely to be indiscreet if she was well lubricated. Every time Ginny got anywhere near the bottom of her glass, Taz made sure that it was topped up again.

Across the room from Ginny, Bob and Alice were sur-rounded by a small circle of friends, or possibly sycophants. Taz couldn't be sure, but she took a picture of the group anyway. It would be fun to have a record of the evening, and anyway, it might have its uses one day. Taz had been in two minds whether or not to invite the CO and his wife and had sought advice from Maddy. Maddy had pointed out that the mess wasn't running a party as most of the single officers had used the opportunity of two weeks' disembarkation leave to escape to see their families and friends. Consequently, if there was a mass exodus from the patch to Taz's house it might leave Bob and Alice feeling like pariahs. Maddy had convinced Taz that, despite the fact that she really didn't know Bob and Alice at all well, it would be churlish not to include them, especially as she had enjoyed their party at Christmas. 'After all,' Maddy had concluded, 'they can always turn you down.'

When she had phoned Alice to extend the invitation, Alice had accepted for herself and Bob but declined on Megan's behalf. Megan had been offered a princely sum in return for a spot of babysitting that night and, like most teenagers, was too broke to even consider turning it down. Having ascertained various details such as time and dress, Alice then needed to know the address. Taz had been quite gratified to hear the note of approval in Alice's voice when she realized precisely which house in the village was hers. Alice's approval had been even more patent when she had arrived on the doorstep and had noted that the interior of Taz's house was equally as lovely as its pretty exterior, if not more so. Taz knew at that instant that, despite her gaffe at their Christmas drinks party, she had attained social acceptability with the highest echelon in the regiment.

Long before midnight, Ginny was well on the way to becoming comprehensively plastered. Not that she was in a minority. A number of the men had probably also had more than was good for them. Taz didn't mind. All she cared about was giving everyone a good time. Their future headaches and hangovers were no concern of hers. Alice, she noticed, was looking at the rowdy crowd with an air of disapproval. She remembered what Maddy had told her about Alice being teetotal. In Taz's experience people were teetotal for one of two reasons: either they were ex-alcoholics or they were control freaks. There was nothing about Alice that would remotely suggest that she had once been a lush, but as Taz observed her she began to think that the control freak option seemed really very likely. There was something very guarded about Alice, almost as though she was scared of something. Again Taz's curiosity was awakened. What on earth could Alice be so worried about? Surely, of all the women in the regiment, her position had to be the most unassailable. Taz decided that she could only work on one thing at once and shelved her ponderings about Alice.

* * *

Ginny was watching Bob. Around her the party ebbed and flowed, but she was isolated by her thoughts and oblivious to the noise and activity that surrounded her. People were laughing and joking, chatting and bantering and Ginny was on a solitary island made up of dark thoughts. When she saw Bob and Alice arrive she had almost fled the party. She didn't think she could cope with being in a social environment with him, with the danger that they might be forced into any sort of proximity. She had been just about able to cope in Kosovo before she had flown back, and she was dreading it when work resumed after the holidays were over, but she hadn't been prepared for meeting him again this evening. Ginny had been just about to turn on her heel and leave when Maddy had caught her arm and whispered that it would cause comment. Ginny had felt a sudden shiver of fear – was she so obvious? Had anyone else noticed? Maddy had assured her that she had only noticed because she knew how Ginny would be feeling. She took Ginny to one side and told her to brace up, hold her head high, keep on the other side of the room, pretend she didn't care, and think 'up yours, Bob'. So Ginny took Maddy's advice and decided she would front it out. But fronting it out took courage and Ginny found that the easiest source of courage came out of a bottle. Luckily there seemed to be an endless supply.

There was still some time to go before midnight and Ginny knew she had had too much to drink. She was aware of feeling faintly tipsy but who cared? It was New Year's Eve after all, and if a girl couldn't let her hair down then, when could she? Besides, she had no one to give a damn about what sort of state she got into. If she made a complete fool of herself she was only going to embarrass herself, no one else. The depressing thought made her remember her feelings towards Bob, so there she was, glowering malevolently at him across the room, and even more malevolently at Alice. What had that dried-up, charmless, humourless, cow got that she hadn't? What hold had Alice got over Bob that he would choose to spend his days with *her* and not Ginny? Why was she excluded from long-term relationships? Why couldn't she find love and happiness? She was dreading midnight. Everyone else would be hugging and kissing and making promises and having hopes for the new year, and what had she to look forward to? Fuck all, that's what.

Ginny was so wrapped up in her own dark misery that she was unaware of Maddy approaching until Maddy grabbed her arm and steered her out of Taz's drawing room and into the kitchen, which was mercifully empty apart from a couple of men from the village whom Maddy didn't recognize. They were deep in a conversation about some local issue and barely glanced at the two women as Maddy propelled Ginny through the kitchen and into the scullery at the back.

'What do you think you're doing?' she hissed at Ginny. 'You couldn't make how you feel about Bob much more obvious if you had a neon sign flashing on your forehead.'

This was the last straw for Ginny. She was already feeling utterly down and dejected, and to have her best friend bawling her out on top was too much. She dissolved into sobs. Huge, body-wracking gulps of sheer misery. 'I – I – I – I'm s-s-sorry,' she wept. 'I-i-i-it's just I – I – I – I'm s-s-so m-m-miserable.' Maddy took her in her arms and hugged her, but this show of kindness only made Ginny feel worse. Not only was the party ruined for her but now she was spoiling it for Maddy. I – I – I – I'm s-s-s-sorry,' she repeated through her gasping sobs. 'I – I – I – I'm j-j-j-just b-b-being s-s-silly.'

It was at this moment that Taz, wondering why the light was on in the scullery, came out to investigate and found them. 'God, I'm sorry,' she said, a little stunned at the scene. She wasn't used to finding casual acquaintances having a traumatic time in her utility room. 'Can I do anything to help?'

This further display of kindness brought on a fresh wave of unhappiness in Ginny. Maddy shook her head and Taz retreated tactfully. It was several minutes before Ginny's emotional storm began to abate. Slowly she brought herself under control and her sobs were reduced to an occasional stuttering intake of breath.

'You really are down in the dumps if that was all brought on by Bob,' said Maddy.

'No,' said Ginny. 'It's not just him. New Year isn't a good time to be single and alone. It just all got too much.'

'But Bob being here hasn't helped matters.'

'Well, no. Not really.'

It took a while, but Maddy persuaded Ginny to rejoin the party and made sure that the slight smudge under Ginny's eyes, where her mascara had run a little, was repaired.

'You look fine,' Maddy assured her. 'Honestly. I'll tell you, if I'd cried my eyes out like that my face would be all red and puffy and my eyeballs would be so bloodshot that my friends would worry that if opened them too wide I'd bleed to death.' Ginny smiled wanly at Maddy's attempt at humour. 'That's a girl,' said Maddy. 'Now head up and think "fuck 'em".' She pushed her out of the scullery and into the kitchen and towards the noise of the party.

They had barely gone two steps when the kitchen door was pushed open and Taz led Bob in.

'I'm so sorry about that,' their hostess was saying as she led Bob across to the sink and picked up a cloth. 'Someone caught my elbow just as I was pouring and – well, you got the benefit. I hope it won't stain.' From the angle the two were standing at they did not immediately see Maddy and Ginny who were stopped in their tracks, unsure whether to proceed or retreat. Taz began to mop some spilt red wine off Bob's jacket. As she did so, he looked up and saw the two women standing staring at him. He also saw the fleeting look of longing flit like a shadow over Ginny's face. His smile slowly faded.

'Good evening,' he said to them. His voice was cold and unfriendly. He hadn't wanted this encounter. Taz glanced up from her ministrations and took in the look that passed between Bob and Ginny. She didn't know what its significance was but significant it certainly was.

'Something wrong?' she asked brightly, pretending to ignore the sudden tension she felt in Bob through the sleeve of his jacket and the change in atmosphere.

'Nothing,' said Ginny, squaring her shoulders. She walked out of the kitchen followed by Maddy.

Outside the kitchen Ginny leant against a door jamb. 'Fuck,' she said, exhaling slowly. Maddy raised her eyebrows.

'Not the most welcome of meetings.'

'Do you think Taz guessed anything?'

'No. I mean, why should she even suspect anything in the first place? And if she did notice a slight animosity between you, well, he's your boss and it's not unknown for superiors and subordinates to fall out.'

'Yeah. I'm just oversensitive at the moment. Sorry. Come on, let's party.'

And Ginny, over her tears and determined to put her unhappiness behind her, plunged into the noisy crowd.

In the kitchen, Taz, having finished with Bob, was putting another batch of sausage rolls in the oven. Not only had she seen the look between Bob and Ginny but she had also felt Bob stiffen with tension. Something was going on between Bob and Ginny, and Taz was sure she knew what it was. Having only been interested in Ginny's unfortunate liaison from a personal point of view, things had suddenly taken an unexpected turn. The news that Colonel Car Crash had not only been involved in another smash, but had also bonked a junior officer might have any amount of mileage in it. She'd have to find out a great deal more. She thought perhaps, as Ginny was going to be on her own in the mess for the remainder of the holiday, she might appreciate a bit of home cooking. She considered inviting Ginny to supper but then dismissed the idea. She didn't know Ginny well enough for the implied intimacy that was involved in a supper invitation. No, it should be lunch. Lunch with lots of booze should do the trick.

New Year's Day brought a quiet morning at Montgomery House. Megan was still in bed, not having got home from her babysitting job until the small hours of the morning. In the kitchen, Alice was rereading the previous day's New Year's honours list, checking that she hadn't missed some old friend or acquaintance to whom she should send a congratulatory note. Bob was nursing a cup of sweet tea and a hangover with equal care.

Alice lowered her paper and studied him. 'Headache, Bob?' she asked without a trace of sympathy in her voice.

'Not really, my dear,' he replied, hoping she hadn't noticed the wince as the sound of his words crashed and reverberated through his throbbing temples.

'You deserve one.' She folded the paper and put it on the kitchen table.

'Do I, darling?'

'You know very well that you were quite . . .' Alice paused. She wanted to say drunk. That's what he'd been, for heaven's sake, but it was an ugly word with ugly implications. 'You were quite merry.'

'Only a bit,' said Bob weakly, wishing she would shut up and go away. He had gone beyond being afraid he was going to die and was now afraid he wasn't. It would be a happy release under the circumstances.

'Well I would say you showed a remarkable lack of self-control. I don't know what people like Richard and Alisdair thought of your behaviour.'

'They wouldn't care. They were pretty well oiled themselves.'

Alice sniffed. 'I think you ought to put a stop to your officers drinking to excess.'

Bob sighed. 'Why, for heaven's sake? We work hard, we play hard. What on earth is your problem with that?'

'You should set an example.'

Bob wasn't feeling at all well, and this lecture from Alice was beginning to grind down his seriously reduced supply of patience. All he wanted was to be left in peace. He knew he'd overdone things the night before, he was painfully aware of it and he didn't need her nagging on and on about it.

'I was off duty, we were all off duty, it was a splendid party, we all enjoyed it. Whether or not I had too much to drink is irrelevant,' he said quietly. 'My officers know that I am a good CO and they know that I only demand of them the same standards I set for myself.'

'Huh,' sniffed Alice. 'Some standards if last night was anything to go by. Take Ginny Turner—'

'I don't think Ginny Turner has any place in this discussion.'

'Oh no? I think she has. She was disgustingly drunk. She was reeling.'

Alice had gone too far. What had happened between him and Ginny was still a raw and tender memory. He'd seen her reaction when he'd arrived at the party and he had a fair idea why she and Maddy had disappeared. He'd pretended not to watch her but he'd been conscious of every move and gesture she'd made, and of her long black stares that seemed

143

to swing between malevolence and longing. It had unsettled him because he knew he was the cause, and the guilt he felt at his adultery was now compounded with guilt over what he had done to Ginny. She had enough to contend with without Alice having a go at her too. He lashed out.

'So what if she was drunk? At least she's got more life in her than some I could mention. At least she's natural. At least she's not shit-scared she'll let something slip if she gets pissed. At least she can let her hair down, which is more than can be said for you. You never enjoy yourself because you're frightened you might forget your elocution lessons and revert to your roots. But that doesn't mean the rest of us have the same hang-ups. And the sad thing is, no one would give a stuff if they found out your father was only a staff sergeant. It doesn't matter. You're the only one with a hang-up about rank. No one else gives a flying fuck.'

'Lose a house point for bad language, Dad,' said Megan, yawning and sleep-dishevelled from the doorway. 'And he's right, you know,' she said laconically to her mother.

Alice had gone completely pale, an expression of horrified disbelief etched on to her face. She had never been spoken to like that before and Bob had done it in front of their daughter. How could he? And not only that but Megan had supported him. She felt betrayed by them both. They had ganged up against her. They knew how vulnerable she felt about her background, that she hated anyone referring to it, that it was taboo. She felt humiliated but more than that she felt angry. How dare they? How dare they mention that her father had never been commissioned?

Suddenly she felt she couldn't bear the sight of either of them. She had to get away from them both but Megan was in the doorway and Alice was afraid that if she went close to her daughter she might strike her. There was only one route of escape and, banging her chair backwards, she headed for the back door.

'Damn you both!' she snarled at her family with such uncharacteristic force that she succeeded in shocking them both as, dragging her cardigan around her, she stormed out into the grey, damp morning.

Alice had no plan of where she was going, she just knew she couldn't stay in the house. She was close to tears and shaking with suppressed rage. She stamped down the path and on to the pavement. She nearly bowled someone over in the process.

'Hey!'

Alice looked up. It was Sarah. 'Sorry,' she mumbled. Part of her was terrified she was going to burst into tears and have to explain, but part of her wanted hugs and sympathy.

'Is something wrong?'

'Nothing.'

Alice was aware that Sarah was studying her. She was nobody's fool; Alice knew that. No coat, no make-up. She would guess that Alice wasn't out for a constitutional or planning on going visiting. Sarah would surely realize that she had left the house in a hurry and might even realize that she had rushed out because she was upset. But Alice was so numb with the shock of Bob's dreadful outburst that she wasn't sure if she cared if Sarah knew or not.

'I don't know about you, but I'm gagging for a cup of tea. Would you like one?' she heard Sarah ask.

Although Alice had lived on the patch for the best part of nine months, this was the first time anyone had invited her for tea or coffee on a whim. Feeling raw from her recent set-to with her family, and suddenly grateful for this unexpected gesture of friendship, Alice accepted. Besides which she was suddenly aware that it was too chilly, and she was too inappropriately dressed, to stay out of doors for long, and she couldn't return home until she'd calmed down thoroughly.

Sarah looked at the taut expression on Alice's face and realized that things were far from well with her neighbour. She made a stab at conversation, as a silence would be too awkward. 'I was just out posting the kids' thank you letters. I needed to blow the cobwebs away after last night,' said Sarah.

'Oh.'

Sarah glanced at her neighbour again. Her voice was toneless and flat and she didn't sound a bit like her normal self, but Sarah was too tactful to mention anything. She knew that unlike herself, Alice couldn't be suffering from a hangover, but something was definitely wrong.

They turned into Sarah's garden. 'Here we are,' she said brightly, putting the key in the lock. She led the way indoors. 'Sorry about this,' she said. The curtains downstairs were still drawn and Sarah whizzed through the sitting room and the dining room pulling them back and letting in the daylight. 'You must think me a dreadful slut.' But judging by Alice's expressionless face, she wasn't thinking anything, let alone that. 'Right,' she breezed on and led the way into the kitchen. 'Tea or coffee?'

'Oh, um, coffee please.' Alice sat down on a kitchen chair and stared blankly out of the window at the dreary day.

'I'm afraid it's instant,' she admitted hesitantly. She knew for a fact Alice hated instant.

'Oh, fine.' Sarah thought that definitely showed something was wrong. Alice, when offered instant, would normally make some excuse and ask for tea instead. She filled the kettle under the tap, plugged it in and went to the fridge to get the milk.

'I've forgotten, do you take sugar?'

'No.'

Sarah began to wonder if Alice was going to get beyond monosyllabic words. She would never have called Alice chatty – in fact Sarah had once heard Alice comment that she abhorred gossip in any shape or form – but she was always assiduously polite, very conscious of social niceties, and that included proper replies to questions. Sarah made banal small talk while she waited for the kettle to boil and put her curiosity on hold.

'There you go,' she said, putting two steaming mugs on the table. 'Last night was good fun, wasn't it?'

'It was kind of Taz to invite so many people,' Alice replied, not looking anywhere in particular but certainly not at Sarah.

'Bob enjoyed himself, didn't he?'

Alice looked at her and Sarah saw her bite her lip, her eyes dull with misery. Suddenly Sarah knew what had happened. Alice's views on alcohol were no secret and Bob's overindulgence the night before had been the cause of some ghastly row. That was why she had rushed out of the house like that. Sarah reached her hand across the kitchen table and rested it on Alice's.

'Do you want to talk about it?' she asked gently.

146

'No . . . I . . .' Alice shook her head.

'You and Bob had a row?'

Alice nodded.

'It's not the end of the world. Alisdair and I have had our moments too, and look at us. We haven't ended up in the divorce courts.' Though she didn't add that it had come a bit too close for comfort on at least two occasions.

'It's not that.'

'Then what is it?' Sarah was no longer asking out of nosiness, but from genuine concern. Alice was obviously distraught. Something had been said which had gone beyond the normal hurtful words of a marital bust-up.

Alice shook her head again and the tears hovering on the edge spilled over and ran down her face. Sarah got up and put her arm round her.

'Alice,' she said. 'You can't bottle everything up inside you. You need to let it out, otherwise it'll poison you. It's like lancing a boil.' Sarah didn't know if Alice had taken in what she'd said or not because she continued to cry silently. Sarah stood beside her, patted her shoulder and stroked her hand and hoped that her family would keep to their normal holiday routine of not emerging until nearly lunchtime. Eventually Alice began to quieten down. Sarah went across the kitchen and returned with a roll of kitchen towel.

'Here,' she said, proffering it. 'Have a jolly good blow and dry your eyes.'

'Thanks,' mumbled Alice and did as she was told.

'Now, drink your coffee before it gets cold.'

Alice dutifully obeyed.

'So, you had a go at Bob for having one over the eight last night?' Alice nodded over the brim of her mug. 'Well, he wasn't the only one. I think everyone was a bit merry.'

'Yes, but he should have set an example,' said Alice and blew her nose again. 'That's all I said.'

'Well, it doesn't sound too bad as rows go. You ought to hear what Alisdair and I have been known to say to each other.'

'Yes, but that's the point. It didn't end there.' Sarah waited for Alice to go on. She didn't want to pry. If Alice wanted to tell her, she would. 'He said some dreadful things to me and Megan heard.'

'Oh.' That was different. It was one thing to have a row; it was another matter entirely to have it in front of the kids. 'But what could he find about you to cause him to say dreadful things? You never do anything wrong.'

'Well, apparently, compared to the sainted Ginny, I do.' Alice's voice was sour with bitterness.

'Ah, Ginny.' There was a pause as Sarah digested this. Ginny seemed to crop up a deal too often in connection with Bob. Part of Sarah wondered if she only noticed because Ginny was a woman. She didn't suppose she would read anything into it if, say, Richard's name kept getting linked with Bob's. There was no way it would cross her mind for an instant that Richard and Bob would be having a 'liaison'. Although, and Sarah had to suppress a smile at the thought, it wasn't beyond the bounds of possibility in this day and age, however unlikely a scenario it was.

'Apparently, compared to Ginny I'm riddled with hang-ups and I don't know how to enjoy myself.'

Bob had a point there, thought Sarah, although she said, 'Oh, I don't know about that.'

Alice looked dangerously close to tears again. She blew her nose and sipped her coffee and then said, 'But he's right. I don't.'

It was such a bald, true statement that Sarah wasn't sure how to respond. 'Well . . .' she started, and then stopped. She couldn't refute it. They both knew that. 'Well, we all enjoy ourselves in different ways.'

'No, you don't. I see you and the other wives on the patch. You laugh and joke together and go to each other's houses and go on shopping trips together. But not me. No one wants me to tag along. I don't find the jokes funny and I always seem to put a damper on things. Besides, you all know I'm too busy making sure everything is perfect at Montgomery House.' There was more than a touch of self-pity in Alice's voice. Her exclusion obviously hurt more than she had let on in the past.

'But Montgomery House is a showpiece. Your house is always exquisite and you cook beautifully and . . .'

'And I don't have fun.'

'Perhaps "fun" isn't your cup of tea.'

'Perhaps if I told you why, you'd understand.'

'Try me.'

'My father was in the army.'

'I didn't know that.' Ah, thought Sarah, Alice was scarred by a dodgy boarding school with puritan values. That would explain a lot. But as she listened she discovered she was wrong.

'I haven't gone around bragging about it. He was a staff sergeant, and I spent my life watching the kids from the officers' patch and longing to be like them – to go to boarding school not the local secondary mod, to drive around in an estate car, to talk with a posh accent, to have a Labrador for a pet and learn to ride for a hobby.'

Sarah didn't know what to say. She had no idea. A staff sergeant! Good God. Everything about Alice seemed so right, so authentic. If she had heard that Alice's father had been in the army she would have assumed he had been a general at the very least, but a staff sergeant. 'So how come . . . ?'

'You mean how come I made it?'

'No. Yes, I suppose so.' Sarah wasn't quite sure what she wanted to know, but the option offered by Alice seemed as good as any.

'As I got older I worked out that there were ways of joining the officer classes. You didn't have to be born or bred for it. I discovered I could go into the army myself as an officer or I could train to be a nurse or I could become a teacher. Whichever I chose I'd end up living in the officers' mess. I'd always liked kids and I knew I'd make a good primary school teacher so I went down that path. Once I got out to Germany I made friends with the female officers and copied them – the way they dressed, their hobbies, what they read, how they behaved. I read books on etiquette, I made sure I always said and did the right things, I had private elocution lessons to lose my accent, I bought a cashmere sweater and a string of pearls. And then I asked for a transfer to another school in Germany, in a different garrison miles away where no one knew me and I could start again – only this time everyone thought that I came from a pukka background. I fitted in right away, never put a foot wrong but that was because I have always been careful to watch my step. I decided that I couldn't do that and drink, so I stopped drinking.'

149

'So that explains it.'

'And no one guessed it was all a facade.'

'Even Bob?'

'Even Bob. We dated, we fell in love and I always managed to find excuses why we couldn't go back to England to meet my parents, so we didn't. Then we got engaged and I said I wanted a regimental wedding, so it was arranged out in Germany and I lied at the last minute and said my father was too ill to come and my mother was staying in England to look after him. Of course, the truth was I never told them. I think Bob was smelling a rat by this time, but whether he was too much in love to care, or too much of a gentleman to make the accusation, I don't know.'

'You don't know? Haven't you discussed it since?' Sarah was aghast. Besides which, surely Bob must now know about Alice's father.

'Not discussed it, no. What was there to discuss? He had the perfect army wife who would do everything just so, and no one else knew, so Bob just accepted it.'

'But your dad?'

'Of course I had to tell Bob. I did it after the honeymoon. Bob's always said he doesn't care. And do you know, I don't think he does. He's always been great with my dad. They talk like old friends. If he comes to visit they go off down the pub together. Dad won't go into the officers' mess. Bob says it doesn't matter but Dad won't all the same. Says it's wrong, that he's not entitled and that's that. In his way he's just as much of a snob as me.'

'I never realized your background was anything but the best.'

Alice managed to raise a wan smile. 'I suppose that's one of the best compliments I've ever had. Because I've always felt as though I was playing a part, I couldn't ever let my guard down.'

'So no fun.'

'I thought it best not. I thought fun might be as dangerous as drink.'

'And Bob raked this up again this morning?'

'Not as such. It was mentioned in the course of the row. He told me that no one would give a monkey about Dad. Actually his words were "no one would give a flying fuck".'

150

Sarah had to keep her teeth clenched to stop her mouth dropping open. She'd never heard Alice swear before, and certainly not like that.

Alice continued. 'So is he right? Now you know the truth, what do you think?'

Sarah drew in a slow breath to give herself time to think. 'Well . . .'

'You *do* think he's right.'

'I'm not sure. I mean, I don't think any the less of you because of what you've told me. In fact I probably think more of you. I can't think of many people who would have been that single-minded to go for an ambition like that. It's real Eliza Dolittle stuff. And it's even more admirable that you got away with it.'

'But?'

'But if people find out, there will be talk. There's bound to be. You know what a regiment is like for gossip, it's worse than the village post office, and this would be the best story they'll have heard in ages. But it'll blow over in a few days. Five minute wonder,' Sarah added hurriedly, seeing the look of utter horror on Alice's face.

'You're not going to tell anyone are you?'

'Of course not.'

Alice gave a sigh of relief. 'Thank God for that.'

'But if you want to loosen up a bit then you've got to stop worrying about anyone finding out. It isn't as if anyone's going to pry into your background. After all this time everyone just accepts you for what you are. I think, now I've had time to think about it, Bob is probably right. I don't think anyone will care—'

'Or give a flying fuck,' said Alice, dryly.

'I couldn't have put it better myself.' Sarah saw a trace of a smile appear around Alice's mouth. 'How about another coffee?' she offered.

'I don't wish to be rude, but could I have tea this time rather than coffee?' Sarah turned away to hide her smile. Alice must be feeling better.

Ginny tottered out of her bed and over to the washbasin in the corner of her room. When she reached it she hung on to the sides while she slowly raised her head to look at the reflection in the mirror above it. Her skin had a greasy, unhealthy sheen, her hair was lank and matted and her eyes were bloodshot.

'Ugh,' she shuddered. She felt slightly nauseous but she didn't think she was actually going to be sick. That was something to be thankful for, she supposed. But all the same her mouth tasted disgusting. She vaguely remembered a line from a book about some small animal of the night dying and making someone's mouth its mausoleum. Frankly, the way her mouth tasted it had gone beyond that. She wouldn't have minded if the animal had just laid down and breathed its last, but this one seemed to have shat itself to death. She lowered her gaze again and concentrated on the co-ordination required to put toothpaste on to her toothbrush. She noticed that her hand was shaking slightly as she tried to get the white goo on to the bristles and gave up the task. She squirted a gob of paste directly into her mouth and then moved it around in a desultory fashion with her brush until she had eradicated the worst of the repellent reminder of the previous night's excesses. She rinsed and spat some but it made her head feel worse, so she filled a glass with water, grabbed a bottle of aspirin and took herself back to bed. As she crossed the floor she wondered why her carpet looked as if someone had been indulging in a spot of light pruning and leaf sweeping while she'd been asleep, but in her delicate state of health it was far too hard a question to address. Tucked under her duvet again she took a couple of pills, washed them down with water and tried to remember the night before. It was all pretty clear up to the point where she had run into Colonel Bob in the kitchen. After that . . . No, a blank. She racked her brains. She must be able to remember something, surely. Scarily blank. What had she done? Oh God, please don't let it be something embarrassing. Still a blank. She was going to have to ring Maddy to check what did happen. Always assuming Maddy could remember. She'd been pretty far gone too.

Mercifully, the mess was deathly quiet. Usually in the morning of any given day at any time of the year, the air throbbed with the sound of half a dozen different stereo systems competing for supremacy. So there were some advantages to being the only person left in the building, thought Ginny weakly. She contemplated putting her own radio on but even that seemed too much effort. Then, as she lay there, sleep overtook her and gave her some respite from her churning stomach and pounding temples.

She became dimly aware of a voice invading her dream.

'Come on you slug,' a sergeant major was yelling at her. Ginny tried and tried to climb the six-foot wall but the silvery slug-slime that covered it meant she couldn't get a grip.

'Come on you slug.' She was being shouted at louder but it was no good. 'Oi, Ginny, wake up.'

Ginny opened her eyes and blinked against the sudden brightness. 'Maddy?' Where had the sergeant major gone? For a second she was completely confused. Then consciousness became complete. 'Maddy. You woke me up.'

'Oh, well done Einstein. It was like raising the dead. I'm not surprised though.'

'Ah.' Ginny winced as she tried to sit up. It hurt. She made a mental note to make no sudden movements. Her head wasn't up to anything other than complete immobility.

'You may very well say "ah".'

'Ah,' said Ginny again, wishing Maddy would moderate her voice a little.

'And how are we feeling today?'

'*I* am feeling bloody awful if you must know, but I suspect *you* are feeling disgustingly OK.'

'I wouldn't go as far as that,' said Maddy, sitting down on the end of Ginny's bed. 'But I bet I'm feeling better than you.'

'That wouldn't be hard,' muttered Ginny with feeling.

'So I'm here to get you dressed, march you round to Taz's to apologize and then take you back to mine for lunch, TLC and a hair of the dog.'

At the word apologize Ginny's eyes widened in horror. 'Apologize?' she repeated. 'Oh God.' She stared at Maddy and then shut her eyes again as if that would make everything better. 'What did I do?'

'Well, after nearly flooding her scullery with tears—'

'I remember that bit.'

'Well, after the tears you livened up . . .'

'Go on.' Her brain cells began to connect.

153

'And you suggested everyone should dance.'

'Yes.' Ginny nodded her head weakly as a vague memory stirred.

'Which seemed a good idea at the time.'

'Yes.' It had seemed like a good idea. She remembered that bit now.

'So you chose one of Taz's compilation CDs.'

'Yes.' Had she?

'Do you remember which one?'

'No.' Not a clue.

'Does "Best Film Themes of the Nineties" ring any bells?'

'It should, shouldn't it?' She opened her eyes as if a glimpse of Maddy's face would give her inspiration.

'The theme to *The Full Monty*?'

'Oh my God, I didn't. Tell me I didn't. Please. Oh shit.' Ginny closed her eyes again and swayed back on to her pillow.

'No, actually you didn't.' Maddy was killing herself laughing. Ginny's eyes snapped open and they had a dangerous glint in them. 'But it was close,' added Maddy hastily. 'It was only because Richard and I got to you before you got your clothes off that you didn't.'

'And that was all I did?'

'Well . . .'

Ginny sighed and looked exasperated. 'Look, Maddy. I feel absolutely shite. I haven't the strength for games. Please tell me the worst, put me out of my misery and then I can get up and eat humble pie for a week.'

'You didn't want to leave but Richard and I thought it best. So you gave us a bit of trouble when we got you out of the house.'

'What sort of trouble?'

'You clung to some of the shrubs in Taz's garden.'

'That explains the leaves.'

'What?' It was Maddy's turn to be confused.

'Look,' Ginny gestured at the carpet by the basin. 'I couldn't think where all those leaves had come from.'

'From Taz's prize shrubs, that's where. It'll be a wonder if some of them recover.'

'Sounds like a big apology. So how many witnesses were there to this carry on?'

154

'Not many. I mean as far as *The Full Monty* was concerned I don't think many people realized how close you got to stripping. I don't think they were paying much attention, and as for the fracas in the bushes – it was just me, Richard, Taz and a couple of people from the village.'

'Not Bob?'

'No.'

Ginny sighed thankfully.

'Why should you care if Bob witnessed it?'

'I don't really.'

Maddy peered at her. 'You don't still hold out hope that you and he . . .'

'No,' said Ginny sharply. 'No I don't. And don't suggest for a minute I do.' But even to her own ears she sounded remarkably unconvincing.

Maddy gave her a long hard look. 'Whatever you say. I'll wait for you in the ante-room. See you in a few minutes.'

Ginny rubbed her face as Maddy closed the door behind her and braced herself to get out of bed. She looked at her watch. Nearly midday. Perhaps some lunch at Maddy's would make her feel better. That was something to look forward to, but she didn't fancy her first task of the new year, which was to make amends with Taz.

Ginny wasn't too sure what the garden had looked like before her ministrations but Maddy assured her that it had looked a great deal better than it did after.

'Honestly, it was so neat and clipped and tidy and now her hedges look as though they've had someone dragged through them backwards.'

'Ha bloody ha,' said Ginny, entirely without humour as she rang the doorbell.

Taz answered. She was still in her dressing gown.

'Oh God. I'm sorry. I didn't mean to get you out of bed,' blurted Ginny.

'You didn't. Since when has a single mother ever had a lie-in till gone midday? Come in, come in.'

'No. We won't stop. Honestly.'

'Why? I've got a big pot of coffee made, the house is almost straight and you're not interrupting anything. I can't see what the problem is. Unless you don't like my company?'

'No,' said Ginny and Maddy in unison. 'No, it's not that,' continued Ginny. 'It's just I only came round to apologize, not to take up any of your day.'

'Don't be silly. Come in.'

'OK then,' said Maddy. 'But we won't stop for long. Just a quick cuppa.'

They stepped over the threshold into a house that was clean, swept and didn't smell of cigarette smoke or alcohol or give any indication that a big, boozy party had been held in it the night before.

'But this is amazing,' exclaimed Ginny, impressed.

'How have you done it?' asked Maddy.

'A team of leprechauns came in while I was sleeping,' said Taz. 'No, Amelia had me up at five, so once I had got her sorted there wasn't much point in going back to bed so I cracked on. To be honest it was only a question of filling and emptying the dishwasher a few times and pushing a hoover around.

'Oh yeah,' said Maddy. 'Go on, admit it. You've been working like a navvy.'

'No.' Taz laughed. 'Come on, coffee.'

They followed her into the kitchen where the only evidence of the previous night's party were several cardboard boxes filled to the brim with empty bottles and a couple of black plastic sacks bulging with rubbish.

By the big pine kitchen table Amelia sat patiently in her high chair happily playing with some pasta shapes.

'Sorry about the mess,' said Taz as she reached into a cupboard for some mugs. 'I'm going to take it all out to the garage when I'm dressed, then that'll be the house done.'

Ginny and Maddy exchanged looks. She called a couple of boxes of bottles and some full bin bags a mess? This woman was in a different league to most members of their sex. Most of the women they knew would still be in bed after such a monumental party, not having got to bed until the last guest left, and tidying up would certainly wait until the next day or possibly the day after.

Before she poured the coffee Taz gave Amelia a biscuit and a beaker of juice then turned her attention to her guests.

'How do you do it?' said Maddy in admiration. 'You throw a party for the whole area, you've cleared up before

156

lunch, your daughter is a paragon and I feel totally inadequate.'

'I'm lucky with Amelia, I grant you. She's just a naturally placid child. Give her a few bits to play with and she's happy for ages. In a minute I'll give her some lunch and while she's having her afternoon nap I promise you I'm going to crash out too.'

'Well, that's something. I was afraid I was in the company of a robot. How much sleep did you have last night?'

'A couple of hours.'

'Is that all?' shrieked Ginny, and immediately regretted her outburst as her head exploded with a bolt of pain behind her eyes. Taz caught the wince of pain that flickered across her brow. She dished out coffee. Gratefully Ginny took a slurp, then she squared her shoulders a little and looked at Taz across the table. 'Taz, I gather from what Maddy says that I was far from the perfect guest last night.'

'Not at all,' said Taz. 'You were fantastic fun.'

'Yeah right. Sobbing in your kitchen, trying to strip and then trashing your garden.'

'I'm the only one apart from Maddy who knows about your tears, so you hardly made an exhibition of yourself. All very discreetly handled. As for the strip – you didn't. So what's to apologize for there? And my garden? Plants grow. By spring it'll all be as it was before without me even having to raise a finger.'

'But none of it should have happened – or got close to happening. So I do apologize. OK?'

Taz looked at her visitor and smiled. 'OK. I'll accept your apology on one condition.'

'What's that?' Ginny had a momentary worry that Taz might expect her to repay her by doing some gardening or something. And she didn't know one end of a pair of secateurs from the other.

'Come and have lunch with me.'

'What?' Ginny was a little taken aback. Surely if anyone was issuing lunch invites it should be her. Then she realized how bad mannered her response had been. 'Sorry, but I wasn't expecting that. It should be me giving you lunch.'

'But where is there to eat round here? And don't tell me

157

the officers' mess, because I know it's pretty well shut till the regiment comes back off leave.'

'Well, there's always the village pub.'

'Have you eaten there?'

Ginny had to admit she hadn't; drunk there certainly, but not eaten.

'Well don't, that's my advice.' Taz looked at Ginny expectantly. 'So you'll come?'

'Yes, thanks. It's really kind of you.' And she made a mental note to bring something really nice for both her and Amelia to show how much she appreciated Taz's kindness.

Taz suddenly yawned hugely. She looked at her visitors, horror-struck. 'I am *so* sorry. How rude!'

'No, we've stayed too long,' said Maddy, draining her coffee and standing up. 'It's us who are rude. Come on Ginny, time to go.' And before Taz had time to protest or to stop them Maddy had shepherded Ginny out of the kitchen and through the front door.

They were at the end of the path when the door opened again and Taz yelled to Ginny, 'Saturday at twelve. It's just us so come as scruffy as you like.'

'Thanks,' called Ginny back. 'I'll look forward to it.'

The phone in the officers' mess was ringing off the hook when Ginny finally got back from Richard and Maddy's that evening. She thought quite hard about answering it because she didn't think it was very likely to be for her. Most people she knew phoned her on her mobile and she couldn't be bothered to hunt around for a pencil and paper to take a message for one of her absent colleagues. But then a sense of duty took over. She was glad it did.

'Ginny. It's Netta. Where on earth have you been?'

'Out, why?'

'I couldn't get hold of you.'

Even at a distance of several hundred miles Ginny could hear the note of exasperation in her sister's voice. 'So what's wrong with my mobile if you wanted me so urgently?'

'It's switched off.'

'Is it?' Ginny delved into her handbag to discover her sister was right. 'Sorry,' she mumbled into the handset.

'I was ringing to wish you a happy New Year. I tried to ring you last night but couldn't get you then either.' Then Netta added suspiciously, 'Have you only just got in from celebrating?'

'No I haven't. Anyway, what's it to you if I have?'

'Jealously, that's what,' replied Netta with a laugh. 'I love the Isles of Scilly but trust me, you don't move here for the social life.'

'Or the shopping.'

'No. But out of the tripper season I can go out and leave my front door open and the kids wander around the farm or play on the beaches with their friends in complete safety, so there are some advantages. And I wouldn't swap it for the world.'

'So, how's the new sprog?'

'Bloody late, that's what, but I think it'll be any moment now.'

'I thought it was due around Christmas.'

'It was, but apparently it's changed its mind. Anyway, how are you, apart from, I assume, hungover?'

'I'd like to be all upbeat and tell you how fantastic things are but frankly it's all going to rat shit.'

'You shouldn't have got involved with Bob in the first place,' said Netta sternly.

'You can't choose who you fall in love with.'

'I know, but you're too grown up not to know better.'

Ginny remained silent. She knew Netta was right but she wasn't up for a lecture on the subject; she was feeling too raw and too hungover for anything other than sympathy.

'So when are you coming over to see us?' demanded Netta.

'Soon, I promise.'

'I thought you might come at Christmas.'

'I know but I did explain. Apart from problems with travel if the weather really clamped down, I honestly didn't think you would want me there if you were about to go into labour. Anyway, Petroc wouldn't want me getting under his feet if you weren't there.'

'Don't be so silly. You know he loves you to bits. And you don't get under his feet, you're always a great help.'

'Maybe. But you don't need me. You've got Petroc's mum

159

and all his relations to help you out. When the novelty of the new baby wears off and they stop rushing around to help, I'll come. I'll come in the spring, I promise.'

'You better had. It's been a year now since we've seen you and it's too long. The kids can hardly remember what you look like or even who you are.'

'I promise. Neither hell nor high water will keep me away. I'll put in for three weeks' leave, if you can bear to have me for that long, so it gives me ample travelling time too.'

'You're on.'

Maddy was buying some tonic water in the Naafi when she ran into Sarah. Sarah seemed to be on a similar mission but she was also stocking up with inordinate quantities of bread, beans, and cereal.

'It's having the kids home,' explained Sarah as Maddy glanced in her trolley. I give them three square meals a day and yet they seem to spend the intervening hours consuming vast plates of beans on toast or huge bowls of cornflakes.'

'I expect they're growing,' said Maddy, who couldn't imagine what it would be like to have kids as old as Sarah's. They seemed so terribly grown up compared to Danny.

'Jen had better watch that she only grows upwards and not outwards,' said Sarah. 'At her age it's all too easy to develop a bit of podge.'

'But didn't I see them out for a run with their father yesterday? If they're doing all that exercise then surely they can eat loads too?'

'Maybe. Listen, I'm glad I ran into you.' Sarah had a quick glance around the shop to see if they might be overheard. 'Is something up with Ginny? Alisdair says I'm imagining things but she doesn't seem right to me. You're a friend of hers. Do you know what's going on?'

Maddy wasn't about to betray any confidences but equally she wanted to know what Sarah's suspicions were. 'In what way?' she asked.

'I don't know. But I noticed she didn't turn up to Alice's and Bob's drinks—'

'She *was* duty officer,' interrupted Maddy.

'I know but she could have dropped in for a few minutes.

And she's asked for a posting. And I noticed that she seemed quite upset the other evening at Taz's.'

'Just a bit maudlin I think,' said Maddy lightly.

Sarah gave her a hard stare. 'I think it's more than that. To me it seems as though something happened while they were out in Kosovo and I think someone has done something to really upset her. Should I ask Alisdair to have a word with her?'

'No!' Sarah looked startled by the vehemence of Maddy's reply. 'No, don't bother him. I'm sure it's something trivial and it'll blow over.'

'It can hardly be trivial if she's after a posting. Is there something going on between Ginny and someone else in the regiment?'

Maddy really didn't want to continue this conversation. It was getting into seriously dodgy territory. She pretended to look at her watch. 'Look, I'm going to have to dash. I've left Richard holding the baby, so to speak, and I promised I wouldn't be long.' Maddy made her way to the checkout to pay and as she did so she was aware that Sarah was staring after her, apparently deep in thought.

When Maddy got home she put the tonic away in the cupboard and then leant against the kitchen sink and gazed the length of the garden, although she didn't see the bleak wintry scene. Things were getting serious. Sarah was beginning to put two and two together, and if *she* was, then how many other people were noticing and coming to some sort of conclusion? And what about Richard? He really ought to know that matters in the regimental headquarters were far from plain sailing. For heaven's sake, he worked with both of them and he had a right to know. If the shit hit the fan he would be one of the main people who would have to cope with the mess. But if she told him she would be betraying Ginny's trust. And things were further complicated by Richard's position in the regiment. As the adjutant he was the CO's right-hand man. He was the link between the junior officers and the CO and he was expected to know of anything that might upset the smooth running of the unit and tell the CO before things came to a head. But wouldn't it put Richard in an impossible position if he had to tell his boss that there were rumours about one of his officers and him? Maddy groaned.

'Aren't you feeling well?' said Richard, just behind her. Maddy jumped as if she had been touched by a cattle prod.

'God!' she shrieked. 'Don't creep up on me like that.'

'I didn't creep,' said Richard, aggrieved. 'I walked into the kitchen perfectly normally. You were miles away. Anyway, back to my original question – don't you feel well?'

'Why do you ask?'

'Because people don't normally groan for no reason.'

'Oh.'

'So?'

'I was just thinking about something.'

'And?'

'Nothing really.'

'Liar. Something is really bugging you. I've seen you deep in thought a few times recently. So, tell me what it is.'

'No.'

Richard put his hands on her shoulders. 'You're worrying me. If something is getting to you, I want to know. It can't be anything so bad that we can't overcome it.'

'It's not to do with us.' She saw Richard's face clear a little. 'Honestly, I'm worried about someone I know. They've done something a bit silly and I'm not sure how to help. Or even if I should. OK?'

'So, who is it?'

'I can't say.'

'I see.' His face hardened, resentful at being shut out.

'Honest, it's not important.'

'But it has to be because it's worrying you.'

'Well, it isn't.'

'Is it someone I know?' Maddy wasn't going to lie to Richard so she didn't say anything in reply. 'Is it someone in the regiment?'

'Please Richard, don't keep asking me. I'm not going to tell you.' And although a few moments earlier she had been undecided about whether to tell Richard, she suddenly made up her mind that he didn't need to know. Or at least, he didn't need to know unless Ginny did something even more foolish. As things stood, it looked like Ginny had accepted that the affair was not going to continue, and that the best thing for her to do was to quietly leave the scene. Maddy

162

might tell Richard after she had gone but she wasn't going to right now.

'If you're not telling me, it's because this isn't just a bit of gossip is it? If I find out I might have to take action, is that it?' Maddy shrugged. 'So it *is* someone here.' Maddy remained shtum. 'And it's got to be an officer.' Richard's face lightened as the answer came to him. 'It's Ginny, isn't it?'

'Please, Richard. I can't tell you what it's about. I'd be breaking my promise to her. Believe me, if she wanted you to know she'd tell you herself.'

'Is this about her wanting a posting?'

'I'm not telling you anything.'

Richard began to get exasperated. 'For heaven's sake Mads, I'm her adjutant.'

'Yes, and I'm her friend.'

'What on earth was it that made her so unhappy all of a sudden?'

But still Maddy kept quiet. She wasn't going to let the cat out of the bag.

Richard began to think out loud. 'Why would a normally bouncy woman suddenly become miserable and introverted?' He stared at Maddy as if he expected her to provide the answer. 'Oh, God! How could I be so stupid? It was love, wasn't it? Someone ditched her – that's why she wants to leave. So, who was it?'

'What?'

'I want to know who it was. Ginny's the best regimental admin officer I've ever come across. I'd far rather we got rid of the little toerag who has screwed Ginny up than lose her.'

'I can't possibly tell you.'

'Why?'

She looked away. 'Because I don't know who it is.' There. She'd lied, but if she gave Richard a clue that she *did* know, he'd try and worm it out of her.

Richard had seen Maddy look away from him. 'You're lying,' he said.

Another silence.

'I'm going to have to ring the CO about this.'

'Don't.'

'This is something that is going to affect the regiment and he has a right to know.'

'Trust me. Don't.'

'Maddy, this isn't just about Ginny. This is about the regiment too. The regiment is bigger than just one woman, even if she is a good friend of yours. The colonel isn't going to have a go at Ginny. She'll probably never even know that he knows. But the regiment must come before an individual.'

'Bollocks,' said Maddy. 'I don't care what twaddle you spout at me about the regiment. Please, just take my advice and don't go to the colonel.'

They glared at each other until Richard realized that Maddy wasn't going to give in and he walked out of the kitchen in a huff, muttering to himself.

The subject of their altercation was blissfully unaware of the ructions she had caused and was cheerfully tucking into a gin and tonic at Taz's house. Taz was frying some chopped onions and Ginny was sitting at the kitchen table watching her hostess stir them around with a wooden spatula. Amelia was sitting in her high chair gnawing on a breadstick.

'It's paella. I hope you like it,' said Taz.

'Sounds scrummy.'

'It's something Amelia will eat too.'

'What very sophisticated tastes you have,' said Ginny, addressing the little girl. Amelia gave her a smile displaying her tiny, perfect teeth and pushed her breadstick in Ginny's direction. Ginny pretended to nibble it and then pushed it back to Amelia who giggled deliciously and demanded that the game be repeated.

Taz watched them for a while as she stirred. Then she said, 'So how come you're so good with kids?'

'I've a sister with a huge brood. And I like kids.'

'Don't you want some of your own?'

'Well . . .' Ginny shrugged. 'One day, perhaps.' Taz looked at her and Ginny knew what she was thinking. 'I know, I'm no spring chicken.'

'I wasn't thinking anything of the sort.'

'Liar,' said Ginny with a smile to show there were no hard feelings. 'It's just a question of finding Mr Right.'

'It isn't always essential,' said Taz, indicating Amelia. She pulled a green pepper on to a chopping board and began to deseed and slice it.

'Maybe not for you, but in my job there's so much upheaval and going away suddenly, it just wouldn't be fair on a kid not to have at least one parent providing a bit of stability.'

'So with all those men to pick from you still haven't found the right one.'

'Pathetic, isn't it?'

'No one even close?' Taz swept the little bits of pepper into the pan with the onions and reached for a tin of tomatoes.

'Well . . .'

Taz opened the can and tipped it into the mixture. 'So, what does "well" mean?'

'I found him but I couldn't have him.'

'Unfortunate.'

'Very.'

Taz saw that Ginny's glass was empty and reached for the gin bottle. 'How about the other half?' she offered.

'Great.' Amelia held up her hands to show that she'd now finished her breadstick. 'Ginny, be a poppet and get Amelia another stick out of that cupboard by you.'

While Ginny was engaged doing that, Taz sloshed a vast slug of booze into Ginny's glass and topped it up with tonic and some more ice. She handed it to Ginny who took it with thanks.

'Cor, that's a meaty one,' said Ginny after she'd tasted it.

'Oh, I'm sorry, is it too strong?' said Taz innocently.

'Good job I'm not driving.' But she didn't complain. After all, it was the weekend, she was off duty, and she didn't even have to contemplate work until Monday. The thought that on Monday she would have to face Bob again made a knot of apprehension grip her. She frowned involuntarily.

'Something wrong?' asked Taz.

'No. I just remembered something I wish I hadn't.'

'Which was?'

'Work on Monday.'

'Ah. That would certainly explain it.'

Taz turned her attention to her paella and Ginny played with Amelia again. After a minute or two Taz said, 'So why couldn't you have your Mr Right, if you don't mind me asking?'

'The usual. He's married.'

'And the army doesn't approve of that I take it.'

'They'll turn a blind eye if the marriage is on the rocks and the affair pretty much happens as the divorce becomes inevitable. However, affairs between male and female officers when the spouse of one still thinks the marriage is OK aren't generally considered to be favourable to one's career.'

'But if you love each other isn't it worth sacking the career?'

'I would. He's got a bit more to lose.' Ginny didn't know why she was telling Taz all this. Part of her wondered if it was the gin loosening her tongue, or whether it was because Taz was nothing to do with the army and couldn't possibly affect anything.

Taz put the lid on the paella, turned the heat down and left it to simmer. Then she lifted Amelia out of her chair, picked up her glass with her barely touched drink and said, 'Let's go through to the sitting room so Amelia can play with her toys and we can chat in comfort while lunch finishes cooking.'

Suddenly Ginny found the idea of unburdening herself to someone completely unconnected with everything extremely appealing. And Taz was so sympathetic – and such a good listener.

Richard waited until Maddy took Danielle to the swing park before he phoned Bob that afternoon.

'I'm sorry to bother you at home, Colonel,' he began, 'but I need to talk to you about something a bit tricky.'

'Now?'

'Well . . .'

'Come round, then. Alice has taken Megan shopping for more school uniform so we won't be disturbed.'

'I'll be with you in five minutes.'

It was less than that when Richard rang the doorbell at Montgomery House. Despite the proximity of his house to the colonel's, he was chilled to the bone by the icy wind that cut through his jeans and sweater. He was glad when Bob opened it almost immediately. Richard felt he must have been looking out for him.

'Come in, come in, out of the cold,' Bob said. 'Tea? Coffee?'

'Neither, thanks,' said Richard rubbing his hands together.

'Let's go into the kitchen. Warmest room in the house.'

Richard followed him along the hall and into the kitchen. The Saturday paper and its variety of supplements were spread over the table and a large mug of tea steamed beside it.

'Sure about the tea?' asked the colonel. 'The kettle's only just boiled.'

'No, honestly.'

'So what's so urgent to drag you out of a nice warm house to come and see me?' The colonel sat down on one of the pine ladder-backed chairs and gestured to Richard to sit too. Richard pulled the chair out and settled himself. He put his elbows on the table and rested his chin on his clasped hands.

'It's about Ginny.'

'Go on.'

'I think I know why she wants to move. I don't think it's anything to do with her family.'

'Really?' said the colonel. He sounded quite edgy, almost angry. 'So what has she said?' Richard was slightly surprised at the tone of the CO's voice.

'She hasn't said anything as such; I've sort of deduced it for myself. Well, she hasn't said anything to me. I think she's spoken to Maddy.'

'Has she?' His lips tightened and Richard could see a muscle pulsing near his ears as the colonel clenched and unclenched his teeth. Richard felt as though he was upsetting Bob but he didn't have a clue why. He was painfully aware that Maddy had warned him against doing this and now it seemed she was being proved right. He wondered what the hell she knew.

'And what has she said to Maddy?'

'I don't know. Maddy said she was told in confidence and she won't tell me.'

'Oh.' The muscle stopped pulsing. 'So what have you deduced?'

'She's had an affair with someone in the regiment and it's ended badly.'

The colonel nodded. 'And who do you think she's had the affair with?'

'I don't know. But I think we should find out. Ginny's the best admin officer I've ever come across, and I feel we would be better keeping her and ditching whoever has made her so unhappy.'

'And how do you propose to find out?'

'That's just it, Colonel. I haven't got a clue. I was rather hoping you might have an idea.'

The colonel examined his fingernails thoughtfully. 'To be honest, I haven't. I mean, I can hardly haul her into my office and demand an answer. And supposing you're wrong? Supposing it *is* something to do with her family. After all, that's what she told me.'

'I don't think I am wrong. Maddy as good as confirmed I was right. She said she doesn't know who the other party was but I bet she does. Ginny and she are as a thick as thieves. They tell each other everything.'

The duty officer at the Department of Corporate Communications in the MoD had settled down in the duty bunk with a plate of sandwiches and the TV guide. The previous week had been quiet – the press had been engrossed in a scandal involving a leak at the Ministry of Transport and all the media's attention had been focused in that direction. 'And long may it stay like that,' he murmured to himself as he noticed that there was a particularly good documentary about the English Civil War on that evening. He was just about to bite into his cold chicken sandwich when the phone rang. He removed the sandwich, unbitten, from his mouth and picked up the receiver.

'DCC Army, duty officer speaking,' he said into the mouthpiece.

'This is Marcus Hepplewhite here.'

'Hello, Marcus. What's the *Mercury* on to this time?'

'I've got a story that one of your commanding officers has been dipping his wick.'

'So?'

'Well, for one, he's married, and secondly, it's his regimental admin officer he's been knocking off.'

'Female RAO I assume?'

'God, yes, although it would probably make a better story if it wasn't.'

'No doubt,' the press officer said dryly. 'And who have you got in your sights?'

'Colonel Car Crash.'

'Bob Davies?'

'The one and only.'

'Are they back from Kosovo?'

'Indeed they are, according to my source. They got back just before Christmas. So what is the official comment from the army?'

'Absolutely nothing. I know nothing about it.'

'So we can print it?'

'I can't stop you, you know that. I assume the story's got legs?'

'I wouldn't have bothered you if it hadn't. The "Other Woman" was given the bum's rush by Colonel Car Crash when he came to his senses and she told our trusty reporter Tabitha Alabaster every juicy detail imaginable. We've got it from the horse's mouth.'

Ginny had been back from Taz's house for a couple of hours when her mobile rang.

'It's me, Bob,' said the male voice, although she'd recognized it instantly. 'We need to meet. There's a problem.' No preamble. No how are you? Just straight to the point.

Ginny was taken aback. This was the last thing she'd been expecting. But even though she was surprised, she managed to keep her cool. She wasn't going to be bounced into a meeting just because Bob had got the wind up him about something.

'It's not convenient tonight.'

She could hear the exasperation in his voice as he replied. 'It is urgent.'

'Tomorrow.'

'I mean *really* urgent.' He sounded almost desperate. It must be serious.

'OK. Give me half an hour.'

'Where?'

'The disused airfield. Where the gliding club meets. I'll be by the hangar at six.'

'Right.' The line went dead.

Ginny flipped her mobile shut and sat down on her bed. Something had rattled the boss. She wondered what it was but she knew that it could really only be one thing. Unless Bob had said something, Alice wouldn't have found out and no one in the regiment knew, apart from Maddy. Ginny was sure Maddy wouldn't tell a soul. She was her friend and friends didn't do that sort of thing to one another. So what on earth could it be?

Outside in the corridor she could hear the mess phone ringing. Other single officers were about now – they had started to drift back ready for work on Monday – and Ginny hoped someone else would answer it. The phone stopped. Problem solved, she thought. A few seconds later it began to ring again. Ginny went to the door of her room and looked out. There didn't seem to be a soul around. Perhaps the few other current inhabitants had gone out again. It wasn't beyond the bounds of possibility – after all, it was Saturday night. Reluctantly Ginny walked to the alcove that housed the phone and picked it up.

'Hello.'

'Is this the officers' mess?' asked an unknown voice.

'Yes,' replied Ginny.

'Can you tell me if it would be possible to speak to a Miss Virginia Turner?'

'Speaking. Who's this?'

'I'm Marcus Hepplewhite.'

The name was faintly familiar to Ginny, she knew she'd heard it somewhere but she couldn't place it. 'I'm sorry but . . .'

'I'm the news editor of the *Mercury*.'

Now she remembered the name. 'Yes,' said Ginny slowly. Her mind was reeling. What on earth would the press want with her?

'We are going to run a story tomorrow about a liaison between you and Lieutenant Colonel Bob Davies, the man who became familiar to our readers earlier this year as Colonel Car Crash.'

170

'I beg your pardon?' Ginny slumped against the wall. How the hell . . . ?

'I believe you had an affair with Colonel Bob Davies while you were on tour with his regiment out in Kosovo. I am ringing to offer you the chance to give your side of the story. Is it true that now the affair is over you are being forced to leave the regiment?'

Ginny slid down the wall until she was sitting on the corridor floor. Her heart was pounding and she felt quite sick.

'Miss Turner, are you there?' said Marcus's voice in her ear.

'I don't know where you got this from, but it's all a lie.' Ginny hoped she sounded convincing.

'I don't think so. One of the country's top freelance journalists has told me that she heard the story from you yourself.'

'Don't be so ridiculous.' Ginny was now more angry than scared. Since when had she talked to a journalist?

'You told Tabitha Alabaster only this afternoon.'

'I did no such thing.' Now Ginny was absolutely steaming. 'I don't know who did speak to this hack, but it wasn't me.'

'I expect you know her as Taz.'

Ginny felt as though she had been punched. Taz? Taz! Surely not? She was a friend.

Marcus continued. 'You told Taz and she has filed the story. Is there anything you would like to say?'

'Go to hell,' snarled Ginny down the receiver and slammed it back on to its rests. She stayed slumped against the wall for a few minutes. That explained why the colonel was so worried. The press must have phoned him too. The shit was about to hit the fan and no mistake. And she still couldn't believe that Taz had betrayed her. She'd told Taz because she seemed so sympathetic – she seemed to care. And all the time she'd been wheedling information out of her to make a quick buck. Ginny felt a surge of anger. No one, *no one* did that to her and could hope to get away with it. After she'd seen the colonel, Ginny decided she would go round to Taz's and have a word with her. In fact she was going to have several words, and most of them would be very direct. She glanced at her watch. If she was going to meet Bob on time she was going to have to get a move on. The airfield was only just behind the barracks but it was a good fifteen-minute walk over to the hangar. At this time of day, and in the dark, they should be safe from any other prying eyes, although if it was going to be all over the papers the next day, did it really matter?

Ginny returned to her room and flung a coat over her shoulders. She rummaged in her pockets to find a pair of gloves and put them on. She noticed her hands were shaking dreadfully. Ginny breathed deeply and left her room. Whatever was going to happen now was largely her fault. She had been indiscreet and now the proverbial chickens weren't just coming home to roost, they were booking into the best bedroom and asking for room service.

She walked swiftly out of the mess and through the barracks to the gate that led on to the airfield. It was a derelict area of land that the regiment used for the occasional training exercise and that the dog owners of the barracks used to walk their pets. The physical training instructors bullied the troops around its perimeter track in an effort to keep the regiment up to a peak of fitness, and randy squaddies used it as a trysting place with local girls during the warmer, lighter months of the year. However, on a miserable winter's evening, Ginny and Bob could be almost certain of having the entire area completely to themselves. Ginny passed through the wicket gate in the chain-link fence and on to the concrete perimeter track, rutted and pockmarked as age took its toll on the surface. The moon was up but clouds kept scudding in front of it and in the near pitch-black Ginny had to watch her step. Several hundred yards away loomed the dark shape of the old hangar. Ginny picked her way along the old roadway until she reached it. She peered into the darkness, trying to see Bob, but the shadow was too deep. She approached the huge doors and there seemed to be no sign of him. She resigned herself to a wait in the cold. She hoped he wouldn't be long, it was perishing.

'Nice one, Ginny.'

She leapt at the unexpected proximity of his voice and gave a little gasp. 'God, you frightened me,' she hissed.

'Not half as much as your little revelation to the press has frightened me,' he snapped back.

'So they phoned you too. I realized just after your call why you wanted to meet me so urgently. The *Mercury* got hold of me just after I put the phone down to you. Even so, it's no reason to be lurking in the shadows waiting to scare the wits out of me,' she said in a low voice.

'I'm lurking for two reasons. Firstly I wanted to be sure that it was you, not some lad on a hot date, and secondly I wanted to make sure you hadn't got an entourage of paparazzi trailing along with you.'

'That was below the belt.'

'Was it? And which of us has gone to the press?'

'But I didn't. At least, I didn't *know* I did.'

'Ignorance is no defence in law.'

'Do you honestly think that I am so mean-spirited as to tell the tabloids about our fling in Kosovo?'

'I don't know. You tell me.'

'Look, I may not like the fact that things are over between us, I may want a posting so I don't have a constant reminder of how unhappy I am, but I am not mean and I am not vindictive.' The anger that Ginny had felt as a result of the phone call was welling up again and if Bob was going to level accusations at her and not believe her, well, he could take a running jump.

'So how do they know then? Thought transference?'

Ginny shot him a withering look but it was wasted in the gloom. 'You've met Taz, haven't you? I think Maddy and Richard took her along to your house for Christmas drinks.'

'Yes. So what?'

'I had lunch with her today. We got talking about men. She was nice, she was sympathetic and I told her that I didn't seem to have much luck. She's nothing to do with the army, she's just a friend, so I told her about you. It turns out she's one of Fleet Street's finest.'

'Fuck.'

'That pretty well sums it up. I got fucked by you in all senses of the word and now she's done much the same.'

'So what do we do now?'

'You tell me.'

Bob passed his hand over his face and sighed heavily. 'We could deny it.'

'I expect if Taz is sneaky enough to use a story one of her friends told her, she's sneaky enough to record it.'

'We don't know that.'

173

'And the press are going to be so much more lenient if they can call us liars too,' said Ginny, her voice heavy with sarcasm.

'You're right.'

'Have you told Alice yet?'

'No.'

Ginny was silent. She didn't know what to say. She might have been hurt by Bob but she was recovering and she would move on eventually. Bob's life was about to come crashing round his ears. He had a wife and daughter to consider – to say nothing of his career. If Ginny lost her job she could find another; she didn't have a family to think about housing, or a daughter to educate at an expensive school. If she thought things were going to be difficult for her, they would be hell for him.

'Bob? I'm sorry.'

Bob looked at her and shrugged. 'Yeah, well. You weren't to know, I suppose. What's done is done.'

'If I'd known I wouldn't have breathed a word.'

'You told Maddy.'

'How did you know that?'

'Richard came to see me this afternoon. Oh don't worry,' he added, seeing the look of horror on her face. 'She didn't tell him anything except that you'd been unlucky in love. Richard came to try to persuade me to wheedle the details out of you so we could post the cause of your unhappiness instead and persuade you to stay on as admin officer.' He gave a tight laugh. 'If only he knew.'

'He will soon.'

'Won't they all. I suppose I'd better go to Brigade and come clean before the *Mercury* goes to press. Thank God it doesn't come out on a Sunday. At least it gives us twenty-four hours.'

'Do you want me to come to Brigade with you?'

'I don't think that'll be necessary. It's my guts they'll want, not yours.'

'Bob, I'm so, so sorry.'

'I know you are Ginny, But in many respects it's my fault too. What happened in Kosovo never should have taken place. I don't know what I was thinking about. I knew in my heart it would end up with me hurting someone, but I never guessed to what degree, or how many. You, Alice, Megan. And Alice and Megan are the innocents in all this.'

'I know. What can I say?'

'I don't think there's anything either of us can say.'

'So what are you going to tell her? I don't mind if you want to make me out to be the scarlet woman in all this. Couldn't you tell her that I seduced you, that I got you drunk and took advantage of you?'

'I'll tell her the truth. That we were two frightened, lonely people who clung together for comfort and then animal instincts took over. I'm going to tell her that it was barely more than a one-night stand, that it doesn't mean that I love her any less and that I want her to forgive me.'

'Yes, that sounds good.' Ginny tried to keep the hurt out of her voice but inside part of her felt as though she was being destroyed. She was glad of the dark. She was dangerously close to tears and she didn't want to show any weakness. Bob had enough to worry about without her entering the equation too. She cleared her throat. 'Once the story gets out it's going to be horrible around here. All the press will descend. Remember when they all wanted to interview Colonel Car Crash?'

'Don't. This is going to be a nightmare.' He thought for a second or two. 'In fact, I think it might be better if we got you out of this. You'd better go away on leave.'

'I can't. Not just like that.'

'You can and you will. Your assistant can cover and the chief clerk can help.'

'Well . . .'

'Is there somewhere you can go that's out of the way?'

'I've a sister in the Isles of Scilly.'

'Perfect. I doubt if the press will find you there. Especially if you keep your head down.'

'OK, I'll go.' Ginny reached up and put a hand on Bob's shoulder. He leaned his head over so his cheek rested on it and then drew her towards him.

'If it had been under any other circumstances; if I had met you before I met Alice; perhaps if I didn't have a kid to think about, it might have been different.'

Ginny rested her head on his chest and felt the warm

comforting wave of love sweep through her. She wondered what it would be like to feel like this all the time, to be wanted and cared about, to be held and cared for. She screwed her eyes shut to stop the tears escaping and nodded. 'If only,' she said quietly into the lapel of his coat.

After a few minutes Bob drew away from her. 'I think we had better go and see Richard. He needs to know what is going on. And then I'll go and tell Alice.'

Ginny nodded. 'You go ahead. I'll follow in a couple of minutes. We don't want anyone to get the wrong idea about us, do we?' she said, trying to make a brave attempt at humour.

Bob kissed her on the forehead. 'That would never do.' He turned and walked back towards the wicket gate.

After he had gone Ginny let the tears roll down her cheeks. They were tears of self-pity because she had lost him forever, and tears of anger at Taz's betrayal, and tears of worry because she had no idea what the future would hold, but she was certain it wasn't going to be pleasant. Then she made her mind up that crying wasn't going to achieve anything. She sniffed and ran her hands over her cheeks to sweep the tears away. She dabbed her nose on the back of her sleeve and said, 'Stuff you Tabitha. I hope the money chokes you.' Then she squared her shoulders and followed the colonel back to the barracks.

'You don't have to leave us, Maddy,' said Bob as he took a seat in the Greenwoods' sitting room. 'This isn't a social call—' He was interrupted by the sound of the doorbell. Maddy got out of her seat to answer it. Bob could hear a murmur of voices in the hall and then Maddy, looking concerned, showed Ginny into the sitting room.

'Maddy, I think you probably know what this is about,' began the colonel.

'I'm glad someone does,' said Richard, looking around at everyone. Ginny was pale, the colonel looked strained and Maddy looked deeply uncomfortable.

'I have to tell you that Ginny and I have both been contacted by the press about an unfortunate incident which took place in Kosovo.'

Richard's brow creased. 'I'm sorry, Colonel, but nothing unfortunate happened. Apart from a couple of minor incidents it was a completely uneventful tour. Oh, except your car crash of course.'

The colonel gave Richard a long look and then said, 'Richard, if you stop wittering just for a moment, I'll tell you everything.'

'Oh, right, yes, certainly.'

'It's all about the car crash. That night Ginny and I spent on the mountain – well, we didn't just spend it trying to keep warm.'

Maddy looked at the carpet, pink with embarrassment, and it was almost possible to hear the penny drop in Richard's brain.

'You mean . . . ? Oh God,' he said to Maddy. 'So that's why you didn't want me to go and see the colonel about this.'

'Yes,' said Maddy sadly. 'But I couldn't tell you, because I knew that the fewer people who knew, the safer the secret would be.'

'Precisely,' said Bob. 'But now the press know.'

'But how?' asked Maddy.

'You're not to blame in any way, but you know your friend Taz?' Maddy nodded. 'Do you know what she does for a living?'

Maddy shook her head. 'Not really. I got the impression she was some sort of consultant for a company up in London.'

It was Bob's turn to shake his head. 'No, she works for a London company all right – several of them in fact. She's a freelance reporter. She's the one who has sold our souls for forty pieces of silver.'

'Taz?'

'Taz.'

'So now you know why she was so friendly to all of us,' said Ginny. 'That's why she wanted me to go over for lunch. I thought she was being nice and sympathetic, and all the time she was after a story. She must have got an inkling at her New Year's do, when I got upset. All I did today was walk into a trap she'd set and answer a load of questions that I foolishly thought were quite innocent.'

Maddy shook her head in disbelief. 'Now I understand,' she groaned. 'This wasn't the first story she's filed.'

'There've been others?' asked Richard.

'"Colonel Car Crash" for one. I told her about the accident. I thought she was just a friend in the village, I had no idea she was connected to the press. And then there was a piece in the *Mercury* about a regiment somewhere in Britain. We all loved it because the wives that were described in it seemed so like us. I see now it *was* us.'

'And now she's got a real scoop,' said Ginny bitterly. 'Some friend she's proved herself to be.'

'Anyway,' said Bob, 'I'm sending Ginny away on leave for a while till this all dies down.'

Richard nodded. 'But what about you, Colonel? What are you going to do?'

'I'll have to stay and face the music. I'm going to speak to the brigade commander later this evening and see what he has to say.' He grinned ruefully. 'Quite a lot, I should imagine. Especially considering some of the other high-profile cases that have been in the press in the last couple of years.'

Richard nodded again. 'Do you think . . . ?' he began, but then he realized that what he was about to say sounded incredibly tactless. 'No, forget it.'

'Did you want to ask if I am likely to be court-martialled?' Richard shrugged, embarrassed. Bob passed a hand wearily over his face. 'To be honest, I don't know. Obviously I hope not, but the brass may want to make an example of me. We'll have to wait and see.'

Megan and Alice sat in stunned silence as Bob finished talking.

'I'm sorry,' he said.

Bob couldn't judge what Alice was thinking because she was looking down at the carpet.

'The slag,' said Megan angrily. 'The utter bloody slag.'

'Don't swear,' said Alice, quietly and automatically.

'That's not fair on Ginny,' said Bob, equally quietly. 'She wasn't the only person involved in this.'

'But she was our friend. My friend,' said Megan. 'How could she? What a whore.'

'That's enough, Megan,' said her father with force.

Megan shot him a look and stormed out of the room. Silence followed.

'So,' said Alice with icy calm looking up at her husband. 'I wouldn't have known about your liaison,' she said the word as though it was distasteful to pronounce, 'if it hadn't been for Tabitha Alabaster selling the story to the *Mercury*?'

'No,' said Bob, unable to meet her eye.

'I see.' There was a pause. 'Why?' she asked. 'Why did you do it?'

'I don't know. We had just come through a fairly frightening ordeal, we were alone, it was dark and cold.'

'And she was available.'

'You make her sound cheap.'

Alice sniffed. 'Well, isn't she? I've always thought her fast. I've always thought she had the morals of an alley cat and now she's proved it to everyone. The shame of it is that she has to drag us through the gutter too.' Alice sounded close to tears. 'Everything we've ever worked for and she has to come along and destroy it.'

'We don't know that.'

'You think they'll let you keep command of the regiment after this?' Alice's voice was shrill with anger and pain.

'Well . . .' But the thought had gone through Bob's head too. He knew that with a scandal like this making the papers he would lose the respect of his men and the army wouldn't countenance that. It was almost a certainty that he'd have to go.

'I gave up everything to help your career and you have thrown everything away for a sordid little affair. How could you? How could you do it to me and Megan?'

'There's nothing you can say that'll make me feel any worse about all this than I do already.'

'So when is the story going to run?'

'Monday, I believe.'

'How many other people know?'

'Ginny, obviously, and Richard and Maddy.'

'You told them before you told me?' Alice was aghast.

'Maddy already knew. Ginny confided in her when she got back from Kosovo.'

'Crowed about her conquest.' The bitterness in Alice's voice was almost tangible.

'Ginny's not like that.' Bob regretted the words as soon as he'd uttered them.

'Well, you would know. After all, you know her intimately, don't you?'

Bob didn't rise to the bait. Alice had every right to feel bitter. If she had transgressed he would have felt the same. 'In a minute I'm going to have to phone the brigadier.'

Alice sighed at the thought of yet more people being privy to what was, in reality, a personal matter. 'Yes, I suppose you must.'

'And I think I'm going to have to tell Alisdair and Sarah. If I'm relieved of command, they will be affected too.'

'How long do you think we've got?'

'I think we'll know what action is going to be taken on Monday.'

'So soon? Dear God.' She leant back in her chair and shut her eyes.

'Alice, I want you to know that I still love you. What I did was wrong and foolish, but it doesn't change my feelings about you at all.'

Alice's eyes snapped open. 'Are you asking forgiveness, is that it?'

Of course he wanted to be forgiven but he felt it was too much to ask just yet.

'I don't think I can,' she continued. 'I'm not even sure I love you.'

Bob nodded. He had no right to expect her to love him any more. He'd betrayed his family, he'd broken his marriage vows, he'd delivered his career a mortal blow and destroyed Alice's ambitions.

Megan lay on her bed and stared angrily at the ceiling. Over and over she asked herself how Ginny could have done that to them. How could she have slept with her father? The two people she loved best in the world had ruined her life. No wonder Ginny had been funny with her that day she'd gone to see her in the mess. It all made sense now. And was that why Ginny had made friends with her? Had she done it just to wheedle her way into her father's affections? Probably, thought Megan bitterly. What a cow! And it was going to be in the papers, so everyone at school would know about it. How gross. The teachers would be all concerned and fuss about her and ask her if she wanted to talk about it. As if. And she knew some of the kids would snigger and whisper and some of the others would be snotty and not talk to her. Hot tears began to roll down her face. It was horrid at home and it was going to get worse at school. She felt she wanted to die.

Downstairs she could hear the faint murmur of her parents' voices. Why didn't her mum shout at her dad? She ought to give him a piece of her mind. She ought to throw him out, thought Megan. That would serve the bastard right. See how he liked it if his life turned to rat shit. She didn't stop to think that his life already had. She could only see things from her perspective.

She picked up her mobile and pressed buttons until the number of her friend Zoë appeared. She pressed 'call' and hoped Zoë had hers switched on. She really needed to talk to someone. After half a dozen rings her friend picked up.

'Zo? Can you talk? Something dreadful has happened.'

In the mess, Ginny was lying on her bed, her room in chaos. On the floor were a couple of half-filled cases, clothes spilling out, hangers strewn over the carpet, personal effects littering surfaces, but Ginny was oblivious to it. She was staring at the ceiling, anger churning through her body as she thought about Taz's betrayal. What sort of person could do that? she wondered. How selfish did you have to be to sell stories about people who thought they were friends? Very, was the obvious answer. It just beggared belief that anyone could be so . . . So what? Ginny didn't know whether Taz had been motivated by greed, ambition, jealousy or just plain old-fashioned nastiness. And it was unlikely she would be able to find out. After she had left Richard and Maddy's she had gone straight round to Taz's cottage, but it had been deserted.

She leant on the doorbell just in case Taz was inside but, despite pressing the button until her thumb was sore, there was no response. 'Scuttled back down the drains,' muttered Ginny. She felt like hurling a stone through the window but it wouldn't help her case to be charged with criminal damage on top of everything else. Unable to vent her spleen she had stormed back to the mess and begun to throw her kit into cases, until she realized that she should phone her sister to warn her of her impending arrival. However, Netta's phone had been engaged. 'Bugger,' she swore. She lay on her bed to give it a few minutes before she tried again and found that her anger at Taz took over her thoughts.

Ginny made an effort to calm down before she tried to call again. Netta didn't need her yelling and screaming down the phone about some woman in the village. She breathed deeply and slowly a few times and then pressed the redial button. The phone rang. Ginny was surprised at how puffed Netta sounded.

'Have you been running?'

'What?'

'You're panting.'

'I'm doing my breathing. The baby's coming. I thought you were the midwife.'

'Oh. Where's Petroc?'

'Getting the car out. Is this call important Ginny? Only I need to get to the hospital.'

'No. Well, it is a bit. Can I come and stay, tomorrow?'

There was a gasp from Netta followed by some frantic puffing. 'Hell's bells Gin, you pick your moments. Yeah, whatever. You'll have to fend for yourself. Look, Petroc's outside with the car. I've got to go.'

The line went dead. Ginny said, 'Good luck Netta,' to the ether.

Ginny switched off her phone and put it on her bedside table. Good luck to you and me both, she thought. Then she turned her attention to her packing. An hour later she put two bags in her car and slipped out of the barracks. She felt like a rat leaving the proverbially doomed vessel but she knew it was the right thing to do. As she passed under the raised barrier by the guardroom, she was aware of two men in raincoats standing on the corner of the road. She risked a glance in their direction. One appeared to have a camera, but Ginny was lucky with the traffic and had pulled away before he was able to get a shot.

The sharks are circling, she thought, and she felt a surge of pity for Bob and Alice. She was able to escape but he would be stuck there until things got sorted out.

'I should go and see if Alice needs any help,' said Sarah

after Alisdair had broken the news to her on Sunday morning.

'Is that wise?' asked her husband.

'Why not?'

'You don't think she might think that you're . . .' he paused. 'That you're gloating? I mean you've never been that fond of her and you haven't always disguised it. And let's face it, as I am more than likely going to have to take over the regiment until a replacement for Colonel Bob is found, she might well feel that you want to snoop round Montgomery House to measure it up for curtains, so to speak.'

'Surely not?'

'Well . . .'

'But if I don't go she'll think she's being abandoned. She'll think she's some sort of pariah.'

'True.'

Sarah sighed as she thought over the dilemma. 'I don't know what to do for the best.'

'It's not the sort of thing one comes across on a regular basis.'

'Thank God for that.' Sarah thought again and then came to a decision. 'I am going to go round. I think I'll wait till she's on her own. You said that Bob's got to go and see the brigadier today. When he goes I'll nip round. I discovered recently that she's more vulnerable than I would have dreamed. I think she'll need a shoulder.'

'If that's what you think is best. And,' said Alisdair with raised eyebrows, 'I've got to hand one thing to you.'

'What's that?'

'You haven't said "I told you so". Didn't you tell me just before we went off to Kosovo that you thought there was something going on between Bob and Ginny?'

'Well . . .' Sarah shrugged. 'It's not exactly something to be proud of, is it? Anyway, I don't think there *was* anything particularly "going on" just then.'

About an hour later Sarah saw the colonel's staff car draw up outside Montgomery House and the colonel, in full number two dress, get in. She allowed a decent interval of around fifteen minutes to elapse before she walked down the road to Alice's house. She took a deep breath and rang the doorbell. Despite rehearsing in her mind what she was going to say she was so shattered by Alice's appearance when she came to the door that all her prepared platitudes went out of her mind.

'Yes?' said Alice warily, her face puffy from crying and her hair tousled.

'I just came . . . I just came to say . . . Oh, God, Alice, I am so sorry.'

'Come in,' said Alice dully. She held the door open wide. Sarah crossed the threshold and glanced into the sitting room to her right. The curtains were still drawn, newspapers were strewn over the coffee table and the sofa cushions were unplumped. Sarah could never remember seeing Alice's house in anything less than perfect order. But then she thought that if her world were crashing down, she wouldn't be too fussed with tweaking and tidying either. Alice led the way into the kitchen. The sink was piled with dirty mugs and plates and there were toast crumbs over the big pine table.

'Coffee?' she offered tonelessly.

'Tea if you've got it, please.'

Without a word Alice reached into a cupboard and extracted a packet of tea bags. She dumped one into a mug.

No teapot and Crown Derby, thought Sarah. Things must be bad. Then she pulled herself up for even thinking such a thought. Of course things were bad. They could hardly be much worse.

'So, you know the news.' Alice said it as a statement of fact.

'Yes. Alisdair told me about it a little while ago. I came to see if there was anything I could do to help you.'

Alice gave a mirthless laugh. 'We're beyond help, I think. Bob's gone to see the brigadier and then we'll know what's in store for us.'

The kettle boiled and Alice slopped the water into a mug. Then she took a plastic container of milk out of the fridge and poured some into the mug. Finally she fished the tea bag out with a spoon and dropped it in the sink on top of the other debris.

'How's Megan taken the news?' asked Sarah gently, accepting the proffered mug.

'Not well.' Alice poured herself a cup of coffee from a

cafetière as she spoke. 'I haven't seen her since yesterday evening. I tried to talk to her but she's locked the door to her bedroom.'

'This sort of thing is always hard on the kids.'

'It's no picnic for the wives either,' said Alice tightly.

'No. I didn't mean . . .' Sarah tailed off. She didn't know what she meant. She didn't have a clue what Alice was going through. 'I just want you to know that I'll do anything I can to help you. I really mean that. If you want someone to answer the phone, to vet your calls, or go shopping for you so you don't have to talk to or face anyone you don't want to.'

'The whole world, you mean.'

'Whatever.'

'That's kind. At the moment I really don't feel as if I could face anyone. And we haven't even seen the story in the *Mercury* yet.' Alice took a sip of her coffee. 'I'll be the laughing stock of the barracks.'

'I don't think so. I think most of the wives will be thinking it could so easily be them in your shoes. Let's face it, every time the men go away, doesn't it always cross our minds that they might stray?'

'No,' said Alice. 'Maybe I was naïve. Maybe I had no imagination, but I never once thought that anything like this might happen. I always assumed that Bob loved me too much for that.'

'I never felt that confident,' said Sarah, surprised at herself for admitting such an intimate fear. But as she had, she carried on. 'Personally, I always felt that as long as I didn't know and he didn't come home with some nasty disease, I would be able to live with it. It's probably fine in theory. I expect I would look upon it differently if it happened for real.'

'I hope you never have to put it to the test.'

Sarah nodded.

'Put what to the test?' asked Megan from the door.

Sarah looked round. 'Hello Megan,' she said. She noticed that Megan looked as though she had been doing her share of crying too. 'Nothing really. Your mum and I were just talking about trusting people.'

'Huh,' snorted Megan. 'I'm *never* going to trust anyone again. Look where it gets you.' She stared at her mother

185

and Sarah angrily as if she was daring them to contradict her.

'You may feel differently one day,' said Sarah gently.

Megan just shot her a killer look. 'Where's Dad?' she said.

'He's gone to see the brigade commander,' said Alice.

'To get sacked?'

'I don't think it should come to that. I told him to deny everything. There's no point in him admitting to anyone that the story is true. I doubt if there's any evidence – unless someone saw them at it, and from what your father has said I don't think they did.'

'Oh.' It was obvious that Megan wasn't sure if she should be pleased at this.

'If your father has to leave the army, we lose this house, his pay, we probably won't be able to afford to keep you at your school – it'll be a nightmare. We'd all be punished for what he did.'

'I see.' Megan looked even more subdued.

Alice pushed her chair back and stood up. 'Would you like some toast?'

'I'm not hungry.'

'I know how you feel,' said Alice, 'but you must eat.'

'I said I'm not hungry.'

Alice ignored her and put a couple of slices of bread in the toaster anyway.

'I'll be getting along,' said Sarah. She sensed that Megan and Alice probably needed to be on their own. 'If you want to talk, you know where I am,' she added as she gathered up her handbag. 'And just tell me if you want anything from the supermarket or anything.'

'Thanks.'

'You stay here with Megan. I'll see myself out.'

'Sarah,' said Alice diffidently. 'I really appreciate you coming round. I was afraid I'd have to cope with this on my own.'

Impulsively Sarah leaned forward and put her arms around Alice. 'It's what we do best, us army wives – stick together.'

Alice nodded, not trusting herself to speak.

*   *   *

186

Ginny had driven through the night, apart from a stop for a couple of hours at a motorway service station where she had dozed in the car. It had been a miserable journey. The weather had been diabolical. Mostly it had just rained, but as she neared Dartmoor the temperature dropped and at first the rain had turned to sleet and then it had begun to snow. After a few miles the flakes had swirled thicker and larger, dashing themselves on her windscreen like some sort of frozen suicidal insects. Ginny found herself mesmerized by the wet flakes and had to concentrate to keep her eyes on the road ahead and not be drawn into watching the dancing flurries in the beam of her headlights. The blizzard continued until Ginny was only a few miles short of Plymouth. She began to get worried. Snow was building up at the edges of the road and on the central reservation of the dual carriageway and she could see dirty-coloured ridges and ruts of muddy slush running parallel to the rapidly disappearing white lines. If it carried on like this she might not be able to get through to Penzance. And then, as suddenly as the rain had turned to snow, it turned back into rain again and the road reverted to slick, black tarmac.

Outside Plymouth, Ginny stopped for a late breakfast at a roadside truck stop. Despite the fact that it was Sunday morning, the car park was already full of enormous pantechnicons from any number of different countries. Ginny squeezed her little car between two monstrosities and looked at the wheel hubs level with her as she sat in her vehicle. She hoped that the driver noticed the car when he pulled away again. She didn't fancy coming out of the cafe and finding a flattened pile of metal where her trusty Renault had been.

Ginny locked the driver's door and made her way across the puddled car park and into the steamy truck stop. She was assaulted by the smell of cigarette smoke, hot fat, bacon and coffee. After such a long journey she didn't think she could have come across anything more delectable. She made her way across to the counter, very aware that she was the only woman in the place apart from the large, aproned lady presiding behind the spotless counter. The place was packed with, what seemed to Ginny on first impression, solidly built middle-aged men in check shirts and jeans, although one or two wore the livery of larger haulage companies. For their part the truckers gave her a cursory appraising glance and then ignored her.

Ginny cast her eye over the menu on a blackboard by the door into the kitchen. Full fry and a pint of tea for under a fiver – that had to be the best value ever, she thought. She ordered it and took and paid for a newspaper and then settled herself at a table to wait for her meal. She had been aware of a faint stir of interest in her when she had made her entrance into a predominantly male domain, but she had quickly regained her anonymity. But would that be the state of affairs after the story ran in Monday's press?

For a while she stared at the front page of her own paper and wondered what it was going to be like to feature in a national tabloid. Would people recognize her as a result? Would she be able to go out and about without people staring at her and pointing? She had never been in the public eye and the thought of it horrified her. Fifteen minutes of fame was all well and good if you courted it, if it was for something positive, but to get into the headlines for a failed love affair was verging on the tragic. And that was the point – it was a personal tragedy for all concerned. What right did the public have to poke its nose into her and Bob's business? Ginny wondered how long interest in the story would last. Would the press try and find her? Would they be able to track her down at her sister's? And then other thoughts began to crowd in. What would happen to her career? Would she be out of a job? Would anyone in the army ever talk to her again? It was a nightmare, but there was nothing she could do now to alter things. She wondered briefly if it might have been better to make a comment, to have put across a defence. Perhaps not. Least said, soonest mended, and all that.

'Penny for them,' said the ample lady proprietor as she placed a plate laden with bacon, eggs, beans and fried bread in front of Ginny.

'Not worth that much,' said Ginny.

'Come far?' she asked, placing a huge mug of steaming tea on the table too.

'Yeah. I've driven most of the night but not much further now.'

'This should help you to keep going then.'

188

'Thanks.' Despite her worries, Ginny suddenly realized she was absolutely famished and that she hadn't eaten since lunch the previous day. She tucked in with gusto, the hot food reviving her flagging spirits and energy levels quickly. By the time she had finished she was able to feel more pragmatic about how recent events were going to affect her, although she was worried sick for Bob and still consumed with bitterness regarding Taz's perfidy.

Bob stood ramrod straight in front of Brigadier Robbins. The interview had not been easy for either party. Jim Robbins had known Bob for a number of years – he had taught him at Staff College, he had been on a major field exercise in Germany with Bob and had met Alice socially on several occasions.

'And you can absolutely guarantee that this story about an affair with your admin officer is a complete fabrication?'

Bob swallowed with guilt and shame. 'Yes, Brigadier,' he replied.

'But for God's sake! What on earth happened that made her go to the press like this?'

'I don't know.'

'And you're sure there was nothing. I mean, Ginny's an attractive woman. I would understand the reason why if you . . .'

'Yes, but I didn't,' Bob insisted, hoping that God would forgive him for this dreadful, dishonourable lie. But Alice was right. There was more at stake than just honour, a great deal more.

'Well you know what'll have to happen now? Regardless of your innocence, a serious allegation has been made and it has to be investigated. You are suspended from all further duties. You must go home, pack, leave the barracks and find somewhere to stay. You may not stay on army property. You'll have to find a friend or relation to put you up.'

Bob paled with shock at the harshness of the immediate action. 'What about Alice and Megan?'

'They may stay in the quarter until further notice.'

'Yes, Brigadier.'

'And where's Virginia Turner?'

'I sent her on a fortnight's leave.'

'She will have to be suspended too. Get your adjutant to ring her and tell her to stay wherever she is until she is contacted.' The brigadier rubbed a hand wearily over his face. 'This is a God-awful mess Bob. I hope Alisdair is capable of holding the fort until we get a replacement for you.'

'He's very competent.'

'Glad to hear it. He's going to have to be. Right, you'd better get back and pack. I'll start to tell those who need to know.'

Bob saluted and left wondering where on earth he was going to stay. He supposed he would have to ask his brother if he could let him have a bed for the foreseeable future.

'So how was it?' asked Alice when he returned home. She was waiting for him in the kitchen, not having moved since Megan had returned upstairs to her room with her toast, having refused to discuss events with her mother.

'Grim,' said Bob.

'I don't doubt. What's going to happen?'

'I've been suspended from duty.'

'Oh.' Alice thought about it for a second, then she added, 'Well, it'll be nice to have you around for a bit.' She got up from the table and leant against a work surface. She relaxed slightly at the prospect that things might not be so terrible after all. She had half expected that they might have had to move straight away.

'It's not like that. I have to leave the barracks immediately. I may not return. I may not stay on army property anywhere.'

Alice exhaled slowly as the implication sank in. 'Or pass go or collect two hundred pounds,' she said with a bleak attempt at humour.

'That's about the size of it.'

'Then what?'

'Some sort of investigation, I suppose.'

'And if they find out the truth? Court martial?'

'With any luck it may not come to that. Let's hope to God it doesn't.'

'And if it does?'

'Well . . .' said Bob.

'I see.' Alice's mouth tightened into a thin line as she swallowed back tears. She turned away from Bob and busied herself folding a tea towel. She didn't trust herself to speak. She was afraid she was going to cry and she didn't want Bob to see how upset or frightened she was. Instead of folding the towel up she crumpled it into a ball.

'I'll go and start packing,' said Bob hesitantly, wondering if he ought to do something to try to comfort his wife.

'Good idea,' said Alice, still with her back to him.

He left the kitchen and Alice sat down on one of her treasured ladder-back chairs and put the scrunched tea towel on the table in front of her. She looked about her. This house had seemed the epitome of everything she had strived for, and now it would forever be associated in her mind with dishonour and scandal.

And what would become of them if Bob had to leave? Neither knew any other way of life. The army had been everything to both of them. All their friends were in the army; they had spent all their adult lives with it, and now what? They didn't even have their own house. Alice knew they had some savings but it wouldn't be enough for a decent house, not somewhere nice. After living in such luxury she didn't think she would be able to settle in some little suburban box on an estate.

She yawned. It didn't help matters that she was so tired she could hardly think straight. She hadn't slept a wink the previous night. She'd spent the sleepless hours going over the possibilities of what might happen and possible courses of action. One of the things she had considered was leaving Bob. Anger didn't even come close to describing how she felt about what he had done. He had betrayed her, he had let her down, he had gone with that woman – but was his crime so dreadful that it was worth sacrificing sixteen years of married life? Certainly leaving had been her first instinct, but if she went, where could she go to? It had been humiliating enough to break the news to her mother who had never been convinced that Alice's marriage, above her station as it was, would last. Alice had thought she'd been able to detect a note of triumph in her mother's voice over the phone line.

And what would become of her if she did leave him? She hadn't worked since she got married. The last thing she wanted was to have to return home to her mother and see her gloat. It was conceivable that she might be able to get a job but Alice didn't know if her qualifications would still be considered adequate. Anyway, she'd only taught in a couple of small primary schools in Germany; it would be a whole different ball game teaching in a school in Britain with the much-publicized problems regarding discipline, truancy, literacy, inspections and funding. It all seemed such a jungle compared to the cosy sort of school that she had started work in a couple of decades previously. And if she left Bob, what would happen about Megan's schooling? Would the army continue to help carry the cost, or would they have to find the full fees themselves? If Bob lost his job that could be very tricky indeed.

But there was one overriding reason to stick by Bob. If she left, she would leave the way clear for Ginny to try to snare Bob for keeps. Alice wasn't convinced by Bob's argument that it was over between him and that trollop, and there was no way she was going to roll over and let Ginny get any of the remaining spoils. She wasn't sure if after this debacle there were going to be any, but any that might finally emerge out of the ruins were going to be hers and not Ginny's.

She yawned again and wished there weren't so many imponderables. Nothing seemed certain, and she didn't seem to know anything very much any more. She didn't even know if she was hurting or numb inside. Part of her didn't seem to feel anything and yet another part of her ached more than she thought possible without any obvious wound. She had made Bob sleep in the spare room – the first time they had slept apart when they hadn't been physically separated by distance. Bob had looked hurt but had not complained and had trailed off silently. And after he had gone Alice had regretted what she had done. She didn't want to be alone in the double bed but she was too proud to go to him and change her mind.

Ginny pushed her greasy plate away and turned her attention to her tea. As she sipped it she looked at the words on the page in front of her but nothing was going in. Hopeless, she thought. She folded the paper back up again and stared out of the big plate-glass window. What with the condensation on the inside and the raindrops on the outside she could only make out blurry shapes, but no matter. It wasn't as if she was the least bit interested in the view, or lack of it.

With a start, Ginny remembered that Netta had been in the throes of having a baby when she had phoned the night before. She looked at her watch. It had been over twelve hours since she had phoned; there should be some news. She thought about phoning from inside the cafe but she didn't think that using a mobile would go down a storm with a load of hairy-arsed lorry drivers. Perhaps she would wait till she got in her car. The cafe owner came over to her table and swapped her plate for a bill.

'You look better for that,' she remarked conversationally.

'It was great, thanks.'

'You looked all in when you pulled up here just now.'

'Yeah, well, I've not had a great weekend.' And ain't that an understatement, thought Ginny.

'Ah,' said the large lady, knowingly, as she checked Ginny's left hand for a ring.

Ginny put her hand under the table when she saw the direction of the look. She didn't know why. Perhaps she felt that it was yet another intrusion, albeit kindly meant, on her private life. She rummaged in her purse for a fiver and gave it to the lady, then followed her across the cafe to get her change.

'You drive safely now, and just remember there's plenty more fish in the sea.'

Not when you get to my age, thought Ginny, but she didn't voice her pessimism out loud.

Ginny took her change and braced herself for the inevitable blast of cold air when she opened the cafe door. She gathered her coat around her shoulders and scuttled across to her car, still nestled between two monstrous trucks. She settled herself in and then dialled her sister's number. The phone rang half a dozen times before it was picked up.

'Hello,' said the sleepy voice of her brother-in-law.

'Hi, Petroc. It's Ginny. How's Netta?'

'She's OK. Tired but fine. She had another little girl who's just great.'

'I'm so pleased. What are you going to call her?'

'Dunno yet. We were both too whacked after it all happened to sit down and try to think of names.'

193

'It all went all right then?'

'Yeah. This one took its time. I've only been back from the hospital for a couple of hours so I'm a bit knackered.'

'Oh sorry, did I wake you?'

'Yup, but don't worry. My mum's got the rest of the kids till Netta comes out of hospital so I can catch up on my sleep any time. What's this about you coming to stay?'

'I've got some problems. I need a bolt hole for a while. Netta said it would be OK.'

'She mentioned it. So when are you arriving?'

'This afternoon, if I can get on the chopper.'

'Oh.' Petroc sounded quite stunned. 'I didn't realize it was quite so soon.'

'Don't worry about doing anything for me. I'll try and be as much help as I can, rather than a hindrance. I realize that the last thing you want when you've got a new baby is a visitor too, but I wouldn't ask if it wasn't important.'

'So what sort of scrape have you got yourself into now?'

'I'll tell you when I see you, honest. Now you go back and get some kip. I'll let you know from Penzance if I can get on the flight or not. Bye, and give Netta and the new sprog a big hug and kiss from me.'

Ginny flicked her mobile shut again. Then she switched on the engine, slipped the car into gear and headed for the Tamar Bridge and the far south-west.

'Is that very loyal?' asked Alisdair when he saw Sarah reading the *Mercury* on Monday as she made a pot of tea and poached him an egg simultaneously. He was tense with anxiety about what the day would hold for him now he was in charge. That would have been bad enough without all hell breaking loose as far as the regiment was concerned. And, to cap it all, it was all happening on their first day back after the long Christmas break.

Sarah looked up guiltily. 'I just needed to know what Taz had told them. I felt that forewarned was forearmed.'

'Thinking of giving interviews to the press yourself then?' he said tightly, flicking some minute motes of dust off his epaulettes and straightening his stable belt.

'For God's sake, no. I thought if I was going to go and

194

give Alice some moral support I needed to know what line the paper had taken. And it's awful. Look!' she said with a certain amount of indignation as she pushed the paper towards her husband.

'"Colonel Car Crash says 'Roger, Over and Out',"' read Alisdair. '"First he *rogered* her, then he told her it was *over*, then he threw her *out*." Good God, how do they think of these headlines,' he said in disgust. 'And it's not even right. Bob didn't throw her out.' He scanned further down the page. 'This is dreadful!' There were pictures of Ginny, Alice and Bob taken at Taz's party. 'Alice must be in bits about this,' he commented. 'Though, thinking about it, I don't suppose she's seen it. I can't imagine they take this rag, and I can hardly see her nipping down to the Naafi for a copy.'

'No. But even so, I've no doubt she knows the general gist of the story. There are probably a few insensitive souls who have rung up to tell her. That's why I thought I would go round in a minute. I thought she might need someone to hold her hand.'

'Megan might need some sympathy too. It can't be much fun for a teenager to have this sort of stuff written about your dad in the gutter press.'

'Poor kid,' agreed Sarah, thinking how Will and Jen would react if they were in Megan's position.

'And remember, Bob is denying this story. OK?'

Maddy too was poring over the paper. 'This is worse than I imagined,' she muttered as she cut up toast soldiers for Danielle.

'What is?' asked Richard.

'Guess,' answered Maddy. 'I feel so guilty about all this. If I hadn't become friends with that woman this would never have happened.'

Richard sighed. 'There's no point in you beating yourself up about it,' he said. 'What's done is done.'

'Which means you agree – it's all my fault.'

'No,' he said with a shade too much emphasis. 'No, I don't mean that at all. The woman was obviously going to get stories out of the regiment if no one knew who she was. If she'd introduced herself to you as a London hack you'd never have said a word.'

195

'No I would not,' said Maddy hotly. 'Bl—' She was about to swear but remembered that Danielle had got to the stage when she was prone to repeat words, any words, that were new to her. Only the day before, she had been toddling around the house yelling 'bugger, bugger, bugger', which Maddy had explained to Richard was a mispronunciation of the word butter, but Richard had been loath to accept that. She certainly wasn't going to give him any grist for his mill by lapsing in his hearing. 'I tell you, when I see her again, I'll give her a piece of my mind.'

'I don't think she'll be back here for a bit; certainly not until the dust settles.'

'What I've got to say can wait.'

Richard dropped a kiss on Maddy's nose and on the top of Danielle's head, grabbed his beret and briefcase and took himself off to work. Maddy spread a little Marmite on a finger of toast and fed it absent-mindedly to her daughter as she reread the piece in the *Mercury*. Her sense of outrage grew until she was almost shaking with suppressed rage.

The phone rang. 'Yes,' she snapped down it.

'Maddy,' said the bemused voice of Ginny.

'Ginny. I'm so sorry. How are you?' Maddy tucked the phone under her chin and with both hands free she lifted Danielle down from her chair so she could run off and play and leave her mother in peace with the phone.

'I'm OK. I've seen the paper.'

'Ghastly, isn't it?'

'What's the reaction in the barracks?'

'Too early to tell. I've only just read it myself and I haven't had the chance to test the temperature of the water.'

'Will you? And then let me know.'

'Sure. Good journey?'

'Not bad. I got here yesterday afternoon. Netta's just had number five so there's going to be plenty to keep me occupied and to stop me from brooding.'

'Good.' There was a crash followed by a wail from the sitting room. 'Oh Lord. Danny's done something. Must dash. Phone me this evening.' Maddy put the phone back on the hook and went to rescue her daughter.

As she picked up the overturned lamp, dried the tears

and soothed her little girl, she wondered how she could see what other people thought without looking as though she was either revelling in Alice's misfortune or taking an unhealthy interest in other people's unhappiness. Perhaps, she thought, a trip to the Naafi might do the trick. She glanced at her watch. It wouldn't be open for a bit. Time for another cup of tea.

Maddy made the tea then pottered round the house for a while, Danielle trailing behind her, making beds, tidying toys away, doing a spot of half-hearted dusting until she reckoned it was time to make a sortie to the Naafi. She dressed Danielle in her coat and woollen hat and then popped her in the pushchair before throwing on her own tatty old jacket and heading out the front door. In the drive opposite, Caroline was unloading supermarket carrier bags from her car. The big store in the next town was open twenty-four hours and Caroline often went at the crack of dawn because, as she said, if Grace had had her up and about for hours, she might as well use her time constructively. Maddy was only thankful that Danny seemed to like a more leisurely start to the day.

'Hi,' called Maddy.

'Hi there. Off for a walk?'

'Just popping to the Naafi for a couple of bits and pieces.'

'OK. Hey, Maddy, do you know what's going on? There's a crowd of people outside the barrack gates. It looks like reporters. Are we expecting some VIP visitor or something?' Caroline knew that Maddy was often privy to advance information, being the wife of the adjutant.

'You mean you don't know?' said Maddy, amazed. She'd have thought everyone would have heard the news via the regimental grapevine by now – or seen the paper. After all, Bob had told Alisdair and Richard on Saturday – thirty-six hours was usually more than enough for such important news to get round.

'Obviously not,' said Caroline.

Unusually for Maddy a sense of propriety overtook her. 'Look, I don't think the middle of the patch is the best place for this. How about I drop in for a coffee on my way back and I tell you everything?'

'Deal. But don't be too long. I don't think my curiosity can hold out.'

Maddy hurried off. As she made her way along the roads through the married quarters she was aware of a few knots of wives standing outside their houses or on street corners, chatting animatedly. The hot news was being disseminated, thought Maddy as she saw a few of the wives glance at her and look a little guilty, perhaps ashamed at indulging in gossip so publicly.

In the Naafi a couple of the soldiers' wives were poring over a copy of the *Mercury* and chortling.

'How the mighty have fallen,' said one, with obvious Schadenfreude.

'Serve her right, toffee-nosed cow,' said the other. They ignored Maddy, probably because they had no idea who she was and Maddy, in her ancient jacket, didn't look like an officer's wife.

Maddy longed to say something to put the record straight but she knew it was better not to. She grabbed a wire basket, threw in some milk, a packet of biscuits, a pack of loo rolls and a bag of chocolate buttons for Danny and headed for the checkout. The checkout girl began to zap Maddy's purchases.

'Bit of a turn-up for the books, ain't it?' she said.

'What is?' asked Maddy innocently.

'The colonel knocking off Captain Turner. Mind you, she's not bad looking. I reckon half the lads in the regiment would have her given a chance. And I've always thought she was a bit of a goer. Not like the colonel's wife – she wouldn't give the lads a second glance.'

'Well, I very much doubt Captain Turner would have given the lads a second glance either,' said Maddy tautly. 'And besides which, you shouldn't believe everything you read in the papers.'

The checkout girl looked up from her till and saw the expression on Maddy's face and then coolly looked down again. 'That's two pounds and forty-seven pee,' she said.

Maddy handed over the money, got a few coppers in change and left the shop. She'd known that the news was bound to generate a lot of interest but she had expected, perhaps naively, that most members of the regiment would feel sorry for the three main protagonists in the sordid story. How wrong she had been.

The groups of wives were still gathered around as she returned to Caroline's. How much was there to discuss? thought Maddy. Plenty, obviously. Caroline was looking out for her on her return to their road and had the front door open as Maddy pushed Danielle up the garden path.

'Come in, come in,' she welcomed as she grabbed the front of the stroller to pull it over the doorstep. 'Kettle's boiled,' she said to Maddy, 'and Grace has got all her toys out ready for you to play,' she said to Danny as she unclipped Danny's straps and helped her off with her coat. Danny toddled along the corridor and into the sitting room while Caro led Maddy into the kitchen.

'Now, tell me before I burst with curiosity,' ordered Caro.

As Caroline poured boiling water on to the coffee granules in one of the mugs Maddy said, 'Colonel Bob had a fling with Ginny Turner and it's in the papers today.' The sound of hot coffee spilling over the side of the mug, trickling across the worktop and splashing on to the floor made Caro realize she ought to stop pouring. Still looking agog, she grabbed a dishcloth and mopped up the mess.

'You're kidding me.'

'Straight up,' said Maddy.

'Good God.' She slopped the excess coffee out of the mug and into the sink.

'Well, to be honest, it's only in the *Mercury* but the other papers have obviously dispatched some of their reporters here to glean more gossip. Hence the scrum at the gate.'

Caro finished clearing up the mess and making the two cups of coffee. She handed one to Maddy.

'Let's go through to the sitting room so we can keep an eye on the girls.'

Maddy followed her through, although the two children were playing perfectly happily, albeit separately, and patently didn't need supervision.

'How's Alice taken it?' asked Caro when they had settled into armchairs.

'I don't know. I don't know what to do. I mean, she must know that I know. I feel I ought to go round but it's a bit

199

hypocritical. Especially as Ginny's my friend and I knew all about it before she did.' Caroline's mouth dropped open again. 'Ginny told me when she came back from Kosovo.'

Caroline's mouth shut again and she nodded. 'Oh.' She digested the information. 'And all this time you kept shtum?'

'Had to. I knew if the story got out, I'd be the first person Ginny would think had ratted on her.'

'So how did it get out?'

Maddy explained about Taz.

'What a cow!' shrieked Caroline in indignation and disbelief. 'How could she?'

'I expect she got paid a decent amount of money.'

'But to knowingly ruin two friends' careers for the sake of a scoop . . .'

'I know, I know. It beggars belief, doesn't it?'

'Have you said anything to her?'

'Not yet. She's flown the coop.'

'I'm not surprised.' Carol whistled. 'Well, she won't be invited into the regiment again, will she?'

Maddy shook her head. 'You realize that the other piece in the *Mercury* was down to her too?'

'Yeah,' said Caroline. 'The penny was just beginning to drop.' She looked at Maddy. 'We should have guessed.'

'It's easy with hindsight. Do you know, at the CO's Christmas drinks, Sarah was introduced to Tabitha and she knew she'd heard the name recently. And neither she nor I made the connection.'

'Sorry,' said Caro, 'Who is Tabitha?'

'Taz. Taz is short for Tabitha – Tabitha Alabaster. So it's no wonder we didn't twig. She never gave anyone a clue about what she did, and we didn't know her real name.'

'Devious cow.'

'Anyway, the official line from the regiment is that we know nothing, but it would probably be better if we say nothing at all if the press corner us.'

'They'll get nothing from me,' confirmed Caroline.

Ginny had arrived at Petroc and Netta's farm the previous evening after an uneventful but rather bumpy helicopter flight from Penzance. On the way from the heliport to the farm

Ginny had divulged to her brother-in-law the reason for her unexpected visit.

'You've done it good and proper now, my duck, haven't you?' he'd said with a chuckle. But then he'd seen how completely devastated Ginny looked and had put his hand on her knee to give her a reassuring pat while thundering along the tiny lanes in his battered old Land Rover and steering with the other hand. 'Well, you're in the best place. The press won't find you here and you'll get a chance to have a good think about it all.'

After they had dumped Ginny's kit at the farm they had driven the mile into Hugh Town to visit Netta in the little hospital. Netta, looking radiant, was sitting up in bed, and not for the first time Petroc was struck by how similar the two sisters were. Facially they were almost identical except that Netta's skin had a semi-permanent tan from her outdoor life and her hair was shoulder-length compared to Ginny's curly bob. Netta was feeding her baby contentedly and was so engrossed in watching the infant sucking at her breast that she didn't see her visitors until they were at her bedside. Despite the fact that this was Netta's fifth, Ginny had never met any of the other children until they had been several months old. She was astounded at how incredibly small a newborn was.

'Look at her little finger nails,' she said in amazement. 'They're so tiny but so perfect.'

'Aren't they just,' said Netta running her own finger gently over the back of the infant's minute hand. 'You can hold her, if you like, when she's finished guzzling.'

Ginny wasn't sure if she wanted to. The baby looked so incredibly fragile and vulnerable. Netta read her expression correctly. 'Babies don't break, you know. You'll be all right.'

Ginny nodded. 'Well, if you're sure.'

'So why are you escaping?' asked Netta.

Ginny repeated her tale.

'Nice one, Gin. You've really done it this time, haven't you?' she said, not without sympathy. 'Well, I can see why you want to get out of the spotlight, that's for sure.'

'It's not so much just getting out of the spotlight as being told to keep out of the way. I had a phone call from the adjutant while I was waiting at the heliport at Penzance. I've been

201

suspended from duty until further notice so I can't go back to the regiment even if I wanted to.'

Netta sighed and glanced at Petroc. 'You can stay with us for as long as you need. That's OK, isn't it darling?' she said.

Petroc nodded in agreement.

'But it could be weeks,' said Ginny, touched by their kindness. 'I'll help out as much as I can. I know I'm a hopeless cook but I'm a terrific skivvy. You just tell me what needs doing and I'll do it.'

'I know you will, and you may regret making an offer as open-ended as that. With a farm to run and five kids you may find you've taken on more than you bargained for.'

The baby finished her feed and Netta handed her to Ginny. 'Look, hold her up against your shoulder and rub her back to get any wind up.' Ginny did as she was told, scared she might damage or bruise the minute, warm bundle but Netta didn't seem the least bit concerned. 'That's right,' she said as Ginny manoeuvred the infant into an upright position. The baby rested its tiny downy head against Ginny's cheek and made funny little mewing sounds. Ginny rubbed her back gently and nuzzled against the child. She smelt wonderful – sweet and clean and delectable. She was suddenly aware that she wanted part of this. She wanted to be a mother. This was the whole point of being a woman. Before, she had always been rather frightened at the idea of being wholly responsible for another life, and even more scared of the commitment that went with motherhood. She'd often joked that if it turned out she didn't like it she could hardly hand the kid back and ask for a refund. But holding this minuscule scrap of human life was what nature really intended her to do in life. She hadn't been put on earth to organize expeditions or to make money or to order people around, but to have babies. And as Ginny cuddled the baby she realized how much she was missing out on life. She was silent as she assimilated her thoughts but she stroked the little bundle rhythmically and in a couple of minutes the baby had dozed off contentedly.

Netta yawned too.

'We must go and let this pair get their beauty sleep,' murmured Ginny, not wanting to disturb the baby.

'Here, give her to me,' said Netta.

Reluctantly Ginny passed back the baby and Netta placed her gently in the perspex cot by the bed and covered her with the utilitarian hospital blanket – pink for a girl.

They hadn't stayed much longer after that as Netta looked ready to drop. 'Not much sleep available in a hospital,' she had explained, so Ginny and Petroc had said goodbye and drove back to the farm.

'Make the most of the peace and quiet,' Petroc had said as they had sat companionably in the sitting room, sharing a bottle of wine. 'I told Granny Flo you've come to stay and that we'll have the kids back here tomorrow. She sounded quite grateful. Her house is not really big enough for her to have our brood for long.'

'It'll be nice to be able to make myself useful,' said Ginny, although she was wondering how on earth she would cope with looking after four children when Petroc was going to be involved with running the farm. She'd been used to helping Netta, but that was just it – she'd helped Netta. The thought of being virtually in sole charge was totally terrifying.

Petroc laughed. 'You should see the look on your face,' he chortled. 'Don't worry; Granny Flo said she will come over to give you a hand. I'm not going to throw you in at the deep end completely. God, it would be like chucking Christians to the lions.'

But on the Monday morning Ginny was feeling very much like a Christian in the Coliseum. She was in her sister's warm kitchen gazing glumly at the paper spread out on the vast, ancient pine table that dominated the room and wondering how much more horrid and humiliating life could get than to see your failed love affair plastered all over the first four pages of a national tabloid.

The kitchen was wonderfully cosy, despite the howl of a January gale coming straight off the Atlantic and tearing round the house, causing the trees to thrash about wildly and anything loose to flap and whip madly, trying to tear itself apart and be carried away by the wild storm. On the walls, Netta's collection of copper jelly moulds gleamed softly in the electric light and on all the cupboard doors were paintings and drawings done by the children of round yellow suns in blue skies, stick figures with starfish fingers, spiky hair and bright-red smiles, and blobby white flowers in green fields. The Aga behind Ginny warmed her back and under her feet the bright rag rugs on the aged flags stopped any hint of cold from the stones striking up. Opposite her was the battered, tatty sofa that Netta's cats used as a scratching post despite the expensive, purpose built and still unused one that Ginny had presented the animals with a couple of years previously in an effort to save the upholstery. And all around her were the thick granite walls that ensured the farmhouse was cool in the summer but totally weatherproof in the winter. But despite the cosiness of the kitchen, Ginny felt numb and cold as she read and reread the tacky story.

The back door opened and a gust of wind tore into the kitchen and picked up the sheets of newsprint. Ginny grabbed them before they could fly on to the floor and weighed them down with a half-drunk mug of tea. Petroc came in, stamping his feet in his wellingtons on the huge, thick doormat to get the worst of the mud off them.

'Staring at it isn't going to make it go away,' said Petroc, taking off his waxed jacket and rubbing his hands. Ginny had been engrossed in the paper when he had gone out to see to some farm business thirty minutes earlier. 'God, it's wicked weather out there and no mistake. Get the kettle on, flower.'

Ginny didn't appear to hear what he said. 'But it isn't even what I told her,' she moaned. Despite the homely warmth of her surroundings she shivered and rubbed her hands together as if to restore feeling to them. She was hurt by the betrayal but even more so because someone she had thought of as a friend had distorted the facts to make the story seem even more lurid. 'If people believe this I'm never going to be able to stay in the army. They'll think that no man is safe anywhere near me,' she complained with more than a hint of self-pity in her voice.

'It'll be a five-minute wonder, mark my words.' Petroc shifted the huge kettle that lived permanently on the Aga across on to the hotplate himself.

'But the damage is done.'

Petroc sighed. It wasn't as if they hadn't already been over the same ground a dozen times since he'd nipped to the newsagent in Hugh Town to get a copy of the *Mercury*. He hadn't told Ginny that the newsagent had pointed at the picture of Ginny splashed over the front page and remarked at how much 'that army bird' looked like Netta.

'Does she?' Petroc had remarked, hoping to deflect any further curiosity.

'Anyway, why you buying the *Mercury*?' the newsagent had inquired. 'You don't normally.'

Petroc had prided himself on the speed of his response. 'Netta's asked for it. She's just had the baby and it makes her hormones go all funny. And you know what women are like when that happens.'

The mention of the baby had done the trick and by the time the newsagent's wife had been called through from the back of the shop to hear the news and all the necessary details had been passed on for immediate dissemination into the island grapevine, the matter of which paper Petroc was buying was completely forgotten.

'So what are you going to do with yourself today?' asked Petroc. 'I'm afraid I've got stuff to do on the farm so I won't be any company.'

'I'll walk into Hugh Town in a while to see Netta and the baby, then I thought I'd pop into Granny Flo's to say hello to her and the kids.'

'Do you think you'll be around at lunchtime?'

'Do you want me to be?'

Petroc shrugged. 'It's just there's a load of veg in the fridge that needs eating up and when that happens Netta usually makes soup.' He looked at Ginny hopefully like a labrador wanting to be taken for a walk.

Ginny wrinkled her nose. 'I'm not sure about soup. I'm not much of a cook.'

'All you do is chuck it in boiling water and cook it up in a big pan. I'm sure that's all Netta does.'

'I'll ask Netta when I see her,' said Ginny, not convinced.

The kettle boiled and Petroc dropped a teabag into a mug and slopped the hot water on top. 'Do you want a cup?' he asked.

Ginny looked at the revolting scummy dregs in her mug and went right off the idea of tea. Through the kitchen window Ginny saw the sun suddenly blaze across the farmyard. The strong wind had chased the storm clouds away. She got up and leaned across the wide windowsill and peered out. The sky was the colour of speedwells and although the wind was still whipping across the countryside Ginny suddenly had an urge to get out in the fresh air.

'Thanks, but no thanks,' she said. 'I'm off out while the sun is shining. I need to get the cobwebs blown away.'

Petroc nodded. He understood entirely. He couldn't bear to be stuck indoors for too long either.

'You'd better wrap up,' he advised. 'That wind is bitter.'

Ginny found a coat and Petroc lent her a pair of gloves and a scarf and then she opened the door and stepped out into the gale. The sun was still shining brightly but Petroc was right – the wind was perishing. It cut through the denim of her jeans and made her face sting. Undeterred, Ginny set out briskly for the mile or so walk into Hugh Town. In the sky above her the fluffy picture-book clouds were being harried across the blue expanse like sheep being herded by a collie, but on the horizon Ginny could see the dark line of a threatening squall heading towards the islands. She hoped she would make it to the hospital before it struck – she didn't fancy being caught in a downpour. On either side of the road – little more than a lane despite the fact that it was one of the island's main thorough-fares – were tiny fields of daffodils. No nodding yellow heads to be seen though, as the blooms were picked whilst still in tight bud and shipped off to London and the big markets there. In the stone-walled fields were armies of pickers – January was the height of the daffodil season for the islanders and it was a case of all hands on deck until the crop was harvested.

Ginny breathed deeply as she swung down the road. The air was undeniably fresher here and the tangy smell of the sea made her feel invigorated despite her mood resulting from the newspaper story. The road sloped down towards the town – well, not really a town, despite its name, but more just a fishing village. Ginny could see the harbour with its little fleet of fishing boats bobbing in the hyacinth-blue sea, and the narrow spit of land that separated the harbour on the north from the beach on the south and joined the main part of the island to The Garrison, the circular peninsula at the extreme western end of the island.

Along the narrow neck of land was the main part of Hugh

Town; some of the houses were grey granite and some were painted pastel colours, which gave the village a vaguely Mediterranean air. It looked so idyllic. Ginny felt almost jealous of Netta; with Petroc, the kids, the farm and this scenery. In the past Ginny hadn't envied her sister one jot, feeling that she had sold herself short by marrying Petroc when she had been barely twenty. She thought Netta had given up the chance of a career and life in the fast lane to be a farmer's wife with virtually no financial security on an island booted off the end of England and into the Atlantic. Yet now Ginny had to admit that there was something to be said for Netta's lifestyle. She might not have access to the bright lights, and she might not be able to shop for the latest fashions, but maybe the things she did have were worth more than the glitzy trappings of consumerism. She might not have money to burn but the house she lived in had been in the Pengelly family for generations and, short of some terrible global disaster, it was likely to stay that way. Their overheads were minimal, the kids' school was terrific, the crime rate was almost zero, their health was fantastic, and so the list went on. She weighed up what she had going for her in her own life: a room in an officers' mess that she could no longer use since she had been suspended, a dodgy bank balance, a car and a handful of passing friends – some of whom had turned out not to be her friends at all. Frankly, she thought, it didn't add up to a hill of beans. Yeah, she'd travelled a bit, been places, seen things, but would that keep her happy in her old age? Everything about her life was so ephemeral, so transitory, so superficial. But Netta had a real life with love, family, security and happiness. Netta had got it right all along and, Ginny had to admit to herself, she had got it wrong.

A cloud scudded in front of the sun and the temperature plummeted still further. Ginny looked at the sky and saw that the threatening squall was almost on her. She broke into a jog and scooted the last few hundred yards past a scattering of granite cottages to the hospital that was down towards the beach. She paused at the entrance to catch her breath just as the first few fat drops of rain that presaged the next shower splattered heavily on to the ground. The door behind her banged open and a youngish man with wildly curly hair barged out. He was so busy pulling up the zip of his jacket and turning up his collar that he almost knocked into Ginny.

'Whoops,' said Ginny as she stepped backwards to avoid him.

'Uh,' he said, looking up and noticing her. He stared at her hard. 'Good grief,' he then said.

'I beg your pardon,' said Ginny, faintly put out. She had half expected an apology as *he* had nearly banged into *her*.

'Nothing,' he said gruffly. 'You just look familiar.' He stared at her so hard it verged on the rude. And no sorry, no excuse me. 'In fact I know just who you are.'

Ginny felt a frisson of fear. Even here in the Isles of Scilly someone had made the connection between her and that awful picture on the front page of the *Mercury*. She didn't know why she thought that they wouldn't. Why, just because they lived on an island, would they not read the national papers and look at the pictures? And then recognize the subject when they saw her. She supposed it was because she felt so far removed from her normal life, so far from the regiment that it was almost like being in a foreign country. How ridiculous, she thought. What a nit she'd been. And because she'd been such a nit she'd let her guard down and now someone knew who she was.

'Do you now?' said Ginny stonily, staring back just as rudely, hoping against hope that her defiance would protect her, make him doubt his certainty. Two could play at that game. He looked at her impatiently as though he expected her to own up to who she was and confirm his suspicions but she was damned if she was going to explain anything to him. Why should she to a complete stranger who seemed to have had a bypass operation on the bit of his brain governing manners? As she stared, she noticed that his eyes were hazel – almost green in fact – and his skin was the most wonderful shade of olive, and he had an incredibly neat nose.

'Well, if you don't mind getting out of my way so I can get on?' he said.

'Me! In your way? You ran into me!' Ginny said, shrill with indignation.

He gave her a puzzled look as if unable to comprehend her problem and stomped off into the rain. Ginny shrugged and went through the doors from the freezing cold of a

January morning to the stifling heat of the cottage hospital.

Netta was sitting on the edge of her bed in her dressing gown when Ginny got to the women's ward. She kissed her sister and peeked into the cot where the baby was sleeping peacefully.

'Hiya Net,' she said. 'How are tricks?'

'I'm fine. How are you, more to the point? I saw the *Mercury* this morning. One of the nurses showed me. She wondered who the woman was who looked so like me.' She raised her eyebrows. 'Just what I needed.'

Ginny bit her tongue to stop herself saying that the impact on her own life was rather more than it was going to be on Netta's.

'Have you told Mum and Dad?' asked Netta.

'Do you think I ought to?'

'For God's sake Gin! Someone is bound to tell them. To say nothing of the Internet. You know how Dad catches up with the British news on the Net. They're going to be shocked to their socks if they find out from someone else – of course you've got to phone them. Thank God that it's the middle of the night there and Dad probably won't be aware of what's going on for a few more hours. You're to phone them this evening, understand?'

Ginny was sometimes surprised at how bossy her little sister could be. 'Yes, Netta,' she said meekly.

'And don't think you will get away with pretending to forget. I'm being allowed out, providing the doc gives me the all-clear, so I'll be there to make sure you jolly well do.'

'Great news that you're being allowed out.'

'Don't change the subject,' said Netta sternly. 'Really, Ginny, the story was appalling.'

'It was a complete exaggeration,' retorted Ginny hotly. 'That bloody woman Taz made loads of it up.'

'I'm glad to hear it. Mum isn't going to be best pleased when she sees it.'

'Fingers crossed she doesn't.' Ginny sighed heavily. 'It's a mess, isn't it?'

'Frankly, yes. Still, I expect it'll blow over soon enough. Tomorrow's fish and chip wrappings and all that. Right, what do you think about the name Rose?'

Ginny considered it for a minute. 'It's all right. Yes, I like it.' Better than Florence which the eldest girl had got lumbered with as Petroc had insisted that she be named after his mother. Although now the whole family called her Flossie which seemed to suit her.

'You don't sound sure.'

'It's not for me to say though, is it? What does Petroc think?'

'I haven't told him yet. If he hates it I'll think again.' She looked at the baby. 'Flossie, Barnaby, Jack, Lisa and Rose,' mused Netta. 'It goes with the others, don't you think?'

It was hardly a matching set, thought Ginny, but names were a subjective business. Anyway, it wasn't really down to her to have an input in labelling this little scrap. 'Rose Pengelly? Yes, it's OK.'

'Good, that's settled. Now what news?'

'Hardly any really. I'm on my way to see Granny Flo and the kids. Oh, and Petroc wants me to make vegetable soup for lunch. He says I just throw it all into boiling water – is that right?' Ginny wrinkled her nose. She didn't enjoy domesticity and making veg soup was her idea of hell.

'No, it isn't,' said Netta with a laugh. She told Ginny what to do. Ginny felt more and more at sea as Netta went through the details of frying onions and garlic, adding the chopped veg, covering it with water, adding stock cubes, simmering, puréeing . . .

'Can't I just open a tin?' pleaded Ginny finally.

'Not if that veg is going to waste.'

'But you'll be home this afternoon.'

'All right. Forget it, open him a tin and I'll sort out the soup this evening.'

Ginny sighed with relief. 'Thank God for that. At least something will be guaranteed to go right today.'

'So what has gone wrong, apart from the story in the paper?'

'Oh it's nothing. I just met this wild man who barged into me and then accused me of being the one to get in his way, and then as this altercation was going on he realized who I was. He must have seen the paper.'

'Who was it?'

210

'How on earth should I know? He recognized me and was perfectly piggish, so I didn't quite get around to exchanging calling cards.'

Netta laughed. 'What was he like?'

Ginny described his untamed hair and his almost green eyes and his complexion.

'You seem to have noticed an awful lot about a man who barged into you and then shoved off without an apology.'

'Did I?' She had, hadn't she? If he hadn't been so rude Ginny wouldn't have minded finding out who he was and getting to know him, but his half-decent looks had been completely negated by his appalling manners.

'Well, I can't think who it might have been,' said Netta. 'There's a smashing guy who runs a family hotel in Hugh Town and he's got curly hair, but he is charm personified and wouldn't dream of being so rude. Frankly, I don't know anyone as boorish as the bloke you've just described.'

'Perhaps he wasn't local. After all there's no rule that says that anyone who might recognize my picture in the paper has to be a resident here.'

'No there isn't. It's just that a local is less likely to relish the idea of the press descending on the island. We like tourists here but we don't want masses of London hacks here raking up muck. I just hope he doesn't go around tipping off the tabloids that you're here. I don't fancy having the paparazzi camped out round the farm.'

The thought hadn't crossed Ginny's mind. She gasped involuntarily. 'Oh, God. You don't think he'd tell anyone, do you? I mean, the papers may pay for a tip-off like that and there are people out there who will do anything for a bit of cash.'

Netta shrugged. 'I don't think your story is *that* news-worthy.'

For some reason Ginny felt a bit nettled by Netta's put-down. Huffily she said, 'It's all right for you to say that. It's not you in the papers.'

After Ginny left Netta she tramped through another sharp shower to Granny Flo's house. She could hear the squeals and yells of the children playing as she opened the gate in the low garden wall and walked up the gravel path to the bright-red front door. She rapped the highly polished dolphin-shaped brass knocker sharply to ensure it would be heard over the children. Granny Flo, little, white-haired and rosy-cheeked – a picture-book granny – opened the door and held it wide for Ginny to enter.

'Hello, me 'ansome,' she chuckled in her Scillonian burr, as Ginny bent to kiss her. 'You've been and gone and done it proper this time and no mistake.'

Ginny smiled sheepishly. 'You've seen it then.'

'Bit hard to miss, flower. I haven't shown the kiddies.' She led the way through the dark hall into the south-facing kitchen with its big window overlooking the bay and across to the headland and the Star Castle Hotel. As Ginny walked into the room, the last vestige of the heavy shower was blown away and the sun lit up the view. Instantly the sea turned from murky grey to brilliant azure, flecked with dazzling white wave crests. Ginny felt as though it was a show put on for her benefit – just to demonstrate to her how wonderful the islands could be. In the kitchen, Netta's brood were grouped around Granny Flo's table. Flossie and Barnaby were tall enough to stand, but the younger two, Jack and Lisa, were kneeling up on chairs. They were playing with some rather grubby-looking pastry that they had fashioned into shapes and pretend tarts and cakes and which had obviously, judging by the pastry's grey tinge, been keeping them occupied for a while. Flossie, standing opposite the door, looked up and caught sight of Ginny first.

'Aunty Gin,' she shrieked, throwing her lump of dough down and running around the table, nearly knocking her little sister off her chair in the process.

In a second Ginny was clasped by both Flossie and Barnaby, and Jack was clambering off his chair, determined not to be left out. Only Lisa, who could not be expected to remember an aunt who had last visited her when she was barely nine months old, was indifferent to Ginny's arrival. Instead she used the opportunity of her siblings' absence from the table to gather up their share of the pastry and start to eat it. Granny Flo swooped down on her from across the kitchen and gently removed the unsanitary mixture, but Lisa objected and protested lustily. The resulting bedlam in the kitchen was indescribable as Flossie and Barnaby shouted all the louder to

212

get Ginny's attention, Jack yelled because everyone else was and Lisa bawled because she had been thwarted.

In the middle of the mayhem Ginny sat on one of the kitchen chairs. She pulled Jack on to her lap, which quieted him as he was instinctively aware that he was occupying a prize spot, and Flossie and Barnaby were each able to access an ear into which they could simultaneously and in stereo tell Ginny all their news. At the same time Granny Flo placated Lisa with a digestive biscuit. The noise abated.

'Aren't you two big ones at school today?' asked Ginny.

'We go back on Thursday,' said Flossie, aware that she was the eldest child and it was her duty to impart the intelligence.

'I'm going to school too,' lisped Jack proudly.

'Only nursery,' said Flossie dismissively. Jack looked as though he was about to cry at this put-down.

'I'm sure it's very like school,' said Ginny, staring hard at Flossie and daring her to contradict. 'So who wants to come back to the farm with me?' she said, changing the subject.

'Now?' asked Barnaby.

'If you want. Mummy's probably coming home this evening. How about it?' Ginny looked at Granny Flo for confirmation.

'You can do whatever you want my ducks,' she said. 'I was only going to cook you eggs for your lunch, so if you want to go home now . . .'

'What sort of eggs?' asked Flossie.

'I thought we could have nice boiled eggs with soldiers.'

Flossie considered the offer. 'Well . . .' She looked at Ginny. She liked boiled eggs and fancied them for lunch but equally she wanted to go home.

Ginny felt a twinge of apprehension. Suppose they wanted to go home and yet demanded boiled eggs from her. How the hell did you do boiled eggs? Was it five minutes or ten? And would she be a laughing stock if she admitted to being such a hopeless cook that she couldn't even boil an egg?

'Or we could go with Ginny up to the farm and I could cook you eggs there,' offered Granny Flo, as though understanding everyone's unspoken thoughts.

Ginny suppressed a sigh of relief. 'That would be wonderful,' she said. 'And Petroc wants me to make him some soup and, I'll be honest, I haven't a clue. You wouldn't be a honey,

213

Granny Flo, and give me a hand? Netta said she'd supervise when she gets back this evening but I don't think she should. She ought to rest or something, oughtn't she?'

'Well, she ought to, but I know Netta. We might persuade her to put her feet up for a little while.'

'Come on then children,' said Ginny. 'That's settled. We'll all go home to see Daddy and Granny Flo will do you eggs there. Flossie, you find everyone's coats and hats. Jack, you help Granny clear up here, and Barnaby, how about you take me upstairs and help me put everyone's bits and pieces into a case?'

'That's right my ducks, you do what Aunty Gin says. Come on Lisa, you can help me too.'

The children bustled off importantly, happy to help Ginny and Granny Flo get them ready for departure. Ginny followed Barnaby up two flights of stairs into the attic bedroom that served as the older children's dormitory when they stayed with Petroc's mother. Lisa was deemed too young to manage the steep stairs, so she slept with Granny Flo, which the older children saw as her loss but which Lisa rather liked. She found something very comforting in knowing that Granny Flo was only a few feet away from her. The attic was light and airy as it had two skylights that looked over the roofs of Hugh Town towards the quay. Ginny went to have a look at the view while Barnaby gathered up pyjamas, knickers, socks and other discarded clothes from the floor of the bedroom. As Ginny looked out she saw a helicopter clatter over towards the airport. It wasn't the one that provided the scheduled twice-daily service between the island and Penzance, but Ginny's curiosity wasn't aroused. Helicopters were a common enough sight as they were one of the main forms of transport to and from the island. Ginny turned her attention away from the window and she trailed around after Barnaby picking up things that he missed – a couple of teddies, a hanky and some picture books – and stuffing them into the holdall, gaping open on one of the beds.

'Is that everything?' she asked once the room looked relatively clear.

'There's our toothbrushes in the bathroom,' he volunteered. 'And Lisa's stuff in Granny Flo's room.'

'Gosh! Well done you for remembering those,' said Ginny, who believed that young kids had to have loads of positive encouragement to give them the requisite amount of self-esteem. She had already made a mental note to check Granny Flo's bedroom and the bathroom but Barnaby wasn't to know that. Barnaby swelled with pride and led the way to the tiny, old-fashioned bathroom, where they found not only the toothbrushes, but also Flossie's hairbrush and two flannels. Then they went into the front bedroom and found Lisa's few things. As they returned downstairs, Ginny heard the helicopter whine overhead as it departed for the mainland. It hadn't hung around for long, she thought. Had it been dropping someone off or picking up?

Twenty minutes later they all left Granny Flo's. Ginny carried the holdall hefted on to her shoulder. Granny Flo pushed Lisa in her buggy and Flossie and Barnaby raced on up the road out of the town with Jack running behind, his stubby legs whirling as he yelled at them to slow down, a request that his elder siblings pointedly ignored as the gap between them grew. Behind them, from the west, the weather threatened further rain. Granny Flo and Ginny both noted the impending squall and hurried after the other children. As they followed the road as it swung slightly inland, or as far inland as it could go on an island that measures barely two miles by three, a man with a large holdall came into view from the opposite direction. He was wearing a belted raincoat and a baseball cap. Beneath his coat, visible between the open lapels, Ginny could see he was wearing a collar and tie. She was reminded of the men she'd seen hanging around the gates of the barracks when she had fled at the weekend. She thought about the recent helicopter and wondered if this man might have been a passenger – it was not inconceivable that he could have been, and the road they were on went past the airport. Feeling as though she was overreacting slightly to what was, after all, a vague hunch, Ginny pulled her scarf up until it was over her nose and swapped the holdall over to her other shoulder so that it came between her and the approaching stranger. Granny Flo threw her a faintly curious look but didn't say anything. The stranger passed, giving them a long look as he ambled down the road.

'So what was all that about?' asked Granny Flo when the man was out of earshot.

'What?' said Ginny, trying to appear casual.

'You didn't want that bloke to see you. Who was he?'

Granny Flo never ceased to amaze Ginny. She might be in her mid-seventies but nothing got past her. Her sharp blue eyes saw everything and her mind was still able to put two and two together faster than an accountant with a calculator.

'I don't know.'

Granny Flo halted and stared at Ginny with raised eyebrows, disbelief obvious.

'OK, I haven't a clue who he is but I just wondered if he might be a reporter. Someone recognized me today and I'm worried they may have tipped off the papers.'

'Who recognized you? A local?' Granny Flo was livid with the idea that an islander might betray one of her relations.

'I don't know who the hell it was. It was just someone I ran into at the hospital.'

'What, a nurse?'

'No, a bloke in a hurry.'

Ahead of them, Jack, still trying to catch his brother and sister, was tiring. He stumbled and then fell. Even against the wind from the west Granny Flo and Ginny could hear the roar. Ginny dropped the holdall, and ran up the road until she reached the small figure lying sprawled on the tarmac. She bent down and scooped up the little boy. Holding her nephew tightly in her arms she managed to haul up the leg of his jeans and take a look at his knee. It was red from the bang on the road but the skin was intact. There would be a bruise later but there was no real damage done.

'Ooh. Poor Jack. Aunty Ginny'll kiss it better.'

Ginny bent her head to his knee and Jack roared all the louder. Flossie and Barnaby returned down the road to investigate. Flossie looked at his knee.

'Don't be a baby, Jack. There isn't even a proper bruise,' she said witheringly.

'It looks very sore,' said Ginny firmly. Really, she thought, what a little madam Flossie was growing into. And so like her mother in many ways. Ginny could well remember the crushing put-downs Netta had delighted in scoring against her big sister.

216

She pitied Rose. If this was how she treated Jack, only four years her junior, Flossie was going to boss her littlest sister horribly. Just like Netta had bossed her. Ginny reckoned that there was a dominant bossy gene on that side of the family. She half wished she had it too. Despite ten years in the army, she was, sadly, sometimes lacking in assertiveness. Obviously this was not a trait that Flossie was going to be lumbered with. She gave Jack a sympathetic squeeze and he, aware that for once someone was sticking up for him, stopped bawling and smiled smugly at his aunt. Flossie, having been proved right that Jack's knee wasn't as sore as he had made out, gave Ginny a look that couldn't have said 'I told you so' more clearly if she'd had it tattooed across her young forehead, before continuing on her way up the road towards the farm.

Petroc was still out when the family thundered into the kitchen. Instantly Flossie made a beeline for her room to make sure everything was as she had left it. Barnaby embarked on raiding the cupboards and the fridge for crisps and milk, and Jack stomped off calling the names of the cats. Ginny felt that if the cats had any sense they would keep their heads well down. Lisa, seeing most of her nearest and dearest had abandoned her, put her arms up as a signal that she wanted out of her buggy. Granny Flo bustled about; she sorted out Lisa, put the kettle on to boil, peered in the fridge to check out the selection of vegetables, put on an apron and got out a chopping board and knife almost before Ginny had her coat off.

'Make yourself useful, me flower, and scrape these,' said Granny Flo, handing Ginny a couple of potatoes, a carrot and a swede. Ginny looked about the kitchen vaguely for the potato peeler. 'It's in the drawer by the sink,' said Granny Flo reading her mind.

Ginny got busy. She had just finished cleaning the veg when the phone went. She dabbed her hands on the front of her jeans and went over to the dresser where the phone lived.

'Hello,' she said. 'Pengelly Farm.'

'Can I speak to Ginny Turner please,' said a man's voice. A voice Ginny had never heard before.

Ginny caught her breath. Shit, she thought. 'I think you have the wrong number,' she said, praying her voice sounded

217

steady because she certainly didn't feel it. Granny Flo stopped chopping and looked across the kitchen at her.

'But you said Pengelly Farm,' accused the voice.

'I'm sorry, there's no one of that name here. Goodbye,' she said and slammed the receiver down.

'Who was that?' asked Granny Flo calmly.

'I don't know. Someone who knew I'm here but I didn't recognize the voice.'

Granny Flo raised her eyebrows. 'Ah,' she said. 'You think it might be the press.'

'Dunno. But if it was, how did they find me?'

'You said yourself you'd been recognized.'

'But that wouldn't have given them an address.'

'It's a small island, ducks. And it isn't as though there aren't a lot of grockles around at the moment. Someone is bound to know who Netta's sister is and that she has come to stay.'

'What am I going to do?'

'Sit tight and ignore them. That's my advice.'

Ginny was just considering Granny Flo's words of wisdom when the back door opened and in came Petroc. He greeted his mother, looked approvingly at the signs of the soup being prepared and then went to the door that led into the rest of the house and yelled, 'Kids. Dad's home.'

There was the sound of a small herd of large creatures approaching. It never ceased to amaze Ginny just how much noise four small children could make. Flossie erupted into the kitchen first with whoops of joy as if she had been away from her father for years, not just a couple of days. Jack managed to make it through the door just ahead of Barnaby who was still eating crisps, and Lisa toddled in last of all. One after the other they flung themselves at their father and despite the bedlam there was something about their arrival that reminded Ginny of the children forming up for Maria's inspection in *The Sound of Music*. A thought struck her that made her smile, despite her worries about the imminent arrival of the press on the doorstep. She wondered if Netta was going for seven so she could form her own musical troupe.

'Daddy, Ginny says Mummy may be coming out of hospital today. Can I go with you when you get her?' demanded Flossie once the excitement had died down.

218

'And me,' clamoured the others.

'We'll see,' said Petroc vaguely. 'There may not be room in the car for everyone.'

'I asked first,' said Flossie firmly, shooting a filthy look at her siblings.

The brewing row was interrupted by the phone ringing. Petroc grabbed it. He listened for a second then he held it out.

'It's for you,' he said to Ginny.

Gingerly, Ginny took it. 'Hello,' she said.

'Is that Ginny Turner?' asked the voice Ginny recognized from the earlier call.

'Sod off,' she yelled into the receiver and then slammed it back on its rests.

She turned back to the others, shaking slightly. 'I'm sorry Petroc. I shouldn't have sworn in front of the kids.'

'Who was it?' he asked, bemused.

'The press I think. I don't know how they've tracked me down but they have. If anyone else calls for me please don't tell them I'm here. The people that I need to speak to have my mobile number so they shouldn't call on your phone.'

'OK.' Petroc shrugged. 'But in a place this size if someone wants to find you they will.'

'It'll only be a five-minute wonder. In a couple of days there'll be some other story for them. I reckon I can keep my head down until then.'

'Well, I won't let them on the farm, that's for certain.'

The kids, realizing that their father was busy, began to drift off to do other things. As Jack toddled out of the kitchen he was crowing 'sod off, sod off', to the tune of 'Baa Baa Black Sheep'.

Alice was staring glumly at the paper. Sarah, sitting across the kitchen table from her, was at a loss for words. They had gone over and over the story, nit-picking every word, examining every detail, looking at every nuance, every double entendre, each smutty innuendo until Sarah was fed up with the whole thing. Not that she could say so. Alice needed her support and if this dissection was what Alice wanted to do, then so be it.

'It's so much worse than I thought it would be. It's all so . . .'

Alice stopped, searching for the right word. 'So seedy. And to think we're in the middle of it.' She looked up at Sarah. Sarah thought Alice looked as though she had aged a dozen years since the party at New Year. Her normally immaculate grooming had been neglected; her hair was lank and in need of a wash and looked flat and thin, and her skin, devoid of make-up, was pale and lined. There was even a mark down the front of her sweater. 'You know, you read of other people going through this sort of thing and it's just words on a page. Yes, I felt quite sorry for Hillary Clinton when that dreadful Monica Lewinsky was front-page news, but I had no idea about the awfulness of finding out that one's husband has been unfaithful and that the whole world knows and, what's more, knows all the grubby details. The reality is so ghastly. Sickening.'

Sarah nodded sympathetically. She couldn't imagine the turmoil and hurt that was besieging Alice.

'Have you heard from Bob?' she asked gently.

Alice nodded. 'He's phoned a couple of times. Last night to say he'd arrived safely at his brother's house and then this morning after he had seen the paper.'

'What did he think about it?'

Alice snorted. 'He was quite ashamed. As well he might be.' There was a catch in her voice and Sarah pushed the box of tissues towards her. Alice shook her head and straightened her shoulders, refusing to give in to more tears.

'And Megan?'

'She won't talk. She's shut herself in her room. She says she's been betrayed by the only two people in the world she loved.'

'You haven't done anything.' Sarah was angry with Megan for blaming her mother, who was as much of a victim as she was.

'She meant Ginny,' said Alice icily.

Oh God, thought Sarah. To have Megan make hurtful comments on top of everything else was appalling. Poor, poor, Alice.

'I knew their friendship was wrong. I knew I should have stopped it. I've always thought she was a bad influence, but no, Bob insisted that Megan would like to go to Alton Towers

220

and he wouldn't listen to me. I knew no good would come out of that trip, and it hasn't.' For a second Alice looked almost triumphant at having been proved right but then she seemed to collapse again. 'What I don't understand was why she did it.'

'What?' Sarah didn't follow Alice's train of thought.

'Why she felt she had to have Bob and Megan? They are my family, nothing to do with her, so why did she try to take both of them away from me? What was she trying to prove?'

'Do you think it was as deliberate as that?'

'I don't know.' She sounded almost defeated.

The phone rang. Sarah looked at Alice who nodded. Sarah went across and picked it up.

'Yes,' she said guardedly.

'Alice?' asked a woman's voice.

'No. Who's speaking?'

'It's Maddy.'

Sarah relaxed. 'Hi Maddy. It's Sarah here. Can I help you?'

'I wanted to speak to Alice. I feel I owe her an apology.'

'Hang on.' Sarah put her hand over the mouthpiece and relayed the message to Alice.

'Does she want to come round?' said Alice lifelessly.

'Do you want her to?'

'I can't stay a recluse forever.'

'OK,' Sarah told Maddy.

'I'll be round in a tick.'

Sarah replaced the receiver.

'Did she say why she needs to apologize?'

Sarah shook her head. 'No. I'll put the kettle on, shall I?'

Alice sighed. 'Tea. The British cure-all. The great panacea. Only it doesn't work.'

'No, I don't expect it does. Not for things like this.'

'No. It doesn't put a ruined marriage back together.'

'Is it as bad as that? Is it ruined?'

Alice looked up bleakly. 'I don't know. I don't know if I can forgive him. If I can ever trust him again. Was this the first time? What else will I find if I dig around? After all,' she gave a hollow laugh, 'he hardly volunteered this information, did he? He only came clean when he had no choice. I've got all these questions and doubts and I can't answer them. And worse, if I ask Bob, how can I be sure that I'm getting a truthful answer?'

The doorbell rang. 'That'll be Maddy,' said Sarah, stating the obvious. She went to answer it.

'Hello,' said Maddy loudly, then more quietly, 'How is she?'

'Hi,' Sarah said brightly. Then, 'How do you think?' sotto voce. 'Come in, the kettle's on.'

Sarah shepherded Maddy into the kitchen. Maddy looked uncomfortable and embarrassed.

'Hello, Maddy.'

'Alice, how are you?' She sounded genuinely concerned.

Alice looked at her somewhat coldly. 'As well as can be expected, under the circumstances.'

'Yes, sorry. Stupid question.'

Silence fell. On the work surface the kettle hissed and Sarah fussed around with mugs and milk. Maddy shifted awkwardly but Alice did not ask her to sit down.

'Look, Alice, I've come to apologize. I feel responsible for Taz. If I hadn't made friends with her, none of this would have happened.'

'You think so?'

Sarah passed them both a mug of tea. Maddy pulled a chair back and sat down, despite the lack of invitation. Alice didn't comment.

'I do. But I also want you to know that I had no idea she was a journalist.'

'Really?'

'Honest. Even when we saw a story by her in one of the papers we didn't twig that Taz and Tabitha Alabaster were the same person.'

Still Alice looked utterly sceptical.

'We didn't,' confirmed Sarah. 'In fact I discovered that Taz was short for Tabitha at your drinks party and I still didn't make the connection.'

Alice looked from one to the other as if trying to work out if this was some further conspiracy or if it was the truth. They both stared steadfastly at her, willing her to believe them. She dropped her gaze and looked at her mug.

'All right, I believe you.' She took a sip of tea. 'And it's not true.'

'What?' said Maddy and Sarah together, not following her.

'About none of this happening if you hadn't met Taz. Bob and Ginny happened, and Taz had nothing to do with that.'

'But no one would have known if it hadn't been for Taz,' protested Maddy.

'You knew,' shot back Alice. 'Ginny told you and then Taz, and after that who knows how many people she would have bragged to about her conquest if the papers hadn't got hold of it.'

That was true, thought Maddy. To confide in one friend was one thing, but two? She must have known the story was more likely to become common knowledge with the more people she told. Had she done it on purpose? Maddy began to wonder. Perhaps Ginny was more scheming than she had thought. Suddenly Maddy didn't feel quite so sympathetic to her friend as she had done.

'At least,' continued Alice bitterly, 'Taz brought it all out in the open. If it hadn't been for her, I might never have known what had happened.'

'Mightn't that have been better?' asked Sarah gently.

'I don't know.' She seemed close to tears again. 'You mean, what the eye doesn't see and all that?' She sniffed and blinked a few times. 'But it still doesn't mean that something didn't happen between them. We'd still have been living a lie. And as it is we're now living another one. Bob's telling everyone that nothing happened, hoping against hope that they won't be able to prove anything when of course a number of us know full well that it did. And I'm now wondering what else I don't know about. What other truths are hidden?'

'I suppose so,' said Sarah, who had in her time wondered about her own husband's fidelity when he'd been away and had long since decided that as long as she knew nothing she wouldn't get excited about the subject. She knew she was being an ostrich but the alternative seemed much worse.

Maddy finished her tea. 'I must be getting back,' she said. 'I've left Danielle with Caro and I said I wouldn't be long.'

'Does Caro know the reason for your visit?' asked Alice dully.

'You mean . . . ?'

'Yes.'

'Well, I suppose the whole patch knows what happened by now.' Maddy dodged a direct answer as she wasn't going to admit that she'd had a gossip session with Caro earlier that morning.

Alice sighed. 'It was only to be expected, wasn't it?'

Sarah forbore saying that she was surprised it hadn't been round the barracks the day before. She showed Maddy out then returned to the kitchen.

'Do you want to get off home to your kids too?' asked Alice.

'They're both old enough and ugly enough to fend for themselves. They don't need me, you do.'

Alice nodded. 'Thanks. I appreciate your support.'

'It's OK. What about lunch for you and Megan?'

'I'm not hungry.'

'How about if I scramble some eggs?'

'I don't want to put you to any trouble.'

'Alice, it's no bother. I'll do some for Megan too.'

'She won't come down.'

'Then I'll take lunch upstairs to her.'

'I don't really like food upstairs.'

Now, why didn't that surprise Sarah? But whatever Alice felt about things normally, now wasn't the moment for her to insist on her exacting standards. 'Don't you think that just for today it's important that she eats something and that it doesn't really matter where she eats it? Circumstances are hardly normal, are they?'

Alice nodded.

The phone rang and Sarah answered it again. It was Bob.

'Sarah, I don't know how Alice is going to take this but the military police want to come and search the house for evidence.'

'What? What on earth for?'

'I don't know. But they're on their way and because it's military property there's nothing we can do to stop it. Can you warn Alice?'

'Yes, I suppose so.'

Sarah put the receiver down. 'Alice, I'm sorry, that was Bob. The military police want to have a look around.'

'Well, they can't,' said Alice flatly. 'This is my home and I shan't let them in.'

Sarah explained what Bob had told her. Just as she finished, the doorbell rang. The two women stared at each other for a moment then Alice shut her eyes as if by doing so she could blot out the increasing horror of what was happening.

'You let them in,' said Alice. 'I must tell Megan.' Wearily she got up from the table and made her way up to see her daughter.

Sarah went to the door. On the doorstep were a middle-aged man in a suit and a warrant officer in uniform. Irrationally, Sarah thought that the man in the suit bore an uncanny likeness to John Thaw's Inspector Morse.

'Mrs Davies?' said the TV lookalike.

'No, I'm Sarah Milne, a neighbour.'

'Colonel Milne's wife?'

Sarah was just about to correct him that her husband was only a major but then she remembered that her husband had been given acting rank in order to take over from Colonel Bob. 'Yes, yes I am. And yes, he phoned to tell me you were on your way. Mrs Davies is upstairs telling her daughter you want to search the house.'

Morse/Thaw shuffled a little awkwardly. 'I think it would be better if we spoke indoors.'

'Yes, of course.'

Sarah stood back to allow them to pass. As they entered the hall, Megan and Alice were coming down the stairs. The man in civvies and his sidekick introduced themselves to Alice as Major Griggs and Mr Watson. There didn't seem much point in introducing Alice to them – they obviously knew who she was – and Megan made it perfectly plain she wanted nothing to do with them. She gave them both a filthy look and then stormed off into the kitchen.

'I'm sorry about this, Mrs Davies, but we need to see if there is any evidence of what your husband has done,' said the major.

'I very much doubt there is,' she said coldly and formally.

'The alleged affair, according to that dreadful scandal sheet, took place in Kosovo. I suggest if you want evidence that you look out there.'

'There is a possibility that they had a liaison here too.'

Alice looked horrified at the suggestion. 'Don't be ridiculous,' she snapped. 'Anyway, there was no affair and there certainly wasn't one here.'

Both men had the decency to look shamefaced.

Sarah couldn't help but admire Alice's cool, but she didn't think Alice would be able to maintain it indefinitely. 'I don't know if it's possible, but would it be all right for Mrs Davies and her daughter to wait in my house while you conduct the search? I really don't think either of them wants to witness it.' She looked at Alice for confirmation. Alice nodded with a look of relief on her face that she didn't have to watch two strange men rummaging through her personal possessions. Sarah continued, 'I'll be happy to escort you round the house. If you gentlemen would like to wait here, I'll just take Mrs Davies and her daughter over to my house and when I return you'll be able to make a start.'

Alice and Sarah made their way into the kitchen to join Megan and to explain to her what was going on. She was standing by the sink staring out of the window, her hands resting on the work surface.

'Sarah has said we can go round to her house while the police are here,' said Alice.

Megan didn't turn round. 'Oh, goody,' she said, sarcasm dripping from every syllable.

'There's no need to be like that,' chided Alice.

'Like what?' shrilled Megan, spinning round to face her mother. 'Dad's about to be thrown out of the army, my best friend has told the papers that she screwed him and consequently completely screwed my life too, and the police are about to paw through all my things. What the hell do you expect me to be like?' She was white and shaking with anger. She turned away from them again and stormed towards the back door. Sarah and Alice followed silently.

Megan was waiting for the two women by Sarah's front door.

'Have you rung the doorbell?' asked Sarah, ignoring the earlier outburst.

'No. I didn't know if Jen and Will were up.'

'Doubt it. It's only just lunchtime.' Sarah opened the door and showed Megan and Alice into her sitting room. It was clean but hardly tidy with the previous day's paper strewn across the coffee table, the cushions flat and squashed, two dirty coffee cups on the mantlepiece and the curtains only half drawn. With a practised hand, Sarah swept up the paper and tucked it under her arm, plumped and straightened the cushions, grabbed the cups and pushed the curtains fully open. In about thirty seconds she had transformed the room.

'Sit down,' she suggested. 'I'll bring you a cup of tea each and then I think I'd better get back to Montgomery House. I'm sorry about lunch. If Jen or Will make an appearance get them to rustle something up. They're perfectly capable when I'm not around. Otherwise I'll do something when I get back. It can't take too long.' But even as she said this Sarah knew she was kidding everyone. Two men, searching an entire house for slivers of evidence – letters, mementoes, keepsakes – it would take an age.

She left Alice and Megan sitting in silence, then whizzed into the kitchen to put the kettle on and then belted upstairs to Jen's room. Will might have been the elder but Jen was the more sensible.

'Jen,' she said as she pushed her daughter's door open. A scene of total chaos hit her – make-up littered the dressing table, cotton buds were spilled on the floor, dirty clothes were left lying where they fell, magazines and hangers were higgledy-piggledy on the bedside rug. There were CDs out of their boxes by the hi-fi, bits of school work on the desk and, incongruously, a large cardboard cut-out of David Beckham in the middle of it all. Sarah wondered where the hell that had sprung from. She was sure it hadn't been there the day before. She ignored the mess and the cut-out and said 'Jen,' again, more sharply.

'Uh.'

'Jen, wake up.'

'Wassamarra?'

'I need you to get up.'

227

'Uh.'

The conversation seemed to be going round in circles. Sarah picked her way through the obstacle course on the carpet to the curtains and drew them back.

'Whatdaya wannado that for?' slurred Jen, woozy from sleep.

'Wake up,' ordered Sarah. Jen opened her eyes and then screwed them tight against the light. 'I've got Alice and Megan downstairs. I'm going to make them a cup of tea and then I have to go out again. I want you to get dressed and go down and make them some lunch – eggs or something – understand?'

'Now?'

'Of course now. It's lunchtime.'

'Where have you got to go?'

'Out.' Everything was too complicated to go into details. And besides, in Jen's sleep-befuddled state she wasn't likely to take anything in. 'Come on, get up.' Sarah hurtled downstairs again into the kitchen just in time to hear the kettle click off. She made two mugs of strong tea, sloshed milk in both, put them and a sugar basin on a tray and carried it through into the sitting room.

'I put milk in both but I wasn't sure if you took sugar, Megan.' She wasn't going to start apologizing for the lack of a Georgian silver tea set or bone china cups. In her house it was like it or lump it. 'Jen will be down in a minute to look after you,' she added. 'Right, I'll go back and make sure the military police are behaving themselves.' Alice gave her a bleak smile but Megan looked stonily at the carpet. 'Right, till later then.' Sarah left them, almost glad to escape, although she didn't think things would be much more comfortable back at Alice's place.

When she walked through the front door of Montgomery House, the two policemen were where she had left them. When she had told them to 'stay there', she hadn't expected them to obey her like a couple of gun dogs. She'd thought they would have had the nous to find a place to sit at the very least.

'OK then,' she said. 'Where do you want to start?'

Ginny, Granny Flo, the children and Petroc were sitting down for lunch when Ginny's mobile rang. At the first bar of 'British Grenadiers' she leapt up to answer it. Grabbing it from her bag she offered the family an apologetic grin and then retired to the sitting room to talk. She knew that, realistically, it was probably either a close friend or someone from the barracks trying to get in touch with her. In either case it probably wasn't a conversation she wanted to have in public.

It was Richard. 'The military police have to search your room,' he announced after a few quick pleasantries.

'Why?'

'Who knows?' said Richard wearily. 'There's a couple of them turning over Montgomery House. I suppose they want to find proof.'

'What on earth for? I've hardly denied anything, have I?'

'I think that if there's going to be any disciplinary action, they're going to need it.'

'Oh.' Ginny felt quite shaken at that piece of news. Disciplinary action implied a court martial and all the dreadful things that went with it. 'Oh, I see.'

'They have asked for another woman to be present while they go through your things. I thought I ought to ask if there is someone you would prefer.'

Ginny rolled her eyes. This was getting worse and worse. 'Would Maddy do it?'

'I think it has to be someone military.' Richard didn't tell her that he'd already approached Maddy and she'd refused point-blank. After the initial shock of the revelation in the press and the subsequent repercussions, feelings had become more focused and Alice, the innocent victim, was getting all the sympathy with none at all left for Ginny.

'Oh.' What would be worse? Someone she worked with, or one of the female soldiers she barely knew? She didn't know. She didn't care. 'Anyone, Richard. It doesn't matter. Find someone who can be spared.'

'OK.'

'So how are things in the regiment?' She tried to sound bright, as though she was making a general, conversational inquiry.

But Richard's reply was shot from the hip. 'Pretty grim. The troops are a bit shocked about it all, half of them are

229

wandering around as if they're lost sheep and the other half are too busy chewing the fat to be any use. Poor old Alisdair has been dropped right in it and is desperately trying to pull everything and everyone together, and it doesn't help matters any that we haven't got an admin officer either.'

Poor Richard, thought Ginny, he sounded as if he was having a tough time too. 'It doesn't sound a bundle of laughs,' she said guiltily.

'It can't be any better for you.'

'Yeah, but I've got no one to blame but myself.'

'That's not strictly true, is it?'

'It's very sweet of you to say so but I'm a big girl now. I'm as responsible for this horrid state of affairs as anyone.'

'Look, I'd better go. It's pretty busy here. I'll talk to you again soon. Bye.'

'Bye,' said Ginny, but she thought the line was cut before she had got the word out. It sounded to her as if someone had interrupted Richard and he hadn't wanted to have to admit to talking to her. Well, she thought, so this is what it's like to be a persona non grata. She returned to the lunch table and tried to put her worries about possible disciplinary action out of her head, but every time there was a lull in the conversation she couldn't help letting her thoughts slip back to the news of the military police's involvement in the affair.

Granny Flo returned to her own house in the afternoon and Ginny was left in sole charge of the four children. Outside, the weather had taken a turn for the worse; the showers had banded themselves together to form a steady downpour, the temperature had dropped and although the wind was no longer as strong or as gusty, it was still very blowy. All in all, it was a miserable January afternoon. Before Petroc had returned outside to carry on with whatever jobs needed doing on his land, he had lit a roaring fire in the sitting room. Ginny had found the cupboard containing a great pile of kids' games and was now teaching them all how to play Mousetrap. She had fallen on it with great glee having remembered it from her own childhood. In fact, as she looked at the box, she was convinced that it was the very game that had been given to her on her tenth birthday, and when she examined the pieces she was sure, as the little white mouse was missing its tail –

just like the white mouse in her game had done. Typical of Netta to snaffle it from the family home when Ginny's back was turned, without even asking her, she thought. But then, what would she have done with it? It was hardly the sort of thing she would have dragged around the world with her for the past ten years.

'Your mummy and I used to play this when we were little girls,' she told her charges.

'Did you?' said Flossie. 'And did you argue over things like Barnaby and I do?'

'Probably,' acknowledged Ginny. Actually they had fought like cats and on one occasion their father had been so incensed that a game designed to be fun had caused such discord that he had confiscated it and forbidden them to play it for weeks. Ginny just hoped things didn't degenerate to such an extent this time. 'Come on then,' she said, lifting the lid off the box. 'You and Barnaby will have to play on your own. I shall help Lisa and Jack.'

Ginny and the children settled themselves on the big rug in front of the fire with the board and the plastic components of the giant Heath Robinson mousetrap. The rain splattered against the little cottage windows and the wind whistled round the corner of the house but they were quite content and warm in the low-ceilinged room with its cheerful chintz curtains and covers and its rough plaster walls that had been standing for generations. The flames from the fire made the shadows dance and weave on the walls and the glow of the lamps made the room seem warmer still.

Lisa leaned against Ginny, happy to let her throw the dice and move her little plastic mouse. Jack was much more independent, although he needed help when it came to assembling his bit of the trap. Needless to say, Flossie directed him as to exactly how he should do it. After they had been playing for a while, and despite the chatter and occasional squeal or shout, Ginny realized that Lisa had fallen asleep. She picked her up and laid her on the sofa, wedging her with cushions so she couldn't roll off. She was a picture of contentment with her eyes shut tight, her fat little thumb crammed into her mouth and a half smile on her face as if she were dreaming about something agreeable. Ginny returned to the game, more than

231

happy to play on her own behalf instead of Lisa's. She'd forgotten how much fun board games could be.

There was a sharp rapping on the front door. Ginny sighed and excused herself to the children. 'I won't be a minute. Don't throw the dice till I get back, Barnaby, and don't touch anything, Flossie. That way there can be no arguments.' There had been a couple already but nothing major, but Ginny didn't trust Barnaby and Flossie not to have a good set-to if she wasn't there to referee. She uncurled her legs from under her and staggered to her feet. 'God, I'm too old to sit on the floor,' she muttered under her breath as her muscles twanged painfully. She tottered across to the sitting-room door. As she opened it she was struck by a cold draught. She shivered and glanced longingly back at the roaring fire before she shut it again behind her, isolating herself from the warmth of the room, but there was no point in letting the heat out. She opened the front door.

'Hello,' said the wild-haired man from the hospital.

Ginny stared at him and then went to slam the door again. But the man was too quick for her and got his foot in the way before she could get it closed.

'Ow,' he hollered as she leant her whole weight on the door.

'Get out,' she hissed at him.

'I can't. My foot's trapped.'

Ginny eased fractionally with the idea that he would withdraw his foot but instead he shouldered the door and got half his body through it.

'Go away,' she snarled.

'Ginny, listen to me.'

'No.' She heaved against the door.

'Why won't you talk to me?'

'Because the last time I talked to you, you told the press where I was.' Her voice came out almost as a series of grunts as she put all her effort into trying to evict her visitor and shut the door.

There was a guffaw from the man. 'Press! Press? What do you mean I told the press?'

'Of course you bloody did, now bugger off.'

'Wait till I tell Petroc that one.'

232

Ginny relaxed slightly at the mention of her brother-in-law's name, but she still kept her weight pressed firmly against the door. 'You know Petroc?'

'Course I do. We went to school together.'

'Prove it.'

'What?'

'Prove it.'

'Now?'

'If you want to talk to me, yes.'

'How?'

'How should I know? It's your problem not mine.'

'His mum's called Flo.'

'Not good enough. Anyone could have told you that.'

'His wife is Netta, his kids are Flossie, Barnaby, Jack and Lisa.'

'And?'

'And what?'

'If you're such a good friend of Petroc's you'd know what I meant.' Ginny gave the door another shove and was gratified to hear a gasp of pain from the stranger.

'You mean she's had the baby?'

Ginny relaxed again but the door didn't move.

'Hey, that's great. I didn't know.'

If this guy wasn't a friend then he was a remarkable actor who knew a lot about the family, thought Ginny. Which didn't necessarily mean he hadn't gone to the press but it did make it rather less likely. She took her weight off the door. The wild-haired man half fell sideways through it at the sudden release. He regained his balance and rubbed his shoulder and his hip, then he flexed his foot and winced.

'Sorry,' said Ginny, not sounding sorry at all.

'Yeah, well. Christ, you're strong for a woman. What do you do for a living? Kick-start jumbos?'

'I beg your pardon?' She stared at him stonily.

He breathed out heavily. 'My turn to apologize. That was rude.'

'Hmm.' What was it with this man that he had to be so horrible? It was the second time that day she had found his manners obnoxious. She wasn't sure she was inclined to accept his contrition.

233

'I'm just feeling a bit battered and I'm not at my best when I'm in pain.'

Ginny couldn't feel any sympathy for him. He'd put his foot in the door when all was said and done. Flossie appeared, intrigued by the odd noises coming from the hall and curious about what was delaying Ginny.

'Oh, hi Uncle Chris,' she said.

'Uncle Chris?' queried Ginny.

'I told you, I've known Petroc all my life and so of course the kids know me.'

'Are you coming to play Mousetrap with us?' asked Flossie.

'I hadn't planned on it, but if you'd like me to . . .'

'I'm sure Uncle Chris is far too busy to stay for games,' said Ginny firmly.

'Oh no I'm not,' said Chris, equally firmly. 'And Mousetrap is one of my favourites.' He shot Ginny a look of triumph.

'Great,' said Flossie, grabbing his hand and dragging him into the sitting room where he was greeted with yelps of delight from Barnaby and Jack. Lisa slept on.

The game continued. The kids didn't notice the tension between Ginny and Chris or that they didn't exchange a word except for things like, 'Pass me the dice, please,' or 'Help Jack to move his mouse.' As far as they were concerned the grown-ups were having just as much fun as they were. But Ginny was just going through the motions and all the time she was longing for the game to finish so she could get shot of this rude, self-assured man. She hadn't wanted him here, she hadn't invited him, she didn't trust him, and hell, she didn't even like him. The sooner he went, the better, as far as she was concerned, even if he was Petroc's bosom buddy.

It was getting dark before the children tired of playing Mousetrap and decided they would rather watch television. They gathered round the set, Flossie naturally calling the shots as she had the remote, while Ginny tidied the game away and then finally woke Lisa who blearily stumbled off the sofa and went to join her siblings, still with her thumb plugged firmly into her mouth.

'She won't sleep tonight,' said Chris.

'And you are the great expert,' said Ginny.

'No, but I know that Netta doesn't like her to sleep too long in the afternoon otherwise she's awake half the night.'

'So why the hell didn't you tell me?'

'You didn't ask.'

Ginny sighed angrily and stomped off to the kitchen. Chris followed. She hadn't wanted him to do that. She'd hoped he would get the hint and just bugger off. Ginny thumped the big kettle on to the hotplate and opened the door of the big freezer. She thought she could probably cope with fish fingers, chips and beans for the children's supper but she wanted to make sure she had everything before she made rash promises to them. If Petroc was going into Hugh Town to fetch Netta, he could always collect any shopping required at the same time.

'Are you making tea?' he asked hopefully as Ginny, having found what she wanted, slammed the freezer door shut and then went to the cupboard where the mugs were kept.

Ginny didn't reply but she took down two mugs and the teapot. Obviously she wasn't going to get rid of him that easily.

'Anyway,' said Chris, unperturbed by Ginny's chilly attitude, 'you are probably wondering what I am doing here?'

'Not really,' said Ginny leaning against the warm rail at the front of the Aga.

'I just wanted to say sorry for being so odd at the hospital this morning.'

'I didn't realize that you were behaving oddly. I thought bad manners must have just come naturally.'

'Ouch.'

Ginny didn't care. Why should she? She had enough problems of her own without worrying about the sensibilities of a man who didn't seem to care about other people's.

'Look, I'm eating humble pie here.'

Ginny hoped it would choke him. 'So what do you want, a round of applause?'

'No, just a cup of tea actually.'

Ginny turned away as she felt dangerously close to smiling. This man was incorrigible.

'I'm really sorry though that I was so odd. It's just you caught me completely off my guard. I was taking in someone who had cut himself badly with a kitchen knife and I was worried about him and not really thinking.'

'So?'

'It's just you look so like Netta.'

'So I'm told.'

'Only you weren't pregnant.'

'Ten out of ten for observation then.'

'But apparently, as Netta has now had the baby, neither is she, although I didn't know that this morning.'

'Perhaps you had better get on to whoever runs the bush telegraph.' Ginny paused as she thought about what Chris had told her and about their encounter at the hospital. Then she said. 'So when you said, "I know exactly who you are", you recognized me as Netta's sister and not the person on the front page of the *Mercury*?'

'You? Front page of a national? Yeah, right.' It was Chris's turn to be disbelieving.

Ginny pulled that day's copy of the *Mercury* off the dresser shelf and showed him. Chris looked at the picture, looked at Ginny, gave a long low whistle and read the story. As he did so, Ginny made two cups of tea and got the milk from the fridge. She pushed one of the mugs across the table to Chris, together with the sugar basin and a spoon, then she got three more mugs and a baby beaker, filled them with milk and arranged them on a tray, tipped some biscuits from a packet on to a plate and carried the lot through to the sitting room. When she returned Chris had finished reading.

'So no wonder you're a bit paranoid about the press,' he said. 'Is it true?'

'If you want to know if it's true that Colonel Bob and I had a brief affair in Kosovo, yes it is. Most of the rest is pretty much lies.'

'Which is why you've escaped here to Netta's. I can't think of a better place to be than with Netta and her family.' He sounded terribly sympathetic.

'Yup, that's what I thought. I hoped I would be able to lie low until another story came along but I think someone has tipped off the press. I had a couple of calls today from a strange man.'

'Not me, honest.'

'No, it wasn't your voice.'

'Hallelujah!'

236

Ginny raised her eyebrows. 'Which means?'

'You believe something I've said!' This time Ginny allowed the smile to escape. 'You're even more like Netta when you smile, did you know that?'

'Actually, Netta's like me when she smiles.'

Chris took a sip of his tea. 'Do I take it from that that you are the elder?'

'That's right.'

The back door burst open and the gust of freezing wind that shot into the kitchen seemed to carry Petroc with it.

'Oh, great girl Ginny. Pour us a cup,' he said seeing the pot on the table. 'Hi, Chris. I see you and Ginny have met. Any news about Netta?' As he said all this he stripped off his boots and waterproofs. He went over to the Aga to warm himself.

'No, she hasn't called yet,' said Ginny. 'I hope it doesn't mean there's a problem.'

'I'll ring. Are the kids OK?'

'They're next door watching TV.' Ginny poured Petroc a cup of tea and passed it to him. 'We tired them out with a marathon game of Mousetrap.'

'Except for Lisa,' Chris reminded her.

'Yeah, sorry, she slept through it.'

'Great,' said Petroc with a grimace. 'Never mind though. With a new baby coming home I don't suppose there'll be many unbroken nights for a bit.'

The phone rang. Ginny started and Petroc and Chris both looked at her, understanding the reason for her reaction.

'If it's for me, I'm not here. Say I've returned to the mainland, anything, I don't care.'

But it was Netta with news that she'd been passed fit to go home. 'I'll go and get her,' said Petroc, draining his tea. 'Do you want a lift back?' he asked Chris.

'Would you mind if I waited here? I'd like to see the new addition and I'll walk back later. Is that OK with you too?' he asked Ginny.

'I don't mind.' She was surprised and a little flattered at being consulted.

Petroc pulled on his waterproofs before setting off again. After he had left, Ginny directed Chris to make sure the fire in the sitting room was still OK and the guard was properly in place while she went around the house pulling the curtains and snuggling the building down against the vile weather outside. The lowering clouds had killed any last vestiges of light from the setting sun and it was now pitch black despite the fact that it was barely five o'clock. What a day to bring a baby home, thought Ginny as she returned to the warmth of the kitchen.

Chris was sitting at the table when she returned. 'The kids asked for a video. I put *Cinderella* on for them – Flossie's suggestion – is that all right do you think?'

'Why ask me? If it's what they wanted, why not?'

'I just wondered if Petroc and Netta have any views on them watching telly for more than a set number of hours each day.'

Ginny guffawed. 'I don't think Netta has totally signed up to the anything-for-a-quiet-life school of motherhood, but she comes pretty close to it sometimes. Frankly, if *Cinderella* is going to keep the little darlings happy for a while so I can get on with their supper, then who's to worry?'

At that point Flossie banged into the kitchen dragging Lisa behind her.

'Lisa needs the loo,' she said, letting go of Lisa's hand and dashing back into the sitting room before there could be the least suggestion that she might do something about it. Ginny took Lisa upstairs to the bathroom and helped the toddler with the tricky business of her trousers and pants before lifting her on to the loo. She sat on the edge of the bath and waited patiently for Lisa to finish, which seemed to take an age. Finally they were free to return.

Chris was cracking eggs into a bowl.

Ginny stood by the door, her eyebrows raised and said, 'Hungry?'

'No, but the children are.'

'And I was just about to make them fish fingers, chips and beans.'

'But you haven't, so I thought I'd make them cheese and tomato omelettes with a salad and brown bread and butter which is a healthier option.'

'Oh, puh-lease,' said Ginny. 'Anyway, they probably won't eat it.'

'Yes they will.'

'How do you know?'

'Because I've cooked it for them before.'

Ginny rolled her eyes. 'What, a man cooking? Come off it. What's your real reason for putting on a pinny?'

'What, you think I'm cooking just to try to impress you, is that it?' He gave her a steady look as if to dare her to challenge the implication.

Ginny felt unaccountably flustered. 'Yes. No. I don't know.' She regained her composure. 'All right, what are your motives then?' she demanded.

Chris went on whisking the eggs in the bowl. 'You're in the army, right?'

'So?'

'You fire guns but you don't do it to pull the blokes, to impress them or anything.'

'No, it's my job – sometimes. I still don't get your point.'

'Cooking – it's what I do.'

'Ah, so Chris isn't your real name. What is it then – Jamie, Gary, Ainsley?'

Chris gave her a withering look and began to chop some tomatoes. Although Ginny would not admit it she was suitably impressed by the way his knife reduced the round red fruits into a pile of tiny chunks in seconds.

'No, I'm not a TV chef; I run a hotel in the town. Like most people here I support my family through the tourist industry. OK?' As he said this he gave her a look which defied her to make fun of it.

'Oh.' Ginny felt a little foolish. She remembered him talking about the reason for his trip to the hospital – an accident with a kitchen knife. She should have made the connection earlier. In the ensuing, rather chilly silence, she noticed that she felt a small sense of disappointment that yet another man whose acquaintance she had made came complete with a ready-made family in tow – which made him unavailable. Not that she wanted him to be available, as she didn't find him at all attractive. Not in the least, she told herself firmly. Not one jot.

Chris got out a pan and put it on the Aga. He melted some butter and then tipped the eggs into it. Ginny watched him work and wondered how long it took to become such an expert, as he

239

obviously was. He moved the eggs around in the pan until they began to set then he tipped in some of the chopped tomatoes and cheese and flipped the omelette over so it folded in half. When it was done he slid it out of the pan and on to a plate which he put in the Aga to keep warm. Then he began the process again.

'Look, rather than watch me, would you grate some more cheese?' he asked.

Ginny nodded and went to the fridge for a lump of cheddar. She found a board and a grater and set to work. The silence changed from cool to companionable. Chris carried on making omelettes and then, when they were all done and keeping warm in the oven, he whizzed up a salad.

'Call the kids for me,' he said.

Ginny went into the sitting room and told the children to come through.

'What's for supper?' demanded Flossie.

'Omelettes,' said Ginny.

'Ooh, goody,' said Barnaby. 'Did Uncle Chris make them?'

Ginny nodded and had to move out of the way to avoid the stampede of small people all racing to get to the table first. Ginny watched Chris lift Lisa into her high chair and serve the children their food. She wondered if he treated his own family with the same care that he seemed to lavish so effortlessly on Netta's brood, but if he did, why was he up in Netta's kitchen and not back at home with his own?

Jen was sitting in Megan's room, flicking through a copy of *Cosmo*. As soon as Sarah had got back from Montgomery House she had dropped a heavy hint to Jen that it might be a good idea if she and Megan made themselves scarce so the two mothers could talk. Will had gone out to see a friend, and it wasn't that Sarah cared if Jen overheard anything – she was old enough to be discreet and she wasn't directly affected – but she felt it was unfair on Megan. Jen had instantly picked up the unspoken suggestion and, with a quickness of wit honed by years of having to find excuses for being terminally disorganized at school and rarely being able to hand her homework in on time, she had told Megan her CD player was at school and she wanted to listen to a new album she'd got for Christmas.

'I don't suppose you've got a stereo we could use?' she had asked innocently.

'There's one in my room. We could go back to my place if that's OK with you?'

Sarah had given Jen a broad smile and told her not to hurry back. As Megan had left the room, Jen mouthed at her mother that she owed her one. She liked Megan well enough, but she was three years younger for heaven's sake, and she really hadn't fancied spending the dying remnants of the afternoon in her company.

Still, it had come as a pleasant surprise that Megan had a copy of the latest *Cosmo* and now Jen was slouched in the rocking chair, half looking at the pictures of the hottest styles in accessories and half listening to Megan, who was lying on her bed, feet at the pillow end, telling her in detail about her school. In the background, Jen's Travis album was playing.

'And I swear that Mum chose it because she has a complete thing about pink and the headmistress is called Miss Pink.'

'Miss Pink? Is that her real name?' Jen turned another page.

'Has to be. The old bag hasn't the imagination to change it.'

Jen looked around Megan's room. 'Your room's not so bad, pink's all right. At least your mum does it up. Mine just takes what we're given. She thinks that by putting a few pictures up on the walls and shoving the ornaments on the mantelpiece it's going to look like home, but it never does. It just looks like another gross army quarter.'

'Yeah, but your mum doesn't mind mess.'

'You mean we live in a tip,' said Jen dryly.

Megan flushed with embarrassment. 'No, I didn't mean that at all. Your house is great, it's comfortable. It looks lived in.'

'And so does a pigsty.'

Megan laughed. 'You may not like your place, but try living with my mother. I bet you'd soon change your mind then. I can't even sit on the sofa without her twitching the cushions straight. Every meal we have has to be at the table with napkins and place mats and crap like that. I bet you're allowed to eat on trays and watch TV.'

241

'You mean, you don't?'

'See!'

Jen whistled to express her disbelief. 'It sounds as bad as boarding school.'

'Yeah, and on Thursday I'm back there. I swap this place for school, great.'

'I quite like school,' said Jen.

'I *did*.'

'So what's changed?' Even as Jen said that, she knew she'd put her foot in it. 'Oh, God, I'm sorry. Of course.'

Megan turned away and shrugged. 'It's not your fault,' she mumbled.

'You think it'll be bad when you go back?'

'Dunno. The girls I like, my friends, they'll be all right but there are some right stuck-up cows there.'

'Yeah, we've got ones like that too. But they won't read a rag like the *Mercury*, will they?'

'But they'll all know about it. They may not read the *Mercury*, but they'll have *heard*, won't they?'

'Yeah,' said Jen. She shut the magazine up and tossed it on to the floor, creating a small island of mess in the perfect room. 'So what do you think'll be the worst; the ones who blank you or the ones who act all concerned but aren't?'

'It'll all be gross. And the teachers'll be awful.' She put on a silly voice. '*Megan, you know you can always talk to me if you need to.* Huh! They just want to pry when they say that. They don't care at all, skanky lot. I expect they're already laying bets as to what is going to happen to him.'

'What do you think that'll be?'

'I overheard Mum talking to your mum. They were talking about a court martial.'

'Gross.'

'And if he gets found guilty of misconduct your mum thought it might mean he has to resign.'

'Shit,' said Jen.

'I know. And if Dad's out of a job, what will happen to us?'

'He'll find something else,' said Jen with a confidence that was entirely false.

Megan didn't answer her; she just stared at her with an expression of utter disbelief until Jen dropped her eyes.

'The thing that worries me though . . .' said Megan. She stopped, diffident about voicing her concerns.

'Yes?'

'Well, what if Mum and Dad split up?'

'You think they might?'

'Dunno.'

'But they've been married for ages.'

'Yeah, but it's a pretty awful thing Dad's done, isn't it?' There was another silence as both girls thought about the implications of Bob's actions.

'I hope Ginny loses her job too,' said Megan angrily.

'At least she's been sacked from the regiment, so you don't have to see her.'

'The cow.'

'But you liked her.'

'Two-faced bitch. I reckon she was only nice to me to get at my dad. She used me. Can you believe it?' The pain and bitterness that she felt was evident in her voice. Jen thought she sounded close to tears. She hoped Megan wasn't going to break down. She wasn't sure she could handle it.

Megan sighed heavily again and blinked rapidly a couple of times. She got herself under control. 'I just can't believe my dad did that, went with her like that.'

'No.'

Megan looked at Jen. 'Do you think your dad's ever done anything like that?'

'I don't reckon. I mean, I love him and all that but I can't imagine him being able to pull a bird. He's hardly a looker is he? Ugh, think about it, it's gross.'

Megan giggled at the thought of Alisdair trying to pull a woman. 'But look at my dad, he's old. I can't imagine why Ginny fancied him.'

Jen didn't say that she thought Megan's dad was lush. She understood exactly why Ginny had gone with him if the story in the press was to be believed. She was old enough to know not to believe everything she read in the papers, but equally she knew about there being no smoke without fire.

'Did they find anything?' Alice asked Sarah tonelessly when they had settled down in her sitting room with a cup of tea.

243

'I don't think so. They've taken away a whole load of papers from the study, bank statements and the like.'

'I suppose they're looking for evidence of hotel rooms.' Sarah wasn't sure what to say.

'Oh don't worry,' said Alice. 'I don't think Bob and Ginny got up to those sort of shenanigans. I mean, when? Until they went to Kosovo he didn't have to go away overnight at all. Besides which, what was the point when they knew they would have six whole months with me well out of the way?'

'But it wasn't like that. It wasn't planned, was it? And it was only very brief.'

'Bob says so, but can I trust him? For all I know they were at it like rabbits for the whole time they were there.'

'For what it's worth, Alisdair thinks Bob is telling the truth.'

Alice bit her thumbnail. 'Which begs the question, if it was such a meaningless affair, why did it happen at all? That's the thing I want to know.' She sounded cold and bitter. 'Why did Bob take such an enormous risk with our marriage, his career, everything for a few rolls in the hay with that woman? I can't believe he was so foolish. It doesn't make sense.'

'Isn't it a throwback to the hunter-gatherer instinct? The thrill of the chase and all that? That men can't resist going after things, especially things that involve an element of danger.'

'I'm rather hoping *she* went after *him*,' said Alice tartly.

'Yes.' Sarah could understand that sentiment. It was easier to bear. Both women sipped their tea contemplatively. 'Have you made up your mind what you're going to do?' asked Sarah.

'You mean, am I going to leave him?'

Sarah shrugged. It was one of the matters that needed addressing.

'I don't know. I've got to stick by him publicly until the investigation is over – you know, like politicians' wives. If I go now I'll just confirm things, which will hardly help him. And if he gets sacked then life will be awful for all of us whether I'm with him or not. But part of me feels like I want to punish him. What he's done is terrible. It's not just the infidelity. I think I could cope with that if that was all it was. No, it's the shame and the publicity. That's what I find so hard to forgive.'

'To err is human, to forgive is divine,' murmured Sarah almost without realizing she had voiced the thought out loud.

'You think I should forgive him?' said Alice sharply.

'I don't know. I don't feel in a position to comment.'

'No. The thing is, part of me feels that I'm also to blame. That because I don't do things like Ginny, that's why he found her so attractive. If I was a bit more fun he might not have gone off with her. Perhaps everything that happened is really my fault.'

'I think that's ridiculous.'

'Is it? I'm prissy. I know enough about myself to know that. I'm all repressed and uptight. I'm a goody-two-shoes. And Ginny, well, she's more of a free spirit, isn't she? She does things and has no regrets, whereas I would always worry about the consequences so I don't do things in the first place.'

'But haven't you *ever* done anything you regretted?'

Alice thought for a while. 'No,' she said simply.

'Never?'

'No.'

'You mean you've never got drunk and wound up in an embarrassing position?'

'No.'

Sarah was impressed. 'Not even when you were a student?'

'No. I suppose I'm terribly dull like that.'

'No, you're not,' said Sarah who was wondering what Alice had ever done in her life apart from eat and breathe.

'Have you?'

'What, embarrassed myself?'

'Yes.'

'Countless times. If Alisdair knew about some of the things I did before I met him I think he'd be shocked to his socks.'

'Really?'

Sarah nodded.

'Like what?'

'You don't want to know,' said Sarah darkly.

Alice looked disappointed, although she said, 'I didn't mean to pry.'

'Oh, I don't suppose nowadays it would be considered so very shocking, not compared to the things you hear going on in some of those clubbing holiday resorts in Cyprus and

Spain, but I did more than my share of drinking and twice I woke up in places and didn't have any idea how I'd got there.' Alice's eyebrows were hovering near her hairline in horror. 'And I slept with more boys than I care to remember. Of course in those days the only thing to be frightened of was getting pregnant, and the pill pretty well took care of that. I have horrors of Jen carrying on like me, what with Aids and everything. Not that she knows about my misspent youth, of course.'

'No,' said Alice automatically.

'So you didn't do any of this?'

'No. Once I made up my mind I was going to get into the officers' mess I never drank.'

'Well, I sort of knew about that. You said that last time we had a chat.' Alice nodded. 'But I didn't know it meant that you've never been on the pop. But what about men?'

'No.' Alice looked almost ashamed. 'There's only been Bob,' she said quietly.

Sarah exhaled slowly. 'Good heavens.'

'I suppose you think I'm odd.'

'No, not at all. In a way I'm almost envious.' Alice made a small noise of disbelief. 'No, I am. You see, I've never really lied to Alisdair; I have just been economical with the truth about how many boyfriends I had had before I met him. It wasn't a detail I thought he needed to know. In fact I always felt it would be better for him not to know everything about my past. Too many skeletons. But you, you don't have to hide anything. I think that's very commendable.'

'No. But the thing is . . .' Alice stopped, reddening with embarrassment. 'The thing is, I don't think I'm much good in bed. I think that could be why he had a fling with Ginny. I expect she was much more exciting. I haven't got the first clue what to do, well, apart from the basics.'

Sarah looked at Alice and her heart went out to her. 'But Bob must have known he was the first.'

'I suppose so. I mean, I didn't tell him as such. I was a bit inhibited about talking about things back then.'

God, thought Sarah, she's inhibited enough now. How inhibited must she have been then? 'But he guessed?'

'I think so. I mean, it did hurt a lot and there was quite a bit of, you know . . .' A pause. 'Blood.'

'He would have known,' said Sarah. 'So, if you know nothing about sex, whose fault is it?'

'I don't understand,' said Alice.

Sarah moved to sit on the edge of her chair so she could look Alice right in the eye. 'Look, I've slept around. I'm not proud of it but I learnt a lot about what men like. You have only slept with Bob. So how are you supposed to have learnt anything? If he hasn't told you, taught you, how are you supposed to know?'

'Well, there are books.'

'Cobblers. It's not down to you. There's an old saying that it takes two to tango. You mustn't blame yourself if you don't know all the tricks of the trade. If Bob wants a different sort of sex, new positions or whatever, he should have told you and taught you. Whatever Bob did in Kosovo isn't your fault. He'd have probably done it anyway. It's got nothing to do with acrobatics in bed, so you mustn't blame yourself. Understand?'

Alisdair had almost finished for the day and was breathing a sigh of relief at having got through his first day as commanding officer without too many moments of angst. He was stacking papers and checking he'd signed everything Richard had prepared for him when there was a sharp rap on his door. He looked up and saw Major Griggs and Mr Watson standing outside in the corridor.

'You want to see me?' asked Alisdair, although it was obvious that was exactly what they wanted. They came in and, rather ominously, shut the door behind them. Alisdair buzzed through to Richard that he was not to be disturbed, but that he would like one of the clerks to bring in three cups of coffee.

'Take a seat,' he told the two men. They waited in silence until a clerk with a tray of mugs appeared and disappeared again discreetly.

'I thought you ought to be given an update on our investigation,' said Major Griggs. When he had introduced himself to Alisdair, he hadn't volunteered a first name and Alisdair found that he didn't particularly want to know it anyway. He didn't fancy having this man for a friend so if things stayed formal that was fine by him. 'We have been unable to find any concrete evidence that anything untoward went on between Colonel Davies and Captain Turner.' He sounded almost disappointed.

Alisdair felt irritated by the tone. 'What did you expect? Colonel Davies has denied there was any affair at all and even the *Mercury* alleged that the affair only consisted of a one-night stand on the side of a mountain in the middle of bloody Kosovo, followed by a few grabbed moments in the billets.'

'Yes, sir, but we thought that there might have been other assignations either before or since.'

'Assignations? You mean you hoped that they might have been rolling around together in a local hotel, with bills and witnesses all over the place so you could have them bang to rights.' Even as Alisdair said this, he realized that the phrase 'bang to rights' wasn't the best one to use in the circumstances, but he was angry and hadn't been thinking as clearly as he should have been. The fact of the matter was that this whole incident had incensed him. Not what Bob and Ginny had got up to, he couldn't have given a damn about that – apart from the fact that it was a lousy thing to do to Alice – but the official investigation into everything had got right under his skin. The army's attitude was that extramarital affairs undermined discipline, were bad for morale and were prejudicial to the establishment. The fact that the rest of the human race could be unfaithful without their personal possessions and private lives being pawed over by policemen, followed by horrendous disciplinary proceedings and the ruination of their careers, seemed to make it all grossly unfair. And it was precisely because the army got so upset by this sort of peccadillo that made it front page news when some poor chap got caught with his trousers down. Alisdair had no doubt that married bank managers had been known to bonk attractive female tellers; that doctors had had it away with receptionists – and a couple of MPs had certainly knocked off their researchers – and they had all retained their posts, their status and their perks. But if an army officer stepped out of line, first it hit the front pages, then the shit hit the fan, and then he or she hit the proverbial skids. And now this pair of goons sitting in front of him seemed to be positively disappointed that their investigations had drawn a blank and they wouldn't be able to crucify Bob and Ginny.

Major Griggs and his stooge shifted uncomfortably in their seats, aware that they were causing a senior officer to view them with a great deal of displeasure.

'And you were unaware of anything untoward going on between Colonel Davies and Captain Turner.'

'Nothing at all. And seeing how well I know both of them, I think I would have done.'

Griggs looked unconvinced. 'We will have to take statements from both of the parties,' he said. 'And of course we'll need to talk to Tabitha Alabaster.'

'The first two are easy enough; the chief clerk has their current addresses. As for Tabitha Alabaster, you'll have to get hold of her through the paper. She left her house in the village the weekend before the story appeared and no one has seen her since.'

'She worked out she wouldn't be the most popular inhabitant then,' said Mr Watson.

'Precisely.'

After the military policemen had gone, Alisdair rang Bob. 'They haven't found any evidence,' he told him.

'Of course not. There wouldn't be any.'

'Let's hope they don't find anyone who might be prepared to give them any.' Alisdair chose his words carefully. He was pretty certain no one would be listening to the phone call but you never knew. And if he was going to support Bob convincingly then he had to be sure that he didn't let slip any hint that he knew Bob was lying.

'Let's hope indeed.'

'I don't want you to be cashiered. Apart from anything, it would destroy Alice.'

'Ginny?'

Ginny recognized Chris's voice at the other end of the line. 'Yes.'

'I've got a bloke booked in to the hotel who I think might be press.'

'Really?'

'Apparently he flew in this morning, but not on the scheduled chopper. He came on a private charter.'

'And what makes you think he's press?' Although Ginny was certain he was right. She recalled the bloke walking into Hugh Town from the airport and, although the man she'd seen and the man at Chris's hotel might have no connection at all, she reckoned that two and two made four whichever way you looked at it.

'He's been asking questions of my staff. He wants to know where Netta lives.'

'Shit.' That pretty much confirmed it.

'Don't worry, they're playing dumb. They all know Netta's a friend of mine.'

'Have you seen this guy?'

'No. He'd gone out again when I got back here from the farm. I imagine he'll be in for dinner tonight. I'll see if I can't find out more about him then.'

'Will you let me know anything that you do glean? Forewarned is forearmed and all that.'

'Sure thing.' There was a pause. Ginny got the feeling that Chris wanted to chat but she didn't feel like encouraging him. He was nice enough and he was good with the kids, and Netta and Petroc obviously adored him, but Ginny had had enough of people for the day. She had not had a chance to be on her own – apart from her walk into Hugh Town – since she had got up. Now all she really wanted was to go to her room, shut the door and think about recent events. Not that that was an option until the kids had been bathed and put to bed and she had helped with supper for the grown-ups. The silence continued. Chris got the hint. 'Right, bye,' he said eventually.

Ginny replaced the receiver.

Netta, sitting on the battered sofa cradling the baby who was sound asleep, looked at her sister askance. 'What was that about the press?' she asked.

Ginny plumped herself down beside her. 'Chris thinks he's got a journalist booked into his hotel. Apparently he wants to know where you live.'

'Me, why me?'

'Presumably because whoever tipped him off knows I am your sister. Find you, find me.'

'Sorry, I swear I get stupider every time I have a baby.'

'Impossible.'

'Cow,' said Netta with a smile. 'So what are you going to do?'

'Nothing. Keep my head down, stay on the farm, that sort of thing.'

'It's going to get pretty boring for them if you won't talk or even make an appearance.'

'That's what I'm banking on. It should make them all go away. Which'll be great until the court martial. Then they'll all swarm out from under their stones again.'

'Will it come to a court martial?' asked Netta, shocked.

'I expect so.'

'But you told me what happened was just one of those things. It isn't as if he raped you or anything, or you are blackmailing him over what he did. I just can't see why on earth it'll have to go that far.'

'Because officers are forbidden from having sex with their subordinates.'

'So, let me get this straight, it's what *he* did that was wrong, not what *you* did. Colonel Bob is going to be court-martialled, not you.'

'Probably.'

'But regardless of which of you is senior, you are just as much to blame as he is. And you were the one who told a reporter, which is what has really caused the trouble,' said Netta indignantly. The baby stirred and Netta rocked it in her arms automatically.

Ginny didn't want to hear this argument. She knew what Netta was implying, that the outcome of her indiscretion was that Colonel Bob's career was going to be destroyed and nothing would happen to her. Well, not officially anyway. But she would hardly get away scot-free. At the very least there would probably be a number of social repercussions, she would be pretty unpopular until memories faded, but she would be able to soldier on while Bob would, in all likelihood, be thrown out.

251

'Thanks for the sisterly support,' she sniped. 'Things aren't a picnic for me you know.'

'It's still worse for him.'

'Huh.'

'Look, I know the story in the *Mercury* was horrid, and I appreciate it must be hateful having to hide from the press, but don't you think you're being just a bit selfish in your attitude to Bob?'

'Oh, and he's just brimming with altruism? There am I, thinking I'm in the middle of a dream come true, that I am the love of his life, and then out of the blue he hauls me into his office and tells me that he's made a mistake. He's terribly sorry but everything that had happened had been a complete aberration and would I please forget about it.'

'Yes, I read your side of the story in the paper, remember? I think you waxed even more eloquently to Tabitha.'

'But the thing is that I feel so rejected. It wasn't just an opportunistic affair. I know he really wanted me, he told me that he had done for years. I know he has real feelings for me. It wasn't one of those affairs that start because both parties have had too much to drink. We were stone cold sober for heaven's sake. And I was the one who tried to resist. I was just as aware as anyone that he was married and that it wasn't a good idea, but he . . . he made it impossible for me to stand firm. I couldn't. You see, I love him,' said Ginny hopelessly. 'I have done since I first met him.'

Netta looked at her sister sadly. 'Poor Gin.'

'I thought I'd died and gone to heaven when I found I was posted to his unit. I thought that being around him every day might make him realize that he'd made a dreadful mistake in marrying Alice and that he would ditch her and marry me.'

'You mean you wanted to wreck his marriage?'

'No, not wreck. But I just thought that having me around would make him see sense. He can't possibly love her. She's such a cold fish. No one likes her. All the wives think she's a complete joke. Her attitudes are antediluvian, she disapproves of women working, she's the most appalling snob . . . He can't be happy with her.' Ginny looked at Netta defiantly, daring her to say she was wrong.

Netta shook her head. 'But you can't go after someone else's husband, even if you don't do it actively. You'd have split up a family.'

'I wasn't going to do anything active. I wasn't going to act like some bunny boiler. I was just going to be there. You've never met his wife. You have no idea how awful she is. I could have given him so much more than she ever did. She's so unbelievably icy. And she has no emotion, no spirit, she spends her life clearing up from one dinner party and arranging the next. There can't be any fun in their life, she wouldn't allow that. They've got a teenage daughter who thinks the height of rebellion is to read *Cosmo* . . .'

'Now you're exaggerating.'

'I'm not,' said Ginny earnestly. 'Alice is a total control freak. Everything in her house has to be perfect. There's no clutter, there's nothing personal, there are no pictures stuck up on the kitchen units, she keeps a record of the food and guests for each dinner party, she doesn't drink—'

'She isn't normal,' Netta butted in. 'But presumably she suits him or he wouldn't have married her in the first place.'

'I don't know, but it doesn't seem very likely. And he's such a live wire. He has done all sorts of way-out things; he's led expeditions up the Amazon, he's done a jungle survival course, he climbs, he sails, he skis—'

'And opposites attract.'

Ginny looked defeated. 'Perhaps that's it.'

'Do you think Alice will stick by him if he gets chucked out?'

Ginny thought for a minute. 'I don't know. She's incredibly old-fashioned and I don't know whether that would make her more or less likely to go. She'll be horrified that he even dreamed of being unfaithful, but I think she will forgive him eventually. She is so army-barmy I can't see her giving up the lifestyle.'

'But you'd like her to. If she left Bob, the way would be clear for you, wouldn't it?'

Ginny didn't have to say anything. Netta could tell that was exactly what she hoped for. There didn't seem much point in commenting, so Netta got up from the sofa and prepared to put the baby in her Moses basket by the Aga.

'Come on lazy bones,' she said to her big sister. 'It's time I

253

got supper on the go. You have a choice; either you can bathe the kids or you can cook a stroganoff for the grown-ups.'

'I'll do bathtime,' said Ginny. 'I know my limitations.'

'You'll have to get Chris to teach you how to cook while you're here.'

'No chance. I'm a lost cause in that department.'

Towards the end of the week, Chris phoned to report that the press had given up. He'd checked at the other hotels and boarding houses on the islands to make sure there weren't any other journalists hanging around.

'Thank goodness for that,' said Ginny. 'Did you find out how he knew I was on the island?'

'Simple. One of the nurses in the hospital recognized you. Of course, she knew who Netta was and got the address and phone number from Netta's records.'

'What a cow.'

'I don't think she thought about any consequences. She probably just needed some cash. Anyway, no harm done. The story is history now.'

'And a good thing too. I'm going stir-crazy up here on the farm.'

'It can't be so bad. The kids went back to school today.'

Ginny presumed that that meant his kids had too. For some reason she wanted to know more about the family he supported with the hotel. She made a mental note to ask Netta about them. 'Yeah the kids are at school, or at least, the big ones are, but I want to get out, go for a walk, stroll on the beach, go for a drink.'

'How about you come down to my hotel and have a drink with me this evening?'

Ginny was surprised by the invitation. She hadn't felt they had seen eye to eye enough at their last meeting to merit such an offer. 'You just want me to drink in your place so I don't spend my money anywhere else,' she said.

'You guessed,' said Chris with a laugh. 'Oh well. I'll take it that's a no then.'

'No!' It almost came out like a yelp. God, it sounded eager, desperate even. She tried to sound more casual. 'Er, no. It would be lovely to get out for an hour or so. And apart from the family and Granny Flo I don't know a soul hereabouts.'

'You know me.' He sounded almost affronted to have been left out.

'Well, yes. Where's your hotel?'

'It's the Trelisk and it's near the museum. Netta'll tell you how to find it.'

'What time?'

'Nine-ish suit you?'

'Great.'

Ginny put the phone down and felt inordinately pleased with the invitation. At least here she wasn't a social pariah. Not like back at the regiment. She'd been on the phone to Maddy earlier that day to find out the reaction to the scandal in the barracks.

'I wouldn't make plans about coming back, even if you are allowed,' Maddy had warned.

'Why not?'

'Colonel Bob was more popular with the troops than we knew. The lads are livid about him being suspended and there are a few unpleasant comments being made. You're not flavour of the month at all. Even some of the wives are a bit anti. In fact,' added Maddy, 'I can't say I'm thrilled about the outcome of what you've done either.'

'What . . . ?' Ginny had started, shocked by Maddy's tone of voice.

'If only you had kept your trap shut, none of this would have happened. Richard might occasionally get home earlier than eight o'clock, the regiment might still have a proper commanding officer, the wives might be able to go shopping at the local supermarket without getting accosted by the press, other scurrilous stories about the regiment wouldn't be popping up in the gutter press like toadstools on a rotten log – no doubt sold by disaffected ex-members, and none of them true of course, but hurtful all the same – and without you and your big mouth life might still be quite normal.' Maddy paused for breath after her outburst.

There was silence from Ginny. She felt completely stunned. She knew that she wouldn't be popular with some people in the regiment, but Maddy was her friend. She had thought Maddy

255

would have stood by her, seen her side of things. In fact, she had half thought that there would be just as much sympathy for her as for the colonel. She certainly hadn't expected this. And what hurt almost as much as Maddy's outburst was the revelation that the troops were against her too. They were her troops too, not just Colonel Bob's. She had worked her butt off to make sure their admin all got done – that they went on the right courses at the right time for the best chance of promotion; that their pay and allowances all got sorted out quickly; that any mistakes in their documentation got rectified immediately – and now they were repaying her by painting her as the scarlet woman. And she hadn't been. She'd been the one saying sex was a lousy idea. How unfair was that? And how dare they! Well, fuck 'em, fuck the lot of 'em. She wouldn't go back to the regiment now even if they begged her to.

But the trouble was, if she didn't go back there, where else could she go in the army? And would it be the same wherever she went? Would there always be a whispering campaign that would smear her name? For the first time in her life Ginny knew what it was like to feel real regret. It seemed as if she had screwed up her life big time. She'd lost her job, her reputation, her friends, pretty much everything. If she could rerun that night on the mountain, undo what had been done, how different things would be now. But that wasn't an option. Magic or time travel was great in theory but Ginny didn't find either was much of a help in real life. It was very tempting to wallow in self-pity, but Ginny knew that it wasn't an answer. It wouldn't achieve anything. Her only course of action was to get over the past and look forward to the future. She would start with the very near future. She would look forward to the evening with Chris. At least he was still talking to her.

Megan sat silently in the car as Alice drove her back to school.

'Do you want the radio on?' Alice asked her.

'Not really.'

'And do you want me to come in with you to have a word with Miss Pink or are you going to be all right?'

'I'll be fine. Stop fussing, Mum.'

Alice glanced across at her daughter. She was very pale

and Alice thought she had lost weight too. Not that that was surprising. Alice knew that she had herself. She had had a problem keeping her blouse tucked into her skirt the day before, a skirt that had fitted perfectly the previous week and which was now hanging off her. It was scary how anxiety, worry, anger and sadness had turned her from a size twelve, ordinary middle-aged woman into a skinny, frumpy crone. When she looked at herself in the mirror she could see lines that had not been there previously, more grey hairs than she remembered, and a hardness and wariness in her eyes that she'd never seen before. She didn't mind so much that her face bore physical witness to the anguish she had gone through since the weekend, but what really tore her apart was that her daughter was suffering too.

'You mustn't let the things people say get to you,' she said 'There are bound to be a couple of the girls there who will think it clever to be unpleasant.'

'Mum,' said Megan wearily, 'I know. I've been through all this with Jen.'

'I'm sorry, dear,' said Alice tightly, hurt by her daughter's tone of voice. 'I only want to help.'

'Yeah, well . . .'

They drove on in silence for a while. Megan slumped in the passenger seat, watched the road and scowled at pedestrians when they drove through towns or villages. Alice kept thinking of things that she felt she ought to say to her daughter, but the mood in the car was so intimidating she refrained. Every now and again she glanced nervously at Megan to see if her mood was improving. It remained steadfastly sullen.

'You'll tell me if things are bad at school, won't you?' she said eventually as they neared their destination.

'If you're so worried about how things are going to be, why on earth are you sending me back?' snarled Megan.

'We've been through all this,' said Alice.

And indeed they had. The day before when Alice had been packing Megan's kit for her departure they had had a huge row on the subject. Megan's point had been that she wouldn't be able to concentrate while she was at school with so much to worry about.

'There's no point in me being there if I'm not going to learn anything,' she had said.

'So what will you do if you stay here? And how long will this go on for? We've no idea if the whole incident is going to be over in days, or weeks, or months. If you're here you'll just mope around. You'll have nothing to take your mind off things.'

'What, like having the school bitches have digs at me? Getting taunted about having a father who sleeps around? And then having to lie and say he didn't, when we all know he did.'

'That's not true.' Megan had stared defiantly at her mother until Alice dropped her gaze. 'Don't exaggerate,' Alice had said as calmly as she could, although she had come very close to slapping Megan. 'A brief affair does not constitute "sleeping around".'

'Huh. If you ask me, if he's done it once, he'll do it again.'

That had been too much for Alice. Before Megan could duck, Alice's hand had flashed out and smacked her sharply across her cheek. Silence followed the crack of the blow. Then, dry-eyed, Megan had turned on her heel and walked out of the bedroom.

Once she had gone Alice felt quite drained by the violence of her anger. She sat down on the edge of Megan's bed. She heard her daughter descend the stairs, walk across the tiled floor of the hall and then the front door was opened and shut. Alice was worried that Megan might be about to do something rash. Heaven knew, with everything that had gone on in the family recently it wouldn't be a surprise if she did something wild like run away. Tiredly, Alice got up, went across the landing into her own bedroom and crossed the floor to the window. From behind the curtain Alice watched Megan walk to Sarah's house. Alice felt a surge of relief. She had gone to talk to her new friend, Jen. Well, that was all right then. She was glad Megan liked Jen. She seemed such a sensible girl; very down-to-earth like her mother, despite her unfortunate taste in clothes and music. Alice had returned to the packing, silently praying that Jen would make Megan see sense – that she would be better off at school, where she could slip into the routine of lessons and have her mind occupied by things other than her problems at home.

When Megan returned some while later, Alice didn't ask about her visit to Jen's. It was enough for Alice that Megan had made no comment about the two cases sitting in the hall, ready to be loaded into the car. The matter had been closed. And now Alice certainly didn't want it brought up again just as they were arriving at the school.

As they pulled up in front of the main door on the wide, sweeping gravel drive, there were several other cars already there. Alice noticed the covert glances in their direction, the nudges and the sotto voce comments made between parents and between other children. Only to be expected, she thought with a suppressed sigh. She and Megan manhandled the cases out of the boot and into the cavernous hall of the school. They were dumped in the growing pile of luggage to await the school groundsmen who would transport them to the girls' rooms later.

'So,' said Alice brightly. 'Do you want me to stay for tea or would you rather I went?'

'You can go if you like.'

'That's not what I asked. I asked what *you* would like me to do.'

'If you go, I can go up to my room.'

Alice understood her reasoning. Megan would be required to play host to her mother if she stayed for tea and perhaps it was too much to expect. 'Right, darling. I'll see you in a few weeks. Ring me at any time if you need to talk.'

'Yeah, OK Mother.'

Alice leant forward and kissed her quickly on the cheek. 'I'll be off then.' She turned and went back to the car, her heart sinking at the prospect of a two-hour drive and then a return to an empty house. She was used to it, it had happened before, as there had been a number of occasions when Megan and Bob had both been away at the same time. But this time it was different; not only was she without her daughter and her husband but this time events had cast her adrift from the regiment. This time she had lost her position too, and without that she had lost much of her raison d'être.

Alice was locking up her car when Sarah waylaid her.

'You must have been looking out for me,' said Alice, attempting a lightness of tone that she certainly didn't feel.

'I was, actually. I'm having some wives round to coffee tomorrow, now the kids have gone back. I'd like you to come too.'

'Thanks, but no thanks,' said Alice firmly.

'Please come,' said Sarah. 'You can't shut yourself away. There's . . .' She paused. 'There's a lot of sympathy for you on the patch.'

'I don't want pity,' said Alice.

'I didn't say pity, I said sympathy. There's a deal of difference. We all know how tough it's been on you this last week and, well, we want you to know that we're behind you.'

Alice looked puzzled. 'I don't understand.'

'Look, there's probably not much any of us can do to make things better for you. You must be going through hell, but we care.' Alice still didn't look convinced. 'Honestly, we do. And if you come along tomorrow you'll see it for yourself.'

'I don't know,' said Alice, weakening. She had certainly felt very lonely since the dreadful news had been broken to her, but she couldn't think that the wives cared much. She was nobody's fool. She knew that she wasn't popular; that the wives viewed an invitation to dinner at her house as a chore, not an evening out; that she was considered odd because she didn't drink and insisted on 'standards'; that she was old-fashioned because she thought wives should concentrate their attentions on their husband's career and doing good work within the regiment, and not on earning money.

'Please,' insisted Sarah.

'Maybe just for a few minutes,' said Alice. It wasn't as if she had anything better to do, apart from some housework.

'Good,' said Sarah with a warmth that surprised Alice. 'About elevenish?'

'Fine.'

Sarah watched Alice go into her house and then walked along the pavement to Maddy's front door and rang the bell.

'Come in, come in,' said Maddy, glad of the company of an adult after a day of toddler talk.

'Alice has agreed to come to coffee tomorrow.'

'That's good. It'll do her good to get out and find how much support there is for her.'

'That's what I told her.'

'You'll never guess who phoned me yesterday,' said Maddy.

'Who?'

'Ginny.'

'No! What did she want?'

'Sympathy I think. Not that she got it from me.'

'But I thought you were friends with her.'

'I know. I was . . . am. I don't know. I was horrid to her and now I feel dreadful. I mean, when she told me about her affair she said Bob had done all the running and I believed her. But now . . .' She shrugged. 'I don't know what to believe. And if she hadn't told Taz – well, none of this mess would have happened. You've got to admit, a lot of it is her fault.'

'The person I really blame is Taz, not Ginny. She was quite calculating about what she did. She wormed her way into our friendship, took what she wanted and then left all the mess behind. If you want my advice,' said Sarah, 'it's Taz you want to vent your spleen on, not Ginny. She's got enough to contend with without getting grief from us too.'

'Now I feel even worse,' said Maddy. 'I wonder if she'll ever forgive me?'

At nine that night Ginny wandered into Hugh Town and made her way along the main street to Chris's hotel. It was on the sea front, overlooking the harbour and the pier where the *Scillonian* docked. Ginny glanced up at the name on the notice above the door giving detail of the licensee. 'Christopher Tregaskis' it said. 'Licensed to sell . . .' Tregaskis, she thought. That sounded like a good local name, but that and the fact that he owned the place was about all she knew about him. She'd decided against asking Netta about him. She had been afraid that Netta would misconstrue her reasons and make some mean comment. She felt battered enough by recent events without dishing out yet more ammunition to be used against her.

She pushed at the front door and entered the hall. Opposite her was a small reception desk. On her left was a neat notice board with details about various activities on the islands – outings to Tresco and Bryher, trips out to sea to look

261

for dolphins, the helicopter timetable, details of flights to Newquay and Exeter and other bits of information likely to appeal to tourists. On her right was a large mirror, obviously positioned to give the small hall a feeling of greater space. By the desk was a vast pedestal flower arrangement, mostly and unsurprisingly consisting of daffodils, and then there was an elegant flight of curved stairs leading to the upper floors. In the air there was a pleasant smell of furniture polish mingled with the scent of the flowers.

Ginny walked to the desk and pinged the bell. A small, neat woman with curly brown hair and a label on her lapel announcing her to be Mrs Carole Tregaskis appeared from a back office. She looked really nice, thought Ginny. Chris was a lucky man.

She switched on a smile. 'Hello,' she said. 'My name is Ginny Turner and I'm staying with Netta and Petroc Pengelly.'

'Hello, there,' said Carole. 'Chris told me you were on the island. Of course I can see you're Netta's sister. You're so very like her. Chris said you would be coming down this evening for a drink. He's in the office. Would you like to go through or do you want to wait for him in the bar?'

'I'll go through to the office, if that's all right?' Ginny didn't particularly fancy propping up a bar on her own and, being out of season, she didn't think there would be anyone else to keep her company.

'Of course. If you go through this door here and follow the corridor to the end you can't miss it.'

Ginny followed the directions and found herself outside the centre of operations for the hotel. Chris was sitting at a desk covered with mounds of paper. Ginny had never seen a more chaotic office in her life.

'Hi,' he said as she entered. 'Take a seat. I won't be long.'

Ginny looked around for a chair and located one eventually, hidden under a stack of box files. She moved them on to the floor and sat down.

Carole appeared at the office door. 'The kids have just phoned. I need to get home. The dog has cut its paw and is bleeding all over the house. He won't let them examine it.'

'Go then. If blood gets all over the carpets it'll be a pain to get it out.'

Carole nodded in agreement and left.

Ginny was surprised. She would have thought that they would have lived over the shop. 'Don't you live here?' she asked.

'What?' He wasn't really listening.

'Do you live here, at the hotel?' She rephrased the question to make it clearer.

'We have a room upstairs for whoever is duty manager. But otherwise, no.' He sounded impatient. Obviously he didn't want to have small talk interrupting his work. He continued his frantic tapping at the calculator, stopping every now and again to write down the figures and then shuffle through some papers on his desk before resuming the tapping once more.

'VAT return,' he said. 'Hate the things.'

'They're not so bad to do,' said Ginny.

'What do you know about them?'

'I understand accounts, if that's what you mean,' she answered.

Chris looked up at her. 'You do? But I thought you are in the army?'

'I am, but that doesn't mean that I have no qualifications. Admin is what I do; it's what I specialize in. I spend my life doing accounts and paperwork and stuff like that.'

'Really?'

'Yes. Don't sound so amazed. I'm rather good at it actually.' Which she knew to be a total understatement but she could hardly say she was one of the best in her field.

Chris carried on with his figures for a few minutes until with a groan he muttered under his breath that the bloody thing didn't add up. Ginny was tempted to ask if there was something she could do but restrained herself. She instinctively knew that no man wanted to be shown how to do something by a woman. However, she did wonder when she was going to get the promised drink. At this rate it would be too late. Chris put down his pen and passed his hand wearily over his face.

'Enough of paperwork,' he said standing up and grabbing at a pile of files as they threatened to slide off the desk. 'Let's go and get a drink. And I want you to tell me about yourself.'

He led the way out of the office and along the corridor back to the main bit of the hotel. En route they passed Carole, who now had her coat on and her handbag slung over her shoulder.

'I thought you were off home,' he said.

'Got caught by another phone call and I could hardly tell a future guest to shut up.'

'No,' said Chris. He remembered his manners. 'Have you two met?'

'We did the introductions when Ginny got here,' said Carole.

'Oh good,' said Chris. Carole moved towards the front door. 'I hope the dog is not too bad,' he added.

Carole nodded and disappeared.

Ginny thought that Carole seemed remarkably relaxed about her husband going to have a drink with a strange woman, especially one who had just been splashed across a national tabloid for having an affair with someone else's husband. Still, though, perhaps that just proved that some couples trusted each other implicitly. But no matter, Ginny thought. She wasn't about to make the same mistake twice. Chris was safe from her attentions if Carole was at all worried. In fact, any married man was as safe as houses as far as attentions from Ginny were concerned.

Chris pushed open a heavy panelled door and allowed Ginny to pass through. The bar was small and cosy, with a log fire opposite the bar itself and two big French windows opposite the door, which opened on to a terrace and a spectacular view across the harbour.

'This is lovely,' said Ginny.

'Nice isn't it? You should see it on a sunny day. It's wonderful to sit outside with a glass of cold beer and watch the boats come and go.'

Ginny could imagine it so. She wondered why Netta had never suggested that she should come and visit this bar on her previous visits to the island. It would have been delightful to sit here on a summer's evening.

Chris flipped up the counter and went behind the bar. 'What's your poison?' he asked.

'I'll have a glass of red wine,' she answered.

Chris poured her one and then drew a pint of beer for himself.

'So how come I've never met you before?' said Ginny, staring at Chris over the rim of her glass. 'I mean, you being such a friend of Petroc's, and all that.'

'I don't know.' Chris took a pull of his drink. 'Do you come to the islands often?'

'About once a year.'

'In the summer?'

'Usually.'

'Well then, that explains it. Have you any idea how busy I am in the summer?'

'Ah.'

'Ah, indeed. From June to September I barely come up for air. I work eighteen-hour days, I have no time for socializing whatsoever and Petroc and Netta know this. And besides which, Netta tends to avoid the town when it's chock full of grockles.'

'That's true,' agreed Ginny. 'We spend a lot of the time taking the kids for picnics around the farm and fossicking around on the beaches the visitors don't seem to get to.'

'Precisely. The islands are wonderful out of season but you have to grit your teeth a bit in the summer.'

'Better that than the alternative.'

'Sorry?'

'Well, you'd have a pretty miserable existence if the tourists didn't turn up.'

Chris laughed. 'Point taken.' He had another sip of beer. 'So what made a nice girl like you join the army?'

Ginny shrugged. 'Travel, sport, my total lack of any domestic skills, that sort of thing.'

'Fair enough. But doing admin doesn't seem very exciting.'

'No, but it's very satisfying.'

Chris made a snorting sound.

'You don't agree?'

'Nope. I love this business, I love the guests we have, I love providing a service, I love the thought that I'm giving people a good time, but I hate the bloody paperwork.'

'Hence the state of your office.'

Chris nodded. 'I keep meaning to get my act together but I just hate that sort of thing so much. I do the bare minimum to keep the place going relatively efficiently but VAT and taxes nearly cause me breakdowns.'

Ginny toyed with the stem of her glass. 'Don't you have an accountant?'

'No.'

Ginny raised her eyebrows. 'But surely . . . ?'

'There's only one on the island. We fell out.'

Ginny's eyebrows went higher.

'He complained about the state of my paperwork. He said that unless I got my accounts sorted out so they were legible before I presented them, he'd have to charge me twice as much. I told him to stuff it, that I paid him enough as it was.'

Ginny suppressed a smile. She could easily imagine the exchange. 'So where's the next nearest accountant?'

'Penzance.'

'It's not so far.' Chris stared at her but didn't say anything. Ginny studied him for a second. 'He told you the same, didn't he?'

Chris nodded. 'Except it was a she not a he, but yes.'

Ginny made a sympathetic moue. Then she said, 'I don't want to seem interfering, but would you like me to see if I can sort things out for you? Get things ready for the accountant and sort out your filing?'

'I couldn't allow you to do that.'

'I wouldn't offer if I felt it was going to be such a terrible task.'

'I can't afford to pay you much.'

'Did I mention money?'

'No, but . . .'

'Listen. Money really isn't part of the equation. I'm suspended from the army on full pay. I don't need to be paid twice. Feed me while I'm with you if I need sustenance, let me have an intravenous supply of decent coffee, allow me a free rein to get it organized properly—'

'Hey. How much of a free rein?'

'I didn't get a chance just now to have a proper look at how things are in the office but you don't seem to have much of a filing system for a start.'

'Well, there is a sort of one.'

'"Sort of one" isn't good enough. You really need files for

266

bookings, invoices, contracts with local businesses, catering suppliers, bills paid, bills unpaid, and a zillion other categories I should imagine. Plus a proper system of cross-referencing. I mean, how do you manage? How come you know where anything is in that place?'

'I know. I keep meaning to do something about it but . . .'

'Well, I'm the answer to your prayers. I'll come down for a few hours each day. I'll walk Flossie, Barnaby and Jack to school then give you a hand until it's time for Jack to finish nursery. I'll have to leave at twelve to pick him up. Depending on how I get on I'll see whether I'll need to work afternoons too.'

'And you're sure about this?'

Ginny nodded and drained her glass. 'You can show your gratitude by offering me another drink.'

'I'm so grateful you deserve a cellar full of wine, not just a glass.'

'Don't make rash promises. I might take you up on them.'

Netta was in the kitchen feeding the baby when Ginny got back. When Ginny told her about her plan to use her enforced holiday to help out Chris, she was delighted.

'It's an ill wind and all that stuff, isn't it? It's exactly what he needs. He and Carole are hopeless at that side of the business. I sometimes wonder how on earth they know who they have coming to stay and for how long. And if you decide you can get him sorted out working half a day, you can help me get the cottages ready for the summer season.' The cottages were two little holiday homes made out of a converted stable block. Netta and Petroc, like most island residents, relied on the summer visitors to supplement their family income. The cottages could each accommodate a family of four and they were basic but comfortable. Each had a kitchen because Netta was quite happy to have people staying on the farm but there was no way she had the time to run around after them. If the families didn't want to cook for themselves, Netta had a list of hotels and pubs on the island more than willing to do it for them.

'No rest for the wicked then.'

Netta shook her head. 'And when I consider how wicked you have been . . .'

267

Ginny didn't want to be reminded. 'What needs doing?' she asked swiftly.

'A bit of painting. Some of the gloss needs doing and the walls all need a roller taken over them. I want to take all the curtains down and wash and iron them. And the cookers need a thorough clean.'

Ginny grimaced. 'Ugh, cleaning cookers. Horrid job. One of the reasons I joined the army was to spare myself that sort of thing.'

'Tough. You're in the real world now, where that sort of thing happens.'

Alice was having second thoughts about going round to Sarah's house when the phone rang. The notion of meeting a host of people, all of whom – however noble their outward intentions – were bound to view her as an object of curiosity, was more daunting than she felt able to cope with.

'I'm just making sure you're not going to chicken out,' said Sarah when Alice picked up the receiver.

'Oh, um . . .'

'Absolutely not,' said Sarah with feeling. 'Honestly, I'm sure it'll do you so much good if you come along.'

'I don't think so,' said Alice. 'I'm sorry, but I just don't feel ready to meet a crowd of people at the moment.'

'It's not a crowd. It's just Maddy and Caro and a few of the other wives. Only half a dozen really.'

'I can't—'

'Yes you can,' interrupted Sarah. 'You don't have to stay long and I promise that if you hate it you can make a bolt for the door any time you want.'

'Sarah, I really don't want—'

'And what are you going to do instead? Sit at home and worry about the future?'

'No . . .'

'Yes, you will. I know you. You have nothing else to do unless you get out and about. Come on. It won't be so bad, you'll see.'

Sarah was right. What would she do? The house was spotless, she had no one to prepare a meal for apart from herself and the last thing she felt like doing was eating. And the other wives might laugh at her predicament behind her back but they wouldn't do it to her face. Getting out for a while might not be total hell. 'OK. I'll show my face for ten minutes. I'll be along in a few moments.'

Alice replaced the receiver and made her way upstairs to check her hair and make-up. And to spend a short time composing herself. If she was going to face the other wives, she was not going to demean herself by letting her most private feelings escape. She was going to be certain that she didn't let herself down.

When she felt ready, she walked slowly down the wide, sweeping stairs to her front door. As she did so she remembered the first time she had descended these stairs and how grand she had felt, how it had seemed to epitomize the culmination of all her ambitions. Well, she had got what she wanted. She had got the grand house, the position, the status and with it had come the scandal and the exposure in the press. If she had known the consequences of her dreams, might she have wished for different things? Alice didn't know, but all she could do now was to make the best of the situation. She opened the front door and stepped outside. Right, she told herself, head up, shoulders back. Then she headed for Sarah's house.

Sarah opened the door almost instantly. Alice could hear a hubbub of voices coming from Sarah's sitting room.

'Am I the last to arrive?' asked Alice. She hoped her voice didn't give away how nervous she felt.

Sarah nodded. 'Come on in. I've just made a fresh pot of coffee.' She led Alice into her main room. The conversation faltered for a moment as the other wives noticed her entrance but it picked up so quickly again that Alice almost wondered if she had imagined it. Sarah disappeared over to a table to get her a cup of coffee, leaving Alice momentarily on her own. Alice stopped to take stock of who was present and to wonder how to proceed. She wasn't used to feeling unsure of herself. She'd spent years making sure she knew exactly how to behave in any given situation and suddenly she felt like a small kid at a new school; gauche and alone. But, before she lost her small stock of courage and fled, she was rescued by Maddy.

'Alice,' said Maddy. 'How are you? No, don't answer that.

269

What a crass question that is. You'll be feeling horrible, I've no doubt. How could it be anything else with all that you've gone through recently?' There was a murmur of sympathy from the other wives. Alice felt a glow of warmth that they really did, genuinely seem to care.

Alice rewarded them with a wan smile. 'Well, you just have to get on with life, don't you? There's no point in curling up in a corner, is there?'

Caro approached Alice and gave her a hug. 'You're such a trouper,' she said. 'If anything awful ever happens to me, I shall try to behave with as much dignity as you have.'

'Hear, hear,' said the other wives.

Alice was stunned. She hadn't expected anything like that. 'I don't know what to say,' she stammered shyly.

Sarah came over with a cup of hot coffee. 'Just accept the compliment as heartfelt. A lot of people would have ranted and raved, but you've been amazing. Now then.' She saw that Alice was getting embarrassed by their kind words and deliberately changed the subject. 'Did Megan get back to school OK?'

'After a fashion. She didn't want to go. She was worried about gossip.'

'I'm not surprised,' said Maddy. 'Kids can be horrid to each other, can't they?'

Alice nodded. 'I remember when I was little,' she began. Then she stopped herself. What on earth was she thinking about? She was about to recount a story of how horrid some of the officers' kids had been to her when she had lived on the senior NCOs' patch.

'Go on,' said Sarah.

Then Alice thought, what the heck? As revelations went, this was such a minor one. It certainly didn't even begin to compare with what had come out in the press in the previous few days. And anyway, these women were her friends now, weren't they?

'Well,' she said. 'When my father was a sergeant –,' she looked around, expecting to see mouths agape, jaws dropped, but there was no reaction at all. It was almost as if she'd said nothing more banal than 'When my father was younger'. She brought herself back to her story, '– I longed to join in the games the officers' children played. They always seemed to have so much fun. Their games always seemed so much more imaginative than the ones the kids played on the other ranks' patch. But they would run away from me and hide whenever they saw me. One day I chased them. I was wearing a Laura Ashley dress. I was so proud of it, but one of the boys had rigged up a tripwire. I didn't see it and went headlong. I ripped the dress. The officers' children fell around laughing.' She fell silent and looked around, wondering what the reaction would be to her disclosure. The room was quiet. The other wives were all listening to her but no one looked the least bit deprecating.

'If Danny ever behaves like that when she's older, she'll have to answer to me,' said Maddy with feeling. 'The little bastards.'

'They were kids,' said Alice.

'They knew what they were doing and they knew they were being mean and spiteful,' said Sarah. 'Don't tell me they didn't.'

Alice was surprised that the comments were all about the behaviour of the children. It was almost as though no one had noticed her confession to being the daughter of another rank. Perhaps Sarah had been right, perhaps no one cared about those things nowadays. Perhaps Alice herself was the only person to whom it mattered. And now she had told everyone and the reaction had been so non-existent, it didn't matter to her either. She felt such a sense of relief that she almost laughed. She stopped herself. That would be inappropriate. Old habits die hard, she thought with a private smile.

The conversation moved on from the behaviour of children to schools, from schools to league tables, from league tables to desirable places to live, and suddenly Maddy and Caro were making a move to go to collect Danny and Grace from the friend who was minding them for the morning.

'Good grief, is that the time?' said Alice looking at her watch. She smiled at Sarah. 'You were right to make me come. I only meant to stay a few minutes and I've been here half the morning.'

Alice and Sarah walked towards the front door. 'And no one said anything untoward, did they?'

'No. Everyone was lovely. I felt very welcome. Thank

you Sarah.' She leaned forward and impulsively gave Sarah a hug.

'We're all behind you, you know. Whatever happens, no one wants to see you suffer.'

'It's not in my hands though, is it? If the army decides to believe the story and Bob has to go then there's nothing I can do.'

'Let's hope for the best then, shall we?'

The call from the military police came through on Monday morning, just as Ginny and the three eldest children were preparing to leave for the walk to school in Hugh Town. The kitchen was a scene of chaos as Netta and Ginny found school bags and coats, put sandwiches into lunch boxes, fed Lisa and Rose, cooked breakfast for Petroc, retrieved reading books from down the side of the sofa, and generally got things sorted. The noise of the telephone bell over the racket almost went unheeded until Flossie picked it up.

'Aunty Gin,' she hollered over the noise. 'It's for you.'

Ginny went over to the phone. 'Hello,' she said, holding the receiver tight against her ear and putting her other hand over her other one to block out the noise generated by four children and a baby.

'This is Major Griggs of the Provost branch,' she heard a deep voice with a faint north-country accent say.

Ginny sagged. She had put all the unpleasantness of the investigation out of her mind. She had barely given it a thought over the past few days, but now it was impinging on the safe haven she had created for herself here. 'Yes,' she said wearily.

'I need to get a statement from you. I want to know when I can come and interview you.'

'Whenever,' said Ginny. She didn't care. It would be awful whenever he chose to do it. Sooner, later, what did it matter to her?

'I can't make it over to the islands this week,' said the major. 'Will you still be there next week?'

'Yes,' said Ginny.

'I'll let you know when to expect me.'

'Yes.' Oh, goody.

272

'Goodbye.'

Ginny put the phone down.

'Bad news?' asked Netta, who had been watching her sister's reaction to the call.

'The army. They're coming to get my side of the story.'

'Oh.' Netta gave her a sympathetic smile. 'You knew it had to happen one day.'

Ginny nodded. 'Right,' she said breezily. 'Everyone ready?' The three children were by the back door in their anoraks and boots, school bags on their backs and lunch boxes in their hands. Jack's only contained an apple for his mid-morning break but he wanted to be like his big brother and sister and had insisted that he should have one too. Flossie, of course, had sneered that Jack's lunch box was one that she had discarded a year or so ago, and anyway, as it only had a piece of fruit in it, it couldn't really be called a lunch box but Jack was not to be dissuaded.

'Squad,' she called. 'Squad, 'shun.' The three giggling children obediently brought both feet together and stiffened their backs. 'By the left, quick march. Left, right, left, right.' Netta held open the back door. The children, pretending to march, shambled through it. 'Left wheel,' called Ginny, as her troops exited into the farmyard. She waved to Netta who shut the door behind her. The game of soldiers continued through the yard and down the track until they got to the road. It had been the same the other two times she had taken the children to school, but then she had enjoyed the game. The army then had been consigned to some sort of forgotten foggy limbo. Now, although she played the game for the children's sake, the army had made its presence felt in her life once again and the fun had evaporated. The prospect of a visit from a military policeman hardly promised to be some diverting entertainment, and the thought of being interviewed, of having to divulge intimate details of her affair, made her flesh creep. Still, if the kids wanted to play at soldiers she would humour them, even though her heart was no longer in it. At the gate on to the road, the kids broke ranks and ran along the tarmac, between the dry-stone walls, towards the town.

'Keep in,' called Ginny automatically after them although there was hardly a danger from traffic. She lengthened her

273

stride to keep them in view and then broke into a jog as they threatened to extend the gap between them more than what she felt was acceptable. She caught up with them in a dozen or so strides and grabbed Jack's hand then, having secured his safety, she ran with him till they levelled with the two others. By this time they were almost at the outskirts of the town and Jack was red, dripping with perspiration and flagging with fatigue.

'Phew,' said Ginny, feigning exhaustion for the sake of Jack who would lose face to admit he was pooped. 'Slow down. I'm shattered.'

Obediently Flossie and Barnaby slowed to a walk. Ginny swung Jack, lunch box, school bag and all, on to her hip. If he fell behind Flossie, the little madam was bound to give him a hard time about not being able to keep up, or worse, make him feel guilty that they might be late for school – which they certainly wouldn't be, but Jack wouldn't know as he couldn't tell the time. If she carried Jack there was no chance of that and she would get to the Trelisk Hotel in good time too. Besides, Jack didn't weigh that much and it was largely downhill to the school.

Twenty minutes later, after the kids had safely been transferred to the care of their teachers, Ginny rolled up at the front desk of the hotel to report for duty. A young, unknown girl, labelled Vicki Forbes, greeted Ginny with enthusiasm.

'Chris said to show you to the office and to keep the coffee coming. Is that right?'

Ginny hid her disappointment that Chris wasn't there to meet her himself and replied that it sounded just fine.

'Chris apologizes for his absence,' continued Vicki, 'but he's gone to buy fish.'

'OK,' said Ginny. Reasonable enough. The hotel had to continue to function. She made her way to the office and sat behind the desk. As she gazed at the disordered piles of papers, document wallets, box files, invoices and sundry other bits and pieces, she wondered what on earth had possessed her to volunteer to take the job on. Where to start? she thought. Then she gave herself a mental shake, put her bag on the floor, rolled up her sleeves and began by piling everything that was on the desk on the floor instead. At least with the desk clear she would have somewhere to work. She was halfway through that task when Vicki appeared with a tray with a Thermos jug full of delicious-smelling coffee, a cup and saucer, a jug of cream and a bowl of sugar cubes.

'At least there's somewhere to put it,' said Vicki with a grin. 'I've never seen the top of this desk before.'

Ginny grinned. 'And how long has that been?'

'A couple of years. Since I left school.'

'Well hopefully you and it will soon be well acquainted.'

'It's going to be a hell of a job, isn't it? Are you going to be here long?'

'A week or two. It should be enough.'

The expression on Vicki's face plainly showed that she didn't believe it would be anything like enough time to sort out the chaos, but she didn't contradict Ginny.

With plenty of coffee to keep her going, Ginny got to work. Having cleared the desk, she began arranging different pieces of paper into piles according to subject matter. After about an hour there was no space left on the desk so she began new stacks of paper on the floor. She was crawling around on the carpet, her bottom pointing towards the door, when Chris came to see how she was getting on.

'Not your best profile,' he said laconically from the doorway.

Ginny looked round. 'Cheeky.'

'Exactly,' he said.

Ginny couldn't stop herself from laughing.

'How are you getting on?' he inquired.

'OK. It'll look a lot worse before it gets better, but as long as no one interferes with my system before I start getting things squared away it shouldn't take too long. And anyway, like it or not I've got to stay here for at least another week, so I should have time to do a proper job.'

'You make staying here sound like a penance. Is it because of this?'

'No,' said Ginny hurriedly. 'No, it's nothing to do with sorting this bugger's muddle out. It's just there's other stuff happening that I've got to deal with.'

Chris looked puzzled. 'So what is it? Netta's family?'

'No, and anyway staying with them could hardly be called a penance. They're great. No,' she sighed. 'No, I had a call from the military police today. They're coming to interview me, but not till next week. It's a bit like having the Sword of Damocles hanging over me.'

Chris shook his head. 'I'm sorry. I'm probably being unbelievably thick, but you've lost me completely. What possible interest have the police got in you? I thought you were here to get away from the press – I didn't realize that you're a fugitive from justice too.'

Ginny gave a mirthless laugh and hauled herself to her feet. 'Have you got a few minutes?' she asked. Chris nodded and Ginny explained the army's disciplinary system, and how she and Colonel Bob had managed to breech it, and how she was now the scarlet woman as far as the regiment was concerned, and how both her career and Colonel Bob's hung in the balance.

Chris whistled. 'A bit of a mess then.'

Ginny nodded. 'You could call it that.'

'And are you and Bob . . . ?' Chris looked embarrassed.

'What? An item?'

Chris shrugged.

'Oh no. As far as he is concerned I'm rather an embarrassment, an aberration, a blot on his career plan.' Ginny couldn't hide the pain she felt.

Chris, leaning against the door jamb, shifted uncomfortably. 'Oh.'

'No. He told me in no uncertain terms that he considered his wife a much better bet if his career was to go any further.'

'That, presumably, was before the story got into the papers.'

Ginny nodded. 'And that's all seen as my fault too.' She told Chris about the duplicitous Tabitha and her spat with Maddy.

'You've been a bit hard done by, haven't you?'

Ginny nodded. She was starting to feel quite sorry for herself and she was afraid she was going to lose control.

'Well,' continued Chris, 'it's not just you that's been hard done by, but Colonel Bob and his missus and his kid, and most of the rest of the regiment.'

Ginny felt a flash of anger. No, it wasn't 'just as bad' for the others. It was *she* who had had the worst of it, what with Maddy and the other wives being so horrible, and it had been *her* story that had been all over the press, and it was *her* dreams about Bob that had been so comprehensively shattered. No, it had definitely been worse for her. Why did everyone feel so much sympathy for bloody Bob and his family? She thought of putting Chris straight but, hell, what was the point? He probably wouldn't understand anyway.

'Well,' she said tartly. 'I've got a lot of work to do, so if you don't mind . . .'

'Right,' said Chris. 'Whatever.' He wandered off again, leaving Ginny still simmering with annoyance. She was annoyed that he hadn't been sympathetic; she was annoyed that he hadn't taken her side, and she was annoyed that, having failed so miserably on both those counts, he hadn't intuitively known how he had hurt her and apologized. God, she thought, everyone seemed to forget that she was a victim too.

Just before twelve Ginny tidied up as best she could and prepared to leave to collect Jack and take him back to the farm. She slid past the reception desk, glad that Chris was nowhere to be seen as she was still mad at him for his earlier comments. She was just about to leave the hotel when she heard Vicki calling her name.

'Ginny. Ginny!'

Ginny turned round. 'Yes,' she said, conscious of the time and that if Vicki delayed her, poor Jack would feel abandoned.

'I shan't keep you,' said Vicki, seeing her glance at her watch. 'I just wanted to ask you something.'

'Fire away.'

'I know you were in the army.'

'Yes, why?' asked Ginny guardedly, wondering where this was leading.

'Oh, it's nothing to do with . . .' she tailed off. She'd obviously heard about Ginny's recent past. Ginny raised her eyebrows. 'It's just that I had a booking today. A Major Griggs. Do you know him?'

Great, thought Ginny. 'Of all the hotels in all the world and he has to book into this one,' she said, doing a dreadful parody of Humphrey Bogart.

'Sorry?' Vicki looked completely lost.

'Yes,' said Ginny. 'Yes, I know him. Actually, I know *of* him, if I'm being entirely truthful.'

'Well, that'll be nice for him. He seems to be coming on his own so it's good that he'll have someone to talk to.'

'Yeah, great isn't it?' said Ginny with a total lack of enthusiasm. The trouble was, there was no doubt that he was going to have someone to talk to and that someone was going to be her, whether she liked it or not. Vicki gave her a slightly puzzled smile and Ginny turned and headed towards the school.

She got there just as Jack was coming out. She bounded up to the door and gathered him up, avoiding crushing the large sheet of paper he was clutching in one hand. He was still at an age when kisses from his aunt were to be welcomed and not despised. At least he still loved her unconditionally and wasn't going to make comments about her past or her behaviour.

'What did you do today, Jack-me-lad?'

Jack flourished the piece of grey sugar paper. On it was a bright, swirly daub that could have represented anything.

'That's great Jack! What is it?'

Jack didn't seem to be the least bit affronted that Ginny did not instantly recognize the subject of his oeuvre.

'It's Mummy.'

'It's lovely my sweet. And Mummy is going to love it.'

Ginny took the still-damp painting off him and carefully rolled it up to protect it for the journey home. Then, taking Jack's hand, they strolled out of the playground and headed along the road that led to the farm. For the first few hundred yards he skipped along happily but as the road got steeper and his legs began to tire his steps got smaller and slower. Ginny, deciding that if she wanted to be home for lunch she would have to do something, bent down and got Jack to clamber on to her back.

It was one thing offering a piggyback first thing in the morning and on a downhill slope, but it was a different matter entirely now she was tired after a morning's work and the gradient was distinctly upwards. By the time she got to the farmyard, Ginny was hot and bothered. She let Jack slide to the ground and she leant against the wall of the house while she recovered. Without a backward glance and with no word of thanks to Ginny, Jack grabbed his precious painting and rushed indoors to see his mother. After a couple of minutes Ginny wearily followed.

'Hi,' said Netta. 'You look bushed.'

'Utterly pooped,' confirmed Ginny, flopping down on the sofa by her sister. 'Your son weighs a bloody ton. I gave him a piggyback from the crossroads.'

'More fool you,' said Netta. 'I wouldn't have done. How was work?'

'OK.' She didn't sound very enthusiastic.

'I thought you liked doing admin.'

'The filing was fine. It's just Chris.'

Netta raised her eyebrows. 'Chris? But he's a pussycat.'

Ginny shot her sister a sour look. 'Huh,' was all she said. 'And,' she added after a second or two. 'And, the bastard that is coming to interview me is staying in his hotel.'

'You can hardly blame Chris for that, now can you?'

'I'm not blaming him,' snapped Ginny.

'Sounds like it to me.'

'Don't be stupid.'

Netta got up off the sofa, put the baby in its bouncing chair and moved to the other side of the kitchen where she began to cut slices off a large loaf. She wasn't going to dignify Ginny's last nasty comment by replying. She was obviously in a foul mood.

Ginny looked at Netta's huffy back view and wondered why everyone seemed to be against her.

The next day, Chris seemed to have caught Ginny's bad temper. He thumped around the foyer of the hotel. He found fault with all the staff. He criticized the standard of cleanliness and then he stomped out again.

'What was all that about?' Ginny asked Vicki when she came into the office to replenish the coffee supply.

'Carole's gone over to the mainland for a few days. He's always like that when she goes away.'

'Does she do this often?'

Vicki leaned across the desk and lowered her voice. 'I know I shouldn't say anything, but I think she's got a man that she goes to see.'

Ginny was stunned. No wonder Chris was in a rage. If the hotel staff realized what was going on, he must know too. Poor man. It explained everything. And yet they'd seemed so comfortable with each other. Well, she thought, it just goes to show . . .

Ginny didn't like to ask any further questions. It sounded as though all was not well in the Tregaskis family. But at least feeling sorry for Chris and his troubles took her mind off her own.

By the time Major Griggs was due to arrive on the island, everyone spent their time tiptoeing around Ginny. Even the children were wary of her. Her bad temper and moodiness had become a fixture. Netta finally lost patience with her sister altogether after Ginny had snapped at poor little Jack and reduced him to tears when he accidentally knocked her arm and caused Ginny to slop tea on her jeans.

'He didn't deserve that,' shouted Netta as Jack fled sobbing from the kitchen, followed by Petroc, who threw a baleful glance at Ginny as he went.

'He should be more careful,' yelled back Ginny. 'I could have been scalded.'

'But you weren't.'

'No thanks to him.'

Netta glared at her sister. 'I shall be thankful when Major Griggs has seen you. Perhaps once that is over we can start getting back to normal again.'

'Meaning you can't wait for me to go, to get out of your hair.' Ginny wasn't questioning, she was stating a fact.

'I did *not* say that.'

'It's what you meant.'

Netta sighed angrily. 'No, I didn't.'

'Huh.'

Ginny got up and went to the sink where she grabbed the dishcloth and mopped at her jeans. 'You don't know what it's been like for me,' she said.

'No, I don't,' conceded Netta. 'But if you read about half of what's going on in the rest of the world, I have to say that your personal story, lousy though it is for you, isn't that important in the great scheme of things.'

Netta was right, of course, although Ginny was too wound-up to allow herself to admit it. She turned around so she faced the room. 'I just wish none of this had ever happened.'

'Well, we've only got your say-so that it did.'

Ginny could hardly believe she had heard right. After a second while she digested her sister's words, she took a couple of strides forward. 'Do you think I'm going through all this on some kind of ego trip? Do you think I'm a liar?' she shouted, thrusting her head forward belligerently.

'No,' said Netta. 'No, but you could be.'

'I didn't lie.'

'I don't mean that.'

'Sounds like it to me.'

'What I mean is, you *could* lie.' Ginny frowned, not understanding. 'Suppose you said that you made everything up?'

'But I didn't.'

'I know, I know. But supposing you did. Suppose you said that you made up the whole story just to get even with Colonel Bob because he rejected your advances. That nothing had ever happened in Kosovo. You know, "hell hath no fury" and all that.'

'But he came on to me.'

'I know all that, but the details don't matter. The fact is that if you say the affair didn't happen . . .'

'But Colonel Bob has already admitted what went on to his wife. He's been to see the brigadier.'

'And did he admit it to the brigadier? Do you know that? If the man is as career-minded as you have told me, if he is so set on promotion, then if he had any sense he would have said it was a pack of lies. After all, what has he got to lose?'

Ginny shook her head. 'I don't think he'd do that to me.'

'You don't know that, though, do you?'

'No. His interview was after I'd set out to come here.'

'Well, there you go then. And if he did admit it he can always deny everything if it comes to a court martial. Say he was confused or some such. Tortured into making a confession.'

Ginny snorted at the stupidity of Netta's last remark. 'But why would I have lied?'

'Say it was a nasty act of revenge on your part.'

'But that would make me look awful,' said Ginny, shaking her head.

'And, of course, you look so wonderful now. The woman who is breaking up a family and wrecking a man's career

281

because she got drunk and blabbed to the press is going to be the new "Queen of Hearts" as far as the British public are concerned? I don't think so.'

Ginny's face crumpled and a tear of self-pity ran down her cheek. What Netta was saying was true; her reputation was shot to pieces anyway, and by talking to the press, even unknowingly, she had put herself completely beyond the pale – her row with Maddy had proved that much to her. If by making herself look only slightly worse she could salvage things for Bob, well . . . What did the Americans call it? Damage limitation?

'But everyone in the regiment would hate me,' she said quietly.

'Yeah – like you're Little Miss Popular at the moment?'

'That's true. Even Maddy is barely talking to me.'

'Exactly.'

'But why should I? I mean, he wanted the affair, then he ditched me. It's all *his* fault really. All I did was confide in someone I thought was a friend.'

'I'll tell you why you should. Because you loved him, I think you still do, and you don't destroy the things you love.'

Ginny thought about Netta's idea and realized she was right. She *was* destroying Bob, and his family. There were more people involved in this awful business than just her and Bob, and the others, the innocent bystanders, didn't deserve to be caught up in the fallout. Could she – should she – fall on her sword, so to speak, for the sake of Bob's marriage and his career? The repercussions would probably be dreadful and she'd have to face them alone. If she did this, Bob would cease to be involved. And the *Mercury* would crucify her. If she thought the story before had been bad, she dreaded to think what they would do with this. God, whoever had said that there was no such thing as bad publicity had been *so* wrong.

'It would finish me in the army. I'd have to resign.' She sat down on a chair at the kitchen table and began fiddling with the pepper grinder.

'You could get another job. Chris has been telling me how fantastic you've been sorting out the hotel office.'

'Has he?' Ginny brightened momentarily then sank back

into gloom. 'Yeah, but who would want to employ me after this fiasco?'

'It'll die down. In a couple of weeks no one will remember your name, let alone what you look like. And anyway, what you did only matters to people in the army and the press. I bet Jo Public couldn't give a stuff.'

'I suppose.'

'And if you did this there would be no court martial, would there?'

Ginny shook her head. 'No. There wouldn't be any evidence. As far as I know it's only my word against his.'

'So whatever publicity there was would probably be over quicker.'

'I suppose.' She thought for a moment. 'And I'm not sure about there being no court martial. The army might try me instead of Colonel Bob. They might do me for lying.'

Netta shrugged. 'It's a bit unlikely, isn't it? What would they have to gain? Especially if you resign.'

Ginny nodded. 'Perhaps.' She had a thought. 'Suppose the army doesn't buy it? Suppose they don't believe me? I mean, I will be lying, won't I?'

'That's a point.' Netta thought about the problem for a second or two. 'But don't you think they'll want to believe you? I mean, if you convince them that you were just being spiteful, they will be able to keep a senior officer who has to be more of an asset than a lowly captain. Plus they'll be able to avoid court-martialling him and so there'll be less publicity. Come on, they're bound to go for it.'

'But if they've already interviewed Colonel Bob and he's admitted to seducing me . . . Made a statement . . .'

Netta sighed. 'Can we find out if they've seen him?'

'I'd have to get hold of him before I see Major Griggs.'

'Do you know where Bob is?'

'I haven't a clue.'

'Someone back at the barracks must know.'

'I could ring the regiment,' she said hesitantly. Frankly, the last thing she wanted to do was to speak to Richard or Alisdair – or anyone else for that matter.

'Go on then.'

Ginny nodded. 'OK.'

Netta got up and gave her sister a big hug. 'If you do this I'll think you're the bravest person alive,' she said.

'At least one person will think well of me,' said Ginny. She walked across the kitchen and picked up the phone.

Alisdair had been aware of the rising tone of Richard's voice above the bustle of regimental headquarters, and through the partially closed door that separated their offices. Finally he heard the receiver crash down on to its rests.

'Bloody woman,' roared Richard.

Curious, Alisdair got up from his chair and wandered into his subordinate's workplace. 'Who is?' he asked mildly.

Richard breathed out slowly to calm himself and to regain his composure. 'Ginny Turner,' he replied.

'What on earth has she done now?'

'She wants to get in touch with Colonel Bob.'

'Good God. Has she no shame?'

'She says she needs to talk to him urgently.'

Alisdair looked utterly sceptical. 'Huh. More likely she thinks that as he's been away from Alice for a bit he might be in need of some female company.'

'Exactly what I thought,' agreed Richard.

'Did you say that to her?'

'Not in so many words, but I think she got my drift.'

'And she said?'

'She denied it of course. She repeated her story about it being absolutely imperative that she got in touch with him, that it was almost a matter of life and death. Cobblers of course.'

'Still,' Alisdair paused. 'I know she had a loose tongue—'

'And loose morals,' interrupted Richard.

'But she wasn't a liar.'

'No,' said Richard, with a hint of reluctance in his voice. 'You mean, you think she really might need to speak to him?'

'Dunno. But put it this way, if she wanted to start up an illicit liaison again, she's hardly likely to broadcast the fact by trying to contact him through RHQ.'

'Good point.' Richard fiddled with some papers on his desk. 'So you think I'm being too hard on her?'

'Maybe.'

'Why don't you get hold of Colonel Bob and ask him if he'll contact her? Put the ball in his court.'

'OK.' But it was plain from Richard's mien that he wasn't happy.

'Do you want me to do it?' offered Alisdair.

Richard nodded and Alisdair returned to his office to ring his predecessor.

When Alisdair got home that evening he recounted the news of Ginny's phone call to Sarah. 'But don't go telling Alice,' he warned. 'There's no need to upset her. And if Bob wants nothing to do with Ginny, he won't phone her anyway.'

'And if he does?'

'Well, if he does then that's his problem.'

'Do you believe that Ginny's telling the truth; that she needs to talk to him about something important; that she isn't just trying to start things between them again?'

'I don't know, but I just don't think it's wise, that's all. I mean, why on earth would she need to contact him?' said Alisdair.

Sarah changed the subject slightly. 'So did you get hold of Bob?'

'Yes.'

'How is he?'

'Pretty unhappy. Not much of a surprise about that.'

'Poor man.'

'He told me that the military police are going to interview him soon. And then it's just a question of waiting for the date of the court martial.'

'Then the shit'll hit the fan all over again. Great.'

Hesitantly, Bob dialled Ginny's number. He was very unsure about the wisdom of this action but Alisdair had said that he thought he ought to. Besides, he didn't have to contact her ever again if he didn't want to. The phone was answered almost immediately.

'Have you spoken to the police yet?' asked Ginny as soon as perfunctory and rather cool greetings had been exchanged.

'Why do you want to know?'

'Because I'm going to tell them I lied. That I made it all up.'

285

'I don't understand.'

'It'll get you off the hook. I've got the police interviewing me tomorrow. But I had to be sure that you hadn't spoken to them yet. We've got to tell them the same story.'

'OK. But I still don't understand . . . ?'

'I'll tell them I did it out of spite. That I was angry that you had rejected my advances—'

'But you didn't make—'

'That I told Taz a pack of lies. That I suspected that she was a reporter—'

'But you didn't, did you?'

'Of course not, but I don't think they'll be able to prove anything. I'll tell them that I was jealous of your marriage and did it to break it up.'

'And were you?' asked Bob.

Ginny hesitated. 'I was jealous of Alice. I *am* jealous of her, but I don't want you to suffer.' And then after a pause, 'Or Alice, or Megan.'

'But I don't understand why you are doing this.'

'Because you don't deserve to be destroyed. I didn't set out to hurt you and I have. All I wanted was some sympathy and then all this happened This is the only way I can put things right. So you must deny everything too.'

'But I alread—' He stopped himself abruptly. 'If you insist, then I will. Thank you, Ginny.'

'I'm doing it because I love you Bob. I just want you to know that.'

'Thanks,' he said again. He hadn't wanted to know that. He'd had enough to cope with of late. He didn't need to be burdened with guilt too. Damn woman. He put the phone down. He breathed a sigh of relief that he'd managed to stop himself from admitting that he'd already denied everything; he had come frighteningly close to letting that slip. And if he had, she might have changed her mind again.

Thank God it looked like this dreadful business was now almost over. He knew he wouldn't get back the command of the regiment. He probably wouldn't get promoted again, but he still had a job, he would still get his pension and, he hoped, he still had a family.

*   *   *

286

Marcus Hepplewhite put down the phone on his desk and looked at it for a while. A smile spread slowly across his face. No one noticed the unusual but momentary inactivity of the news editor. As usual the newspaper office was buzzing with conversation and noisy with the clatter of keyboards and the shrill of phones. Then, after a couple of minutes' thought, he picked up the receiver again, flipped open his address book, and dialled.

'You'll never guess what,' he said.

'What?' said Taz, recognizing the voice instantly.

'I've just had the duty press officer from the Ministry of Defence on the phone.'

'And?'

'Your friend Ginny has changed her tune. She's denied everything. Says she made it all up. That she told you a pack of lies to get even with Colonel Car Crash.'

Tabitha snorted. 'If you believe that, you'll believe anything. I was there, remember, when she spilt the beans. She wasn't lying. What I got was the truth.'

'That's as maybe, but the army has dropped the charge of conduct prejudicial to good order and military discipline against him. It was her word against his, and now she's saying she lied, and as there wasn't a shred of evidence there's nothing else they can do.'

'Then Colonel Bob is a very lucky man.'

'Not that we can prove that he is.'

'So are you going to run this?'

'I thought we might if you want to do a piece for me. Got an idea about an angle?'

Tabitha thought for a moment. 'Ginny wants the world to think that she fooled me with lies the last time she spoke to me. Well, if that's what she wants, she can have it. I'll write a piece showing her to be the most devious, scheming, lying little cow that ever walked this planet. That should make her think twice about telling porkies in the future.'

Marcus chuckled. 'That's what I like about you Taz, you're all heart.'

'That's me.'

Ginny knew nothing about the new story in the *Mercury* as

287

she walked into the Trelisk Hotel the next morning. She thought Vicki gave her an odd stare as she squeezed round the reception desk, but thought no more about it as she headed along the corridor to Chris's office. She opened the door to the now transformed place of work, where rows of neat box files lined the walls; two gleaming filing cabinets stood like sentries on either side of the door; the desktop was clear apart from a phone, a blotter, a desk tidy and two filing trays. There was no clutter, no loose pieces of paper, no mess. It was now the epitome of an efficient business centre and, provided she could persuade Chris to keep on top of the filing and the general organization, it should stay that way for years.

She looked around her achievement with more than a little pride as she took off her coat and hung it behind the door and put her bag on the corner of the desk. And she felt her pride was justified. She had undertaken a Herculean task and she had sorted it out so that even a child could understand her system and maintain it. Not that it had been easy. Once or twice she had almost found herself crying with frustration and annoyance at the appalling state into which Chris had let everything deteriorate. Well, today was the last day. All she had planned to do this morning was to dot the i's and cross the t's and then teach Chris how her filing system worked.

But then what? Then she wouldn't have anything to occupy her. Her resignation letter to the army had gone in the post only hours after her interview with Major Griggs. She wasn't sure that his reaction to her change of story was going to be universal in the army, but she had a pretty good idea that it would reflect the opinion of the majority. To say that he had been livid was an understatement. He had railed against her for wasting police time, for ruining the reputation of a senior officer and for bringing the army into disrepute. He had informed her that he would have to go to higher authorities, and he was quite certain that they would want to take the matter further. By the time he had left the farm, Ginny had felt like she had been through a mangle and she was in no doubt that it would be impossible for her to continue her career in the army. And, after the way her friends in the regiment had all drifted away from her and had taken the side of Alice, she wasn't sure she wanted it to continue anyway.

She sat in the chair behind the desk and pondered on her future. From her current perspective it looked pretty bleak. She had nowhere to live – she knew she could stay with Netta for a bit, but not forever – she had no job, she had precious little in the way of savings, she had no man . . . In short, she had almost nothing. She was going to have to start from scratch, to write off the last ten years of her life and begin again. It was a tough prospect, she thought, at an age when settling down should be on the horizon, not a complete change. All in all she felt pretty blue.

Chris came into the office clutching a newspaper. He threw it on the desk in front of her. His face was thunderous. 'Look at this,' he shouted, red with rage.

Ginny pulled the paper towards her and saw her picture, yet again on the front page, and a headline in red. THE REVENGE OF THE SCARLET WOMAN, it blared. Transfixed, Ginny read the story, from Tabitha's byline at the top, to where it was continued on page two, page three, page four and page five. It detailed the original story and what had happened to the main players since. Apart from anything else, it went into significant detail about the fact that Ginny was 'hiding in the out-of-the-way Isles of Scilly and working at the family-run Trelisk Hotel', and worse, it included pictures of the exterior of the hotel and a shot of one of the bedrooms. That slimy reporter who had been around earlier had to be responsible for that. Ginny read on with increasing horror. In front of the desk Chris fidgeted and paced impatiently, waiting for her to finish.

'It is just appalling,' she whispered to Chris as she closed the paper.

'It's worse than that,' he shouted. 'It's a disgrace, it's outrageous!'

Ginny looked at his face and saw the anger, the rage he felt. It was her own fault that her reputation was shot to bits, and no doubt she had brought most of it on herself, but to drag his hotel into the ghastly story too – that was unforgivable. There was no way Chris's business deserved to be smeared with the muck they were throwing at her. She was so, so sorry. Why was it that everything she did these days, everything she touched, became ruined and blackened? It was like the

Midas touch in reverse. She didn't know what to say, and she was too hurt and appalled at the vile article to think straight. And what with everything that had been going on recently, she didn't think she could bear another dressing down – and Chris was obviously on the brink of letting rip. She had to get away. She'd apologize later when he'd had a chance to cool off. She grabbed her bag off the corner of the desk and rushed past him out of the office.

'Hey, Ginny!' he yelled after her, but she wasn't going to stop and risk his opprobrium on top of the poisonous piece in the *Mercury*, so she ignored his shouting and ran out of the hotel, past a startled Vicki and Carole.

Outside, the weather was cold and grey but Ginny was oblivious to the temperature as she rushed blindly along the road. She was so wrapped up in her misery and mortification that she was unaware of where she was going until, finally, the road petered out and she found herself on a white, sandy beach with iron-grey rollers crashing on to it, sending up white salty spray. The noise of the waves was deafening and Ginny sat down amongst the marram grass in a dip in one of the dunes, gazing miserably out towards the horizon and letting her thoughts wash over her like the sea was washing over the beach.

It was the raw weather that eventually brought her back to reality. She slowly became aware that she was shuddering from the cold. Her jeans and jersey were not enough to protect her from the chilly damp breeze that was stirring the sharp grass around her. She had been completely self-obsessed with wretchedness and anger, and had no idea how long she had been there. But one thing was clear; she hadn't solved anything in this self-indulgent wallow in misery. It was time to face the music. She uncurled her stiff limbs and stood up. She looked at her watch. It was gone eleven. She realized with a shock that she had been there nearly two hours. Cold and stiff, she stumbled back towards the road. She slapped her arms around her to try to get her circulation going and to warm herself up. She wasn't exactly sure where she was on the island, but that was the advantage of being in such a small place – she was sure she would soon find some familiar landmark and from there be able to determine her way home.

It was only forty minutes or so later that she arrived back at the farm. She steeled herself before she opened the kitchen door. For a start, she was going to have to apologize to Netta for bringing her family into disrepute yet again. The islanders all knew about Netta's sister's connection to Colonel Car Crash, so this latest story would make the Pengellys the centre of gossip yet again. Then she was going to have to eat yet more humble pie as she apologized to Chris for the lousy publicity she had unwittingly foisted on his business.

Cautiously, she opened the door and peered round. Netta and Carole were sitting either side of the big pine table, each cradling a cup of tea. Rose was asleep in her Moses basket by the Aga, and the cats were dozing on the sofa. It all looked so peaceful in contrast to the turmoil going on in Ginny's head. But although part of Ginny wanted to be enveloped by this warm and placid scene, she was shaken by the sight of Carole. Instantly she wondered why Carole was there. Had she come to tear a strip off her too? Did she want some sort of compensation for the damage Ginny's connection with the Trelisk must have inflicted?

Netta leapt to her feet at the sight of her sister coming through the door. Ginny was so uptight that she almost flinched at the sudden movement. She paused by the door, unwilling to enter the kitchen, on the brink of turning and running again. Netta seemed to sense this. She zoomed across the room and grabbed her sister's arm to drag her in.

'Ginny! There you are! We've been worried sick about you. Where have you been?'

Ginny didn't answer right away. She felt too drained by the morning's events and too shell-shocked. Instead she allowed herself to be dragged across to a chair and sat down.

'You're frozen,' reprimanded Netta, feeling Ginny's hand. She bustled over to the Aga and poured Ginny a cup of tea from the pot warming there. Then she added a couple of spoons of sugar and a slosh of milk. 'Here, get this inside you,' she said, putting it into her sister's hand.

Ginny smiled wanly and clasped both hands round the warm mug.

There was an extended silence while Ginny sipped her drink.

291

When she had nearly finished, Netta asked again where she had been.

'Nowhere really,' she replied dully.

'We were worried.'

'You shouldn't have been.'

'But Chris showed me the article. No wonder you were upset.'

Ginny felt self-pity welling up again. She swallowed hard and blinked to get control of herself. 'It wasn't just the article. I was so ashamed of getting you involved too,' she said to Carole. 'And Chris was so angry.'

'He was,' said Carole. 'I've never seen him so mad. It's the first time he's ever felt really involved in such an awful story.'

There, thought Ginny dully. Even his wife hadn't seen him that angry. It was getting worse. The phone rang. Ginny jumped like she had been scalded and shot Netta an agonized look. God, what if the press were after her again? Hadn't they done enough damage?'

Netta picked up the receiver. 'Hello,' she said. Ginny strained to try to hear the other voice, but it was just a garble. 'No, she's back . . . Fine . . . Yes . . . Yes, please . . . Absolutely . . . See you in a bit. Bye.'

Ginny looked inquiring. 'It was Petroc,' explained Netta. He's been out in the Land Rover looking for you. Now he knows you're safe he's going to the school to pick up Jack.'

'Oh shit! I'd forgotten.' Ginny began to cry. 'I can't be trusted to do anything right. I didn't even remember poor little Jack.'

'But there's no harm done. He doesn't know you've forgotten him, and it's no trouble for Petroc to get him.'

The door to the kitchen opened and Chris came in.

'Ginny,' he said, striding across to her. Ginny felt herself shrivel at the thought of the tongue-lashing she deserved to get from him. 'Ginny, there's something you and I need to get straight.' Here it comes, thought Ginny. He stopped beside her and perched on the edge of the table. Ginny was acutely aware of his thigh almost against her arm. She felt distinctly uncomfortable at his proximity. It would have been bad enough even if Netta had been the only person present, but to have his wife just a couple of feet away . . . The last thing she wanted was to give anyone else a reason to hate her. Weren't there enough in the world already? She braced herself for his anger.

'I've been out of my mind with worry about you.'

'But . . .' Ginny was puzzled.

'Where the hell did you get to? I've had everyone I know looking for you. I thought you'd done something rash, something desperate. I've been imagining every ghastly scenario possible.'

This wasn't how she'd expected the conversation to go. 'But you were so angry with me. All that stuff connecting me with the hotel.'

'Angry? With you?' Chris shook his head. 'God, no. I was furious with the paper for printing that load of shit, but I couldn't give a stuff about the connection with you. There's no way a story like that is likely to affect our business. It didn't say anything bad about the hotel – almost the reverse. I'd have had to pay a fortune to get a picture of it in a national paper. Hell, I didn't realize . . .' He gave Ginny an anguished look. 'Can you forgive me? The last thing I meant was to make things worse for you. I wanted to tell you that I admired you for what you'd done. Netta told me your motives. I think you're fantastic, quite wonderful.' He took her hand.

'No,' said Ginny, snatching it back. 'Chris, please. This is all wrong.' She shot Carole an apologetic look and edged her chair away from Chris. What was the man thinking about?

It was Chris's turn to look puzzled. 'What is wrong? I'm not with you.' He took her hand again.

Ginny didn't know what to say. Had he no shame? Such obvious comments, with his wife just there! Just because Carole was being unfaithful didn't give him the right to drag her into the mess too. 'Chris . . .' she started. Then she looked at Carole. 'Carole . . . I'm sorry.'

'Sorry?' asked Carole, her face clouded with puzzlement. 'What on earth for? Chris has said that you haven't done the hotel any harm. Possibly the reverse. So why are you sorry?'

'Look, I don't want you to think that Chris . . . That I . . . That Chris thinks I . . .'

Carole looked puzzled. 'Why on earth should I care what

Chris thinks about you? Unless of course he was being unfair about you and your wonderful office skills.'

'But . . .' Ginny felt as though reality was bypassing her completely. What the hell was going on between these two?

Then Carole's face cleared. 'Ginny, you don't think I'm married to Chris, do you?'

'But the kids, the dog . . . ?'

Carole and Chris roared with laughter. 'They're mine,' said Carole. 'They're nothing to do with Chris. Christ, if they were it would give the island something to gossip about. We're brother and sister-in-law.'

'But . . .' said Ginny, still not understanding. She looked at Chris. 'But you said you ran the hotel to support your family.'

'So I do. Carole was married to my brother. He was drowned at sea eight years ago. He owned half the hotel, so now I share it with Carole. If we don't make a profit, her kids starve.'

'Don't exaggerate,' Carole admonished gently.

'So you don't live together?' Chris shook his head. 'So when the dog hurt himself and you were worried about the blood on the carpet . . . ?'

'I was worried for Carole's sake. Can you imagine the nausea of getting dozens of little blood-stained doggy paw-prints out of the best Axminster?'

Ginny laughed. 'God, I got it so wrong. And when Vicki told me you had gone to the mainland and that Chris was in a mood because he thought you were having . . .' Her voice petered out.

'Vicki told you what?' asked Carole, still laughing.

'She thought you had gone to the mainland to see a man,' mumbled Ginny, none too clearly.

'I wish!' said Carole with feeling. 'My trip was much more prosaic. I think Vicki just feels I ought to be looking for someone else; that I've been without a partner for quite long enough now. No, I went across for nothing more exciting than a trip to Marks and Sparks. And that puts Chris in a bad mood as it means he has to do more of the chambermaiding duties, which he thinks are beneath him. He always gets in a temper when I escape for some shopping for a day or two.'

And while everyone laughed, Chris leant forward and kissed Ginny on the cheek.

That was nice, thought Ginny. If he ever wanted to do that again, he'd be most welcome.

Maddy watched the removal men loading Taz's possessions with cool satisfaction. The bitch was going, so that was a result. She wasn't entirely surprised, and felt that she deserved some of the credit for ridding this place of such a troublesome neighbour. It had only been a month ago that she had run into Taz in the village post office.

'Great to see you again,' said Taz. 'Now everything is back to normal, you and Danny must come and have some lunch.'

Maddy gave herself a mental shake to make sure she hadn't misheard the invitation. 'Sorry?' she said. 'Normal? You call things normal?'

'Well, compared to how they were in the new year.' Taz smiled brightly.

'Right.' Maddy nodded. 'Well, for your information I don't think things are normal in the Davies household, and they won't be for some time – if ever. And Ginny has resigned her commission, so she's out of a job. Alisdair is still running the regiment with Richard's help but as there still isn't a second in command, nor an admin officer, they never get home before eight. But hey, I suppose things are pretty normal compared to the way they were when you legged it.'

Taz's expression hardened. 'Oh, for heaven's sake Maddy, you can't blame me for this. I was just doing my job.'

'Just obeying orders, eh? That's an excuse that, traditionally, hasn't gone down too well with the British army. Now, if you'll excuse me, I've got to get on.' And with that she swivelled Danny's pushchair round and swept out. She didn't return home but went straight to Jayne Potts' house to have a word with her about the local toddler group she organized.

Jayne listened as Maddy told her of Taz's involvement in the scandal. 'Blooming heck,' she said. 'I had no idea. Not a very friendly thing to do, was it?'

'No, it wasn't. Look, I don't want to interfere, but I don't think the other mums would want to associate with her if they knew what she had done. I for one can't trust her as far as

I can throw her. She's proved herself more than capable of using her friends to further her career, not caring about the consequences.'

'So you want me to ban her from the toddler group?'

Maddy nodded.

'I can't promise that I will. I'll have a word with some of the other mums – see what they say. If they agree with you . . . Well, it's my toddler group. I can run it how I want.'

A week later Maddy had had an angry phone call from Taz.

'It's your doing, isn't it?' she said without preamble.

Maddy knew exactly what she was referring to but she played dumb. 'What's that then, Taz?'

'That Amelia has been banned from the toddler group.'

'Has she? Oh dear.'

'She has nothing to do with my job. She loved going to toddlers. Why should she get it in the neck because of something I did?'

'I expect that's exactly what Bob and Alice asked when Megan got dragged into things. She was nothing to do with her father's job or his actions, now was she? But she had a terrible time for weeks after.'

'That's different.'

'It isn't, Taz. It's *exactly* the same. If you can't take it, you shouldn't dish it. And personally, if I had people saying the sort of things about me that they're saying about you, I wouldn't want to hang around. No one likes you around here any more. You're not welcome.' And with that parting shot, Maddy put the phone down.

It was nice, she thought as she watched Taz's furniture being loaded into the van, that her advice had been taken. The only fly in the ointment was seeing the ad in the local paper and discovering that Taz was set to make a healthy profit when she found a buyer for her house. Well, you couldn't have everything, thought Maddy as she turned to the postbox and dropped a long letter to Ginny into it.

A few weeks later, Alice watched her removal men pack up her possessions at Montgomery House. Less than a year, she thought. She sighed. She would have liked to stay longer, but it wasn't possible. The new commanding officer was arriving in a few days so there was no way. And she wasn't looking forward to the new place. She had seen the house they had been allocated for Bob's next posting at the Ministry of Defence. It was a poky little four-bedroom box on the outskirts of London. Such a comedown after the space and opulence of this place, but it couldn't be helped. She turned away from the activity she had been observing and picked up the cut-glass bowl from the table beside her. It was her leaving present from the officers' wives. They had presented it to her at a surprise party held at Sarah's house, and she had been genuinely touched by their real expressions of sorrow that she was leaving. She had found it hard not to get weepy but she had just about managed it. She had dragged up some self-control from somewhere and her eyes had stayed dry.

'How's it going?' asked Bob.

'Fine, I think,' said Alice. 'They reckon they'll be done by tonight.'

'That's good.' He sighed. 'I'll be glad to see the back of this place, what with one thing and another.'

'Will you dear?' She looked away so he wouldn't see the regret on her face. She didn't feel a bit like that. She was going to miss this patch. She was going to miss her friends – real friends, not just acquaintances – the other wives who had stood by her and given her strength and who had got her through the darkest of days. The very wives over whom she had once had visions of lording it; to whom she had thought she would be able to show the correct way of doing things. Well, she thought, it hadn't worked like that. She had been the one on the learning curve and she was grateful. She'd come a long way in the past year and she was a better person for it.

'I fancy a beer before lunch,' said Bob. 'Anything for you?'

'A stiff gin and tonic, please,' said Alice. 'I need some medicine to get me through yet another move.'